# black
# margins

# OUR RECENT RELEASES

**Short Fiction**

Inspector Matadeen on the Moon
By Harishankar Parsai
Trans C M Naim

Seven Sixes are Forty Three
By Kiran Nagarkar
Trans Shubha Slee

Selected Fiction: Hindi Short Stories
Trans & Ed Sara Rai

Waterness
By Na Muthuswamy
Trans by Lakshmi Holmström

Downfall by Degrees
By Abdullah Hussein
Trans by Muhammad Umar Memon

The Resthouse
By Ahmad Nadeem Qasimi
Trans by Faruq Hassan

Katha Prize Stories 12
Ed Geeta Dharmarajan

Best of the Nineties: Katha Prize Stories 11
Ed Geeta Dharmarajan

The End of Human History
By Hasan Manzar
Trans by Muhammad Umar Memon

Forsaking Paradise: Stories from Ladakh
Ed and Trans by Ravina Aggarwal

**Non-Ficton**

Links in the Chain
By Mahadevi Varma
Trans by Neera Kuckreja Sohoni

Travel Writing and the Empire
Ed Sachidananda Mohanty

**ALT (Approaches to Literatures in Translation)**

Ismat: Her Life, Her Times
Eds Sukrita Paul Kumar &
Sadique

Translating Partition
Eds Ravikant & Tarun K Saint

Translating Caste
Ed Tapan Basu

Translating Desire
Ed Brinda Bose

**Trailblazers**

Ambai: Two Novellas and a Story
Trans by C T Indra,
Prema Seetharam & Uma Narayanan

Paul Zacharia: Two Novellas
Trans by Gita Krishnankutty

Ashokamitran: Water
Trans by Lakshmi Holmström

Bhupen Khakhar: Selected Works
Trans by Bina Srinivasan,
Ganesh Devy & Naushil Mehta,

Indira Goswami: Pages Stained with Blood
Trans by Pradip Acharya

**Katha Classics**

Pudumaippittan
Ed Lakshmi Holmström

Basheer Ed Vanajam Ravindran

Mauni Ed Lakshmi Holmström

Raja Rao Ed Makarand Paranjape

A Madhaviah: Padmavati
Trans by Meenakshi Tyagarajan

**Katha Novels**

Singarevva and the Palace
By Chandrasekhar Kambar
Trans by Laxmi Chandrashekar

Listen Girl!
By Krishna Sobti
Trans by Shivanath

**YuvaKatha**

Lukose's Church
Night of the Third Crescent
Bhiku's Diary
The Verdict
The Dragonfly
The Bell

**FORTHCOMING**

The Mountain of the Moon
By Bibhutibhushan Bandopadhyay
Trans by Santanu Sinha Chaudhuri

Short Shorts Long Shots
By Uday Prakash
Trans by Robert A Hueckstedt &
Amit Tripurareni

# black margins

## Sa'adat Hasan Manto
### stories

Selected by
M Asaduddin

Edited by
Muhammad Umar Memon

# KATHA

A3 Sarvodaya Enclave
Sri Aurobindo Marg,
New Delhi 110 017
Phone: 41416600, 2652 4511
Fax: 2651 4373
E-mail: kathavilasam@katha.org
Internet address: www.katha.org

Oxford University Press, 2001

Published by Katha in arrangement with the Oxford University Press, Karachi.
This edition may not be sold outside India, Sri Lanka and Nepal.

This collection was published as *For Freedom's Sake* by OUP in 2001.

The translation of "The Dog of Tetwal" as included in this volume
was first published by Katha in 2001.
This Indian edition first published by Katha in 2003
Copyright © Katha, 2003
First Reprint, 2005
Second Reprint, 2009

KATHA is a registered nonprofit society devoted to enhancing the pleasures of reading.
KATHA VILASAM is its story research and resource centre.

Cover Design: Geeta Dharmarajan

Typeset in 11 on 15.5pt AGaramond at Katha.
Printed at Ana Print O Grafix Pvt. Ltd., Greater Noida (UP).

Distributed by KathaMela, a distributor of quality books.
E-mail: marketing@katha.org

Katha has planted a tree to replace the wood used in the making of this book.

ISBN 978-81-87649-40-3

# Contents

# Acknowledgements

The inspiration for this anthology goes to Professor M U Memon, the series editor, a fine scholar of literature and Islamic Studies and a fine translator. It was during his visit to India in 1998-99 that this volume was conceived. I am deeply gratified to him for his suggestions regarding the selection of the pieces included, for going through each piece meticulously and refining the idiom, and above all, for maintaining his patience through the sometimes messy business of transmitting all the materials back and forth electronically between Delhi and Madison, Wisconsin. I would also like to express my appreciation to Jane Shum for going over the materials and offering suggestions regarding English style and readability.

Thanks are due to Dr Shamsul Haq Usmani, who lent me some of the source materials, and to Dr Shikoh Mohsin Mirza, who was the first reader of some of my own translations and who often suggested a suitable turn of phrase.

A special word of thanks to my wife, Nasreen, who enabled me to undertake this project by looking after the more pressing needs of our son, Zubin, to whom I dedicate my work in this volume with the hope that he will read it someday.

M Asaduddin

# Introduction

*If you are not familiar with the age in which we live, read my stories. If you cannot endure my stories, it means that this age is unbearable.*[1]
— Sa'adat Hasan Manto

Toba Tek Singh? Toba Tek Singh ... Oh yes, the name rings a loud bell in the minds of the people of the Subcontinent. The reader vividly recalls the "demented" Sikh lying between the barbed wires marking the borders of India and Pakistan, in the so-called "no man's land," refusing to accept the division of the country. The image captivates one's mind. This image, which has been seen repeatedly in the many dramatized and film versions of the story, would do credit to a famous painter like Van Gogh or Degas. It is the image of a nowhere man, an existential exile, a marginal man whose fate is decided by the politics of attrition indulged in by shortsighted politicians. A man who is the proverbial pawn in the overwhelming events of history. The name "Toba Tek Singh" creates all this resonance ... It is only some moments later that one thinks of Manto, the writer who created the character. It is the classic case of a fictional character overshadowing its creator.

Though sometimes given to exaggerated claims about himself and his writings, Manto makes a largely valid claim in the above statement. The areas of human experience and the liminal spaces that he focused on relentlessly, shocked people out of their complacency into a new awareness of the reality around them. This is particularly true in the context of his writings about the partition of India. Among all the creative writers who wrote on the theme of partition, Manto stands apart. He alone had the capacity to take a hard, impassioned look at the slaughter and senseless violence let loose on the eve of India's independence, without ideological blinkers, pious posturing or the slightest trace of communal prejudice. And that is why, after half a century of independence and partition, when history is being rewritten from new perspectives and magisterial nationalist narratives are being deconstructed, the creative writer most frequently alluded to is Manto. Moreover, Manto had the courage to probe the innermost recesses of the human mind and expose some of the dark forces and the pressing urges that lie dormant there. The sudden eruption of these forces at critical moments causes great damage both to the individual and society.

There are two assumptions underlying the epigraph that need to be defined in clear terms. First, Manto considered himself a writer in the realist tradition, seeking to represent and chronicle the mores and anxieties of his time. But does this mean that he was simply "of his age" and not beyond? Certainly not. Reality for Manto was not simply the external aspects of it. He had a more inclusive concept of reality that incorporated the internal and psychological aspects of people and events. What he asserts in the epigraph is true to some degree, of all great writers of fiction who represent their zeitgeist. But at the same time all great writers also transcend their age because they deal with categories of human experience, emotion and passion that are universal and timeless. This applies to Manto who shows an evergrowing relevance with the passage of time. While many of his contemporaries are slowly passing into oblivion, his reputation continues to grow.[2]

Second, Manto's realism embraces not only those external aspects of reality about which there is general consensus, but also those that are subjective and psychological and, therefore, tend to be more complex and varied. In his best stories, Manto collapses both of these aspects to create the unique vision that he wants to project.

Through the pioneering work of Premchand, Urdu fiction had already divested itself of its obsession with romance and the world of fantasy, by the time Manto began writing. Urdu short fiction had already made its presence felt and was prospering in the hands of Manto's illustrious contemporaries – Rajinder Singh Bedi, Krishan Chander and Ismat Chughtai. However, even among them he has a special place. The density of some of his works is comparable only with the best in fiction. His writings enable us to look critically at history, nation, politics, sex, and some of our assumptions about them. He has created a galaxy of memorable characters – Sultana, Saugandhi, Babu Gopinath, Ustad Mangu, Saha'e, Mummy, Mozel, and Ishar Singh, who will ensure the immortality of their creator.

What is Manto's worldview, his philosophy of life? Though he has propounded no coherent philosophy of life through his fictional and discursive writings, a close reading of them reveals that he gives a higher status to certain values and concepts that may roughly be called his vision of life. These values and concepts include – frankness, honesty, the discrepancy between appearance and reality, the validity of sex in life, the ethics of human relations, and the ambiguous nature of reality. The humanity that shines through in his writings is a hallmark of his fictional art and his sympathy with the downtrodden living on the fringes of society is an integral part of this vision. His acerbic wit and humour and his pitiless irony are the weapons he uses against the spurious idealism and hypocrisy that vitiate social interaction. About his view of man, Mumtaz Shirin, one of the finest critics of Manto, says,

> Manto is not interested in hallowed angels. Manto the writer does not have much to do with pure and innocent angels who can never possibly commit sin. Manto likes men who dare to commit sin. Manto's human being is neither an angel nor a devil. He is an earthling, a creature of the flesh and blood who has the potentiality of Original Sin, mischief, murder and mayhem. But God had ordered angels to pay obeisance to him.[3]

Manto is certainly "of his age," but in his preoccupation with the general human condition he also transcends it. However, it is a kind of transcendence, one must insist, that works because of an intense engagement with his times.

## II

Manto's childhood was rather common and undistinguished. It did not hold any promise of future greatness. He was born in a typical middle class, conservative family of Samrala, Punjab, in 1912. His authoritarian father, Maulvi Ghulam Hasan, was a barrister and a judge. Manto's mother, a woman with a quiet and artistic disposition, was his second wife. One can legitimately say that in Manto's personality the harshness and egotism of his father were combined with the grace and gentleness of his mother.

Manto's three elder stepbrothers had all become lawyers and his father expected him to become one as well. The young Sa'adat was required to study hard at school and at home without wasting time on frivolous amusements. But the boy's mind rebelled against these restrictions, and he began to show interest in literature while still in school. Evidence of this interest can be found in his autobiographical sketch "Agha Hashr se Do Mulaqatein," where he describes how he formed a dramatic club to stage one of the plays of Agha Hashr Kashmiri. "One day my father pounced on us, tearing apart the harmonium and tablas. He told us categorically that he didn't care for such useless frivolities."[4]

The opposition of his arbitrary and domineering father seemed to deepen Manto's interest in literature and the arts. He had very little regard for the prescribed textbooks. At the Muslim High School in Amritsar, his wayward nature and love for mischief earned him the nickname "Tommy." He liked to read books which had a pronounced subversive intent, particularly those considered unsuitable for boys his age.

The country was in great ferment following the Jallianwala Bagh massacre of 1919. The proximity of the city of Amritsar and the periodic patriotic outbursts that took place there must have affected Manto deeply. Of course, he was only seven years old at the time, too young to comprehend the full impact of the incident or react to it in any demonstrable way. But the whole decade following 1919 saw intense political activity and strife in Punjab, and the city of Amritsar resounded with revolutionary and patriotic slogans. Later, all this culminated in the trial of Bhagat Singh who was at the vanguard of the so-called terrorist movement in 1929. Manto was a great admirer of Bhagat

Singh and had a photograph of him on his study table. And when Manto wrote his first story "Tamaasha," the events at Amritsar provided him the raw material for it.

Manto failed twice (in Urdu!) in his matriculation exam. After passing on his third attempt, he was admitted to the Hindu Sabha College, but his performance there was no better. Indifferent to his studies, he paid more attention to films and books outside the college syllabus. He skipped out with his friends, Hasan Abbas and Abu Said Quraishi, to watch Hollywood films and make imaginary plans to get to Moscow clandestinely. It was during this period that he met Abdul Bari Alig whom he regarded as his literary mentor. Bari, an itinerant journalist and a dilettante of sorts, saw the spark of brilliance and the restlessness in Manto and decided to channel his energies into creative activities. He introduced him to the classics of English, French and Russian literature, particularly of the nineteenth century. Manto read avidly from the works of Oscar Wilde, Chekhov, Pushkin, Maupassant, Victor Hugo and others. Seeing his enthusiasm, Bari asked him to translate Hugo's *The Last Days of a Condemned*, a play opposing capital punishment. The translation, though not a remarkable one, must have sensitized Manto to the magic of words, the complex ways language functions and the pleasure of stringing phrases together. Bari's confidence in Manto's potential engendered in him a sense of responsibility. When the translation was published, with the title "Sarguzasht-e Asir" (1935), Manto must have felt a legitimate sense of pride in having accomplished something worthwhile for the first time in his life. He next translated Oscar Wilde's *Vera*, another work with a revolutionary intent, filled with fulminations against Czarist brutality in Russia. He did this translation along with Hasan Abbas (1934). For Manto, it was not simply a literary engagement. It was also an ideological one as is evident from the following,

We felt that Amritsar with its lanes and bylanes was Moscow, and we were eager to see the end of tyrannical rulers. We dragged the coffin of Czarism through Katra Jamil Singh, Kurmaon, Deorhi and Farid Chowk, hammering the last nail into it.[5]

By now Manto was deep into literature and his main interests were reading and radical pronouncements about revolution. After the required apprenticeship as a translator, he made his debut as a writer with the story "Tamaasha" (The Show.) He published it in *Khalq* under a pseudonym.

Meanwhile, failure on the academic front led both Manto and Abu Said Quraishi to leave Amritsar in search of greener pastures. They entered Aligarh Muslim University in 1934. The atmosphere in the university in the thirties was highly charged. The Muslim intelligentsia had been galvanized by the Khilafat Movement and the movement for Indian independence. The Progressive Writers Movement (PWM) was also making its presence felt, though the first conference of the Progressive Writers Association (PWA) wasn't held until 1936. In other words, given Manto's predilections and temperament, it was just the right kind of environment for him.

Although his stay was short, Manto nonetheless enjoyed his time in Aligarh. After barely nine months in the university he was incorrectly diagnosed with tuberculosis. He borrowed money from his sister and went to the sanatorium at Batote in Kashmir. After a stay of three months he returned fully recuperated. As his father had died in 1932 and his mother was not in a position to support him financially, Manto had to look for employment and landed a job with the newspaper *Paras*. But he soon got tired of yellow journalism. A break came when he got an invitation from Nazir Ludhianvi to become the editor of *Musawwir*, a film magazine owned and published from Bombay by Ludhianvi. Manto left Lahore in late 1936, and went to Bombay to take up his new job.

Manto loved his work at *Musawwir* but quit following a disagreement with Nazir Ludhianvi, and began to work for another magazine, *Samaj*. However their differences were soon patched up and he began to edit both magazines. Manto worked as the editor of *Musawwir* till 1940. In addition to editing the two magazines he also began to work in the film industry. He had a boyhood fascination with films and, after he came to Bombay, his proximity to the film world revived this interest. With Nazir Ludhianvi's help he got a job as a dialogue writer with the Imperial Film Company. Later he worked for Film City for a short time, eventually returning to the Imperial Film Company at the request of its Parsi owner, Ardesher Irani.

The film world excited Manto's imagination and he loved being a part of it. Editing the journals also took up much of his time. But he soon realized that none of these activities could give him the deep satisfaction of writing serious literature. He was alive to the changes in sensibility following the endeavours of the authors associated with the PWM and continued to write short stories, his first love, during this period. Most of these stories, written in the realistic tradition of Maupassant and Chekhov, found a place either in *Manto ke Afsane* (Manto's Short Stories, 1940) or *Dhuaan* (Smoke, 1942).

In Bombay, Manto had been living the life of a carefree bachelor. His relationship with his elder sister, who was also living in Bombay, was strained because his brother-in-law refused to have anything to do with him. His stepbrothers also had a contemptuous attitude towards him because of his "lowly" profession, and because of the style of life that he had chosen for himself. Manto's mother was forced by circumstances to stay with her daughter in Bombay. Her constant prodding led an unwilling Manto to agree to an engagement with Safiya whom he married in April 1939. Safiya came from a Kashmiri business family that had migrated to Bombay from Kenya a few years earlier. Safiya was very docile, just the right kind of spouse for Manto. With the birth of their son, Arif, within a year of the marriage, Manto became a contented householder, devoted to his son and wife.

Manto was generally indifferent to his health. Moreover, despite holding several jobs simultaneously, financial difficulties plagued him constantly because of his extravagance and inordinate drinking. In 1940, matters came to a head when he lost his job at *Musawwir*. He applied for employment at All India Radio (AIR), Delhi. Krishan Chander was at the helm there and he offered Manto a position. Manto left Bombay and began a new phase of his career with AIR.

Manto's joining AIR marked a turning point in his career. At that time many literary luminaries like Ahmad Shah Bukhari, N M Rashid, Chiragh Hasan Hasrat, Miraji and Upendernath Ashk were associated with it, and they provided a very stimulating environment for a promising writer such as Manto. Writing features and radio plays on a daily basis gave him an opportunity to hone his art. He wrote extremely fast and was often too confident and proud of his skills as a writer to even take a second look at the script.

One event during this period left a permanent scar on Manto's mind – the death of his son, Arif. His deep personal grief also left an indelible mark on his writings. Besides this, his edginess and touchy temperament were always a source of complication between him and his friends and colleagues. Nevertheless, the eighteen months he spent in Delhi were unusually productive for Manto. More than a hundred radio plays, filling four volumes in print, two collections of short stories and his first collection of essays, *Manto ke Mazamin* (1942) appeared during this period. Manto's career with AIR, Delhi, came to an abrupt end following an altercation with Upendernath Ashk. Manto considered it an insult if anyone suggested changes in his writings, even if these were called for. Krishan Chander and N M Rashid knew how to handle him without hurting his ego. However, when Ashk, whom Manto considered an inferior writer, made changes in his play, *Awara*, it was the proverbial last straw. He not only refused to agree to the broadcast of the altered version, he gave up a job that was providing him with a fairly good salary, something he needed badly. Within ten days he and Safiya were back in Bombay.

A deeper involvement with the film industry and an increasingly turbulent relationship with the "progressives" marked the second period he spent in Bombay. Manto was too sensitive a writer to put his social commitment above the human individual with all his hidden potential. This was something that the Progressives held against him. He began to edit *Musawwir* once again, and freelanced as a screenplay writer.

Meanwhile several lawsuits were brought against him at the Lahore Sessions Court for the alleged obscenity in his stories "Kali Shalwar" (Black Shalwar), "Dhuaan" (Smoke), and "Bu" (Odour). Later on, similar charges were brought against his stories "Thanda Gosht" (Cold Meat) and "Khol Do" (Open It). In the winter of 1945, he travelled from Bombay to Lahore along with Ismat Chughtai, who was being similarly tried for her short story "Lihaf" (The Quilt). The controversy surrounding Manto and Ismat Chughtai created a lot of heat and dust, involving writers, critics and the reading public. Eventually both were acquitted, with Manto paying a fine. After a few months, he began to write scripts for the Filmistan Studio. Included among the films for which Manto wrote the script are, *Mirza Ghalib*, *Begum*, *Chal Chal re Naujawan*, *Aagosh*, *Ath Din* (in which he also played the role of a demented military officer) and, with Krishan Chander, *Keechad*. When he had a falling out with S Mukherjee at Filmistan he began to work for Bombay Talkies where he developed a very good rapport with Ashok Kumar, one of the most popular actors of the time. This was also a period of relative prosperity for him. Close contact with the film industry also provided him with some of the themes for his fiction, which is clear from the stories written during this time.

However, this period of prosperity was short lived. Life began to change for him in 1947. His self-confidence received an unexpected jolt when Ashok Kumar put aside one of Manto's stories in preference to a story by Ismat Chughtai. For a man with a bloated ego this was a bitter pill to swallow. Moreover, the increasing communal tension in Bombay had an impact on the film industry. It was doubtful whether Muslims would be allowed to continue working in the Bombay film industry at all. A true humanist at heart, free from communal prejudices of any kind, Manto was pained by the spectacle of parochialism and cruelty based on religion. A combination of circumstances and an uncertain future in India, his declining career as a writer for films, and Safiya and her relatives constantly prodding him to migrate led him to his final decision (if it was a well thought out decision at all!) to leave for Pakistan.

Manto's experiences in Pakistan were deeply disappointing. He expected to be hailed there as a great writer, but instead he was met with indifference, both from the government and his peers. He had to run door to door looking for jobs but did not find any commensurate with his status. Even when friends did manage to find jobs for him that would at least ensure his livelihood, he could not retain them due to his incorrigible egotism and his sense of unappreciated genius. His financial condition deteriorated day by day. The general air of uncertainty regarding his career, the lack of a stimulating literary environment and, above all, another charge of obscenity levelled against him, left him demoralized and intellectually confused.[6] His short story, "Open It!" was banned in Pakistan, strange as it may sound, for "breach of public peace."[7] He sought consolation in liquor, so much so that he began to live for it, turning himself into an inveterate alcoholic. He had to be admitted to a mental hospital twice. The end finally came on the morning of 18 January, 1955.

Curiously enough, during the last years of his life, filled with much frustration, anger and psychological disorientation, we see him touching a new pinnacle of creativity. During these years he wrote most of his best known stories, with the exception of "Kali Shalwar," "Bu," and "Babu Gopinath," as well as the stories which show his inclination towards innovation and experimentation.

## III

The presence of Manto is pervasive in quite a few literatures of northern India. So much so that he belongs to the literary tradition not only of Urdu fiction, but of Hindi, Punjabi and Sindhi as well. Among all Urdu fiction writers, Manto has been translated the most extensively into these languages as well as into English. Apart from the innumerable translations of his works scattered in journals and periodicals, to my knowledge, at least seven full length volumes of his stories have appeared in English.[8] The translations have strengths and weaknesses of their own. There are areas of cultural and linguistic erasure and omissions, along with moments of excellence.[9] Translation is, in the final analysis, an act of interpretation and the whole repertoire of the translator's literary, linguistic and cultural resources are brought to bear upon his practice of translation. In this sense, translation and criticism are mutually enlightening processes.

The selection of stories and sketches presented here seeks to encompass the entire range of Manto's thematic and formalistic concerns. We have adhered, with some flexibility, to a chronology that will enable readers to gain some understanding of Manto's growth and development as a writer. Inevitably, this volume contains some stories translated earlier. However, it also includes materials translated into English for the first time. It seeks to look at Manto's fiction from the perspective of some of his recent translators.

Manto started his literary career as a translator of French and Russian fiction, and his short stories bear the unmistakable imprint of the kind of realism practised by Maupassant and Gorky. We have the evidence from his friend Abu Said Quraishi that in the early period of his writing career, Manto read writers such as Victor Hugo, whom he specially liked, Maupassant, Gorky, Chekhov, Gogol, Pushkin, Dostoeyevsky, Andrayev and Oscar Wilde.[10]

With respect to both theme and style, quite a few of his stories show a deep affinity with those of Maupassant. In this context, Leslie A Flemming's comment is quite pertinent,

> Impressionistic elements generally disappeared from Manto's short stories after 1943. Instead, the vast majority of his earlier and later stories contain the Maupassant style of well-constructed plot, containing a single episode, the incidents of which follow one another in logical order, in which there are no extraneous incidents and in which the ending of the story resolves the various elements of the plot into a satisfying denouement.[11]

"Naya Qanoon" (The New Law) is written in the classical realistic tradition with a beginning, a well-fleshed out middle and an end. This Manto story "marks his first attempt to grapple. with any degree of psychological realism, with a lower class character."[12]

It is about the aspirations of the common people. Mangu, the irrepressible kochwan has been conceived in vivid detail. His fellow kochwans at the adda consider him knowledgeable about the affairs of the world. Ustad Mangu enjoys his reputation and has his own perceptions about the Russian Revolution, the Spanish Civil War and colonial rule in India. He has great antipathy towards the British rulers of India as well as towards the fawning Indians whom he characterizes as "toady boys." In his unlettered mind he somehow connects the India Act of 1935 with the independence of the country and refuses to put up with the insolent behaviour of the gora. His unrealistic expectations of seeing tangible changes around him make his naivete obvious and reveal the author's sceptical attitude about the efficacy of political processes for bringing about substantial changes in the human situation.

The story makes it clear that the expectations attached to the India Act were misplaced. It would not be unreasonable to say that Manto wove into the texture of the story his own political perceptions regarding the 1935 Government of India Act and the "gradual" home rule that was being doled out in driblets. The story proleptically (and prophetically) shows the disillusionment of the common people with independence in both India and Pakistan. "The law is still the same," says the police officer sternly, summing up how the expectations of the common people will be thwarted.

"Baanjh" (Barren) lends itself to multiple interpretations. It is a story about love's destructive potential, about self-deception taken to its uttermost limits, and about the creative process. The protagonist is barren because of his inability to love. He is aware that love is the vital spring of life. Without it, life loses its meaning and charm. But he is so unfortunate that no one has ever uttered words of love to him. His wanderings around Port Apollo and the Gateway of India in Bombay are in vain. Manto compares this inability to love with the incapacity of writers to create. Just as a man devoid of love cannot procreate anything and remains barren, in the same way, a writer devoid of imagination reaches a dead end. The protagonist asks the narrator,

"Why is it that most writers suffer from vitamin deficiencies?" Whatever the reply of the narrator, the fact that is underlined here is that writers, too, have to struggle with their demons on a daily basis in order to create enduring works of art.

The protagonist loves no one and no one loves him. But his yearning for love is so strong that he creates a fantasy world in which he is the hero of an adventurous love story. He is Naim and his beloved is Zohra, an embodiment of grace and beauty who loves him despite the great disparity in their social status. They elope and lead a happy life. But this happiness is short lived. Zohra dies abruptly, throwing Naim into an abyss of despair and desolation. He narrates this story of his imaginary love and pain to others, which gives him a strange kind of pleasure. His self-deception reaches the point where he even begins to believe it's true. The event that he imagined for himself and the character that he created become the raison d'être of his life. Written in the format of "a story within a story," "Barren" exhibits Manto's greater self-confidence as a writer and his willingness to try out new ideas.

Manto accepts sex in its protean forms as one of the most basic, instinctual and elemental urges of human beings. Hunger for sex is as primal as the hunger for food. Man takes recourse to all kinds of subterfuge for the satisfaction of this hunger and dresses it up in acceptable nomenclatures and relationships. Suppression of this hunger and the puritanical morality associated with it lead to grave imbalances in the mind and personality of human beings. In his stories, Manto examines the nature of this hunger without batting an eyelid and without resorting to moralistic preaching. The subtlety and complexity he shows in the treatment of sex in his stories is without parallel in Urdu literature. It is in this context that the remark of Muhammad Sadiq, the magisterial historian of Urdu literature, seems quite off the mark, "Manto's interest in sex made him enormously popular with the younger generation, but his ostentatious treatment of it comes close to bravado, and impairs the quality of some of his good stories."[13]

"Swaraj ke liye" (For Freedom's Sake) looks at the effect the suppression of the healthy expression of the sex drive can have on people's lives. The scene here is post-Jallianwala Bagh Amritsar where the air is thick with political activity. There is a carnival atmosphere and people are going to jail in droves in support of the Civil Disobedience Movement. Manto deftly blends politics and sex to deliver his message. In the process, he questions the validity of two institutions, marriage and patriotism, which become a sham when they curb people's natural impulses. Ghulam Ali, the protagonist, joins the Congress Party and participates in political agitation against the British not because he is imbued with patriotism or has any abiding faith in freedom, but because it is fashionable to do so. The mocking and derisive tone which the narrator employs to describe Ghulam Ali, Nigar and Babaji (who, according to some critics, stands for Mahatma Gandhi) is indicative of his attitude towards hypocritical piety. In Manto's stories, hypocrisy is a cardinal sin towards which he is unforgiving. Conversely, candour is a redeeming feature in some of the most vile and depraved characters. Here, the narrator takes a wry look at the principle of renunciation and abstinence from sex, which are traditionally regarded as commendable. These life-denying practices, according to the narrator, make people look ugly and cause a curious distortion of their natural selves,

> I had seen the male volunteers of the ashram. True enough, they all took their ritual bath and brushed their teeth every morning, they all spent most of their time out in the open air and chanted bhajans in accordance with the rules of the ashram, but their clothing still reeked of perspiration, didn't it? Quite a few had bad breath to boot. And I never saw on anyone even a trace of the good nature and freshness one associates with outdoor living. Instead, they looked stooped and repressed, their faces pallid, eyes sunken, and bodies ravaged, as blanched and lifeless as the udders of a cow from which the last drop of milk has been squeezed out. (pp. 116-17)

When Ghulam Ali becomes the leader of the local branch of the Congress Party and then the fortieth "dictator," he mouths the usual platitudes from the podium, and the cheer and adulation of the crowd turn his head. He gets "drunk," as it were, with the heady wine of patriotism. His falling in love with Nigar makes him seem more human, but when Babaji says that a true marriage should be free of lust, Ghulam Ali declares that even though they are formally married, he and Nigar will abstain from sex till India becomes free. They do not want their children to be born as "slaves." From that moment on, deception enters their lives. Ghulam Ali is sent to jail and when he returns to live with Nigar after eight months, his perceptions about things undergo a transformation. Finding themselves unable to repress their natural desires, they decide they can remain true to their vow so long as they do not produce children. This goes on for some time. In the process Ghulam Ali develops an abhorrence for rubber, the material which interferes with his sexual pleasure. The heady wine of patriotism turns into poison and vitiates their lives. Ghulam Ali cannot take any more of this self-deception and Nigar's yearning to become a mother is too strong to resist. With an immense sense of relief they break their vow, return to a normal married life and have children. Ghulam Ali looks back upon his former life as a nightmare. In this connection, one is reminded of Manto's statement in the story "Paanch Din" (Five Days) that "to kill a legitimate desire is tantamount to a heinous murder. To kill one's nature is to do violence to oneself."[14] The metaphor of rubber gathers considerable semantic energy and works so effectively that it seems to acquire phantasmagoric proportions, threatening to engulf the lives of the central characters.

"Odour" is a story of great power and energy – reminiscent of D H Lawrence. Predictably, it became a subject of discussion among readers and critics, eliciting for its author the title "prince of pornographers"[15] from some, while accolades from others. The sexual activity in this story is portrayed as something primal, pure jouissance, unhindered by any social convention or any moral taboos or scruples. Randhir, who has had experience with Anglo-Indian prostitutes, is completely transformed after his encounter with a Ghatin woman. Varis Alvi, the noted Urdu critic rightly suggests that their union can be understood as the union of purush and prakriti,[16] where Randhir represents purush (the masculine principle) and the Ghatin woman represents prakriti (the feminine principle). All other distinctions of class, education, et cetera, vanish the moment one meets the other. Manto uses an elaborate repertoire of images and symbols from the natural world to underscore the primal nature of the sexual encounter. By investing the Ghatin woman with breasts which are like "bowls fresh from potter's hands" and which gleam like "muddy water" and, most of all, with an odour that emanates from her whole being, Manto roots her firmly in the earth. Again, rain becomes a potent symbol framing the narrative. First, it accompanies the experience itself and then it evokes the memory of it. Above all, it soaks the parched earth just as the sexual union between Randhir and the Ghatin satisfies their thirsty souls. The narrator contrasts Randhir's sexual experience with the Ghatin with the experiences he had with Anglo-Indian prostitutes and with his newly wedded, sophisticated wife, who is the embodiment of gilded artificiality. Whereas his sexual pleasure with the prostitutes and with his wife was purely physical, his experience with the Ghatin goes beyond the physical, touching his soul and involving his whole being. Freed of all kinds of conventions and commitments, the sexual act becomes pure joy, an end in itself. Here Manto presents a more complex and nuanced understanding of sexual relations than ever attempted in Urdu by his peers. To interpret this story as the perverted sexual indulgence of a bored and bourgeois man, as some critics have done, is to misread it.[17]

A significant number of Manto's stories deal with the life of prostitutes, pimps and other sundry characters associated with the flesh trade. His portrayal of them, far from adhering to the stereotypical formula of "a prostitute with a heart of gold," is both complex and penetrating. It disabuses the reader of the conventional notions of morality and chastity. Besides highlighting the subjugated and secondary status of women in society, such stories hold up a mirror to society's double standards in matters of sexual morality. The best that can be hoped for from "respectable" society in dealing with prostitution is that its existence will be ignored, just as claims about female sexuality are ignored. If it is the male gaze, which converts a woman into a sexual object, it is society's collective indifference that reduces her to non-existence. Manto portrays these women as they are, and as the profession that they have been forced to engage in compels them to be, without maudlin or melodramatic sentimentality. In doing so, he pierces the veils of pretence and hypocrisy which characterize male-female relationships in the Indian subcontinent. He has the courage to probe the blind spots, to mention the "unmentionables" and to speak the bitter truth in the most forthright manner, without subterfuge or exaggeration. In this respect, the comments he made in response to the accusations hurled at him on different occasions, of obscenity and pornography, and his alleged obsession with sex and prostitutes are worth mentioning. "Literature is not a malady, but a response to malady. It is a measure of the temperature of the country, of the nation. It tells us of its health and disease,"[18] "We (the writers) tell others what they are suffering from, but we do not own the chemist's shop,"[19] "The whorehouse is itself a corpse which society carries on its shoulders. Until society buries it somewhere, there will be discussion about it,"[20] and finally, "Why should I take off the blouse of society? It is naked as it is. Of course I am not interested in dressing it up either, because that is the job of drapers, not writers."[21] Manto was interested in the lives of prostitutes because they represent the paradigm of middle class exploitation. In fact, Manto's choice of prostitutes, pimps, and other sundry characters living on the periphery of society as subjects, tied in well with his ideology (as far as he can be said to have had one) which placed the lives of the marginalized and the subaltern in the foreground with a view towards not only questioning the majority discourse about them but also subverting it.

"Black Shalwar" focuses on the total alienation of prostitutes from mainstream society. Curiously, though they are ostracized° from society and live in "sin," they are by no means godless creatures. Manto wonders why many of the women in the sex trade are, in fact, god fearing and have great reverence for devotional icons and images and observe religious rituals. He argues that religion is that part of their lives which they have managed to preserve in the midst of the corrupting influences that surround them, turning it into a means to redeem themselves.[22] Nor are these women amoral. On the contrary, they often show a kind of robust morality which is healthier than the attenuating morals of a hypocritical society. This is shown by the special feelings that both Sultana and Mukhtar have about Muharram, and by their adherence to other, approved social and moral behaviours. However, the crux of the story lies in its portrayal of the uncertainty in a prostitute's life and her unbearable loneliness. In Ambala, Sultana lived close to the cantonment area where she managed to make a living without much hardship. However, when she and Khuda Bakhsh move to Delhi, she lives in the prostitute quarters constructed by the government, and faces stiff competition. She has difficulty finding clients. Khuda Bakhsh stays away most of the time seeking blessings and benedictions from holy men. Sheer boredom and ennui drive her towards Shankar who exploits her situation to the full. Passive and dependent, Sultana is not even dimly aware of her subjection. Patriarchal society has robbed her not only of her freedom but of her awareness of her "self" as well. The narrator highlights the total lack of direction in her life using a beautiful metaphor. Manto himself alluded to this metaphor when defending the story against puritanical and prudish onslaughts,

On that side of the road was a warehouse, stretching from one corner to the other. To the right, under the metal roof lay some big bales along with piles of all sorts of goods. To the left there was an open space, crisscrossed by innumerable railway lines. Whenever Sultana saw the iron rails shining in the sun, she would look at her hands on which the blue veins stood out just like the railway lines. In that long, open space, engines and bogies were moving all the time, this way and that, puffing and clattering. Whenever she got up early in the morning and went out on to the balcony, a strange sight confronted her. Thick smoke would be rising from the engines through the mist, going upward into the overcast sky like fat, burly men. And also the great clouds of steam, surging loudly from the rails, gradually dispersing into the air. Sometimes, when she saw a carriage being shunted and left to run on its own along a line, she thought of herself ... thought how she too had been shunted on to a line and left to run on her own. Others would change the switches and she would move on, not knowing where she was going. Then a day would arrive, after the momentum had exhausted itself, when she would halt somewhere she had never been before. (p. 63)

Saugandhi of "Hatak" (Insult) also accepts her situation passively, but only in the first part of the story. In the second part she crosses the threshold. This story, which somewhat resembles Maupassant's "Boule de Suif," is a powerful narrative that draws attention to the numerous deprivations of a prostitute's life. Saugandhi's relationship with her clients goes beyond the strictly commercial aspect of the transaction. She prepares to entertain a client on the night of the incident, despite her exhaustion and her desire to rest, because she wants to help another desperately needy woman with the money that will be earned. What is notable is that being in a profession which requires that she sell herself on a daily basis has not robbed Saugandhi of her humanity, her quest for genuine love, or her desire to do good. Her generosity and innate goodness can be seen in the fact that she is even willing to give herself to those who cannot pay at the moment. The pimp, Ramlal, also shows his sympathetic concern for Saugandhi's well-being. Manto unfailingly points out that people who are compelled to live outside the pale of so-called civilized society are not necessarily less human or humane than seemingly respectable members of that society.

What triggers Saugandhi's instinct for revenge is the humiliation of rejection. She is willing to be deceived by the flattering words of her lovers, however untrue, because they give her a sense of self-worth and fulfil her desire to love and be loved. Deprived of the sense of solidity and permanence that a family life can give, Saugandhi needs constant reassurance from her clients that she really is "good" and that they "love" her. The Seth's grunt of rejection, "oonh!" instantly robs her of her self-respect and her self-sustaining illusions. Suddenly she stands face to face with the stark reality of her life. It is interesting that this is also the moment when Saugandhi crosses over the threshold from passivity to action. Madho becomes the immediate target of her wrath because he happens to be a living symbol of the deception and betrayal that have characterized her life so far. Her preference for her mangy dog at the end of the story signifies her rejection of the illusions that have sustained her for so long, and her awareness of her existential loneliness. It is also her first step on a voyage of self-discovery. Manto explores the deepest recesses of her mind through her stream of thoughts. Through its psychologically intriguing ending, Manto invests Saugandhi with a feminist vision that seems remarkable in the context of the time in which the story was written.

It is undeniable that Manto's most powerful stories deal with the Partition of India and its aftermath. "Toba Tek Singh," "Cold Meat," "Open It," "Saha'e" and "Black Margins" all depict the unbearable anguish, trauma and savagery of Partition. While stories like "Tetwal ka Kutta" (The Dog of Tetwal)," "Akhri Salute" (The Last Salute) and "Yazid" (the last two not included here) deal with the legacy of the politics of attrition that the vivisection of the land engendered. They pitilessly remind us that "there is no document of civilization which is not at the same time a document of barbarism."[23]

Manto, the man and the writer, was shattered by this cataclysmic event. For the rest of his life, whenever he alluded to 1947, he always associated it with taqseem or Partition of the country and never, not even once, with Independence. Having left Bombay in strange circumstances, he reached Lahore via Karachi on 7 or 8 January, 1948. "For three months," he writes, "my mind was incapable of making any decision. It seemed as though several films were being screened simultaneously before my eyes. Everything was mixed up, sometimes the bazaars of Bombay and its streets, sometimes Karachi's tiny, fast moving trams and its slow mule carts, and sometimes Lahore's noisy restaurants. I could not be sure where I was. Lost in thought, I kept sitting on the chair all day long."[24]

He was internally divided, and the breach that was caused was never to be filled. Some idea of his mental condition can be gauged from the following,

> When I sat down to write I found my mind in a confused state. However much I tried, I could not separate India from Pakistan or Pakistan from India. My mind was invaded by the same puzzling questions again and again, will the literature of Pakistan be different? If so, how? Who has the claim to what was written in undivided India? Will that be divided as well?[25]

While other writers on Partition employed a narrative strategy that depended on the all too familiar "balancing act" between the different forms of communal violence, Manto's stories look at the violence and barbarity of Partition as a plain and simple descent into the heart of darkness inherent in man. He stares violence in the face and is too clearsighted to seek refuge in the rhetorical consolation of spiritual redemption or healing as many of his fellow writers did.

"Saha'e," a semi-autobiographical story, gives us some clue to the reasons for Manto's own migration to Pakistan. It has always been somewhat of a puzzle to Manto's readers and critics that he, with his clear vision, his truly secular outlook, his scepticism about the efficacy of religion as an instrument of politics, and his deep attachment to Bombay, finally decided to leave India and go to Pakistan. No single reason can be cited for such a momentous decision in his life. In fact, "Saha'e," along with "Murli ki Dhun" (Notes of the Flute), a sketch written in memory of his friend Shyam who was a famous actor in Bombay, and Ismat Chughtai's pen-sketch of Manto, "Mera Dost, Mera Dushman" (My Friend, My Enemy), make us aware of the complex web of circumstances that led to his decision. In the opening segment of "Saha'e," we read the following passage which contains obvious echoes of what might actually have happened in those fateful months of 1947,

> The three of us were Hindus. Our relatives in West Punjab had incurred heavy losses in terms of both property and lives ... presumably why Mumtaz had decided to leave. Juggal had received a letter from Lahore informing him about his uncle's death in communal riots, affecting him badly. Still under the impact of the news, he casually said to Mumtaz one day, "I'm wondering what I would do if riots broke out in my neighbourhood." "Yes, what would you do?" Mumtaz asked.
> "I might kill you," Juggal said in all seriousness.
> Mumtaz fell silent, dead silent. His silence continued for nearly eight days, and broke only when he suddenly announced that he was leaving for Karachi by ship, at quarter to four, that very afternoon. (pp. 168-69).

This story also provides an important key for understanding some aspects of the communal violence that occurred during Partition. Most of this violence was in the nature of retributive or retaliatory action prompted by unconfirmed reports or rumours of killing and arson taking place in some distant corner of the country.

"Cold Meat," the story which Ahmad Nadeem Qasimi considered "too hot" for *Nuqoosh*,[26] shows the transformation of human beings into beasts. Ishar Singh's abysmal lust for wealth and bloodshed motivated him to become a member of the frenzied mob that went on a killing spree. After murdering six members of a Muslim family his lust for blood was somewhat quenched, but his more elemental lust for sex remained unsatisfied. To satisfy his lust, he carried off a young girl of the murdered family on his shoulders. The shocking discovery that he was going to copulate with a corpse gave him a rude jolt and rendered him impotent. Violence lies at the core of the story. Ishar Singh's lovemaking with Kulwant Kaur is as violent as his treatment of the Muslim family. Kulwant Kaur is equally violent in her expression of jealousy. However, for Manto, Ishar Singh's impotence is symptomatic of the fact that the voice of conscience had not been totally smothered.

This carries some message of hope for humanity because the story tells us that "even after turning himself into a beast, man does not lose his humanity."[27] Ishar Singh suffers precisely because he still has some remnants of humanity left in him. It cannot be denied, however, that the story does lapse into melodrama in its depiction of Kulwant Kaur's fatal assault on Ishar Singh. As one critic puts it succinctly, "That final dagger thrust was unnecessary. Why should she stab him at all? Why must sexual death be duplicated by physical hurt?"[28]

In the story, "Open It," Sirajuddin asks eight volunteers at a refugee camp in Pakistan to find his daughter, Sakina, from whom he got separated during the chaotic journey from India. They trace her and, as though her trauma on this side of the border was not enough already, they, apparently, rape her repeatedly and then abandon her to her fate. She is brought to the doctor's office in the camp. When the doctor says, "Open it" (meaning the window), Sakina, lying inert on the stretcher, opens her shalwar involuntarily. She has been so brutalized and her relationship with language has become so tenuous that henceforth the phrase "khol do" (open it) will carry just one meaning for her to the exclusion of all others. The ending of the story stands as a telling epitaph to the death of civilized norms. The fact that Sakina's immediate tormentors were, in all probability, Muslims themselves adds another poignant dimension to the story. It underscores, as do all of Manto's stories directly or indirectly, the fact that "the subject of the Partition was first the human being, not the Hindu human being, nor the Muslim, nor the Sikh. The experiences of each community distinctly mirror one another, indeed they reach out to and clutch at one another. No crime, no despair, no grief in exile belongs uniquely to anyone."[29]

Taken together, "Cold Meat" and "Open It" also highlight the fact that in times of fratricidal war and violence, the female body becomes a contested site subject to assault and conquest. It serves as a trophy of victory or a blot on the collective honour.

The vignettes in "Black Margins" (Siyah Hashiyé) are notable for their macabre humour, their subversive intent, their tongue-in-cheek mode and their freewheeling irreverence. The genre, which might be called "existential belle lettre" as it exists in some literatures, is unusual for Urdu. Outside Urdu, a parallel that comes to mind is the Hungarian writer Istvan Orkeny (1912-1979) who developed the genre of the "One Minute Story" to record the trauma of the Second World War in a mode that was dominated by irony and grotesqueness. In these vignettes, Manto tried to capture man's descent into Hobbesian jungle by recreating some apparently funny and absurd, but in fact, deeply disturbing situations. Narrated in a deadpan, emotionless tone, they depict murder, rape, slaughter, and thuggery as the most natural preoccupations of men. It is in this sense that Muhammad Hasan Askari said that "these stories are not about violence, but about human beings."[30] As one reads through the pieces of "Black Margins," one is reminded of what Mario Vargas Llosa wrote about the fictional world of Julio Cortazar where,

... banal reality begins insensibly to crack and to give in to some hidden pressures that push it up to the prodigious without participating fully in it, maintaining it as a sort of intermediary, tense and disconcerting territory in which the real and the fantastic overlap without integrating.[31]

The flippant tone of the vignettes conceals their serious intent. That is why when they were first published they were misunderstood. Manto was accused of sensationalizing a tragedy. He was shocked by the torrent of accusations and abuse hurled at him, mainly by his fellow Progressives. He published his considered response in the preface to his collection of stories, *Yazid*. It is a document of great importance, providing the background and certainly some added insight into these stories. The following extract makes it clear.

The revolution triggered by the Partition of the land had made me a non-conformist. I am one even now. But gradually I came to accept the horrifying reality without allowing despair to touch me. I dived into that ocean of blood shed by man of his fellow man, and selected some pearls [out of them], recording the tireless ferocity with which man had shed the last drop of the blood of his brother, recording the tears shed involuntarily by some who could not make out why they could not say goodbye to their inherent humanity. These pearls I have presented in my book, *Siyah Hashiyé*.[32]

Manto's "Toba Tek Singh" has become a metaphor for the utter absurdity and mindlessness of the entire exercise of Partition. The eponymous story is a devastating indictment of amateur statesmen and unscrupulous politicians who draw shadow line boundaries between peoples and countries. Their actions are so insane that even the hard core lunatics of an asylum seem much wiser than them.

> ... they did not know a thing about its actual location and its boundaries. That is why all the inmates of the asylum who weren't completely insane were thoroughly confused about whether they were in Hindustan or Pakistan. If they were in Hindustan, then where was Pakistan? And if they were in Pakistan, then how was it possible since only a short while ago they had been in Hindustan, and they had not moved from the place at all? (p. 213)

They further surmise,

> Who knew whether Lahore, which was now in Pakistan, would not go over to Hindustan the following day, or the whole of Hindustan would not turn into Pakistan? And who could say with certainty that some day, both Hindustan and Pakistan would not vanish from the face of the earth altogether! (p. 216)

Then, one lunatic says with desperate rage, "I want to live in neither Hindustan nor Pakistan ... I'd rather live on this tree." Bishen Singh, the "mad" protagonist of the story contemptuously rejects the verdict of the politicians to be divided between India and Pakistan and prefers to die on the strip of land that belongs to neither. This is Manto's symbolic rejection of the vivisection of the country, and his considered comment on the stupidity of the entire exercise.

"Toba Tek Singh" is about arbitrary boundaries and borders that divide people, history and culture. For the millions who were caught in the competitive savagery of Partition and driven out of their homes, India and Pakistan were mere territorial abstractions. In studies of Partition it has been pointed out again and again that perhaps never before in human history was the fate of so many decided by so few, and in such an arbitrary and thoughtless manner. The anxieties of the lunatics in the asylum about their precise location in the new alignment have their exact parallel in the actual history of Partition. The cavalier and whimsical way in which the Mountbatten Plan and the Radcliff Award were put into practice is underscored by the fact that, for days and weeks after the announcement of Partition, people in some provinces were uncertain about their precise location in the new structure.

"Toba Tek Singh" is also a story of dislocation and exile – exile from one's natural home and habitat. Home is where one feels fortified by one's past, one's shared relationships, one's memories and the presence of one's ancestors, even if they are dead. All this defines one's identity and gives it a certain solidity. Even in their demented state, some lunatics have not lost their sense of place, which becomes strongest in the case of Bishen Singh. Through a brilliant metonymic process, Bishen Singh becomes Toba Tek Singh, the person becomes the place where he was born and had his roots. They merge with each other, so much so that towards the end of the story, at least in the Urdu text, it is difficult to distinguish one from the other. Manto's genius lies in sustaining this duality and tension right through to the end, which makes the story an exploration of exile as an ontological human condition.

Above all "Toba Tek Singh" is about lunacy, madness. It is the madness of the sane which is a million times more destructive than the madness of the insane. A lunatic causes harm only to himself, but when a group of normal people choose to get themselves into a rage or frenzy, they leave behind a bloody trail which takes generations to erase. Who knows this better than the people of the Indian subcontinent? Bishen Singh straddles two worlds – at one extreme we have the madhouse, at the other the no-man's land – both of them are spaces where the restrictions of the "normal" world are suspended and individuals are set free from their stranglehold.

Set against the beautiful scenic background of Kashmir, "The Dog of Tetwal" shows the absurdity of the political situation in India and Pakistan. After the partition of the country it becomes imperative that even dogs decide whether they are Indian or Pakistani, marking an absolute difference that brooks no ambiguity. It demonstrates how political machinations become complicit in forming the conception of the "Other," an enemy, real or invented, to justify dubious state policies. "Like Pakistanis, Pakistani dogs will also be shot." This is reminiscent of the jingoistic sloganeering that is too often heard on both sides of the border. Mere political labels are enough to justify the killing of human beings as well as creatures in the animal kingdom.

It is an incontrovertible fact of contemporary history that both India and Pakistan exploit the situation at their borders – the contested territory – for maximum political mileage for the party in power. In the context of the wars fought between India and Pakistan (1965, 1971), the story seems as relevant today as it was fifty years ago. Who is a "martyr" and who dies a "dog's death?" It depends not on the valour and the inherent heroism of the act, but on which side of the border you are on and through which lens you examine the events. In its rejection of facile nationalism which thrives on essentializing human identity, and its depiction of the senseless border conflicts involving the taking of innocent lives, the story becomes a parable of the politics of attrition practised by India and Pakistan, not only in times of war but also in times of peace. A special piquancy is lent to the events of the story by verses from the legendary romance of Waris Shah which evoke the vision of a syncretic past that seems irrevocably lost after the division of the country. At an existential level, the story highlights the problematic nature of the concepts of loyalty and betrayal.

Most of Manto's stories do not exhibit any great inclination towards innovation or experimentation in technique, except for the allegorical mode that he adopted occasionally. He was interested in telling a good, exciting and palatable story. However, his last stories, "Phunde"

(Tassels) and "Sarak ke Kinare" (By the Roadside), show his shift towards anti-story. These narratives subvert the conventional notions of plot and character, and the chronological development of events in the story. Conventional narrative and even linguistic structures have been distorted to represent the chaotic and dream-like aspect of reality that the stories seek to convey.

In "Tassels" there is a bare-bones plot. The story spans the life of the female protagonist from her youth until she is no longer young. There is a strong undercurrent of sex in the story, with suggestions throughout of uninhibited indulgence in it by all the characters. At the end, with the passing of her youth, the protagonist finds herself alone. Men, in fact, run away from her. A strand of violence is interwoven with sex throughout the story. The central metaphor is that of tassels, an image that stands for the confusion in human relationships which arises from unrestrained sexual indulgence, and also for the absurd existence of characters who become playthings in the hands of their own libidinal instincts. Placing the amoral, drifting world of sexual pleasure in the foreground, the story emphasizes the absence of a clear aim or purpose which transforms the protagonist's life into a tassel, superficially attractive but in the end, just a tangle of threads, nothing more.

In "By the Roadside" the point of view, even the voice, remains that of the protagonist, an articulate woman. Here certain images and metaphors are repeated again and again. The sexual act is the pivotal event in the story, along with its implications for the man and woman. After the man abandons the woman, she discovers that she is pregnant and she has to deal with the aftermath of a relationship, which was intense and beautiful while it lasted. She wonders, "Whose law is this? ... Earth's? ... Sky's? ... or the Creator's?"

Through subtle repetitions of images and metaphors, Manto builds a relationship between the world of humans and the phenomenal world. The sexual act becomes a creative process, an important part of the scheme of things. By likening the blue eyes of the man to the sky, a contrast is set up between man, identified with the sky that brings rain, and woman, identified with the earth that brings forth life. In the story, the woman is aware that her union with the man is not sanctioned by society, but for her the birth of a child becomes a cosmic experience, leading to her fulfilment. At the end, she abandons her child as she cannot muster up enough courage to face society's onslaughts. Yet, throughout, the conflict between her natural self (motherhood) and her social self is evident. The characters have not been named, nor have they been located in a social context. The entire focus is on the intensity of experience felt by the woman as lover and would-be mother. To depict that experience Manto veers away from his realistic style of narration towards an elevated lyricism. However, the story in itself presents Manto's view that the sexual act is something of a creative act, that it is sacred, since it constitutes the essential part of the cycle of birth and death in life, and in the cosmos. Sex becomes the regenerative impulse in the universe. The story becomes significant in Manto's canon because in it he moves towards the metaphysics of sex, while earlier he dealt with the psychological and physical aspects of it.

*Muraqqa nigari*, that is, drawing pen-portraits, is an interesting genre in Urdu literature. Many Urdu writers, such as Abdul Haq, Farhatullah Beg, Shaukat Thanavi and Rashid Ahmad Siddiqi, are known for the interesting pen-portraits they have drawn of many famed personalities. Manto, Krishan Chander, Upendernath Ashk, Ali Sardar Jafri and Sahir Ludhianvi have also written such biographical sketches about their contemporaries. Manto is said to have taken to this genre after he was hounded in Pakistan for having written stories like "Cold Meat," "Open It" and "Black Margins." Writing biographical sketches was an innocuous diversion that would not raise the hackles of the custodians of law or the minions of morality. Published in two volumes, *Ganjé Farishté* (Bald Angels, 1952) and *Loudspeaker* (1955), Manto's pen-portraits evidence his interest in his contemporaries, the diversity of his acquaintances, his unmistakable eye for detail, and his unquenchable thirst for all kinds of experiences. The title *Ganjé Farishté* (Bald Angels) is also indicative of his intention to demythologize the personalities and expose their feet of clay.

"Ismat Chughtai" is a pen-portrait of another one of Urdu's great writers. Manto and Chughtai had a lot in common – both excelled in the genre of the short story, both were associated with the film industry, both were rebels at heart and delighted in shocking others, both were "progressives" who had great conflicts with some of the more orthodox and inflexible members of the Progressive Writers Movement, both were accused of obscenity and taken to court. It is because of this that many people expected them to marry each other. It is interesting to see how these two mercurial and fearless writers, who managed to live life on their own terms without compromising their integrity, forged a relationship based on total candour and mutual respect. Polite disagreement was the very stuff of their friendship, and both being wits of the first order, could disagree with each other without being disagreeable. Nothing could threaten their mutual trust or the solidarity of their friendship.

In "Ashok Kumar," Manto recounts events which occurred in his presence, so no hearsay is involved. Ashok Kumar, whose image on screen was that of a sophisticated, suave and urbane gentleman, turns out to be quite the opposite in his personal life – rustic, rude to his friends, a visitor at racecourses, and given to ogling women at times. He was, at the same time, very hardworking, methodical and intelligent. The real strength of his character as a human being and his truly secular outlook become evident at the time of Partition. In the midst of widespread rioting and butchery, he kept his sanity intact, never allowing narrow, self-defeating notions of identity and nationalism to cloud his vision.

After taking over, Savak Vacha took stock of the poor condition of Bombay Talkies, and had to face many difficulties. He removed an undesirable person, who happened to be a Hindu, which eventually created many problems. But when his position was filled, I realized that Muslims held the key positions. I was there, as were Shahid Latif, Ismat Chughtai, Kamal Amrohi, Hasrat Lukhnawi, Nazir Ajmeri, Nazim Panipati and the music director Ghulam Haider. When all of them came together, the Hindu employees felt hatred for Savak Vacha and Ashok. When I mentioned this to Ashok, he burst out laughing, "I will tell Vacha and he will give them a dressing down." (p. 262).

Ashok Kumar had great faith in his status as an artist and had the courage to take a shortcut through a Muslim neighbourhood even though his companion, Manto, feared for his life. Ashok Kumar's words, "they don't bother artists" sums up his faith in the vocation chosen by him. This sketch brings to life many legendary personalities like Devika Rani, Raja Mehdi Ali Khan and others. It records interesting anecdotes about the lives of the people associated with films. It also offers glimpses of the intricacies of different aspects of filmmaking. Above all, the sketch succeeds in transforming our awe and envy of Ashok Kumar into affection for, and intimacy with him.

What is noticeable about both of these sketches is that while portraying these two personalities, one a writer and the other an actor, Manto recreates two evocative slices of social and cultural history for us. While assessing their merits as artists in their chosen fields and describing their strengths and weaknesses as human beings, Manto puts them in their cultural and historical contexts thus providing insights into the ethos of the times. The narration is always interesting and the sketches read like well written stories. The language and style used in them have a unique flavour, conversational, idiomatic and witty, with a liberal sprinkling of colloquial, even slang, words.

His self-portrait, "Manto," which appears in some versions with the title "Sa'adat Hasan," touches upon important facets of his artistic preoccupations and offers readers valuable insights into his creative process. Contrary to the popular myth that he was an inspired and effortless story writer, here we see the artist as a struggling pen pusher searching for a subject for his story. It is a useful corrective for those who indulge in myth making about Manto – about his fecundity and his felicity with language. Manto himself demolishes that myth in the most effective way by underlining the difficulty involved in finding the most appropriate words and phrases to convey his experiences. This portrait also offers a perspective to his continued preoccupation with sex and prostitutes. Shortsighted critics often try to establish a direct correspondence between "Manto the writer of Obscene stories" and "Manto the person." They do not realize that Manto had very strong morals and that his artistic vision could encompass both the sunny and seamy sides of life with equal ease, that he could combine horseplay with solemnity, jocular irreverence with high seriousness. His ability to laugh at himself and to show his own feet of clay to others are the highlights of this autobiographical sketch. It also demonstrates his own predilection for what is known in Urdu as fiqre-bazi, that is, witticisms using conceit and wordplay, a tendency he accuses Patras Bukhari of in his pen-sketch of Ismat Chughtai. The objective of fiqre-bazi is to dazzle the reader with startling verbal innovation and an illusion of eloquence which may not be accompanied by a corresponding depth of meaning.

Manto's open letter to Nehru has been included here because it offers us a glimpse of his state of mind after Partition, torn as he was between his love and loyalty for his former country and his present one. "You are the prime minister of the country that was formerly mine," echoes the anguish of an exile from his own land. Even though he had left the country, his heart still bled for Kashmir, particularly for its common people who were very poor. His devastatingly ironical comments about Nehru's latching on to Kashmir while lacking sufficient determination to remove its poverty, reveal Manto's strong concern for the land of his ancestors and the fate of the Kashmiri people, caught as they were between the politics of attrition practised by both India and Pakistan. At the same time, he felt a deep sense of loyalty towards his adopted land. Hence his heartfelt plea to Nehru, whom he held responsible for trying to obstruct the flow of water by constructing a dam on the river Beas. Manto's politics, whatever his disagreement with the Progressives, draws its sustenance from his genuine humanitarianism, his love for the oppressed and his sense of fairness and justice. Read together with the letters known as "Chacha Saam ke Naam Khutoot" (Letters Addressed to Uncle Sam), Manto's letter to Nehru reveals his political self at its best. These letters, along with his stories about Partition and those about social injustice, decidedly register his presence as an intellectual who intervened in the public sphere through his creative writings.

As he grew older Manto wrote excessively, primarily to meet the expenses of his daily drink, as pointed out earlier. The slipshod manner and the extraordinary speed with which he turned out some of these stories ensured that they would not rise very high.

"Sonorol" is a story, included here purely for academic interest. The text of this story was made available for the first time in 1993 in both Devanagri and Urdu scripts.[33]

## IV

A definitive edition of Manto's works is still awaited. Whichever edition one works from, it has to be collated with other available editions for authenticity. I have done this. In addition, I have also compared the Urdu originals with the Devanagri versions of Manto's complete works published by Rajkamal Prakashan (Delhi, 1992), which is, by and large, reliable, though not wholly accurate.

M Asaduddin

Notes

1. Sa'adat Hasan Manto, "Adab-e-Jadeed," in *Dastavez, Manto*, ed. Balraj Manra (New Delhi, Modern Publishing House, 1986), p. 53. Subsequent references from *Dastavez, Manto* are to this edition.

2. A resurgence of interest in Manto can be seen in India, beginning in 1993 with the publication in Devanagri script of his entire literary output by Rajkamal Prakashan. There was also an international conference on "The Life and Works of Manto" at the Indian Institute of Advanced Studies, Shimla, in 1996. Before that we had Maya Krishna Rao's soul-touching rendition of "Khol do" in stylized Kathakali, and, in 1999, we had Manto entering the exclusive precincts of English theatre in Delhi with Barry John's direction of "Manto," the award winning play written by Kishwar Ahluwalia. Outside India, Anita Desai wrote in *Spectator*, "Manto's irony and humanity raise him on a par with Gogol." Salman Rushdie heaps supreme praise on him in his controversial and oft-quoted essay, "Damme, This is the Oriental Scene for You!" (*The New Yorker*, 27–30 June 1997),

and elsewhere calls him "the undisputed master of the modern Indian story," a claim which many will consider exaggerated but which, nevertheless, draws attention to Manto's wide reputation and acceptance.

3. Sa'adat Hasan Manto, *Noori na Naari*, ed. Asif Farrukhi (Karachi, Maktaba Asloob, 1985), p. 60.

4. Sa'adat Hasan Manto, "Agha Hashr se Do Mulaqatein," in his *Ganjé Farishté* (Lahore, Al-Bayan, 1969), p. 38.

5. See his "Bari Sahab," in ibid. p. 103.

6. Manto recorded the first few months of his ordeal in Pakistan in "Zehmat-e-Mihr-e Darakhshaan," his introduction to *Thanda Gosht* (Delhi, Maktaba-e Nau, 1950).

7. Cf. Devender Issar, ed. *Manto Adalat ke Kathahre mein* (Delhi, Indraprasth Prakashan, 1981), p. 33.

8. Hamid Jalal, *The Black Milk* (Lahore, Al-Kitab, 1956); Leslie A Flemming and Tahira Naqvi, *Another Lonely Voice, The Life and Works of Saadat Hassan Manto* (Lahore, Vanguard, 1985); Khalid Hasan, *Kingdom's End and Other Stories* (London, Verso, 1987) and *Partition, Sketches and Stories* (New Delhi, Viking, 1991); *The Mottled Dawn*; Jai Ratan, *The Best of Manto* (Delhi, Sterling Publishers, 1989); Madan Gupta, *Saadat Hasan Manto, Selected Stories* (New Delhi, Cosmo Publications, 1997).

9. The most widely known translator of Manto is certainly Khalid Hasan. For an idea of the problems with his English translations of Manto, see my "Manto in English, An Assessment of Khalid Hasan's Translations," in Alok Bhalla, ed. *Life and Works of Saadat Hasan Manto* (Shimla, Indian Institute of Advanced Studies, 1997), pp. 159–71.

10. Cf. Abu Said Quraishi, *Manto* (Lahore, Idara-e Farogh-e Urdu, 1955), p. 40.

11. Flemming, pp. 96–97.

12. Ibid., p. 44.

13. Muhammad Sadiq, *A History of Urdu Literature*, 2nd ed. (New Delhi, Oxford India Paperbacks, 1997), p. 587.

14. Mumtaz Shirin, as quoted in Farrukhpi, p. 41.

15. Muhammad Sadiq, *Twentieth Century Urdu Literature* (Karachi, Royal Book Company, 1983), p. 305.

16. "Bu aur Bu-e Adamzad," in Gopi Chand Narang, ed. *Afsana, Rawayat aur Masail* (Delhi, Educational Publishing House, 1981), pp. 243–72.

17. Khalilur Rahman Azmi records how Sajjad Zaheer had publicly condemned "Bu" at the All India Urdu Congress, 1944, held in Hyderabad, because, according to him, "the portrayal of the sexual perversion of a self-indulgent member of the middle class, however realistic, is a waste of time of both writers as well as readers." See his, *Urdu Mein Taraqqi Pasand Adabi Tehreek* (Aligarh, Anjuman Taraqqi Urdu Hind, 1972), p. 93.

18. *Dastavez, Manto*, p. 85.

19. Ibid., p. 82.

20. Ibid., p. 74.

21. Ibid., p. 53.

22. Ibid., p. 90.

23. Walter Benjamin, *Illuminations, Essays and Reflections*, ed. and introduced by Hannah Arendt, tr. by Harry Zohn (New York, Schocken Books, 1968), pp. 257–58.

24. *Dastavez, Manto*, p. 108.

25. Ibid.

26. Ibid., p. 110.

27. Ibid., p. 124.

28. Keki N Daruwalla, "The Craft of Manto, Warts and All," in Bhalla, p. 64.

29. Jason Fransisco, "In the Heat of Fratricide, The Literature of India's Partition Burning Freshly," *The Annual of Urdu Studies*, No. 11 (1996), p. 250.

30. Muhammad Hasan Askari, "Hashia Araai," in Sa'adat Hasan Manto, *Siyah Hashiyé* (Lahore, Maktaba-e Jadeed, 1952), p. 12.

31. "The Trumpet of Deya," *The Review of Contemporary Fiction*, vol. XVII, no. 1 (Spring 1997), p. 25.

32. "Jaeb-e Kafan," in Saadat Hasan Manto, *Yazid* (Lahore, Maktaba-e Jadeed, 1951), p. 175. For Manto's anguished response to the ambivalence of the Progressives, see also his "Dibacha" written on 22 August 1950, in his collection *Chughad* (Delhi, Saqi Book Depot, 1991), pp. 172–76.

33. See, respectively, Balraj Manra and Sharad Dutt, *Dastavez, Manto*, vol. 2 (Delhi, Rajkamal Prakashan, 1993), pp. 399-407 and Balraj Manra, ed. *Manto ke Gumshuda aur Ghair-matbu'a Afsane* (New Delhi, Modern Publishing House, 1992), pp. 20–29.

# The New Law

Mangu kochwan, a tanga driver, was regarded knowledgeable by all his peers at the adda. He had never been to school and was a nobody in that sense. Nevertheless, he kept track of the events going on in the world. Tanga drivers at the stand were aware of his vast store of information.

A few days ago Mangu overheard one of his passengers talking about the possibility of a war in Spain. This led him to pat Gama Choudhry on his broad shoulders with the sage declaration, "Just watch out Choudhry. A war will break out in Spain shortly!"

And when Gama Choudhry asked where Spain was, Ustad Mangu had replied solemnly, "In vilayat, where else?" When a war did break out in Spain, all the kochwans sitting at the adda near the railway station, smoking a hookah, appreciated Mangu's foresight in their heart of hearts. At that precise moment, Mangu, driving his tanga along the shiny road of the Mall, was exchanging views with his passenger about the fresh outburst of Hindu-Muslim riots.

That evening when he returned to the adda, his face looked unusually grave. When the topic of Hindu-Muslim riots cropped up during the round of hookah, Ustad Mangu took off the khaki turban and tucking it under his arm began anxiously, "There is surely a pir's curse behind Hindus and Muslims drawing knives at each other every second day. My elders used to say that Emperor Akbar once hurt the feelings of a holy man who cursed him saying, Get out of my sight! And mark my words, your Hindustan will forever be plagued with strife. And, see for yourselves, ever since Emperor Akbar's reign ended, there's been continuous strife."

He took a deep breath, drew on the hookah and resumed, "The Congresswalas want to liberate Hindustan. Well, I tell you, they can't do anything even if they try for a thousand years. At the most, the Angrez will leave, and in their place will come some Italywala or Rooswala who, to my knowledge, are very tough. But Hindustan will always remain enslaved. And, oh yes, I forgot to tell you that the pir also swore that foreigners would always rule over Hindustan."

Ustad Mangu detested the English passionately. The stated reason for his hatred was that the English rule over India used force and committed untold atrocities against its people. But the actual reason was – the goras tormented him all the time. They treated him with utter contempt, as though he were a stray dog. Moreover, Mangu could not stand their colour. He did not know why, but the sight of a gora face nauseated him. He used to say that their faces, crisscrossed with pink wrinkles, reminded him of rotting corpses with their skin peeling off.

After every close brush with a drunken gora, his mood would be spoilt for the whole day. When he returned to the adda in the evening, he would curse the gora to his heart's content while smoking a Plough brand cigarette or taking drags on the hookah.

Muttering filthy invectives, he would swing his turbaned head and say, "They came to borrow fire, and became masters of the house! They've made life miserable, these sons of monkeys, ordering us around as though we were their servants for generations."

He would not be satisfied. As long as there was someone to listen, he would continue to let off steam, "Just look at him ... rotting away like a leper. I could have knocked him down with a single kick ... and he was raising such a racket as if he would kill me. I swear, I first thought of smashing his skull but stopped myself thinking, it's degrading for me to kill a kafir." He would pause for a while, wipe his nose with his khaki shirtsleeve and resume, "By god, I'm fed up with the tantrums of these laat sahabs. The moment I see their baneful faces, my blood begins to boil. Only a new law can bring us relief from their oppression."

And then one day, he came to know from the conversation between two passengers he took from the court that a new law was soon to be enforced in Hindustan. His joy knew no bounds. They were Marwaris who had come to the court in connection with a lawsuit and were now returning home. They were talking amongst themselves about the new law, the India Act.

"They're saying that the law will come into force from the first of April. Will it change everything?"

"It may not change everything, but it's being said that there'll be great changes. And Hindustan will be free."

"Will there be a new law for interest rates too?"

"Can't say. We'll ask some lawyer tomorrow."

Ustad Mangu's spirits began to soar. He usually cursed his horse and whipped it ruthlessly. But that day he turned around frequently to look at the marwaris. Twirling the ends of his moustache with one finger, he loosened the reins on the horse's back and patting it, said affectionately, "Come on beta, come on. Let's see how fast you can gallop!"

After dropping his passengers, he went to Dinu Halwai's shop in Anarkali, drank a giant glass of lassi and belched contentedly. He held the long strands of his moustache between his lips, sucked at them and yelled loudly, "To hell with them."

When he returned to the adda that evening, he was bitterly disappointed at not finding any of his friends there. He could barely contain the great news he wanted to share with them. For about half an hour he kept pacing restlessly up and down under the corrugated iron roof of the station. A thousand thoughts crowded his mind. The stir caused by the new law had transported him to a different world. He switched on all the lights of his brain to think clearly about the implications of this new law. He was thrilled as he recalled the anxious question of the marwari, "Will there be a new law for interest rates too?" He smiled frequently behind his moustache, cursing the marwaris, "They're bedbugs sucking the blood of the poor. The new law will be like pouring boiling water on them."

He was deliriously happy. His heart was soothed by the thought that the goras, the white rats (as he always called them), would scurry into their holes the moment the new law came into force. When the bald kochwan, Nathu entered the adda, Ustad Mangu ran to greet him with his turban tucked under his arm. Taking Nathu's hands into his own he said, "Come, give me your hand. I'm going to give you some great news. It's so exciting that hair will start sprouting again on your head."

Mangu told his friend about the new law and its implications. During the conversation, he slapped Nathu's palms several times and declared, "Wait and watch what happens! This Russian king will certainly come up with something."

Mangu had heard a lot about the current communist regime in Russia. He liked their new constitution as well as the other developments there. This had led to a confusion in his mind about the new law and the "Rooswala badshah." He thought that the changes that were to take effect from the first of April were the direct consequence of the influence of the Russian king.

For some time, the Red Shirt movement had been active in Peshawar and other cities. In Ustad Mangu's mind all these things – the movement, the Russian king, and the new law – had got mixed up. Whenever he heard that some bombmakers had been rounded up in one city or that some people were being tried for treason in another – these seemed to be the harbingers of the new law to him and he felt optimistic.

One day he found two barristers in his tanga, fiercely criticizing the new law. Mangu listened to them silently. One was telling the other, "The second section of the new law deals with the federation. I can't make head or tail of it. No such federation has ever been heard of in human history. From the political point of view also it's a mistake. As a matter of fact, it can't be called a federation at all!"

Since the barristers used a lot of English words in their conversation, Ustad Mangu could only vaguely understand it. He somehow got it into his head that they were against the advent of the new law in the country and did not want India to be free. Influenced by this thought, he looked at them contemptuously a couple of times and then mumbled to himself, "Sons of toadies!"

Whenever he uttered "Sons of toadies" under his breath against someone, he derived immense satisfaction for using the phrase appropriately and also for being able to distinguish between gentlemen and toadies!

Three days later, he heard three students from the Government College going to Muzang, talk among themselves,

"My hopes have been raised high by the new law. If Mr ... is elected a member of the Assembly, he'll certainly find me a job in some office."

"There'll be many other jobs as well. Something might just come our way in the ensuing confusion."

"Yes, of course."

This conversation made Ustad Mangu doubly conscious of the value of the new law and he began to imagine it as an object with a lot of dazzle. "The new law," he would frequently muse, "that is, something new." And each time, the image of his horse's harness would flash through his mind – the harness which he had bought from Choudhury Khuda Bakhsh after a lot of scrutiny two years ago. When it was new, the nickel coated nails on the harness gleamed and the brass shone like gold. The new law also had to be similarly bright.

Mangu heard a lot about the pros and cons of the new law in the following days. But none of this changed his initial perceptions about it. He felt that with the dawn of the first of April, everything would be clear and many pleasing things would come into view.

Eventually, the thirty one days of March passed. Only a few silent hours of the night were left before dawn. The weather was cooler than usual and a salubrious wind was blowing. Ustad Mangu got up early in the morning, went to the stable, yoked his horse to the tanga and drove off. His spirits were high. He was going to see the new law.

In the chilly morning haze, he made several rounds through the narrow and wide lanes of the bazaar ... but everything looked just the same, like the same old sky. His eyes yearned for a new sight, but everything looked old and worn, except for the colourful plumes that adorned his horse's head, bought from Khuda Bakhsh for fourteen and a half annas.

The sound of horse's hooves, the black road with electric poles alongside, the signboards on the shopfronts, the bells tinkling on his horse's neck, people walking about the bazaar – what was new about any of these things? Nothing. But Mangu did not lose hope.

"It's still early in the morning, the shops haven't opened yet," he reassured himself. Besides, he thought, work at the High Court doesn't begin until after nine. It's futile to expect to see the new law before that.

When his tanga crossed the college, the timekeeper beat the gong for nine rather arrogantly. The students emerging from the main gate, though well-dressed, appeared shabby to Mangu. Probably because he was waiting for a dazzling sight!

He turned to the right from there and reached Anarkali in a few moments. About half the shops had opened by then and there were more people around. Buyers thronged the halwai shops and attractive wares displayed inside glass cases at the stationers' invited attention. Several pigeons were engaged in a playful gambol on the electric wires. But Ustad Mangu showed no interest in any of these things. He wanted to see the new law just as he saw his horse.

When Ustad Mangu's wife was pregnant, he could not contain his restlessness for four or five months. He knew that the child would certainly be born one day, but the wait proved excruciating for him. He wanted a glimpse of the baby just once and then it could take its own time. Impelled by this irresistible desire, he often pressed the belly of his bedridden wife with his hands or pressed his ear to it in order to discover something about the child. But all in vain. Once when he could not bear the wait any longer he burst out, "Why do you lie flat like a corpse all the time? Get up woman. Walk about a bit. You'll feel stronger. Nothing will come of lying down like a wooden board. Do you think you can deliver the baby like this?"

Ustad Mangu was, by nature, very impetuous. He also had an inquisitive mind that liked to explore the reason behind things. Seeing his impatience, his wife Ganga Dai would often say, "The well has not been dug yet and you're dying of thirst!"

However, in his wait for the new law, Ustad Mangu did not show his usual impatience. He had come out of his house that day to see the new law in the same way that he had sometimes gone out to witness a procession led by Gandhi or Jawaharlal Nehru.

Ustad Mangu judged the stature of a leader by the tumult his political procession caused and the number of flower garlands presented to him. He would consider a leader great, if he was laden with marigolds and still greater, if there were a few scuffles amongst the huge crowd accompanying his procession. He wanted to judge the new law according to the same standard. Coming out of Anarkali he drove his tanga gently on the gleaming surface of Mall Road. When he reached the auto shops, a passenger hailed him for the Cantonment. After settling the fare he cracked the whip and told himself, "Might as well. Maybe I'll find out something about the law at the Cantonment."

Ustad Mangu dropped the passenger at his destination, lit a cigarette holding it between the last two fingers of his left hand. Then he went and sat in the back seat of his tanga. When Ustad Mangu wasn't looking for a passenger or when he wanted to reflect on something, he would leave the front seat and relax in the rear, rolling the reins around his right hand. During these intervals his horse would neigh a couple of times and slow his pace, as though he understood that it was time to take a break from the grind of fast trotting.

Keeping pace with the horse's trot, Mangu's thoughts also moved leisurely. Each time the horse lifted its hoof to take another step, fresh thoughts regarding the new law came to Mangu's mind. He was wondering what changes might occur under the new law in the municipal authority's manner of allotting numbers to tangas. He was absorbed in this thought when he noticed a passenger hail him. He turned back to see a gora standing near a distant electric pole waving for him.

As already mentioned, Ustad Mangu detested goras intensely. When he realized that his customer was a gora, hatred welled up in his heart. First, he thought of ignoring him altogether and driving away, but then he opined, "It's stupid to pass up a chance to make money from them. I should make them pay the fourteen and a half annas that I foolishly spent buying the plumes. Let's go."

He turned the tanga dexterously on the deserted road and reached the electric pole in an instant. He reined in the horse and still seated comfortably at the back, asked the gora, "Sahab Bahadur, where do you want to go?" His question was steeped in sarcasm. As he uttered "Sahab Bahadur" his moustache covered upper lip curled down scornfully, and the wrinkle that had formed from his nose to chin quivered and deepened. It was as though someone had scored the dark surface of a sheesham board with a sharp knife. His whole face was beaming, the fire inside him had already reduced the gora to ashes.

Standing behind the pole, the gora was trying to light his cigarette shielding it from the wind. As he turned around and came towards the footboard of the tanga, his eyes met Mangu's and it seemed as if two guns were firing at each other point-blank, creating an explosion.

While Ustad Mangu unwound the reins from his right hand and got down from the tanga, he glared at the gora in a way that made him wince. The gora nervously began to brush some invisible lint from his blue trousers, trying to ward off this onslaught.

"Will you go or just create trouble again?" The gora asked in pidgin Urdu as he inhaled the cigarette smoke.

"He's the same character," these words formed in Mangu's mind and began to dance around in his broad chest. "He's the same character!" he repeated the words mentally, sure now that the gora standing before him was the same one with whom he had had an altercation a year ago. The gora had been drunk and had caused trouble. Mangu had to put up with his nasty behaviour. Ustad Mangu could have taught him a lesson then, could have smashed his skull, but he had restrained himself. He knew very well that the wrath of the court usually fell on the kochwans in such matters.

Keeping the previous year's encounter and the new law of the first of April in mind, he asked the gora in a voice sharp as a whiplash, "Where do you want to go?"

"Hira Mandi," replied the gora.

"It'll cost you five rupees," Ustad Mangu's moustache fluttered.

The gora was taken aback. He screamed, "Five rupees! Are you ...?"

"Yes, yes. Five rupees." As he said this Ustad Mangu's hairy right hand curled into a fist. "So, do you want to go or just talk?" Ustad Mangu's tone had a cutting edge now.

The outcome of last year's encounter made the gora forget Ustad Mangu's broad chest. He felt Mangu was again itching for a beating. Influenced by this appealing thought, he advanced aggressively towards the tanga and swung his stick, motioning Mangu to come down. The polished stick brushed Mangu's hefty thighs two or three times.

From his perch, Mangu looked down at the stocky gora, threatening to crush him under the weight of his glare. Then suddenly his fist shot out like an arrow from a bow and landed on the gora's chin. Mangu pushed him aside, got down from the tanga and began to beat him mercilessly.

The gora was stunned. But he soon gathered his wits and tried to fend off Mangu's heavy fists. When he saw that his adversary was in a frenzy, his eyes raining fire, he began shouting for help. His yells aggravated Mangu even further and his blows began to fall hard and fast.

"The same insolence ... even on the first of April!" Mangu screamed between his punches. "It is we who rule now, beté."

A crowd gathered. Two policemen somehow extricated the gora from Mangu's clutches as he stood between them panting breathlessly. Frothing at the mouth but smiling, he surveyed the stunned crowd. "The days of atrocity are over. Now we've got the New Law. The New Law!" And the poor gora, his face distorted beyond recognition, was staring dumbly at Mangu and the crowd.

The police constables took Mangu to the station. He kept repeating, "The New Law," on the way and at the station, but no one paid any heed.

"The New Law! What the hell are you talking about? The law is still the same."

And then they locked him up.

---

"The New Law" has been translated from "Naya Qanoon," in *Manto ke Numayinda Afsane,* Educational Book House, Aligarh, 1989.

# The Black Shalwar

Before coming to Delhi she had lived in Ambala Cantonment, where several white clients visited her. From them she'd learnt a few sentences of English. She didn't use them in ordinary conversation. But when, after coming to Delhi, she couldn't make a go of things, she said to her neighbour, Tamancha Jaan one day, "This life? Very bad," adding that you couldn't even earn enough for your food.

In Ambala Cantonment she'd done very well. The British Tommies used to come to her drunk. Within three or four hours she could handle nine or ten of them, earning twenty to thirty rupees. These Tommies treated her better than her own countrymen. True, Sultana couldn't understand their language, but her ignorance proved very useful. If any of them wanted something extra she would say, "Sahab, I don't understand what you're saying." And if they pestered her too much, she would begin to swear at them in her own language. They would stare at her, completely nonplussed. She would say in Urdu, "Sahab, you're a bloody fool, a real bastard. Do you understand?" And she used a very affectionate tone to deliver this. The Tommies would laugh, and when they laughed they did look like bloody fools.

But since she'd been in Delhi not a single Tommy had visited her. She'd been here for three months now, a city where she'd heard the Big Lord Sahab lived. But only six men had visited her so far, only six, that is, two a month. And as god was her witness, she had got only eighteen and a half rupees out of these six customers. God knows why, but not one of them thought her worth more than three. She'd told five of them that her fee was ten rupees and was surprised when every one of them said, "Not a penny more than three." So when the sixth one came she herself said, "Listen, I charge three rupees each time. Not a penny less. Now it's up to you. You can stay or go." He didn't argue and stayed. When they went into the other room and he took off his coat she said, "And one rupee for milk." He didn't give her one rupee, instead took out a shiny new eight anna piece with the head of the new king from his pocket and gave it to her. She too, didn't argue. She took it without a word, thinking, "Well, it's better than nothing."

Eighteen and a half rupees in three months – and the rent of her place alone was twenty a month. Her landlord called it a "flat," using the English word. In this flat there was a toilet in which, when you pulled a chain the water immediately carried all the filth into the sewer. It made tremendous noise, and initially she had got a fright. On her first day there, when she'd gone to the toilet she suddenly felt a sharp pain in her waist and took hold of this hanging chain to stand up. She'd noticed this chain and thought that since the flat had been specially fitted out for them, it had been put there to give them some support when getting up. But no sooner had she taken hold of the chain, she heard a clanking sound above her and all of a sudden water came out with a rush.

She was so frightened she shrieked. Khuda Bakhsh had been in the next room attending to his photographic equipment and pouring hydroquinone into a clean bottle, when he heard Sultana shriek. He came running and asked her, "What's the matter? Was that you shrieking?"

Sultana's heart was beating fast. "What's this wretched toilet up to?" she said. "What's this chain hanging down like the chain in a railway carriage? I felt a pain in my waist and thought I'd support myself by it, but as soon as I touched it, there was a loud explosion, so loud that ..."

Khuda Bakhsh laughed his head off. Then he explained, "It's a new style toilet. You pull the chain and all the filth goes into the ground."

How Khuda Bakhsh and Sultana got together is a long story. He came from Rawalpindi. After passing his entrance exam he had learnt to drive a lorry. For four years he worked as a lorry driver on the Rawalpindi-Kashmir route. Then he took up with a woman in Kashmir and carried her off with him to Lahore. When he couldn't get work in Lahore, he put this woman to work as a prostitute. This went on for two or three years but then the woman ran off with someone else. Khuda Bakhsh learnt that she was in Ambala and went there to look for her. In Ambala, he met Sultana. Sultana liked him, and that's how they got together.

From the time Khuda Bakhsh joined her, trade began to pick up. She was a superstitious woman and concluded that Khuda Bakhsh was a man of great spiritual power and that's why things had improved. This enhanced Khuda Bakhsh's standing in her eyes even more.

Khuda Bakhsh was a hard worker. He didn't like sitting idle all day, doing nothing. He made friends with a photographer who took pictures with a Polaroid camera outside the railway station. This man gave Khuda Bakhsh a few lessons on photography. He took sixty rupees from Sultana and bought a camera. Gradually he got together a screen, two chairs and equipment for developing film, and set up on his own. He did well, and had established himself in Ambala Cantonment very soon. There he'd take photos of the Tommies. Within a month he had a wide circle of acquaintances in the Cantonment. So he moved Sultana there too, and thanks to him a number of Tommies became Sultana's regular clients and her income almost doubled.

Sultana bought herself earrings and got eight gold bangles made, each weighing five and a half tolas. She accumulated ten, fifteen good quality saris, and furniture for their home. In short, in Ambala she was very well off. Then suddenly – god knows why –Khuda Bakhsh got it into his head to move to Delhi. How could Sultana refuse? She believed Khuda Bakhsh brought her luck. She gladly agreed. She thought that in a large city like Delhi, where the Big Lord Sahab lived, her trade would prosper even more. She'd heard her friends sing praises of Delhi. And the shrine of Nizamuddin, a saint she felt great devotion for, was there too. She quickly sold all her heavy possessions and they moved to Delhi. There they rented a flat for twenty rupees a month.

It was in a long chain of new buildings running along the road. The Municipal Committee had designated this part of the city as the prostitutes' quarter so that they would not establish themselves all over the town. There were shops on the ground floor and two storied flats above them. Because a single design had been used in the construction of all the buildings, Sultana at first had great difficulty remembering hers. But then a laundrywala took the shop on the floor below. His signboard "Clothes washed here," gave her a sure landmark and helped her locate her flat at once. In the same way, she established many other landmarks for herself. For example, her friend Hira Bai, who sometimes sang on the radio, lived above the shop which announced in great big letters that it sold coal. Above "Excellent cuisine for gentlemen" lived another friend, Mukhtar. Above the workshop that made broad tape for beds, lived Nuri. She was in the regular service of the man who owned the workshop, and, since he needed to keep an eye on it at night, he used to stay there with her.

When you first set up a shop you can't expect customers to start coming right away, and when, for the first month, Sultana had no customers she comforted herself with this thought. But after two months had gone by and still no one had approached her, she became very worried. She said to Khuda Bakhsh, "What is this, Khuda Bakhsh? We've been here a full two months and no one has come our way. I know that trade is slack these days, but it's not so slack that throughout the month no one even looks at you."

Although he hadn't said anything, Khuda Bakhsh had also been troubled about this. Now that Sultana herself had raised the matter he said, "I've been thinking about it for some time now. All I can imagine is that people have taken up war work and can't think of anything else. Or maybe it's that ..."

However before he could say anything further, they heard someone coming up the stairs. Khuda Bakhsh and Sultana pricked up their ears. Shortly, there was a knock at the door. Khuda Bakhsh rushed to open it and a man came in. This was their first customer and they settled for three rupees. After that five more came – that meant six in three months, and Sultana got eighteen and a half rupees from them.

Twenty a month went in rent for the flat. Water rates and the electricity bill above that. And all the other household expenses – food, drink, clothes, medicines. And no income. Eighteen and a half rupees in three months hardly fills in as income. Sultana was worried. One by one, the eight bangles of five tolas each, were sold off. When only one was left she said to Khuda Bakhsh, "Listen to me. Let's go back to Ambala. There's nothing here for us. And even if there is, I don't like it here. You too did well there. Come on, let's go back and cut our losses. This is my last bangle. Go and sell it. Meanwhile I'll pack, and we'll leave by the train tonight."

Khuda Bakhsh took the bangle from her and said, "No, my love. We're not going back. We'll make our living here in Delhi. You'll get all your bangles back right here. Trust in god. He provides, and here too he'll provide us with some means."

Sultana said nothing, and took off her last bangle. It made her sad when she looked at her bare arm, but what could she do? They had to find some way to fill their bellies.

Five months went by, and their income still didn't cover even a quarter of their expenses. Sultana grew extremely anxious. These days Khuda Bakhsh also stayed out all day long, which upset her further. Though there were a few neighbours she could go to and pass time, she didn't like going there every day to kill long hours. So gradually she stopped going altogether. Instead, she would sit in her empty house, sometimes slicing betel nut and sometimes mending her old clothes. Occasionally, she would go out on to the balcony and stand by the railing, aimlessly watching the moving and stationary engines in the railway yard across the street.

On that side of the road was a warehouse, stretching from one corner to the other. To the right, under the metal roof lay some big bales along with piles of all sorts of goods. To the left there was an open space, crisscrossed by innumerable railway lines. Whenever Sultana saw the iron rails shining in the sun, she would look at her hands on which the blue veins stood out just like the railway lines. In that long, open space, engines and bogies were moving all the time, this way and that, puffing and clattering. Whenever she got up early in the morning and went out on to the balcony, a strange sight confronted her. Thick smoke would be rising from the engines through the mist, going upward into the overcast sky like fat, burly men. And also the great clouds of steam, surging loudly from the rails, gradually dispersing into the air. Sometimes, when she saw a carriage being shunted and left to run on its own along a line, she thought of herself ... thought how she too had been shunted on to a line and left to run on her own. Others would change the switches and she would move on, not knowing where she was going. Then a day would arrive, after the momentum had exhausted itself, when she would halt somewhere she had never been before.

She would remain thus for hours, aimlessly watching the vivid, lively railway lines with the engines standing or moving along them. All sorts of thoughts would crowd her mind. Even in Ambala, her house had been near the railway station, but thoughts like these had never occurred. Now she compared this network of railway lines, from which steam and smoke were always rising, to a huge brothel – lots of bogies being shunted hither and thither by a few fat engines. Sometimes she felt that these engines were like the businessmen who used to visit her in Ambala. And sometimes when she watched an engine moving slowly past the lines of bogies, she thought it was like a man walking slowly through the red light quarter, looking up at the balconies where the prostitutes stood.

Sultana feared that ideas like these might lead to some mental disorder. So whenever such thoughts came she stopped going to the balcony.

She repeatedly asked Khuda Bakhsh to have pity on her and stay at home, not to leave her alone lying there in the house like a patient. But every time she asked, he would tell her, "My love, I go out to try and earn something. God willing, soon all our problems will be solved."

But full five months had gone by and both Sultana's and his own problems were yet to be solved.

The month of Muharram was drawing near. Sultana had no means of getting black clothes made for herself. Her friend Mukhtar had had a fashionable Lady Hamilton kameez made, with black georgette sleeves. And to match it, she had a black satin shalwar that glistened like eyeliner. Anwari had bought herself a fine silk georgette sari. She told Sultana she would wear a white petticoat underneath it. This was the latest style, she said. And she had also got herself dainty black velvet shoes with it. When Sultana saw all these things, she was saddened that she couldn't afford such clothes for Muharram.

She returned home pained after seeing Anwari and Mukhtar's clothes, as though a boil had begun to swell up inside her. The house was empty. Khuda Bakhsh was out as usual. She put a bolster under her head and lay down on the carpet. She lay there until the height of the bolster began to stiffen her neck. Then she got up and went out on to the balcony, hoping to get these painful thoughts out of her head.

There were carriages standing on the rails, but not a single engine. It was evening. Water had already been sprinkled on the street, so there was no dust in the air. People had begun to pass by, looking about as they went home silently. One of them raised his head and noticed Sultana. She smiled at him and then quickly forgot about him as she'd already focused her attention on an engine that appeared on the railway track opposite. Gradually the idea that the engine too was wearing black formed in her head. To banish this weird idea from her mind she looked down again at the street. She saw the man still standing there by a bullock cart, the same one who had been staring at her lustfully. She beckoned him. He looked around him and then gestured to ask her the way up to her flat. She showed him. He hesitated for a moment, then quickly came up the stairs.

Sultana invited him to sit down on the carpet. To get the conversation going, she said, "You seemed afraid to come up."

He smiled. "What makes you say that? What's there to be afraid of?"

Sultana said, "Because you waited a little before coming up."

He smiled again, "You're mistaken. I was looking at the flat above you. There was a woman standing there taunting some man. I got interested. Then I saw a green light on the balcony, and I waited a bit longer ... I like green light."

He began to size up the room. Then he got up.

Sultana asked, "Are you going?"

"No," he said. "I want to see your flat. Come on, show me all the rooms."

Sultana showed him all three rooms. He looked them over without saying a word. When they returned to the room where they had been sitting, he said, "My name is Shankar."

Now for the first time Sultana looked at him closely. He was of medium height and was nothing special to look at. But his eyes were unusually clear and bright with an occasional strange twinkle in them. He had a firm, small body. Hair greying at the temples. Trousers of warm cloth. A white shirt with a stand-up collar.

He sat there on the carpet as though Sultana, not he, was the client. This worried her a little. So she asked, "What can I do for you?"

He lay back and replied, "What can you do for me? What can I do for you? It was you who invited me up." When Sultana did not reply, he sat up again.

"Oh, I see," he said. "Now listen to me. Whatever you were thinking, you were wrong. I'm not one of those who come up here, give you something and go away again. I expect a fee, like a doctor does. When people send for me they have to pay a fee."

Sultana was flabbergasted, but she couldn't help laughing.

"What do you do?" she asked him.

"I do what you all do," he replied.

"What's that?"

"What do you do?"

"I? I? ... I don't do anything."

"I don't do anything either."

Sultana said crossly, "That doesn't make sense. There must be something you do."

"And there must be something you do," Shankar replied calmly.

"Yes, I waste my time."

"I too waste my time."

"Come on then, let's waste time together."

"Use your head. This isn't a charity."

"No, and I'm not a volunteer."

Sultana hesitated. "Who are these volunteers?"

"Ulloo ke patté," said Shankar.

"Well, I'm not one."

"No, but that Khuda Bakhsh who lives with you, he's a bloody fool."

"Why?"

"Because for days he's been going to a fakir, hoping that he'll change his fortunes when the man hasn't a hope of even changing his own. It's like trying to open a lock that's rusted." And he laughed.

Sultana said, "You're a Hindu. That's why you ridicule our holy men."

He smiled, "In places like this, the Hindu-Muslim question doesn't arise. If Pandit Malaviya and Mr Jinnah were to come here, they'd both behave like gentlemen."

"I don't know what you're talking about. Are you staying or not?"

"Only on the condition I told you."

Sultana got up. "You may leave then," she said.

Shankar got up, completely at ease. Thrusting his hands into his trouser pockets he said as he left, "I come this way every now and then. Whenever you need me, call me. I can do a lot for you."

Shankar went away. Sultana had now completely forgotten about her black dress. She thought about him for a long time instead. What he had said had brightened her mood considerably. If he'd come to her in Ambala, when she was well off, she'd have looked at him in quite a different light – would probably have pushed him out. But here she was depressed ... she liked the way he talked.

When Khuda Bakhsh came home in the evening Sultana asked him where he'd been all day long. Khuda Bakhsh was exhausted. He said, "I had gone to the Old Fort. There's a fakir staying there since some days. It's him I'm going to every day, so that our fortunes may change."

"Has he said anything to you?"

"No, so far he hasn't deigned to. But Sultana, my waiting upon him won't be for nothing. If god is gracious we'll be comfortable soon."

Sultana's head was full of Muharram. She said in a mournful voice, "Every day you're out all day long. And I'm left here like a prisoner in a cage. I can't go anywhere. Muharram will soon be here. Have you thought about that? Has it occurred to you that I need black clothes? We haven't got a paisa in the house. I had my bangles, but one by one all have been sold. How much longer are you going to trail behind these holy men? It seems as if god himself has turned his back on us since we came to Delhi. Heed my advice and start your photography work here. It'll bring in something at least."

Khuda Bakhsh lay down on the carpet. "But to get started I need a bit of capital," he said. "For god's sake, don't say such painful things. I can't bear it. You're right, it was a really bad mistake to leave Ambala. But everything that happens is god's will, and it is for our own good. Who knows? We'll have to put up with all this for a while, and then?"

Sultana interrupted him. "For god's sake, do something. Steal. Rob. No matter what, but bring me material for a black shalwar.

I've got a white kameez, which can be dyed black. And my white muslin dupatta, the one you bought me for Diwali, can be dyed too. All I need is a black shalwar ... some way or the other you've got to produce it. Look, I'm putting you under oath. Some way or the other you've got to get it."

Khuda Bakhsh sat up. "What's the point of going on and on about it? Where am I going to get it from? I don't even have the money for opium."

"I don't care what you do. You have to bring me four and a half yards of cloth for a black shalwar."

"Pray that god sends you two or three clients this very night."

"But you won't do anything. You could get together enough money if you wanted to. Before the war, you could get satin for twelve to fourteen annas a yard. Now they charge one and a quarter rupees a yard. What will four and a half yards cost?"

"All right, if you say so, I'll find some way." He got up. "But for now, forget it. I'm going to bring in some food."

Food arrived. They sat together and somehow got it down. Then they went to bed. In the morning, Khuda Bakhsh again went off to the holy man in the Old Fort. Sultana was left alone. She lay down for a while, slept for some time, wandered from room to room ... After her midday meal, she took out her muslin dupatta and her white kameez and took them downstairs to the laundrywala to get them dyed. He both dyed and washed the clothes.

Having done that, she came back and read film magazines. These magazines published the stories and songs of the films she had seen. She fell asleep while reading. When she woke up, she could see that it was already four as the sun had reached the drain in the yard. She took a bath, wrapped a warm sheet around her and went out on to the balcony. She stood there for the best part of an hour. It was evening now and the lamps were being lit. The road below looked quite splendid. It grew cold, but Sultana didn't mind. For a long time she watched the tangas and cars going by. Suddenly she caught sight of Shankar. When he reached the point in the street beneath her flat, he raised his head, looked at her and smiled. Sultana, without meaning to, beckoned him to come up.

When he came up, she got worried. She didn't know what to say to him. Actually she'd called him without thinking. Shankar was completely relaxed, as if in his own home. He put a bolster under his head and lay down, just like the previous time. After quite some time passed and Sultana still did not say anything, he remarked, "You can invite me up a hundred times and send me away each time. Things like this never upset me."

Sultana didn't know what to do. "No," she said. "Sit down, no one's asking you to go."

Shankar smiled. "Does that mean you accept my conditions?"

She laughed. "What conditions? Are you marrying me then?"

"Marriage? Neither you nor I will ever get married. Those conventions are not for us. Don't talk such nonsense. Say something to the point. You're a woman. Say something to keep me happy for a while. There's more to life than buying and selling."

In her heart of hearts, Sultana had accepted him.

"Speak plainly," she said. "What do you want from me?"

"The same as the others want." He sat up.

"Then what's the difference between you and them?"

"There's no difference between me and you. But there's a world of difference between me and them. There are plenty of questions you shouldn't ask, you should know the answers without asking."

For a while Sultana tried her best to comprehend what he meant, then she said, "I understand."

"Tell me then. What are you going to do?"

"You've won. I've lost. But I can tell you, until today, no one has ever accepted such a condition."

"You're wrong. In this very quarter you'll find women who are so simple they won't believe that any woman can accept the degradation that you regularly accept without even feeling it. They don't believe it, but there are thousands of you. Your name is Sultana, isn't it?"

He got up and started laughing. "And mine is Shankar. What ridiculous names! Come on, let's go to the other room."

When they came back, they were laughing. God knows at what. When he was about to leave Sultana asked, "Shankar, will you do something for me?"

"First tell me what it is," he said.

She was a bit embarrassed. "You'll think I'm trying to make you pay, but ..."

"Go on, tell me. What's stopping you?"

Sultana summoned up her courage and explained, "The thing is that Muharram is coming, and I haven't got enough money to get a black shalwar made for myself. You know all about the trouble we're in. I have a white kameez and a dupatta, which I have given for dyeing today only."

Shankar said, "You want me to give you money to get this black shalwar?"

"No," she added quickly, "what I mean is that if you can ... you could get one made for me."

71

He smiled. "It's only by sheer luck that I ever have anything in my pocket. But anyway I'll do what I can. You'll get your shalwar on the first day of Muharram. So, are you happy now?" Then he looked at Sultana's earrings and said, "Can you give me those earrings?"

Sultana laughed. "Why do you want these? They're ordinary silver earrings. Worth five rupees at the most."

Shankar laughed and answered, "I asked you for the earrings. I didn't ask you what they cost. Are you going to give them to me or not?"

"Take them," she said. She removed and handed them to him. She regretted it afterwards, but Shankar had already gone.

Sultana didn't believe for a moment that Shankar would fulfil his promise. But eight days later, on the first day of Muharram, there was a knock on the door in the morning at nine. Sultana opened it to find Shankar standing there. He gave her something wrapped in a newspaper and said, "It's a black satin shalwar. Just take a look at it. It might be a bit long. I'm off."

And without uttering another word he left. His trousers were wrinkled and his hair dishevelled. It looked as though he had just got up and come straight here. Sultana opened the package. It was a black shalwar, exactly like the one she'd seen Mukhtar wearing. Sultana was delighted. She finally had the shalwar, Shankar had kept his promise. All the regret she'd felt at the loss of her earrings and the "bargain" she'd made, vanished.

At midday she went down to get her dyed kameez and dupatta from the laundry. She had just put them on when she heard a knock at the door. Sultana opened it to find Mukhtar. She looked at Sultana's clothes and said, "Your kameez and dupatta appear to have been dyed, but the shalwar seems new. When did you get it made?"

Sultana said, "The tailor has just brought it." And as she spoke she noticed Mukhtar's earrings. "Where did you get these earrings?" she asked.

"I just got them today," Mukhtar replied.

And for a little while neither of them could say anything more.

---

"The Black Shalwar" has been translated from "Kali Shalwar," in *Sau Kendil Power ka Bulb: Sa'adat Hasan Manto ke Ikkis Muntakhab Afsane,* Modern Publishing House, New Delhi, 1980.

# Odour

It was a day in the rainy season, just like this one. Outside the window, the peepal leaves were bathing in the rain. On the spring fitted teak bed, now moved close to the window, a Ghatin woman clinged to Randhir's body.

In the milky darkness of the night, the peepal leaves fluttered in the rain, while the woman, still holding him tight, sent shivers through his body.

Randhir had spent the whole day reading news and advertisements in an English daily. In the evening, he had come out to the balcony for some fresh air and saw the woman. She probably worked in the adjoining yarn mill and was standing under the tamarind tree to shield herself from the rain. Coughing a couple of times, Randhir drew her attention and then with his hand gestured her to come up.

He had been feeling lonely for the past few days. The war was on, and most of the Christian girls of Bombay who were easily available in the past had joined the auxiliary force. Many of them had opened dancing schools near the Cantonment where only white soldiers were allowed. Randhir was in low spirits. One reason for his melancholy mood was the scarcity of Christian girls, and the second was that Randhir – who was sophisticated, educated, healthy

and handsome – was still not permitted into most of the bars of
the Fort area just because his skin was not white.

Before the war, he had had physical relationships with several
Christian girls near Nagpara and the Taj Hotel. He was well aware
that he was more adept at handling the etiquette of such
relationships than the Christian lads with whom these girls had
brief affairs just out of fashion. And eventually they married some
nincompoop or the other.

Randhir had called the Ghatin inside to get even with Hazel
and her new found haughtiness. At that time, Hazel lived in the
flat below. Every morning when she came out in her uniform, the
khaki hat tilted at a rakish angle over her bobbed hair, she walked
along the pavement in a presumptuous manner as if all the
pedestrians were dying to prostrate themselves before her.

Randhir wondered why he was so irresistibly drawn towards
Christian girls. There was no doubt they exhibited the contours of
their body to advantage. Without the slightest inhibition they
would talk about their irregular periods and recount their affairs
with former lovers. Whenever they heard a rhythmic tune, their
feet would begin to tap involuntarily. All this was true. However,
any woman could have these qualities.

When Randhir signalled the Ghatin to come up, he had not
even dreamt, he would be able to persuade her to sleep with him.
Looking at her wet clothes, he thought she might catch pneumonia
and felt sorry for her. So he said, "Take off those clothes. You'll
catch cold."

The woman had guessed his intent as his face flushed in
embarrassment for a moment. Later, when Randhir took out his
white dhoti for her, she reflected for a moment and then took off

her dress. It looked dirtier after becoming wet. She put aside her dress and quickly wrapped her thighs with the dhoti. Then she tried to untie the knotted ends of her tight choli. The knot had slipped into the cleavage of her shapely breasts.

She struggled with the knot for a long time with her wornout nails, but it had become tighter after getting wet in the rain. Tired, she gave up and muttered something to Randhir in Marathi, which meant, "What do I do? It doesn't open."

Randhir sat down beside her and tried to undo the knot. When he couldn't manage to open it, he grabbed the two sides of the choli and pulled at them with all his might. The knot slipped open, Randhir's hands moved apart and two shivering breasts came into view. For a moment, Randhir felt as if his hands gave the breasts the shapes of bowls made of soft clay, kneaded by an expert potter.

Her healthy breasts had the same rawness and attraction, the same fullness and warm coolness that one finds in clay pots fresh from a potter's hands.

Those youthful breasts, spotless and earthy, had a strange glow. Beneath the fading wheatish tint there appeared to be a layer of light that created the glow ... at times it did not seem like a glow at all. The mounds of her breasts resembled clay lamps burning under the turgid water of some pond.

It was a day in the rainy season, just like this one. Outside the window, the peepal leaves were fluttering. The two piece dress of the Ghatin was lying on the floor in a dirty heap and she clung to Randhir's body. The warmth of her unwashed, naked body gave him a strange feeling – the kind of feeling one experienced while bathing in the barbers' hot but filthy hamams in severe winter.

Randhir and the Ghatin remained in a tight embrace the whole night. As though their bodies had melted into each other. They barely exchanged words, all their communication was carried on through their breath, lips and hands. Randhir's hands explored her breasts the whole night. Her tiny nipples and the large dark areola around them came to life with Randhir's tender touch, and a vibration coursed through her entire body. Randhir himself shivered every now and then.

Randhir had experienced such quivers many times and the feeling was known to him. He had passed many nights with his chest pressed against the firm or soft breast of some girl or the other. Occasionally he had spent nights with girls who were quite raw. Lying beside him, they would babble out intimate stories of their families that should not be shared with a stranger. He had also slept with girls who did his household chores and saw to his comfort. But this Ghatin girl was entirely different.

All through the night, Randhir inhaled the strange odour coming from her body. The odour was loathsome and pleasurable at the same time. It rose from her armpits, breasts, hair, belly – from every part of her body, and mingled with Randhir's breath. It was a source of wonder to him that though she was lying close to him, he would not have felt her closeness with such intensity without that odour. It seeped into every crevice of his mind and heart and mingled with his old and new thoughts.

That odour had fused Randhir and the girl as one for the night. Each had melted into the other, descended into the depths of the other. Reaching there, they had been transformed into mere embodiments of human delight, a delight that was momentary yet eternal, fleeting yet frozen, and still. They had become like a bird, which though flying high in the sky, looks still and unmoving.

Randhir knew the odour that emanated from each pore of the woman well, though he could hardly describe it to anyone. It was just like the aroma released when water is sprinkled on parched earth. But no, this odour was different. It did not have the artificial scent of lavender or attar. It was primal, as primal and eternal as the relationship between man and woman.

Randhir detested the odour of sweat. After a bath he used to dust his armpits with scented powder or some deodorant to neutralize the sweat odour. Yet, surprisingly, he kissed the armpits of that Ghatin several times – yes, several times – and did not feel any revulsion. On the contrary, he felt a strange pleasure. The soft hair of her armpits was damp with sweat. It also emitted the same odour that could not be understood yet was very familiar. Randhir felt that he knew that odour, but could not recognize it. He grasped its significance but could not explain it.

It was a day in the rainy season, just like this one. When he looked out of the window, he found the leaves fluttering in the rain, the wind whizzing past with a rustling sound. It was dark, but the darkness was imbued with a soft, pale light. It seemed as though starlight had descended to earth along with the raindrops.

It was a similar day in the rainy season. There used to be just one teak bed in his room. Now, there was another. There was also a dressing table in the corner. It was raining. The weather was just the same. Light shimmered through raindrops. The air was filled with the fragrance of henna attar.

The second bed was empty. On the bed on which Randhir was sitting and watching the dance of the raindrops on the fluttering leaves, an extraordinarily beautiful girl was sleeping. She seemed to have fallen asleep while trying to cover her naked body in vain. Her red silk shalwar was lying on the other bed. One tassel of its deep red waistcord was dangling. Her other castoff clothing was also lying on that bed. Her golden flowered kameez, bra, panties and dupatta – all were red, deep red. And they were drenched in henna.

Bits of brocade dotted the girl's dark hair like dirt. These bits along with mascara and rouge had left a unique tint on her face – faded and dull. The colour of the bra had run and left small red stains on her white breasts.

Her breasts were milky white, with a tinge of blue here and there. Her armpits were shaven and had a greyish shadow. Randhir, who had been watching her for quite some time thought, "Doesn't she look as though I've just taken her out of a sealed wooden box after prying off the nails, as one takes out books or china? For doesn't her body bear marks at several places like pressure marks on books and scratches on china, stored in such a box?"

When Randhir had untied the strings of her small, tight fitting bra he had noticed what seemed like wrinkles on her back and on the soft flesh of her chest. There was also a trace mark around her waist left by her tightly fastened drawstring. The sharp edges of her bulky studded necklace had bruised her breast in several places, making those spots look as if clawed by fingernails.

It was a similar day in the rainy season. Raindrops tip-tapped rhythmically on the leaves of the peepal tree, just as Randhir had heard them the whole night on the earlier occasion. The weather was very pleasant. A cool breeze was blowing, carrying the pungent aroma of henna.

Randhir's hands roved over the milky white breasts of the girl for a long time. His fingers felt multiple vibrations in that fair form. When his chest touched her breasts, his every pore heard the music coming from her highly strung body. But where was the call that he had heard in the odour of that Ghatin girl? The call that was more comprehensible than the cry of a baby thirsty for milk, the call that had travelled beyond the audible world and had become soundless.

Randhir was looking out of the barred window. Close to him, the peepal leaves were fluttering. But he was trying to see something beyond, far beyond the rustling of the leaves, at a spot where he could discern a strange, fuzzy light in mud coloured clouds, the kind of light he had seen in the Ghatin's breasts. A light which was hidden like a secret ... and yet apparent.

A fair girl was lying beside Randhir. A girl whose body was soft like flour kneaded with milk and ghee. Her sleeping body emitted the fading scent of henna. Randhir felt revulsion for this dying, gasping scent. It was acrid, like the acridity felt in the belches of indigestion. Dull, insipid, tasteless.

Randhir looked at the girl lying by his side. When milk goes sour, small white lumps lie still in colourless water. In the same way the femininity of this girl was frozen in the shape of white blotches ... As a matter of fact, Randhir's mind languished in the odour of the Ghatin girl, the odour that had no external stimulus. It was lighter than the scent of henna yet more enduring. It did not need to be inhaled ... it found its way to its destination naturally ...

As a last resort, Randhir ran his hands over the girl's milky white body. But he did not feel any tremors in his veins. His newly wed wife, the daughter of a first class magistrate, a BA, and who had been the heartthrob of hundreds of boys in her college, could not accelerate Randhir's pulse! In the dying scent of henna he was searching for the odour of that unwashed body of the Ghatin on just such a day when, outside his window, the peepal leaves danced in the rainwater.

"Odour" has been translated from "Bu," in *Sau Kendil Power ka Bulb: Sa'adat Hasan Manto ke Ikkis Muntakhab Afsane*, Modern Publishing House, New Delhi, 1980.

# Insult

Exhausted after a hard day's work, Saugandhi hit the bed and fell asleep immediately. The Municipal Committee's sanitary inspector, whom she called Seth, had just left for his home after a gruelling session with her that left her bones cracking and her body aching all over. He would have stayed the night – were it not for the great concern he had for his wife who loved him deeply.

The money earned from this seth for her physical labour, was sticking out from her tight fitting, spittle stained choli. Sometimes, heavy breathing displaced the silver coins and their jingle merged with the uneven beatings of her heart. It seemed as though the silver of the coins melted and dripped into the blood of her heart.

She could feel the heat in her chest. This was partly due to the half bottle of brandy the seth brought with him, and partly due to beora, the local brew, which they had with water after the soda had run out.

Now she lay face down on the large teak bed. Her arms, bare to the shoulders, looked like the bows of a kite from which the paper had slipped after becoming wet with dew. A lump of flesh bulged out of her right underarm, turned bluish from excessive squeezing. It looked as though a piece of skin from a plucked chicken had been pasted there.

The room, littered with odds and ends, was small. Under the bed there were a few old, weathered sandals on top of which lay a mangy dog making faces at some invisible object in his dream. The hair on his body had fallen out at places, making him appear bald. Seen from a distance one could easily mistake him for a footmat, made of sackcloth, folded double and left carelessly on the floor.

There was a small shelf on the wall. Make-up items lined it – rouge, lipstick, face powder, comb, and metallic hairpins used to shape hair into a bun. Nearby, from a long pole hung a parrot's cage. The parrot seemed asleep, with its head hidden inside its feathers. The floor of the cage was strewn with small pieces of guava and stale orange peels – small, black mosquitoes and moths hovered over them.

Close to the bed was a cane chair with its headrest dirty from overuse. On its left was a beautiful tripod with a portable His Master's Voice gramophone on it. The black cloth covering it was in tatters. Rusted needles lay scattered on and around the tripod. On the wall, just above the tripod, hung four frames with pictures of different men. Near these pictures, on the left of the entrance door, was a portrait of Ganeshji done in bright colours. It was adorned with both fresh and wilted flowers. The portrait had probably been torn out of a length of fabric and mounted. Close to the portrait, on a small shelf, sat a cup with oil to light the diya that was lying near by. It had probably gone out because of lack of air as its wick stood erect like a tilak on someone's forehead. On this shelf, small and large pieces of incense also lay scattered.

When her first pickings of the day came, she touched Ganeshji's picture with the money, tapped it on her forehead before tucking it inside her choli. She had ample breasts, so the money lay safe there. However, when Madho came over from Poona on holidays, she had to hide away some of the money in a hole she had dug for this very purpose under one of the bedposts.

It was Ramlal, the pimp, who gave Saugandhi the idea to keep money safe from Madho. He was incensed when he heard that Madho came from Poona and wangled money out of Saugandhi.

"Since when did you fall for that bastard? This certainly is a strange love affair! The fellow doesn't spend a paisa from his own pocket and yet enjoys a good time with you. And, on top of that, he robs you of your money. Saugandhi, there must be something wrong somewhere. What do you see in this fellow that makes you so enamoured of him? I have been in this business for the last seven years and I know very well the weaknesses of girls like you."

Ramlal, who pimped in different parts of Bombay for girls costing between ten and one hundred rupees, exhorted her further, "Stupid woman, don't waste your money like this. Some day that motherfucker will snatch the clothes off your back. Dig a small hole under the bedpost and hide all the money there. And when that lover of yours comes, tell him, I swear to you Madho, I haven't seen even a paisa since morning. Please send for some tea and Aflatoon biscuits. I'm famished. Understand? Meri jaan, these are bad times. This bloody Congress has ruined our business by putting a ban on liquor. You, at least get something to drink from somewhere or the other. By god, when I see the bottles emptied here at night and smell the stuff, I feel like ... changing places with you!"

Among all the parts of her body Saugandhi admired her breasts the most. Once Jumna had advised her, "Keep those canon balls under a tight leash. If you wear a bra they'll remain firm."

At this Saugandhi had laughed, "Jumna, you think everyone is like you. For ten rupees you allow guys to ravage your body. And then you imagine that it happens to everyone. Let a fellow try take liberties with me! Oh yes, I must tell you what happened yesterday. Ramlal brought a Punjabi last night at two. We settled for thirty rupees. When we got into bed and I put out the light you should've seen him! He got such a fright. In the dark, all his uppishness vanished. I said, Come on, don't waste time. It's almost three. It's going to be dawn soon. He implored, Roshni, roshni! I said, Roshni, what do you mean? He replied, Light, light! Hearing his squeaky frightened voice I couldn't stop laughing. No, I'm not going to turn on the light. Saying this I pinched his fleshy thighs. He leapt up in pain and turned the light on. I wrapped myself with the sheet and said, Don't you have any shame, you scoundrel? He came back to the bed and I got up to turn off the light. Again he was scared. I tell you I had great fun. Sometimes light, sometimes dark. When the first tram car of the day rumbled by, he put on his trousers and took to his heels. The bastard must have earned the money imagining he would spend it just like that. Jumna, you're a simpleton. I know a hundred tricks to handle these fellows."

Saugandhi did know a lot of tricks which she even shared with some of her friends. In fact, she used to share her tricks with everyone. "If the fellow is a gentleman, be mischievous, tease, tickle, play with him. If he has a beard, run your fingers through it and pluck a hair or two, if he has a large belly, drum it. Don't allow him a moment to take the initiative. He'll go happily and you'll be spared.

The quiet guys are the most dangerous. If they have their way, they'll break your bones."

But Saugandhi was not as clever as she made herself out to be. A very emotional girl, she had just a few customers. That is why all the tricks she knew descended from her head to her belly which, after the birth of a child had stretch marks. When she had seen those lines for the first time she thought her shabby mongrel had made them with his paws. When a bitch passed by without taking any notice of him, the dog used to scratch lines on the ground to hide his shame.

Saugandhi lived in her mind. But a soft word melted her immediately, and that spread to the other parts of her body as well. In her mind, she considered the union between man and woman gratuitous, but the rest of her body thirsted for such a union. The limbs of her body yearned for exhaustion – the kind of exhaustion that comes after they have been left aching. And then to be drowned in sleep – the kind of sleep that comes when the body is bone weary. Such sleep is truly pleasurable. The oblivion that comes after the body has taken a beating and all the joints have come loose. Sometimes you feel you are there and sometimes not. And in this state of being and non-being you sometimes feel as if floating high in the air, with nothing but air on all sides. Even choking in this sea of air seems pleasurable.

As a child, while playing, Saugandhi used to hide in her mother's large wooden box. The twin fear of suffocating and getting caught by her peers made her heart beat wildly. But what a pleasurable sensation that was!

Saugandhi wished that she could spend her whole life hiding inside such a box, searched for by admirers who would go round and round that box. Sometimes they would find her ... so that she also had a chance to find them. The life she had led for the last five years was like a game of hide and seek. Sometimes she looked for someone, sometimes they looked for her. And thus life passed. Every night there would be some man or another on her large teak bed and Saugandhi, who knew lots of tricks to handle men, told herself repeatedly that she would not let him take advantage of her, that she would treat him in a businesslike manner. However, she would be swept away by her emotions and in the end, would remain a woman thirsting for love.

Every night her lover, old or new, would say to her, "Saugandhi, I love you," and Saugandhi, although knowing that he was lying, would melt in his embrace and feel as if the man really loved her. Love – what a beautiful word! She wanted to dissolve it and rub it all over her body, or shrink herself, crawl inside it and put the lid on. Sometimes, when the desire to love became very intense she felt like taking the man lying by her side into her lap and put him to sleep by patting on the back, singing lullabies.

Her desire to love was so intense that she could love each man who came to her and remain true to it too. She was loyal in her love for the four men whose portraits hung on the wall. She always felt that she was very good and often wondered why such goodness was not found in men. She could not understand this. Once, while looking in the mirror, she blurted out involuntarily, "Saugandhi, the world has not treated you well!"

This period – five years of these days and nights – was an inseparable part of her being. Though it did not bring her the happiness she yearned for, she wanted her life to continue in the same pattern. She had no ambition to build a palace, so why should she hanker after money? Her usual rate was ten rupees, out of which Ramlal got two and a half rupees as commission. That left her with seven and a half rupees per day which was enough for her needs. When Madho came from Poona to "raid" her, as Ramlal put it, she could offer him ten or fifteen rupees. She made this offering because of her special feelings for him. Ramlal was right. There was something in Madho that had taken her fancy. Now, why hide the truth? Why not admit it ...

When Saugandhi met Madho for the first time he had said to her, "Aren't you ashamed of bargaining like this? Do you realize what you are bargaining for? And do you know why I have come here? Tsch, tsch, tsch. Ten rupees out of which two and a half go to the pimp, as you say. That leaves seven and a half rupees, doesn't it? Now, for this meagre amount you're promising to give me something that is very difficult for you to give. And I have come to take something I can't really take. I want a woman. But do you, at this hour, want a man? For me, any woman would do. It is enough if she's just a woman. But do I appeal to you as a man? What binds us together after all? Nothing, except these ten rupees, a quarter of which will go as commission. The rest will also disappear. The coins that bind us together – you can hear their jingle, so can I. Your mind is on one thing, mine's on another. Why not talk about something that answers the needs of us both? I am a havaldar in Poona. I'll come once a month for three or four days. Give up this business. I'll give you enough money for your expenses. Well, what's the rent for this kholi?"

Madho had said a lot more. It made a deep impression on Saugandhi and for a few moments she began to consider herself as the havaldar's wife. After he finished talking, Madho arranged the things scattered about in proper order. He tore off the nude pictures that hung over Saugandhi's bed. He said, "I can't allow these here. And this water pitcher, look, how dirty it is! These rags and sheets, how they stink! Throw them out. And you've ruined your hair ... and ... and ..."

Saugandhi and Madho talked for three hours ... bringing them close. Saugandhi felt as though she had known him for years. Till that day no one had ever noticed the smelly rags, the dirty pitcher or the nude pictures. No one had ever made her feel that she had a home that could look like a home, if she made an effort. Men came and went without ever noticing the dirty bed. No one had ever said to her, "Saugandhi, your face is flushed today. You may be catching a cold. I'll get some medicine for you." Madho was so nice. Everything he said made a lot of sense. How he scolded her! She began to feel that she needed Madho. The bond between them became deeper.

Once a month Madho came from Poona and when leaving he would always say, "Look Saugandhi, if you start your business again, we can't be friends anymore. If you allow a man to stay with you here even once, I'll pull you by your hair and turn you out. Look, I'll send you this month's expenses by money order as soon as I reach Poona. Oh yes, what's the rent for this kholi?"

But Madho never sent money from Poona nor did Saugandhi stop her business. Both knew what was going on. Saugandhi had never asked Madho, "Why do you keep mouthing this nonsense? Have you ever given me a paisa?" Nor had Madho ever asked Saugandhi, "How do you come by all this stuff when I don't give you anything?" Both were liars. Both were living in a make-believe world. But Saugandhi was happy. Those who can't get real gold, settle for imitations.

Extremely tired, Saugandhi was sleeping. She had forgotten to switch off the electric bulb over her head. Its bright light was hitting her eyes but she was in deep sleep.

There was a knock on the door. Who would come at two in the morning? Still half asleep, the sound of the knock echoed like a drone in Saugandhi's ears. As the knocking became insistent, she woke up with a start. Two different kinds of drink and the bits of fish stuck between her teeth left a bitter taste in her mouth and thick, slimy saliva dribbled down her chin. She cleaned this smelly drool with the corner of her dhoti and started rubbing her eyes. She was alone in the bed. Lowering her head, she looked underneath. Her mongrel was sleeping. As usual his head was resting on the weathered sandals, and he was making faces at some invisible object in his dream. The parrot too slept, resting his head in his wings.

There was a knock again. Saugandhi got up. Her head throbbed. She went over to the pitcher, took a mouthful of water from the ladle and gargled. She took a second mouthful, drank it and opened the door a crack.

"Ramlal?"

Ramlal had got tired knocking for so long and looked annoyed, "Has a snake bit you that you were sleeping like someone dead? I have been knocking for an hour, where on earth were you?" Then he lowered his voice and whispered, "There's no one in there, I hope?"

When Saugandhi answered "no," Ramlal raised his voice again, "Then why the hell did you not open the door sooner? This is the limit! What sort of sleep was that? If I have to spend two hours striking a deal for every girl, I won't have much of a business left. Now don't keep staring at me. Take off that dhoti and put on your floral sari. Then powder your face and come along with me. There's a seth waiting for you outside in the car. Now, get going, hurry up."

Saugandhi plonked down on the armchair and Ramlal began to comb his hair in front of the mirror.

Saugandhi picked up the bottle of balm from the tripod. As she opened the lid she said, "Ramlal, I'm not well today."

Ramlal put the comb on the shelf and turning, said, "Why didn't you tell me earlier?"

Saugandhi rubbed the balm on her forehead and temples and then explained, "It's not that, Ramlal. I just drank a little too much."

Ramlal's mouth watered, "If there's any left get it for me. Let me taste a little too."

Saugandhi put the balm bottle back on the tripod and said, "If I had left any I wouldn't have this splitting headache. Look Ramlal, the fellow sitting outside in the car, why don't you bring him in?"

Ramlal replied, "No, he won't come here. He's a gentleman. He even had qualms about parking the car outside. Change your dress and come with me to the corner of the lane. Everything will be all right."

Given her bad headache, Saugandhi would not normally have agreed to the deal just for the sake of seven and a half rupees. But she needed the money badly. In the adjoining kholi, a Madrasi woman's husband had been run over by a car. The woman had to return to her village with her grown up daughter. But she had no money and needed some help. Only the day before Saugandhi had consoled her, "Don't worry, behn. My man is about to arrive from Poona. I'll get some money from him and make arrangements for your departure."

Madho was due to arrive from Poona. But the money had to be arranged by Saugandhi herself. So she got up and began to change quickly. In five minutes, she removed the dhoti, put on the sari with the floral print and dabbed her cheeks with powder and rouge. She drank a glass of cold water from the pitcher and set off with Ramlal.

The lane, which was a little wider than the ones normally found in small towns, was absolutely quiet. Because of rust, the gas lamps on the poles had gone dimmer. In that dim light, a car could be seen standing at the end of the lane.

In the fading light and the absolute quiet of the late night, the shadow of the car made her feel as if the ache in her head permeated the atmosphere. The air she breathed also seemed thick and sour like the aftertaste of the brandy and beora in her mouth.

Ramlal went on ahead and said something to the people sitting in the car. Meanwhile Saugandhi also came up. Ramlal turned aside and said, "Here she is, a very nice girl, started work only a few days ago." Then he addressed her, "Saugandhi, come here. Sethji's calling you."

Twisting the corner of her sari around her finger Saugandhi walked up to the door of the car.

The seth flashed a torchlight on her face. For a moment, the light blinded her groggy eyes. "Oonh," said the seth and clicked off the light. The next moment, the engine of the car snarled and it sped off.

Saugandhi had no time to realize what was going on. Her eyes were still dazzled by the light. She hadn't even seen the seth's face properly. What had happened? What did he mean by "Oonh," the sound still echoed in her ears. What? ...What? ...

She heard Ramlal's voice "He didn't like you. Okay, I'm off. Wasted two hours for nothing."

As soon as she heard this, she felt a strange sensation pass through her legs, arms and head. Where's that car? So the meaning of "oonh" was that he didn't like me ... A curse rose from inside her stomach and stopped at the tip of her tongue. Whom would she curse! The car had already left. She could just see the taillights disappearing in the darkness of the bazaar. She felt as though those red lights were live coals piercing her chest like a spear. She wanted to call the seth back, O seth, please stop the car, just for a minute. But the seth, god's curse upon him, was already long gone.

She was standing alone in the desolate bazaar. The floral sari, which she normally wore on special occasions, fluttered gently in the late hour of the night. Its rustling sound annoyed her. It resembled the "oonh" of the seth. She felt like tearing it to shreds.

Saugandhi had dabbed her cheeks with powder and rouge and put on lipstick. When she realized that she had done all this to make herself acceptable, she was filled with shame. To offset her shame she thought, I didn't dress up just for that bastard. It's my habit to do so. Not only me, everyone likes to dress up. But, but, at two in the morning? And Ramlal, the pimp, and the bazaar, the car, the flashlight ... As she remembered all this, spots of light began to float before her eyes, she could hear the snarl of the engine with every gust of wind.

The layer of balm on her forehead, thinned out from applying make-up, was now beginning to run into her pores with perspiration. Her forehead no longer felt her own. When a gust of wind blew over her sweaty forehead, it felt as though someone had cut a piece of cool serotin and pasted it there. Her head still throbbed, a pain restrained by the cacophony of thoughts crowding around it.

Saugandhi tried several times to revive the subdued pain, but in vain. She wanted her whole body to ache, every part of it – her head, legs, stomach, arms, hands – everything should be drowned in pain. And the pain should be so intense that she would forget every other thing. Something snapped in her heart when these thoughts crowded her mind. Was it pain? For a brief moment her heart shrank ... and then expanded. What was it? God's curse! It was that "oonh" which was causing her heart to suffer such pain.

She was about to turn towards home when she stopped in her tracks. She wondered, Ramlal thinks that he didn't like my face. No, he didn't mention that. He just said, Saugandhi, he didn't like you! If he didn't like my face, so what? I also don't like the faces of many men. That fellow, who came on the night of amavasya, how ugly he looked! Didn't I wrinkle up my nose at the sight of him? Wasn't I repulsed when he slept with me? I was almost going to throw up. So? But Saugandhi, you didn't turn him away, you didn't scorn him. This car-borne seth, he spat in your face. His "oonh" had no other meaning. A face like a gecko, and doing up her hair with jasmine oil! What a face and what great expectations! O Ramlal, where did you find this gecko? You were praising this girl? Ten rupees for her? What's wrong with a mule ...

Saugandhi was engrossed in thought and her whole body, from top to toe, was burning. She was angry with herself and with Ramlal who had robbed her of her rest, waking her up at two in the morning. But soon she pardoned herself and Ramlal, and began thinking about the seth. At the thought of him different parts of her body – her eyes, ears, arms and legs – went on alert to see the seth again. A strong desire to observe the whole episode once more, just once, overcame her. She would move slowly towards the car. A hand wielding a flashlight would appear from the car and throw light on her face. Then the sound of "oonh" would come and she ... Saugandhi would pounce on the seth, scratching his face with her two hands like a wild cat, digging deep with all her nails, which were long as in vogue then. She would pull him out of the car and pulverize him with her fists until she was completely exhausted ... and when all her energies were spent she would sit down and weep.

Saugandhi thought of weeping because the intensity of her anger and helplessness had already brought three or four large tears to her eyes. Why do you weep? What has happened to you that you've started dripping? she asked her eyes.

For a while the question floated in her tears, hanging precariously on her eyelashes. Through these tears she kept staring at the void left by the seth's car.

Phur, phur, phur! Where had this sound come from? Startled, Saugandhi looked around but no one was there. Ah, it was her heart beating wildly. Her heart – what had gone wrong with it? It was beating normally when suddenly it began to flutter, garrh ... garrh ... like the sound of the gramophone needle stuck somewhere on a worn out record, and the line, "The night was spent counting the stars," reduced to a repetitive, "stars, stars."

The sky was studded with stars. Saugandhi looked at them and said to herself, "How beautiful they are!" She wanted to divert her thoughts to something else, but the moment she formed the word "beautiful," the thought flashed through her mind, "The stars are beautiful, but you're ugly. Only a little while ago your face was scorned."

"Saugandhi, you are not ugly!" This thought brought back all the images of the past five years – images of herself that she had seen in the mirror. There was no denying that she was not as attractive as she had been five years ago ... when she still lived with her parents, without a care in the world. But, even now she was not ugly. She looked like the average woman, ogled at by men while walking down the street. She had all the qualities that a man considered essential in a woman, with whom he wished to spend a night or two. She was still young and had a well proportioned body. Sometimes, while taking bath, she looked at her thighs and was pleased with their rounded softness. She had a pleasant face. There was hardly a man who had gone away from her unsatiated in the last five years. She was very kind and amiable. Some time ago, during Christmas when she lived at Golpeta, a young man had come to her. In the morning when he went to the other room and took his coat from the peg, he found his wallet missing. Saugandhi's servant had stolen it. The fellow was very upset. He had come from Hyderabad to Bombay to spend his holidays and was now left with no money for his return ticket. Saugandhi took pity on him and gave back his ten rupees.

"What is lacking in me?" Saugandhi asked this question of whatever object was before her – the dimmed gas lamps, the iron lampposts, the square stones of the pavement and the dislodged pebble lying on the road. She looked at each of them in turn. Then she looked at the sky that was hanging over her. But she got no answer.

The answer lay hidden within her. She knew that she was not bad, in fact she was nice. But she wanted someone else to corroborate this. Someone, anyone, to put his hands on her shoulders and say, "Saugandhi, who says you're bad? Whoever says this is bad himself." Even this much wasn't needed. "Saugandhi, you're very good," would be sufficient.

She began to wonder why she wanted someone to praise her. Never before had she felt this need so intensely. Then why today was she looking at even inanimate objects, trying to convince them of her goodness? Why was every atom of her body crying out to be a mother? Why did she want to take every object into her arms? Why did she yearn to cling to the lamppost and rest her cheeks on its cold iron, letting her warm cheeks take away the chill?

For a moment she felt that all these objects – the dimmed gas lamp, the iron lamppost, the square stone and all the other things that lay around her in the stillness of the night – were looking at her with pity. And that sky hanging over her, which seemed like a mud coloured sheet with countless holes in it, understood what she was saying. And she, in turn, felt that she could understand the blinking stars. But what was this tumult going on within her? Why did she feel inside the yearnings that usually came just before the rains? Saugandhi desperately wished that all the pores of her body would open up and whatever smouldered within her would come out through them. But how could that be? How?

She was now standing by the mailbox at the corner of the lane. Whenever the metallic tongue over the mouth of the box rattled, Saugandhi's eyes involuntarily turned to look in the direction of the car. But there was nothing to be seen. She longed for the car to come once more and ... and ...

"To hell with it. Why should I make my life miserable? Let me go home and have a long, restful sleep. What's the use of all this? Just a lot of bother for nothing. Come on Saugandhi, let's go home, drink some cold water, rub a little balm on your forehead and go to sleep. You'll fall into a sound sleep and everything will be all right. To hell with the seth and his car!" Saugandhi felt better now. It was as though she had emerged from a cool bath. She felt light, the way she usually felt after the puja. The heavy burden of thoughts now cast off, as she proceeded towards home she tripped a couple of times.

When she reached near her kholi the whole episode came to her once again. Intense pain coursed through her body. Her steps grew heavy. She felt overwhelmed that a man had sent for her, flashed a light on her face in the bazaar and insulted her only a little while ago. She felt as though strong fingers were poking her ribs – the way people do when they go to buy a sheep or a goat, to see if there is enough meat on the animal.

That seth. May god ... Saugandhi wanted to curse him but then she thought, what was the use? What could she gain by cursing him? The enjoyment was – had he been standing before her, she could have cursed every single part of his existence, she could have said things that would have made him anxious for the rest of his life. She could have torn off her clothes, stood before him stark naked and said, "This is what you came for, didn't you? Take it all for free. But remember that whatever I am and whatever is hidden inside me, neither you nor your father can ever buy."

Saugandhi was thinking of all the innovative ways in which she could take her revenge. If she could meet the seth once, just once, she would do this ... no, no, not that, she would do this. She would take her revenge like this ... no, no, not that way but this way. Well, she would even be satisfied if she could just utter a small curse to his face that would stick like a fly on his nose and stay there for the rest of his life.

Lost in this confused maze of thoughts, she reached her room on the second floor. She took out the key from her choli and extended her hand to open the lock, but her hand came back with air. There was no lock on the door. When she pushed on it, someone undid the latch and the door creaked open. Saugandhi entered.

Madho smiled behind his moustache, and while he was closing the door said to Saugandhi, "So you've taken my advice today? A morning walk is very good for health. If you go out for morning walks regularly it will cure all your lethargy and the waist pain that you're always complaining about. You went up to the Victoria Garden, didn't you?"

Saugandhi didn't reply, nor did Madho expect one. As a matter of fact, when Madho talked he didn't expect her to participate, and when Saugandhi talked, it wasn't necessary for Madho to take part. They had to keep the talk going, so either of them would say something without expecting any response from the other.

Madho sat down in the cane chair with the greasy headrest, left so by his oily head. He put one leg over the other and began to twirl his moustache.

Saugandhi sat down on the bed and said to Madho, "I've been waiting for you to come today."

Madho was startled. "Waiting? How did you know that I was coming today?"

Saugandhi's pressed lips eased a little and a fading smile appeared on them. "I saw you in my dream last night. I got up immediately and looked around. There was no one, so I thought of going out for a walk and ..."

Madho was pleased. "And here I am! Great people have rightly said that hearts reach out to one another. When did you have that dream?"

Saugandhi replied, "At about four."

Madho got up from the chair and sat next to Saugandhi. "And I saw you in my dream at two, standing by me wearing that sari with the floral print, the same one you're wearing now. And your hands? What was there in your hands? Oh yes, a bag filled with coins. You put the bag in my lap and said, Madho, why do you worry? Take this bag. Does it matter whether the money is yours or mine? I swear by your life, I got up immediately and bought a ticket to Bombay. What can I tell you? I'm in a mess. There's a lawsuit against me, out of the blue. If I had twenty or thirty rupees, I could grease the palm of the inspector and get out of the mess. I hope you're not tired? Why don't you lie down? Let me massage your legs. If one's not accustomed to walking, one gets tired easily. Here, lie down with your legs towards me."

Saugandhi lay down, resting her head on her two hands. She started in a strange voice, "Madho, who is that rascal who has implicated you in a lawsuit? If there is any danger of a jail sentence, tell me now. What's twenty or thirty rupees? In such circumstances, even if you pay fifty or a hundred rupees to the police, it will benefit you. If the life is saved, millions can be earned. Leave it, that's enough. I'm not that tired. Stop massaging and tell me the whole story. My heart's beating fast at the mention of this lawsuit. When do you plan to return?"

Madho smelled liquor on Saugandhi's breath. He thought it was a good opportunity and said, "I've to return by the afternoon train. If I don't give the inspector fifty or a hundred rupees by this afternoon ... there's no need to give so much. I think fifty would do."

"Fifty," repeated Saugandhi as she got up leisurely and moved slowly towards the four frames hanging on the wall. The third

100

frame from the left contained Madho's photograph. He was sitting on a chair in front of a curtain with a large floral print with arms resting on his knees. He was so impressed with the idea of being photographed that every part of him seemed to cry out, "I'm getting photographed, I'm getting photographed!" He was staring wide-eyed at the camera. The picture looked as though he had been in pain while it was being taken.

Saugandhi burst into peals of laughter so contemptuous and derisive that Madho got uncomfortable. He rose from the bed and went over to Saugandhi. "Whose photo is making you laugh so loudly?" he asked.

Saugandhi pointed to the first picture on the left. It was the Municipality Inspector. "This one ... the Municipalty Inspector – just look at his funny face. He bragged to me one day that a princess had fallen for him. A face for a princess indeed!" Saying this she pulled at the frame with such violence that its nail was also uprooted from the wall. Before Madho could gather his scattered wits about himself, he saw Saugandhi fling the frame out of the window. From the height of the second floor the frame crashed on the ground. When Saugandhi heard the sound of the glass breaking she said, "When Rani, the cleaning woman, comes in the morning, she'll take away my prince."

Again, peals of stinging, derisive laughter rained from her lips. It sounded as if a knife or a blade were being sharpened. Madho somehow managed a faint smile. Then he laughed, hee, hee, hee ...

Saugandhi now pulled off the second frame as well and threw it out of the window. "What's this bastard doing here? No ugly face can be allowed to remain? Right Madho?"

Madho smiled with difficulty and then laughed, hee, hee, hee.

Saugandhi then stretched out one hand and pulled down the photo of the man wearing a turban, and her other hand moved towards the frame that contained Madho's photo.

Madho cringed as though Saugandhi's hand had moved towards him. Within a second, the frame was in her hand along with the nail. Saugandhi burst into resounding laughter and, saying "oonh," threw the last two frames out of the window.

When the frames landed with a bang, Madho felt something inside him breaking too. He managed to laugh with difficulty and said, "Well done. I didn't like that picture either."

Saugandhi moved slowly towards Madho and said, "You didn't like the picture ... But I ask you, what is there in you that anyone should like? This bulbous nose of yours? The hairy forehead? Swollen nostrils? Your foul smelling mouth, the filth on your body? You didn't like the picture – oonh – how could you like it? It concealed all your blemishes. This is the way of the world now. Whoever hides his blemishes will be punished."

Madho stepped backwards. When he touched the wall, he raised his voice with an effort and said, "Look Saugandhi, it seems you've started your business again. I'm warning you for the last time." Saugandhi cut him off in mid-sentence and began to mimic his tone, "If you start your business again, we can't be friends anymore. If you allow a man to stay with you here even once, I'll pull you by your hair and turn you out. Look, I'll send you this month's expenses by money order as soon as I reach Poona. Oh yes, what's the rent for this kholi?"

Madho was stupefied. Saugandhi continued in her own voice, "I'll tell you. The rent for this kholi is fifteen rupees, and my fee is ten rupees, and as you know, two and a half rupees are for the pimp. That leaves seven and a half rupees, doesn't it? Now, for this meagre amount you're promising to give me something, which is very difficult for you to give. And I have come to take something I can't really take. What binds us together, after all? Nothing, except these ten rupees that jingle. Before, it was ten rupees, now it's fifty. The coins that bind us together, you can hear their jingle, and so can I." Saying all this Saugandhi flicked Madho's hat off his head with her finger.

Madho found Saugandhi's behaviour very disagreeable. He said sternly, "Saugandhi!" Saugandhi pulled his handkerchief out of his pocket, smelled it and threw it on the floor. "These rags and sheets, how they stink! Throw them out. And you've ruined your hair, and ... and ..."

Madho screamed, "Saugandhi!"

"Saugandhi ke bachché! Why the hell did you come here? You think your mother lives here, who'd give you fifty rupees? Or do you think that you're a handsome youth and I've fallen for you? Scoundrel, rogue! Trying to boss me around! Am I your slave? What do you take yourself to be, you beggar? Who the hell are you, I ask? There may or may not be a lawsuit against you in Poona, but there will certainly be one against you here!"

Madho was frightened. He could just manage to say in a subdued voice, "Saugandhi, what has come over you?"

"Your mother's head! Who the hell are you to ask me that? Get out of here, or else ..."

Hearing her loud voice, Saugandhi's sleeping mangy mongrel, staggered to its feet and began to bark at Madho. Saugandhi joined in with swells of laughter.

Madho was now really aghast. When he bent down to pick up

his cap, Saugandhi thundered, "Leave it where it is. Go away! I'll send it to you by money order as soon as you reach Poona." With another resounding peal of laughter, Saugandhi plunked down on the chair.

The mongrel barked Madho not only out of the room but even chased him down the stairs. When he returned wagging his tail, he sat at Saugandhi's feet and kept fluttering his ears. Saugandhi was startled.

There was a terrible stillness around her, something she had never experienced before. She felt every object drowned in emptiness ... like a packed train, which after discharging all its passengers stands alone under the iron shade.

She was frightened by the sudden emptiness that engulfed her. She tried to ignore it, but in vain. She attempted to cram her brain full of countless thoughts all at the same time, but it was like a sieve. One moment she filled it up, the next moment it was empty.

She kept sitting on the cane chair. When, after much reflection, she still couldn't divert her mind, she picked up the mongrel in her arms and climbed on to the large teak bed. Laying him by her side, she drifted off to sleep.

---

"Insult" has been translated from "Hatak," in *Sau Kendil Power ka Bulb: Sa'adat Hasan Manto ke Ikkis Muntakhab Afsane,* Modern Publishing House, New Delhi, 1980.

# For Freedom's Sake

I don't remember the year, but it must have been when Amritsar was reverberating with the cries of "Inquilab Zindabad!" These cries, I recall, were filled with a strange excitement, with a gushing energy one saw only among the blossoming milkmaids of the city as they tore through its bazaars, with baskets of uplas carefully balanced on their heads. It was a wild and woolly time. The dread, tinged with sadness, which had hung in the atmosphere since the bloody incident at Jallianwala Bagh, had completely disappeared and a dauntless fervour had taken its place – the desire to fling oneself headlong, regardless of where one might land.

People chanted slogans, staged demonstrations and were sent to prison by the hundreds. Courting arrest had become a favourite pastime – apprehended in the morning and released by the evening. You could be tried in the court and thrown in jail for a few months. You came out, shouted another slogan, and got arrested all over again.

Those days were so full of life! The tiniest bubble, when burst became a formidable vortex. Somebody would stand in the square, make a speech calling for a strike, and a strike followed. A tidal wave would sweep through, requiring everybody to wear only homespun khadi to put the textile factories of Lancashire out of business. All imported cloth would be boycotted. Bonfires would go up in every square. In the heat of excitement, people would peel off their clothes then and there and throw them into the flames. Now and then a woman tossed one of her ill-chosen saris down from her balcony and people would go wild with applause.

I remember one conflagration in front of the main police station by the Town Hall. My classmate, Shaikhu, became so excited that he took off his silk jacket and cast it on to the pyre of imported clothing. This set off a round of thunderous applause, for he was the son of a noted toady. The applause excited him even more. He peeled off his silk shirt and offered it to the flames too, realizing only later that the shirt had gold buttons and links.

Far be it that I make fun of Shaikhu. The fact is, I felt just as passionate in those days. I would dream of getting hold of handguns and forming a terrorist group of my own. That my father was receiving his pension from the government never crossed my mind. Something inside me was on the boil, wanting to spill out, akin to the heady feeling of a game of flush.

I had never cared much for school, but in those days I positively detested it. I would leave the house with my books and make straight for Jallianwala Bagh. Here, I would watch whatever activity was going on until school ended. Or I would sit under a tree and stare at the women in the windows of houses some distance away, hoping that one of them would fall in love with me. Why such a thought entered my head I have no idea.

Jallianwala Bagh was the scene of much activity at that time. Canvas tents and enclosures were set up everywhere. People would choose somebody as "dictator" every few days and he would be installed with due ceremony in the biggest tent. In mock seriousness, he would receive the greetings of khadi clad men and women for three or four days, at most a fortnight. He would collect donations of flour and rice for the langar khana, the soup kitchen, from the banias, and one day while drinking his lassi (god only knows why it was so readily available in the Jallianwala Bagh area) would be raided by the police, arrested, and whisked away to prison.

I had an old classmate, Shahzada Ghulam Ali. You can get some idea of how close our friendship was from the fact that we had failed our high school exams together twice, and once had even run away to Bombay. Our plan was to reach the Soviet Union eventually. But when money ran out and we had to sleep on the streets, we wrote home to be forgiven, and returned.

Shahzada Ghulam Ali was a handsome young man, tall and fair, with a sharp nose and playful eyes, as Kashmiris generally are. There was something particularly majestic in the way he walked, which also carried a trace of the swagger of professional goondas.

He was not a "Shahzada" during our school days. But as revolutionary fervour picked up and he participated in a dozen or so rallies, the slogans, strings of marigold, songs of patriotic zeal, and the opportunity to talk freely with female volunteers turned him into a half-baked revolutionary. Then one day, he delivered his first speech. The next day I found out in the newspaper that Ghulam Ali had become a "Shahzada."

Soon he was known all over the small city of Amritsar – it doesn't take long for one to become famous or infamous there. Its residents, quite critical of ordinary people and going to all lengths to find fault with them, couldn't be more forgiving to a religious or political leader. They always seem to be in need of a sermon or speech. One can survive here as a leader for a long time. Just show up in different garb each time – now black, now blue.

But that was a different time. All the major leaders were already in prison, and their place was free for the taking. The people, of course, had no need for leaders, at least not so terribly, but the revolutionary movement certainly did. It urgently needed people who would wear khadi, sit inside the biggest tent in the Jallianwala Bagh, make a speech, and get arrested.

In those days, Europe was witnessing its first Dictatorships. Hitler and Mussolini had gained quite a bit of notoriety. Perhaps that's what led the Congress Party to create its own Dictators. When Shahzada Ghulam Ali's turn came, a full forty Dictators had already been arrested.

I headed off to Jallianwala the minute I heard that a strange mix of circumstances had made our Ghulam Ali, a Dictator. Volunteers stood guard outside the large tent. Ghulam Ali saw me and called me in. A mattress was spread out on the floor with a khadi bedcover on it, and there, leaning against cushions and bolsters, sat Ghulam Ali talking to a group of khadi clad banias about, I believe, vegetables. He finished the session quickly, gave instructions to his volunteers and turned to me. He looked far too serious, which prompted me to tease him. As soon as the volunteers had cleared away, I laughed and said, "Hey, Shehzadé, what's up?"

I made fun of him for quite a while. But there was no denying the change in him – it was palpable, and what's more, he was aware of it. He kept telling me, "Sa'adat, no, please don't take me lightly. I know I'm a small man and don't deserve this honour. But from now on I want to keep it this way."

I returned to Jallianwala Bagh in the evening. It was packed with people. As I had come a bit early, I found a place close to the platform. Ghulam Ali appeared amidst tremendous applause. He looked dashing in his immaculate white khadi outfit, the slight swagger mentioned earlier adding to his attraction. He spoke for nearly an hour. Goosebumps broke out on my body several times during his speech. I felt an overwhelming need to explode like a bomb then and there a couple of times. Perhaps I thought that such an explosion might set India free.

God knows how many years have passed since then. Our emotions and the tide of events were in a state of flux, and it is difficult to describe their precise modulations now. But as I write this story and recall him making that speech – all I see is youth itself talking, a youth innocent of politics ... filled with the sincere boldness of a young man who suddenly stops a woman on the street and tells her straight out, "Look, I love you," and then surrenders himself to the law.

I've heard many more speeches since. But in none of them have I heard even a faint echo of the bubbling madness, reckless youth, raw emotion, and naked challenge that filled Shahzada Ghulam Ali's voice that day. Speeches today are laced with calculated seriousness, stale politics and a prudence couched in lyricism.

At that time, neither the government nor the people were experienced. They were at each other's throats, unaware of the consequences. The government sent people to prison without understanding the implications of such a step, and those who submitted to voluntary arrest showed equal ignorance of the true significance of their act.

It was wrongheadedness, and potentially explosive. It ignited people, subsided, and ignited them all over again – creating a surge of fiery exuberance in the otherwise dull and gloomy atmosphere of servitude.

The entire Jallianwala Bagh exploded with loud applause and inflammatory slogans as Shahzada Ghulam Ali ended his speech. His face was gleaming. When I met him alone and pressed his hand to congratulate him, I could feel that it was shaking. A similar warm throbbing was evident on his bright face. He was gasping a bit. His eyes were glowing with the heat of passion, but they also hid the trace of a search that had nearly exhausted itself. They were desperately looking for somebody. Suddenly he snatched his hand away and darted towards the jasmine bushes.

A young woman in a spotless khadi sari stood there. The next day I came to know that Shahzada Ghulam Ali was in love with her. It was not a one sided affair. Nigar loved him madly in return. Nigar, a Muslim, was an orphan. She worked as a nurse in a women's hospital. She was perhaps the first Muslim girl in Amritsar to come out of purda and join the Congress Movement.

Partly her khadi outfit, partly her participation in the activities of the Congress, and partly also the atmosphere of the hospital – all these had slightly mellowed her Islamic demeanour, the harshness which is part of a Muslim woman's nature and softened her a bit.

She was not beautiful, but she was indeed a model of femininity in her own way. Humility – the desire to respect and worship, and adarsh – so characteristic of a Hindu woman's makeup, had come together in Nigar in a most pleasing combination. Back then the image would never even have occurred to me, but now whenever I think of her, she appears to me as a beautiful confluence of Muslim namaaz and Hindu aarti.

She practically worshipped Shahzada Ghulam Ali. He loved her madly too. When I asked him about her, he told me they had met during the Congress rallies, and after a brief time together had decided to tie the knot.

Ghulam Ali wanted to marry her before his imminent arrest. I have no idea why. He could have just as easily married her after his release. Prison sentences used to be quite short in those days. Three months, at most a year. Some would be let off after only a fortnight to make room for others. Anyway, he'd told Nigar of his plan and she was willing. All that was needed was Babaji's blessings.

Babaji, as you must know, was a major figure. He was staying outside the city in the palatial lodgings of the city's richest jeweller, Hari Ram. Ordinarily, he lived in his ashram in a neighbouring village. But whenever he came to Amritsar, he encamped at Hari Ram's. For the duration of his stay, this house would become a shrine for his devotees, who would stand in long queues patiently waiting for his darshan. Babaji gave a general audience and took donations for his ashram in the evening, seated on a wooden platform laid out under a cluster of mango trees at some distance from the house. This would be followed by bhajan chanting and the session ended at his bidding.

Babaji was an abstemious and god fearing man. He was also quite learned and intelligent. These qualities had endeared him to everyone – Hindu, Muslim, Sikh, and untouchables. Everybody considered him their leader.

On the face of it, Babaji was indifferent to politics. But it was an open secret that every political movement in Punjab started and ended at his behest. The government found him intractable, a political riddle which even the brightest government officials could never hope to solve. His slightest smile stirred up a million speculations, but when he proceeded to interpret it himself in an entirely novel way, the populace, already enthralled, felt truly overwhelmed.

The civil disobedience movement in Amritsar, with its frequent arrests, quite clearly owed a lot to Babaji's influence. Every evening at darshan, he'd drop an innocuous word from his toothless mouth about the freedom movement in the whole of Punjab, the fresh and increasingly harsh measures of the government – and, the mighty leaders of the time would scramble to pick it up and hang it around their necks like a priceless amulet.

People said that his eyes had a magnetic quality, his voice held magic, and he had a cool head ... so cool indeed that the worst obscenities, the sharpest sarcasm, could not provoke him, not even for a millionth of a second. This made his opponents writhe in frustration.

He must have taken part in hundreds of demonstrations in Amritsar, but strangely, although I'd seen every other leader, I hadn't caught a glimpse of him, from far or near. So when Ghulam Ali mentioned going to his darshan to seek his permission to marry, I asked him to take me along.

The very next day Ghulam Ali arranged for a tanga, and we arrived at Lala Hari Ram's magnificent mansion.

Babaji was done with his morning ablutions and worship and was listening to a beautiful panditani sing patriotic songs. He was seated on a palm mat spread out on the immaculate white tile floor. A bolster lay near him but he wasn't leaning on it.

The room had no other furnishings besides the mat. The panditani's onion coloured face looked stunningly beautiful in the light reflecting off the tiles.

In spite of being an old man of around seventy two, Babaji's entire body, on which he had only a tiny red ochre loincloth, was free of wrinkles. His skin had a rich dark colour. I was told later that he used to have an olive oil massage before taking bath.

He greeted Shahzada Ghulam Ali with a smile and spared a glance at me. He acknowledged our greetings by a slight widening of the same smile, and then gestured us to sit down.

Today, when I imagine that scene and examine it closely, I find it quite intriguing. A half-naked old man sitting on a palm mat in the style of a yogi. His posture, his bald head, half-opened eyes, soft tawny body, indeed every line in his face radiating a tranquil contentment, an unassailable conviction – he could not be dislodged, not even by the worst earthquake, from the summit where the world had placed him. And close to him sat a just opened bud from the vale of Kashmir ... her head bowed, partly from respect for the elderly man, partly from the effect of the patriotic song, and partly from her own boundless youth, yearning to spill out of the confining folds of her coarse white sari and sing not just a song for the country, but a song dedicated equally to her youth. She wanted to honour not just the nearness of this elderly man, but also that of some healthy youth who would have the spunk to grab her hand and jump headfirst into life's raging fire. In opposition to the elderly man's granite confidence and serenity, her onion coloured face, dark lively eyes, bosom heaving inside her coarse khadi blouse – all seemed to throw a silent challenge – come, hurl me down from where I stand, or lift me up to sublimity.

Nigar, Shahzada Ghulam Ali and I sat somewhat off to one side. I was frozen like a perfect idiot, equally flustered by Babaji's imposing personality and the unblemished beauty of the young

Kashmiri woman. The glossy tiles also had an effect on me, indeed quite an effect. What if the pandit girl would let me kiss her eyes, just once. The thought pulsated through my body, and my mind immediately darted off to my maidservant, for whom I'd begun to feel something lately. I felt like leaving everybody and making straight for home – I might succeed in stealthily luring her upstairs to the bathroom. I just might. But the second my glance fell on Babaji and the passionate strains of the nationalistic song swelled in my ears, a different thought began to run through my body – if I could just get hold of a handgun, I'd rush to the Civil Lines area and start making short work of the English.

And next to this perfect idiot sat Nigar and Ghulam Ali, a pair of hearts in love, somewhat tired of their long and uneventful throbbing, ready to melt into each other to find those other shades of love. In other words, they'd come to ask Babaji, their uncontested political leader, for permission to marry. Obviously it was not the song of the nation that resonated in their heads at that moment. It was their own song, beautiful, but unsung as yet.

The song ended. With a gesture of the hand Babaji gave his blessing to the pandit girl and then turned, smiling, to Nigar and Ghulam Ali, again managing a small glance at me as well.

Ghulam Ali was perhaps about to introduce himself and Nigar but Babaji – goodness, his memory! – quickly said to him in his sweet voice, "Shehzadé, you haven't been arrested yet?"

"No, not yet," Ghulam Ali replied, with folded hands.

Babaji picked up a pencil from the penbox and toying with it, said, "But you are, I think."

The remark went over Ghulam Ali's head. So Babaji looked at the pandit girl and said, pointing at Nigar, "Nigar has captured our Shehzada."

Nigar blushed. Ghulam Ali's mouth fell open. And the onion colour of the pandit girl flushed with good wishes. She gave the pair a look that seemed to say, "How wonderful!"

Babaji looked at the pandit girl once again. "These children," he said to her, "have come to ask for my permission. How about you, Kamal, when are you going to get married?"

So she was called Kamal! The abrupt question caught her off guard and she turned red in the face. "Me?" she said in a trembling voice, "I've decided to join your ashram."

She said this with a trace of regret, which Babaji's perceptive mind registered instantly. He gave her a smile, the soft smile of a yogi, and then turned to Ghulam Ali and Nigar, "So, have the two of you made up your minds?"

"Yes," they answered softly in unison.

Babaji scanned them with his politician's eyes. "Sometimes," he said, "one is obliged to change the decisions one has made."

For the first time in Babaji's lofty presence, Ghulam Ali lost the boldness of his coltish youth, saying, "Even if our decision is put off for some reason, it will never change!"

Babaji closed his eyes and questioned him like a lawyer, "Why?"

Surprisingly, Ghulam Ali didn't lose his nerve at all. His ardent love for Nigar made him say, "Circumstances may force us to put it off, but our decision to free India is irrevocable. Absolutely!"

Babaji, I now feel, didn't think it profitable to query him further on the subject and smiled ... a smile which everyone present must have interpreted in his or her own way. And if asked, Babaji would have given it a radically different meaning. I'm sure of that.

Anyway, stretching further the same smile, he said, "Nigar, come join our ashram! It is only a matter of days before Shehzada will be sent to jail."

"All right, I will," she answered softly.

Babaji changed the subject and asked about the revolutionary activities in the Jallianwala Bagh camp. Ghulam Ali, Nigar and Kamal filled him in for what seemed like a long time about various arrests, releases, and even about milk, lassi and vegetables. During this time I sat there like a bumpkin, wondering why Babaji dilly-dallied so much in giving his blessing to Ghulam Ali and Nigar. Did he have doubts about their love for each other? About Ghulam Ali's sincerity? Had he invited Nigar to the ashram just to help her get over the pain she'd no doubt feel at her husband's incarceration? But then, why had Kamal responded to Babaji's question, "Kamal, when are you going to get married?" with, "I've decided to join your ashram?" Didn't men and women marry at the ashram? These were the kinds of questions that were raging inside my head, as the four of them sat speculating about whether the number of lady volunteers were enough to deliver chapattis for five hundred militants on time. How many stoves were there? How large were the griddles? Couldn't one get a griddle big enough for six women to bake chapattis all at once?

This pandit girl, Kamal, I wondered, would she just chant national songs and religious bhajans for Babaji's edification, once she was admitted to the ashram? I had seen the male volunteers of the ashram. True enough, they all took their ritual bath and brushed their teeth every morning, they all spent most of their time out in the open air and chanted bhajans in accordance with the rules of the ashram, but their clothing still reeked of perspiration, didn't it? Quite a few had bad breath to boot. And I never saw on anyone even a trace of the good nature and freshness one associates with outdoor living. Instead, they looked stooped and repressed, their faces pallid, eyes sunken, and bodies ravaged, as blanched and lifeless as the udders of a cow from which the last drop of milk has been squeezed out.

I'd seen these ashramwalas on numerous occasions in the Jallianwala Bagh. I couldn't imagine Kamal, moulded in her entirety out of milk, honey and saffron, being subjected to the gaze of these men who had nothing but filth in their eyes. Would she, a being swathed all over in the scent of loban, have to listen to them with their mouths smelling worse than the stench of rotting mulch? Perhaps, I thought, the independence of India was above all this.

But this "perhaps" was not something I could understand, what with my patriotism and passion for the country's freedom. I thought of Nigar, who was sitting very close to me and telling Babaji that turnips usually took quite a long time to cook. For heaven's sake, what had turnips got to do with marriage? She and Ghulam Ali had come for Babaji's blessing to get married, hadn't they?

My thoughts wandered off to Nigar and the ashram, which I had never visited. Ashrams, vidyalas, jamat-khanas, takiyas, and darsgahs, all such places inspired only the deepest revulsion in me. I don't know why. I've often seen boys and the caretakers of orphanages and schools for the blind walking in a row along streets asking for alms. I have also seen jamat-khanas and darsgahs – boys donning shar'i pyjamas well above their ankles, their foreheads marked with calluses despite their tender age, the slightly older boys wearing thick bushy beards, the younger ones with a revolting growth of sparse bristles on their cheeks and chins – all absorbed in prayer, but their faces reflecting pure beastliness.

Nigar was a woman. Not a Muslim, Hindu, Sikh or Christian ... just a woman. No, she was more than that. A woman's prayer intended for her lover, or for one whom she herself loved with all her heart. I couldn't imagine her, herself a prayer, raising her hands in prayer every morning as required by the rules of Babaji's ashram.

Today as I recall Babaji, Nigar, Ghulam Ali, the ravishingly beautiful pandit girl, indeed the entire atmosphere of Amritsar, engulfed as it was in those days in the fine romantic haze created by the independence movement – all appear like a dream, the sort one longs to have over and over again.

I still haven't seen Babaji's ashram, but I hate it as passionately today as I did then. I don't care at all for a place where people are subjected to an unnatural way of life. To strive for freedom is fine. I can even understand dying for it. But to turn living people into mere vegetables, without passion or drive, is beyond me. To live in poor housing, shun amenities, sing the lord's praises, shout patriotic slogans – fine! But to stifle the very desire for beauty in humans! What kind of humans have no feeling for beauty, no zest for life? Show me the difference between the ashrams, madrasas, and vidyalas that accomplish this, and a field of horseradishes!

Babaji sat talking about the remainder of the activities in Jallianwala Bagh with Ghulam Ali and Nigar for a long time. Finally he told the couple, who had not apparently forgotten the purpose of their visit to return, and the next day he himself would wed them in the evening.

The two were elated. What greater fortune could there be than to have Babaji himself conduct their marriage! Ghulam Ali later told me that he was so overjoyed he couldn't believe it to be true. The slightest gesture of Babaji turned into a historic event. He couldn't believe that such a great man would personally come to Jallianwala Bagh for the sake of an ordinary man, a man who had become the Congress's Dictator merely by accident. Precisely the headline that splashed across the front pages of newspapers across India.

Ghulam Ali wondered whether Babaji would show up. He was a terribly busy man after all. But the doubt, raised as a psychological precaution, proved wrong. As expected, promptly at six, just as the raat ki rani was beginning to spread its fragrance, and a band of volunteers setting up a small tent for the bride and groom were decorating it with jasmine, marigolds and roses ... Babaji walked in, supporting himself on his lathi, with the patriotic song-spouting pandit girl, his secretary, and Lala Hari Ram in tow. The news of his arrival came at precisely the same moment when Lala Hari Ram's green car pulled up at Jallianwala Bagh's main entrance.

I was there too. In another small tent, lady volunteers were dressing up Nigar as a bride. Ghulam Ali had made no special arrangements. He had spent the whole day negotiating with the city's banias for provisions to feed the volunteers. After that he stole a few moments to talk briefly with Nigar alone. Then, as I recall, he told the officers under his charge that at the end of the wedding ceremony, he and Nigar would raise the flag together.

Ghulam Ali was standing by the well when he heard that Babaji had arrived, and, if I remember correctly, I was asking him, "You know, Ghulam Ali, don't you, how this well was once filled to its mouth with the bodies of people slain in the firing? Today everybody drinks from it. It has watered every flower in this park. People come and pluck those flowers. But strangely, not even a drop carries the salty taste of blood. Not a single petal of any flower has the redness of blood in it. Why is that?"

I vividly remember that as I said this, I had looked at the window of a neighbouring house where, it is said, a young girl had been shot dead by General Dyer as she stood watching the massacre. The streak of blood had begun to fade on the old lime wall behind the window.

Blood had become so cheap that spilling it no longer affected people as it once did. I remember I was in my third or fourth class at school, and six or seven months after the bloody massacre, our teacher had taken us to see Jallianwala Bagh. It hardly looked like a park then, just a dreary and desolate stretch of uneven earth, strewn all over with clods of dried dirt. I remember how the teacher had picked up a small clod, reddened I believe from paan spittle, and showed it to us, saying, "Look, it's still red with the blood of our martyrs!"

As I write this story a myriad of small things keep coming to my mind. But it is the story of Ghulam Ali and Nigar's marriage that I want to write, isn't it?

Anyway, hearing that Babaji had arrived, Ghulam Ali rushed to gather the volunteers at one place. Babaji was given a military salute. The two inspected different camps for quite some time. All the while Babaji, with his keen sense of humour, fired off numerous witty remarks during conversation with female volunteers and other workers.

In the meantime, the evening haze began to settle over Jallianwala Bagh and lights came on here and there in nearby houses. A group of women volunteers started to chant bhajans. They sang in unison, some sweetly, most harshly and out of tune. Together though, they sounded pleasant enough. Babaji listened, eyes closed. Roughly a thousand people must have gathered. They sat on the earth around the platform. Except for the bhajan singing girls, everyone else was hushed.

The chanting tapered off into a silence, anxious to be broken. So when Babaji opened his eyes and trilled sweetly, "Children, as you already know, I'm here to unite these two freedom lovers in marriage," the entire Bagh resonated with loud cries of jubilation.

Nigar, in her bridal attire with her head bowed low, sat in a corner of the platform. She looked very lovely in tri-coloured khadi sari. Babaji motioned her to come closer and sat her next to Ghulam Ali, causing more cries of jubilation to go up.

Ghulam Ali's face was unusually flushed. When he took the wedding contract from his friend and handed it over to Babaji, I noticed his hand was shaking.

A Maulvi Sahab was also present on the platform. He recited the Quranic verse customary at weddings. Babaji listened to it with his eyes closed. The custom of "proposal and acceptance" over, Babaji gave his blessing to the bride and groom. Meanwhile the congratulatory showering of the couple with dried dates, the chuwaras, traditional at such events began. Babaji snatched a dozen or so for himself and tucked them away.

Smiling shyly, a Hindu girlfriend of Nigar's presented Ghulam Ali with a tiny box and whispered something in his ear. He opened the box and put sindoor in her parting. The drabness of Jallianwala Bagh was enlivened again with a round of loud applause.

Babaji got up amidst all the noise. A hush instantly fell over the crowd.

The mixed fragrance of raat ki rani and jasmine wafted by on the light evening breeze. The scene was absolutely breathtaking. Babaji's voice had acquired an extra measure of sweetness today. After congratulating the couple on their wedding, he said, "These two will work for their country and nation with even greater dedication now, because the true meaning of marriage is none other than true friendship between a man and a woman. Ghulam Ali and Nigar will work together as friends for swaraj. Such marriages are commonplace in Europe – I mean marriages based on friendship and friendship alone. People who are able to exorcize carnal passion from their lives are worthy of our respect."

Babaji explicated his concept of marriage at length. He firmly believed that the true joy of marriage was something above and beyond the bodily union of the mates. He didn't consider sexual union as important as generally made to be. Thousands of people ate just to satisfy their craving for flavour. But did this mean that to do so was incumbent on humans? Although people who ate solely out of the need to stay alive were not many, they alone knew the true meaning of eating. Likewise, only those people, who married out of the desire to experience the purity of this emotion and the sanctity of this sacred relationship, truly enjoyed connubial bliss.

Babaji expounded on his belief with such clarity and profound sincerity that an entirely new world opened up before his listeners. I too was deeply touched. Ghulam Ali, who sat opposite me, was deeply engrossed in Babaji's speech seemingly drinking in every word. When Babaji stopped, Ghulam Ali briefly consulted Nigar, got up, and declared in a trembling voice, "Ours will be just such a marriage. Until India wins her freedom, my relationship with Nigar will be entirely like that of friends."

More applause followed, enlivening the dreary atmosphere in the Jallianwala Bagh with its cheery tumult for quite a while. Shahzada Ghulam Ali grew emotional, and streaks of red blotched his Kashmiri face. "Nigar!" he addressed his bride in a loud voice. "Can you bear to bring a slave child into this world?"

Dazed in part by the wedding and in part by Babaji's harangue, Nigar lost her remaining presence of mind when she heard this whipcrack question. "No! Of course not!" was all she could get out.

The crowd clapped again, sending Ghulam Ali to an even higher pitch of emotion. The joy at saving Nigar from the ignominy of producing a slave baby went to his head. And he wandered off the main subject into the tortuous byways of how to free the country. For the next hour he spoke nonstop in a voice weighed down by emotion. Suddenly his glance fell on Nigar and he was struck dumb. He couldn't get a word out. He was like some drunkard who keeps pulling out note after note without any idea of how much he is spending, to suddenly find his wallet empty. The abrupt paralysis of speech irritated him greatly, but he immediately looked in the direction of Babaji, bowed and again found his voice, "Babaji, bless us to remain steadfast in our vow."

Next morning at six, Shahzada Ghulam Ali was arrested. In the same speech in which he had vowed not to father a child until the country gained her freedom, he had also threatened to overthrow the English.

A few days after his arrest, Ghulam Ali was sentenced to eight months' imprisonment and sent to the Multan jail. He was the forty first Dictator of Amritsar and, if I remember the figures quoted in the newspapers correctly, the forty thousandth political activist apprehended and imprisoned for taking part in the independence movement.

Everybody thought that freedom was just around the corner. The astute British politicians, however, let the movement run its course. The failure of the major national leaders of India to reach an agreement pretty much took the teeth out of it.

Following their release, the freedom seekers tried to put the memory of their recent hardship behind and get their interrupted businesses back on track. Shahzada Ghulam Ali was let off after seven months. Even though the revolutionary fervour had considerably subsided by then, people did show up at the Amritsar Railway Station to greet him. A few parties and rallies were also held in his honour. I attended all of them. But they were largely lacklustre affairs. A strange fatigue seemed to have come over people, like runners returning listlessly to the starting line after being suddenly told in the middle of a dash, "Stop! We'll have to do it over."

Several years passed. The listlessness, the exhaustion still hung over India. My own life went through a series of upheavals, some major, some minor. A beard and moustache had sprouted on my face. I entered college and failed twice in my FA. My father died. I knocked about looking for a job and found work as a translator for a third rate newspaper. Fed up, I decided to go back to school and enrolled in Aligarh University. But I contracted tuberculosis and within three months found myself wandering around rural Kashmir, recuperating. Then I headed for Bombay. Witnessing three Hindu-Muslim riots in two years was enough to send me packing to Delhi. But that place, by comparison, turned out to be terribly drab with everything moving at a snail's pace. Even where there was some sign of activity, it had a distinctly feminine feel to it. Well, maybe Bombay wasn't so bad after all, I thought, even if your next door neighbour has no time to ask your name. What of it? Where there is time, you see a lot of hypocrisy, a lot of disease. So after spending two uneventful years in Delhi, I returned to fast paced Bombay.

It has been eight years since I left home. I had no idea what my friends were doing. I barely remembered the streets and bylanes of Amritsar. How could I? I hadn't kept in touch with anybody back home. As a matter of fact, I'd become somewhat indifferent to my past in the intervening eight years. Why think about the past? What good would it do now to total up what was spent eight years ago? In life's cash, the penny you want to spend today, or the one another may set his eyes on tomorrow, is the one that counts.

Some six years ago, when I wasn't quite as hard up, I'd gone to the Fort area to shop for a pair of expensive dress shoes. The display cases in a shop beyond the Army & Navy Store on Hornby Road had been tempting me for some time. But since I have a particularly weak memory, I wasn't able to locate the shop in question. Out of habit I started to browse in other stores, even though I'd come specifically to buy shoes. I looked at a cigarette case in one store, pipes in another, and then I strolled on until I came to a small shop that sold footwear. I stopped and decided to look for a pair there. The attendant greeted me and asked, "Well, sahab, what do you want?"

For a moment or two I tried to remember what I had come to buy. "Oh, yes. Show me a pair of dress shoes with rubber soles."

"We don't carry them."

The monsoons will start any day now. I thought, why not buy a pair of ankle boots? "Well then, how about rubber ankle boots?"

"We don't sell those either," the man said. "Try the shop next door. We don't carry any rubber footwear at all."

"Why?" I asked out of curiosity.

"Boss's orders."

After this brusque but definitive reply, there was nothing I could do but leave. As I turned to go, my eyes fell on a well-dressed man with a child in his arms standing outside on the footpath buying a tangelo from a fruitseller on the street. I stepped out just as he turned towards the store. "You! Ghulam Ali!"

"Sa'adat!" he shouted and hugged me, the child at his chest sandwiched between us. The child didn't like it and began to cry. Ghulam Ali called the man who had attended to me, handed him the child and said, "Go! Take him home!" Then he said to me, "It's been years, hasn't it?"

I probed his face. The swagger, the ever-so-slight trace of rakishness that had been such a prominent feature of his appearance had entirely disappeared. It was a common family man who stood before me, not the fiery young khadi clad speechmaker. I remembered his last speech, when he had energized the otherwise bleak atmosphere of Jallianwala Bagh with his sizzling hot words, "Nigar! Can you bear to bring a slave child into this world?" Instantly, I thought of the child Ghulam Ali was holding in his arms a few moments ago. I asked him, "Whose child was that?"

"Mine, of course," he answered, without the least hesitation. "I have an older one too. And you, how many do you have?"

For a second I felt it was somebody else talking. Hundreds of questions rattled in my mind – Had Ghulam Ali completely forgotten his vow? Had he disassociated himself entirely from his political life? The ardour, the passion to win freedom for India, where had they gone? Whatever happened to that naked challenge? Where was Nigar? Had she been able to bear giving birth to two slave children after all? Maybe she'd died and Ghulam Ali had remarried.

"What are you thinking?" Ghulam Ali smacked me on the shoulder and said. "Come on, let's talk. We've met after such a long time."

I started, let out an elongated "Yes-s-s," and fumbled for words. But Ghulam Ali didn't give me a chance and started to speak himself instead. "This is my shop. I've been living in Bombay for two years. Business is good. I can easily save three, even four hundred rupees a month. And what are you doing? I hear you've become a big short story writer. Remember the time we ran off to Bombay together? But yaar, that was a different Bombay. It was small. This one is huge. Or it seems huge to me, anyway."

Meanwhile, a customer walked in, looking for tennis shoes. Ghulam Ali told him, "No rubber stuff here. Please go to the shop next door."

"Why not?" I asked Ghulam Ali as soon as the customer left. "I was looking for a pair of shoes with rubber soles myself."

I had asked the question only casually, but his face fell. "I just don't like them," he said softly.

"What do you mean, Them?"

"Rubber, I mean things made of rubber." He tried to smile, but couldn't. He let out a laugh instead, loud and dry. "Okay, I'll tell you. It's just a silly thing, but somehow it's had a significant impact on my life."

He seemed deep in reflection. His eyes, playful as ever, dimmed for a second and then lit up again. "That life – it was absolutely phony! To tell you the truth, Sa'adat, I've completely forgotten the days when this thing about being a leader had got into my head. But the past four, five years have been pure bliss. I can never thank god enough for all he's given me. I have a wife, children ..."

"Thanking god enough" got him started about his business venture – the initial investment, the profit he'd made in a year's time, the money he had in the bank now. I interrupted him, "But what's this Silly Thing that had a profound impact on your life?"

The glow once again disappeared from his face. "Ye-e-e-s," he said. "It had a profound impact. Thank god it no longer does. I guess I'll have to tell you the whole thing."

Meanwhile, the attendant returned. Ghulam Ali turned the store over to him and ushered me into his room in the rear. Here, leisurely, he told me why he had developed such abhorrence for rubber goods.

"How I started my political career, you know well enough. And you also know what kind of character I had. We were pretty much alike. I mean, let's be honest, our parents couldn't brag about us being without blemish. I don't know why I'm telling you this. Maybe you get my drift. I wasn't endowed with a strong character. But I had this desire to do something. That's what drove me to politics. But I swear to god that I was not a fake. I could have laid down my life for this country. I still could. All the same I feel, in fact, it's a conclusion I've come to after much serious thought, that India's politics and her leaders are all pretty green, as green as I used to be. A tidal wave rises, but I think it doesn't rise on its own, it's deliberately created.

Perhaps I haven't been able to lay it all out for you clearly."

His thoughts were terribly muddled. I gave him a cigarette. He lit it, took a few long drags and continued, "What do you think, doesn't every effort India has made to free herself, looks unnatural? Perhaps not the effort, maybe I should say the outcome of the effort. Why have we failed to achieve freedom? Are we a bunch of sissies? Of course we aren't. We're men. But the environment is such that our energies fall short of what's needed to reach our goal."

"You mean there is a barrier between freedom and us?" I asked.

His eyes gleamed. "Absolutely. But not like a solid wall or an impenetrable rock. It's like a membrane at the most ... a cobweb, created by the way we conduct our politics, and live our sham lives. Lives in which we deceive others ... and ourselves even more."

His thoughts were still in a jumble. He seemed to be attempting to account for all his past experiences then and there. He stubbed out the cigarette, looked at me and said, "A person should stay the way god made him. He does not need to shave his head, wear red ochre clothes, or cover his body with ash to do good works, does he? You might say a person does all those things out of his own will. That's just it. This novelty, Out of his own will, is precisely what leads people astray, at least that's what I think. Their lofty position makes them indifferent to natural human weaknesses. But they completely forget that it is not their character, thinking or beliefs that will endure in the minds of simple people. As a matter of fact, these disappear into thin air in no time at all. What does endure, rather, is the image of their shaven heads, red ochre garb, and ash-smeared bodies."

Ghulam Ali grew terribly excited. "The world has seen a whole host of reformers. Nobody remembers their teachings. But crosses, sacred threads, beards, bracelets and underarm hair survive. We are more experienced than our ancestors a thousand years ago. I can't understand why none of these contemporary reformers can see that they are disfiguring humans beyond any hope of recognition. There are times when I feel like screaming, For god's sake, haven't you deformed him enough already? At least take pity on him now and let him be! You want to make him god, while the poor thing, he's having a hard time just holding on to his humanity."

"Sa'adat, I swear to god this is how I feel. If it is wrong and false ... then I don't know what is right and true. For two full years I've wrestled with my mind. I've argued with my heart, my conscience, in fact with every pore of my body. In the end, I feel humans must remain humans. If a couple wants to curb their carnal passion, let them. But the entire human race? For god's sake! What good will all that curbing accomplish?"

He stopped briefly to light another cigarette, letting the matchstick burn itself out. Then he shook his head slightly and continued, "No, Sa'adat, you cannot know the incredible misery I've been through, in my body and soul. But it couldn't be otherwise. Whoever attempts to go against nature is bound to pay for it. The day I made that vow in the Jallianwala Bagh – you remember, don't you? – that Nigar and I would not bring any slave children into this world, I felt an electrifying surge of happiness. I felt that with that declaration my head had risen up to the sky. However, when I got out of jail, the painful realization slowly hit me – I had curbed a vital part of my body and soul ... I had crushed the prettiest flower in my garden between my palms. At first, the thought brought an exhilarating sense of pride – I had done what others could not. But then slowly, when my reasoning became clear, the bitter truth began to sink in. I went to see Nigar. She had given up her job at the hospital and joined Babaji's ashram. Her pallid face, her altered mental and physical condition – I couldn't believe it. Spending a year with her convinced me that her torment was the same as mine, although neither wanted to mention it to the other, feeling the noose of our vow tighten around us.

"All that political excitement simmered down within a year. Khadi clothes and the tricoloured flag no longer seemed so attractive. And even if the cry of Inquilab Zindabad did go up now and then, it had lost its previous resonance. Not a single tent could be seen anywhere in the entire Jallianwala Bagh, except for a few pegs left in the ground here and there as reminders of a time gone by. The political fervour had pretty much run out of steam.

"I spent most of my time at home, near my wife." He stopped, the same wounded smile playing on his lips once again. I kept quiet, so as not to interrupt his train of thought.

After a while he wiped the perspiration off his forehead, put out his cigarette and said, "We were both struck by a strange curse. You know how much I love Nigar. I'd think – What kind of love is this? When I touch her, why don't I allow the sensation to peak? Why do I feel so guilty? Like I'm committing a sin? I love Nigar's eyes so much. One day when I was feeling normal, I mean just how one should feel, I kissed them. She was in my arms, or rather I should say, I had the sensation of holding a tremor in my arms. I was about to let myself go, but managed to regain control in time. For a long while afterwards, several days, I tried to believe that my restraint had given my soul a pleasure few had experienced. The truth was, I'd failed. The failure, which I wanted to believe was a great success, instead made me the most miserable man on earth. But as you know, people eventually find ways to get around things. Let's just say I found a way around it. We were both drying up. Somewhere deep inside a crust had started to form on our pleasures. We are fast turning into strangers, I thought. After much thinking we felt that we could, without compromising our vow ... I mean that Nigar wouldn't give birth to a slave child."

The wounded smile appeared a third time, dissolved immediately into a loud laugh with a distinct trace of pain in it, then he continued in an extremely serious tone, "Thus started this strange phase of our married life. It was like a blind man suddenly having sight restored in one eye. I was seeing again. But soon the vision blurred. At first we thought ..." He seemed to be fishing for the right word. "At first we felt satisfied. I mean we hadn't the foggiest idea that we'd start feeling terribly dissatisfied before long. As though having one eye wasn't enough. Early on we felt we were recovering, our health was improving. A glow had appeared on Nigar's face, and a shine in her eyes. For my part, my nerves no longer felt so hellishly strung out all the time. Slowly, however, we turned into rubber dummies. I felt this more than she did. You wouldn't believe it, but by god, every time I pinched the flesh in my arms, it had the feel of rubber to it. Absolutely. As though I didn't have any blood vessels. Nigar's condition, I believe, was different. Her perspective was different too. She wanted to become a mother. Every time a woman in our lane had a baby, Nigar would sigh quietly. I didn't much care about having children. So what if we didn't have any? Countless people in the world don't either. At least I had remained steadfast in my vow. And that was no mean achievement. Well, this line of thinking did comfort me quite a bit, but as the thin rubbery web began to close around my mind, I became more and more anxious. I grew overly pensive, the feel of rubber clung to my mind. At meals, the bread felt chewy and spongy under my teeth." A shudder went through his body as he said this. "It was disgusting! All the time it felt as though soap lather had stuck to my fingers and wouldn't go away. I started to hate myself. I felt all the sap had drained out of me and something like the thinnest of skins had remained behind – a used sheath." He started to laugh.

"Thank god, I'm rid of the abomination now, but after what torment, Sa'adat. My life had turned into a dried and shrivelled piece of sinew skin, all my desires smothered. But, oddly, my sense of touch had become unusually keen, almost unnaturally keen. Maybe not keen, but focused in one direction only. No matter what I touched, wood, glass, metal, paper, or stone, it felt like the same clammy tenderness of rubber that made me sick! My torment would grow worse when I thought about the object itself. All I needed to do was to grab my affliction in two fingers and toss it away ... but I lacked the courage. I longed for something to latch on to for support, the merest straw in this ocean of torment, so that I could reach the shore. I kept looking for it desperately. One day as I sat on the rooftop in the sun reading, rather browsing, a religious book, my eyes caught a hadith of the Prophet Muhammad (PBUH) and I jumped with joy. The Support was glaring in my eyes. I read the lines over and over again. I felt as if water had gushed through the desiccated arid landscape of my life. It was written – It is incumbent on man and wife to procreate after they are married. Contraception is permissible only in the event of danger to the lives of parents. Then and there, I peeled off my affliction and threw it aside."

He chuckled like a child. I did too, because he had picked up the cigarette with two fingers and tossed it aside like some infinitely revolting object.

All of a sudden, he turned serious. "I know what you'll do, Sa'adat," he said. "You will turn whatever I told you into a story. But, please, don't make fun of me in it. I swear to god, I've told you only what I felt. I won't get into a debate over this with you. But the substance of what I've learnt is this – It's no bravery to fight nature, no achievement to die or live starving, or dig a pit and bury yourself in it for days on end, or sleep for months on a bed of sharp nails, or hold one arm up for years until it atrophies and turns into a piece of wood. This is show business. You can't find god or win freedom with show business. I even think the reason India hasn't gained freedom is precisely because she has more showmen than true leaders. And the few leaders who are there, are going against the laws of nature. They have invented a politics that stops faith and candidness from being born. It is this politics which has blocked the womb of freedom."

Ghulam Ali wanted to say more, when the attendant walked in. He had a child, perhaps Ghulam Ali's second boy, in his arms. The boy was holding a colourful balloon. Ghulam Ali pounced on it like a madman. It burst with a loud boom. A piece of rubber dangling from a little bit of string remained in the boy's hand. Ghulam Ali snatched it with his two fingers and threw it away like some infinitely revolting object.

"For Freedom's Sake" has been translated from "Swaraj ke liyé," in *Namrood ki Khuda'i,* and later in *Manto,* Sang-e Meel Publications, Lahore, 1995.

# Khalid

Early every morning, Mumtaz swept all the three rooms. He would clear away cigarette butts, used matchsticks and other odd scraps lying around. He felt comfortable only when the place had been thoroughly cleaned.

His wife slept outside on the veranda. The child lay on his cot.

Waking up early and sweeping all the three rooms had become his morning ritual. He did so because his son had started walking and like all children that age, would put whatever he found on the floor in his mouth.

Though he himself cleaned the room, he was astonished at his son's capacity to ferret out waste from the crevices on the uneven floor.

No matter how hard he tried, Khalid, his firstborn, not even a year old, always managed to pick up something to pop into his mouth.

Cleanliness had become an obsession with him. Every time he saw Khalid pick something up he felt extremely guilty. He blamed himself for not being careful enough.

He loved his son passionately ... to the point of distraction. As the boy's first birthday approached, he grew fearful. He could not understand why, but something told him his son would not live to be one. He shared this fear with his wife. When he mentioned it to her the first time, she could not believe her ears. Her husband was not a man to give in to morbid fantasies. She said, "What is the matter with you? I just can't believe you are saying this. You're not the kind of man to allow absurd notions get the better of you. By the grace of god our son shall live to be hundred! I will celebrate his first birthday in style and put an end once and for all to your morbid fantasies."

His wife's words stung him. He wished as much as she did for his son to enjoy a long life, but nothing could shake off his foreboding.

Khalid was a strapping baby. One winter day the servant had taken the child out for a stroll. When he came back, he told his mistress, "Begum Sahiba, don't use red colour on Khalid Mian's cheeks or someone will cast an evil eye on him."

She exclaimed, "Idiot, as if I would use rouge on my boy's cheeks. They're naturally red."

In winter Khalid radiated health. But with the advent of summer, he lost some of his bloom. Khalid loved to play in water. As soon as he woke up in the morning, he would stretch himself and gurgle down his milk from the bottle. Then his father, about to leave for work, would stand him up in a bucket of water.

Khalid would splash about, to the delight of his parents watching fondly.

Yet Mumtaz's joy was invariably tinged with grief. "Oh god, may it please you to fulfil my wife's words ... I'm confused. I cannot understand why I am constantly haunted by the idea of Khalid's death. Why does such a thought keep crossing my mind? Why would Khalid die? He is in perfect health, much bigger than others his age. Oh dear, I most definitely have gone mad. I love my son to the point of distraction. That is why I'm so jittery. Why must I love my child so? I wonder if all fathers feel the way I do? I wonder if every father lives with the fear of his son's death? I just cannot understand what's the matter with me."

Once all the three rooms had been thoroughly swept, Mumtaz would lay a mat on the floor and lie flat on his back without a pillow. He would enjoy half an hour's peace. That day, as he lay there, he thought, "Day after tomorrow, my son will be a year old. If the day passes by uneventfully, then my peace will be restored and my heart will feel lighter. Allah ..."

He was lying there, his eyes closed, when he felt his son's full weight on his bare chest. He opened his eyes and saw his wife standing next to him. She said, "Khalid has spent a very restless night. He began to shudder in his sleep."

Khalid began to shiver once again as he lay on his father's chest. He touched the child's back and said, "God, please protect my son."

His wife could not conceal her irritation. "For god's sake, you and your delusions. The boy has a mild fever. It will go soon." She left the room.

Khalid continued to lie on his father's chest, his eyes half-closed. Occasionally, a shudder ran through his small body. Mumtaz would then pat the boy on the back.

After a little while, Khalid opened his jet black eyes, looked at his father, and gave him a feeble smile. Kissing his son, Mumtaz asked, "Khalid, what's the matter? Why are you so restless?"

Khalid raised his head and smiled. Then his head drooped and fell on his father's chest.

Mumtaz kept patting the child on the back, praying for his son's long life from the core of his being. His wife had been busy with making the arrangements for Khalid's first birthday party. All her friends had been invited. The tailor had been summoned to make special clothes for the event and the food to be served had been decided too. Everything had been thought of. Yet he found it all distasteful. He just wanted his son's birthday to be over and done with. If only the boy could turn one without his having to hear of it. He preferred to be informed of the boy's birthday after it was over.

As Khalid moved off his chest, he told his son lovingly, "Khalid, beta, are you not going to wish your father well?"

Smiling, Khalid raised his right hand to his forehead.

He blessed his son, "May you live long!" But as the words escaped his lips, he became despondent and panicky.

Khalid paid his respects to his father and left the room.

There was still plenty of time for Mumtaz to leave for the office. He kept lying on the mat, trying his best to get rid of the fear suffocating him.

Suddenly he heard his wife's startled cry, "Mumtaz Sahab, Mumtaz Sahab, do hurry and come here." Her voice was tinged with anxiety.

With a start, he got up and ran out to the veranda. He saw his wife clutching the boy in her arms, pacing up and down in front of the bathroom.

"What happened?" he asked as he took the child from her.

Bewildered, his wife replied "I don't know ... he was splashing water. I tried to get him to clean his nose but he just doubled over."

As the boy tossed and turned in his father's arms it seemed as if life was being drained out of his body.

He laid Khalid on the cot lying in front of him.

By now, both his wife and he were very worried. Khalid kept tossing and turning on the bed as both parents looked on, aghast. They took turns caressing the child, kissing and hugging him and sprinkling drops of water on his face, but the little boy remained lifeless.

After a while the attack subsided and he lay unconscious.

Mumtaz thought his son had died and said to his wife, "He has left us."

Testily, she said, "For god's sake, stop being such a prophet of doom. All the child has had is a few convulsions. He will be up and about soon."

Just then, Khalid opened his huge jet black eyes and looked at his father wanly.

Mumtaz felt a rush of relief. His world, which had stopped, began to move again. In a warm, muffled voice he said, "Khalid, beta, what is the matter with you?"

Khalid smiled weakly.

Mumtaz took the child in his lap and carried him indoors. He was just settling the child on the bed, when his little body was wracked by another convulsion. Like a fit of epilepsy. Mumtaz thought that he too had been seized.

With the second attack, Khalid became even more inert. His eyes sank into his head.

Mumtaz called out feverishly, "Khalid beté, tell papa what is wrong? Beté, get well and start moving. Khalidi, do you want some butter?"

Khalid loved butter. But that day he did not even react. The father asked the son if he wanted milk. The child refused listlessly.

The father clung to his son for all he was worth and smiled at him. Then he handed Khalid back to his wife, "Look after him. I am going to call the doctor."

When he returned with the doctor, his wife looked very worried. The child had suffered three more attacks and was unconscious.

The doctor examined the child carefully and declared, "There is nothing to worry about. Convulsions of this kind are normal in children his age. The usual teething problems. Or maybe worms. I am writing out a prescription. Once he has taken the medicine, he will feel better. Don't worry about it."

That day Mumtaz did not go to work. He spent the whole day with his son.

After the doctor left, Khalid had two more attacks. He lay absolutely still.

When evening came, he thought to himself, "Perhaps god has shown us mercy. It has been some time now since an attack came on."

His wife was relieved, "With god's grace, my boy will be up and about tomorrow."

At night, Khalid had to be given his medicine so Mumtaz decided not to lie down lest he doze off. Instead, he pulled an armchair near his son's cot and kept vigil. Khalid was restless. He kept tossing and turning, and when Mumtaz touched his body he found that his son was running a very high temperature.

In the morning, the child's temperature shot up to 104 degrees.

The doctor came again. All he said was, "There's nothing to worry about. It is a case of bronchitis. I'll write out a prescription and he'll be well soon."

The minute the doctor finished writing the prescription, Mumtaz ran to buy the medicine. Then he gave his son the first dose, but something left him strangely dissatisfied. He decided to go out in search of a specialist.

The specialist arrived. He examined the child and comforted them, "There is nothing to worry about. The child will soon get well."

But Khalid did not get well. The specialist's medicine had no effect. Khalid continued to run a very high temperature.

The servant told Mumtaz, "There is nothing the matter with Khalid Mian. Someone has cast an evil eye on the child. I have a talisman for him. By the grace of Allah, he shall soon be cured."

The talisman was dissolved in the water collected from seven wells and Khalid was made to drink the concoction. A visiting neighbour suggested Unani medicine. He brought the medicine home, but did not give it to Khalid. In the evening, a relative arrived with another doctor in tow. The doctor examined Khalid and said, "It is malaria. Such high temperatures are normal. I will give him a quinine injection. Apply a wet sponge to his forehead."

A cold sponge was placed on Khalid's forehead. His temperature fell immediately. Both his wife and he heaved a sigh of relief. However, their relief was short lived. The child's temperature soared up again.

He put a thermometer in the child's mouth – 106 degrees.

The neighbour came back. She looked at the child and said morosely to his wife, "His neck is broken."

His heart sank. He rang the hospital from the factory below his rooms. He was told not to lose a minute. He called for a tanga, took Khalid in his lap, sat his wife beside him and made his way to the hospital.

He kept on drinking water, but his thirst could not be quenched. As they were going to the hospital, his throat felt terribly dry. He thought he would ask the tangawala to stop in front of a shop so he could get something to drink, but suddenly an inner voice screamed, "Don't quench your thirst. Otherwise Khalid will die."

He lit a cigarette and took two puffs, then threw it away. The voice told him, "Mumtaz, do not smoke, or the child will die."

He asked the tangawala to stop so that he could think for a minute, "Just what's wrong with me? This is nothing but a figment of my imagination. How can my smoking have anything to do with my son's life?" He got down from the tanga and picked up his unfinished cigarette, then clambered back up and just as he was about to take a long pull, it seemed as if an invisible force held him back, "No, Mumtaz, no! Don't smoke. Otherwise Khalid will die!" He threw his cigarette away again. The tangawala gave him a hard stare and he felt that the man was watching and laughing at him. Irritably, to explain away his actions, he told the driver, "The cigarette had gone out." He then pulled his pack from his pocket and took out another cigarette. But he didn't have the courage to light it. He was agitated. His rational mind kept telling him that he was being ridiculous, but that voice, louder and stronger, overpowered his rational mind. He could no longer think. The tanga entered the hospital premises. He crushed and threw the cigarette he was holding. He was feeling sorry for himself – he, of all people, had become the victim of his fantasies.

Khalid was admitted immediately. A doctor examined the child and diagnosed bronchial pneumonia. He said, "His condition is critical."

Khalid was unconscious. Mumtaz's wife sat on the side of the bed and stared at her son with vacant eyes.

Mumtaz was parched. He went to the bathroom next to the ward and turned on the tap. As he cupped his hands the voice spoke, "Mumtaz, just what do you think you're doing? Don't drink that water. Otherwise Khalid will die."

He cursed the voice and drank as much water as his bloated stomach could hold.

As he emerged from the bathroom, his thirst quenched, he found Khalid lying listless, still unconscious, on an iron hospital bed. He just wanted to run away. All his faculties seemed to have abandoned him. Everything appeared unreal. If only he could take his son's illness upon himself. His son looked even frailer than before. "It's because of the water I drank. Why, oh, why did I have to drink so much? Perhaps if I had not been so greedy, my son would be getting better." He reproached himself. And then, it suddenly occurred to him that it was not he but some other person who had fallen prey to these fantasies. "I wonder who it is. It cannot be me. I felt thirsty, so I had some water. How can that in any way influence my son's health? Khalid will soon be up and about again. Insha Allah, we shall celebrate the boy's birthday as planned."

But as he formulated these thoughts in his mind, his heart sank. And the relentless voice said, "Khalid will not live to be one year old." He wanted to stifle that voice and silence it forever.

Then it occurred to him that the voice was nothing but a figment of his own imagination. "Oh god, why does it taunt me?" He felt he couldn't stand it any longer and began to plead with the voice, "Have pity on me, leave me alone. Why are you tormenting me so?"

Evening came. Several doctors had looked at Khalid. Medicine and injections were administered at frequent intervals. But he did not regain consciousness.

All of a sudden, the voice said, "Leave the hospital immediately. If you fail to do so, Khalid will die."

He ran out of the ward. He ran out of the hospital. All he could do was blindly follow the commands of the voice. He had become its slave.

The voice directed him to a bar. It told him to order a drink. When the drink was served, the voice commanded him to throw it away. He threw it away. Then the voice instructed him to call for another drink. He called for another drink and again threw it away. After paying for the drinks and the broken glasses, he walked out of the bar. While the voice shrieked inside his head, he was engulfed by the silence of the space around him.

He walked back to the hospital.

He was going towards his son's ward, when the voice commanded, "Don't go in there. Or your Khalid will die."

He stopped in the park and lay down on a bench.

It was ten o'clock. The grounds were in darkness. The air was quiet. An occasional horn would pierce the silence as a car moved away. In front of him, the hospital clock shone on the high wall of its facade.

He could only think of Khalid. "Will he be spared? Why have a child like this if he is going to be snatched away from you? What is the point of so short a life? I am sure Khalid will ...

And then the voice shrieked in his head. He got off the bench and prostrated himself. "Don't stop till your son gets well," it said.

He remained thus and wished that the voice would grant him a favour. But the voice told him sternly not to ask for anything.

Tears welled up in his eyes. He wanted the favour for his son, not for himself. "Oh god, rid me of this voice. Take my son's life if you must. But please stop this torture."

He heard some voices float across the lawn. On the other side two doctors were sitting on chairs and discussing their patient.

"Such an attractive child."

"The mother has really taken it badly. Poor woman."

"Yes. If she even sees a doctor she begins to plead for her son's life."

"We did what we could."

"I told the mother to pray."

Then one of the doctor's looked his way. He was still prostrated on the ground.

He heard the doctor say to him, "You there, come here."

He rose and moved in their direction.

One of the doctors asked him who he was.

He licked his parched lips and said, "I am the patient."

The doctor told him sternly, "If you are a patient you should be in bed. What do you think you are doing out in the open?"

"Doctor, my son was admitted into the ward over there."

"That was your son?"

"Yes. You were discussing him, weren't you? His name is Khalid."

"Are you the child's father?"

"Yes doctor, I am the child's father," he said, nodding his head sullenly.

"Then what are you doing here? Go back to the ward immediately. Your wife is very worried."

"Yes, doctor."

He rushed off to the ward. He had climbed a couple of stairs

145

when he saw his servant standing on the veranda, tears streaming down his cheeks.

When the servant saw him come up, he began to wail, "Sahab, Khalid has breathed his last."

He entered the ward. His wife lay unconscious on the floor. A doctor and a nurse were trying to revive her.

He came and stood near the bed. Khalid lay there, his eyes shut, his face radiating the peaceful tranquillity of the dead.

He ran his fingers through his dead child's silken hair and in a heartrending voice asked him, "Khalid Mian, don't you want some sweets?"

Khalid's lifeless body refused to react.

Then he pleaded with his son, "Khalid, will you take the voice away, please?"

He swore he saw Khalid nod his head and heard him saying, "Yes."

"Khalid" has been translated from "Khalid Mian," in *Khali Botalen Khali Dibbe,* Saqi Book Depot, Delhi.

# Barren

We had our first encounter exactly two years ago at Port Apollo on this very day. It was evening. In the distance, the last rays of the sun had disappeared behind waves that resembled the folds of a thick, coarse fabric when looked at from the benches facing the sea. I was sitting on the bench on the other side of the Gateway of India, where a man was having his head massaged. I was staring at the ocean stretched out endlessly. At the furthermost point, where the sky and the sea came together, huge waves rose gradually ... as if the sides of a dark coloured carpet were being folded up.

All the lights around the Gateway were on. Their reflection spread in thick, shivering lines over the trembling water. Just below, along the stone wall, rolled-up sails and bamboo poles for the boats stirred gently. The sound of the waves and the voices of the sightseers permeated the atmosphere like a hum. Now and then the honk of an approaching or receding car split the air like an offending "Hunh!" in the middle of an absorbing tale.

It is truly a pleasure to smoke in such an atmosphere. I took out a packet of cigarettes and searched for the matchbox. God knows where I had left it. I was about to put the packet back in my pocket when I heard someone nearby say, "Here, use this."

I turned around. A young man was standing behind the bench. Bombay residents are normally pale, but this man looked frighteningly so. I said, "Thank you very much."

He held out the matchbox towards me. I thanked him again and said, "Please sit down."

The man replied, "Please light your cigarette. I have to go."

I felt he was lying. His tone betrayed the fact that he was neither in a hurry nor had any particular place in mind to go. True, you might ask how one can tell such things from tone. But the truth is, that was precisely how I felt at that time. So I said once more, "What's the hurry? Sit down," and with that I offered him a cigarette, "Please!"

He looked at the packet and said, "Thanks, but I only smoke my own brand."

Believe it or not, I would have sworn that he was lying again. And again it was his tone that betrayed him. This piqued my interest and I resolved firmly that I would make him sit down beside me and smoke one of my cigarettes. I thought this wouldn't be too difficult because in just two sentences he had made it plain that he was deluding himself. He, in fact, wanted to sit down and smoke but at the same time he felt that he should do neither. I could clearly detect yes-no clashing in his tone. Believe me, his very existence seemed to be suspended between being and non-being.

His face, as already implied, was incredibly thin. Besides that, the outlines of his nose, eyes and mouth were so faint that it seemed as if someone had drawn a portrait and then washed it. As I looked at him, his lips would swell at times but then fade away like a spark buried under layers of ash. It was the same with the other features of his face – eyes like two puddles of muddy water, with sparse lashes drooping over them, black hair with hue of burnt paper, dry and brittle like straw. You could make out the contours of his nose more easily, but from a distance it looked pretty flat, because, as I mentioned earlier, his features were exceedingly faint.

He was of average height, neither tall nor short. However, when he stood in a certain way, relaxing his spine, there was a marked difference in his height. Likewise, when he would suddenly stand erect, he appeared to be much taller than his true size.

His clothes were shabby, but not dirty. His jacket sleeves were frayed at the cuffs from constant wear and tear – you could see the threads unravelling. His collar was unbuttoned and his shirt looked like it could hardly survive one more washing. Yet, despite such clothing, he was trying hard to present himself as a respectable man. I say "trying" because when I had looked at him his whole being seemed to have been rocked by a wave of anxiety, and I was left wondering if he was really trying to keep himself hidden from my eyes.

I got up, lit a cigarette, and offered the packet to him. "Help yourself!"

I offered the cigarette and quickly lit the match for him in a way that made him forget everything. Taking a cigarette, he stuck it in his mouth and started to smoke. But then he immediately realized his slip. He promptly removed the cigarette from his mouth, pretending to be coughing. "Cavenders don't sit well with me," he said. "Its strong tobacco irritates my throat right away."

I asked, "So what brand do you smoke?"

He stammered, "I ... I actually smoke very little because

Dr Karolkar has advised me not to. Otherwise I buy 555, which is pretty mild."

The doctor he mentioned was famous in Bombay. His fees was ten rupees. The brand of cigarettes he mentioned, as you may well know, is very expensive. He'd lied through his teeth twice in one breath, which I couldn't digest. But I kept quiet. Though at that moment I desired nothing more than to unmask him, expose his lies, and shame him into apologizing to me. However, when I looked at him I realized that whatever he had said became a part of him. His face did not flush like that of a liar's. Instead, I sensed that he believed whatever he said. His lies were spoken with complete sincerity and conviction, without the least bit of guilt. Anyway, let's drop this. Recounting all these details would require reams of paper and I'd never get around to the story itself.

In a short time, after a little polite conversation, I seemed to have put him at ease. I offered him another cigarette and mentioned how truly exquisite the ocean looked. Since I'm a storywriter, I was able to talk to him about the ocean, Port Apollo and all the visitors there in such a distracting way that even after six cigarettes his throat failed to become the least bit irritated. He asked me my name. When I replied he stood up and said, "You? You're Mr ... I've read many of your stories. I didn't know it was you. I'm very pleased to have met you. Really very pleased."

I wanted to thank him but he continued, "Yes, I remember, just recently I read one of your stories. Can't remember the title. It's the one about the girl who's in love with a man but the fellow deceives her. There's another man, the narrator of the story, who's in love with her. When he discovers the girl's misfortune he tells her, You must go on living. Turn the memory of the moments you spent engrossed in his love, when you were happy, into a foundation you can build your life on. I don't remember it word by word, but do tell me one thing, Is it possible? Forget possible, tell me straight out whether, by any chance, you are that man? Forgive me for asking you such a question. I really shouldn't. But were you the person who had a tryst with her on the rooftop and then went downstairs to sleep in your own room, leaving her alone in the slumbering moonlight with all the passions of her youth?" He suddenly halted and then added, "I really shouldn't be asking this sort of thing. After all, who opens his heart to strangers!"

"I will tell you," I said. "But somehow it seems a bit odd to be discussing everything when we have met for the first time. Don't you think?"

His earlier excitement suddenly cooled. He said softly, "You're right, but who knows whether I'll ever meet you again."

I said, "Bombay is of course a very large city but we can meet again, not just once but many times. I'm an idle person, I mean a short story writer. You'll find me here every evening, provided I'm not sick. Many young women come here to stroll and I come here to find one of them to fall in love with. Love's not a bad thing!"

"Love? Love?" He wanted to say something more but couldn't, and like a rope on fire he fell silent tortuously.

I'd brought up "love" just to be funny. But given the absolutely delightful surroundings, I would have had no regrets about actually falling in love with someone. When the waning daylight and evening shadows meet, when the rows of streetlights begin glimmering in the encroaching darkness, when the air becomes slightly chilled and the feel of romance permeates the atmosphere, one naturally longs to be close to a woman. It is that feeling, that need, which lies hidden in our subconscious.

God knows which story he was referring to. I don't remember all my stories, especially the romantic ones. I've known very few women in my life. The stories I've written about women were done either because of a particular need or just to indulge in a mental gratification of the senses. Since they lack sincerity I don't think much of them. I have observed women of a certain class and have written a few stories about them, but those aren't romances. In any case, the story he'd mentioned must be one of those mediocre romances, the kind I might have written to calm my own ardour. But now I've started telling my own story.

So when he fell silent after uttering "love," I felt the urge to expand further on that. I began, "Well, our forefathers have enumerated many kinds of love, but as far as I'm concerned, whether love is born in Multan or in the icy plains of Siberia, in winter or summer, in the heart of a rich or poor man, beautiful or grotesque, or whether those who fall in it are degenerate or pious ... love remains love. It doesn't change. The manner of love's birth remains unchanged just like that of a child's birth. Of course, it's an entirely different matter if Saeeda Begum gives birth in a hospital, while Rajkumari gives birth in a jungle. Or if a sweeperwoman stirs love in a Ghulam Muhammad while a Natwar Lal is smitten by a princess. Just as children born prematurely remain weak after birth, so is love born before its time. Some children are born after excruciating labour, well, so are some loves – they cause a lot of pain. Just as some women miscarry, so can love miscarry for some people. And just as sterility results in inability to conceive a child, you will find people who turn out to be incapable of love. This doesn't necessarily mean that the desire to love has completely vanished from their hearts, or that the feeling of love has been completely smothered. No, the desire may still be there, but they lack the ability to love. Just as some women are unable to conceive because of some physical imperfection, these people are unable to ignite the spark of love in the hearts of others because of some spiritual imperfection."

I was finding my harangue interesting, so I lectured on without even looking at him. When I did finally look at him, I found him gazing off into space across the ocean, entirely lost in his own thoughts. I fell silent.

The sound of a particularly loud horn suddenly jolted him out of his reverie and he blurted out absentmindedly, "Yes. You're absolutely right!"

I thought of asking him, "Absolutely right? Forget that. Just tell me what I've been saying." But I kept quiet, allowing him a chance to shake off his weighty thoughts.

He was lost in his thoughts for a while and then said, "What you said is absolutely correct, but ... let's drop this topic. It ... well, never mind."

I liked what I'd been talking about. I wanted to continue and have him listen to me, so I repeated, "Well, I was saying that some men also turn out to be barren when it comes to the matters of love. I mean they do desire to love, but are never able to. I think that's due to some spiritual flaw. What do you think?"

He turned paler, as though he'd seen a ghost. The change was so sudden, it worried me. I asked, "Is everything all right? You aren't feeling unwell, are you?"

"No, no ..." He sounded even more worried. "I'm not unwell or anything like that. What makes you think so?"

I replied, "Anyone who saw you now would assume that you're ill, extremely ill. You look frighteningly pale. I think you'd better go home. Come, I'll take you there."

"No, I'll go myself. But I'm not unwell ... I do feel a slight pain in my chest now and then. Maybe it's just ... I'll be okay. You go on."

I remained silent as he didn't look if he could concentrate on anything. But when he insisted I resumed, "Anyway, I was asking what you thought about people who are unable to love. I have no idea what they feel, what their inner thoughts are. But when I think of those barren women – who in hope of conceiving a child, make fervent entreaties to god and disappointed, resort to spells and charms to gain the pearl of their desire, they even bring ash from cremation grounds, recite incantations given to them by sadhus all night long, make votive offerings – it occurs to me that a person who's unable to love must go through a similar ordeal. Such people truly deserve compassion. I feel more for them than I do for the blind."

His eyes brimmed with tears. He swallowed and quickly stood up. Turning his face away he said, "Oh, it's late. I have an important errand to run and I seem to have lost a lot of time talking."

I also got up. He turned towards me and pressed my hand. He spoke without looking at me, "I really must leave now," and walked away.

The second time I met him again at Port Apollo. Although I'm not one for walks, back in those days an evening stroll to Port

Apollo had somehow become part of my daily routine. A month later though, a longish letter from a poet in Agra, which, among other things, made lewd comments about the beauties 'that crowded the port's beaches and how lucky I was to be living in Bombay, pretty much took care of whatever interest I may have had in the place. Now, whenever someone asks me to go there, I'm reminded of that letter and I feel like throwing up. But I'm talking about the time before that letter. Then, I used to go there every evening and sit on the bench next to the place where many people habitually had masseurs repair their skulls.

Day had completely given way to evening, with no trace of light anywhere. The October heat was still intense but a breeze was blowing. Strollers, like exhausted travellers, made up most of the crowd. Behind me, many cars had lined up. All the benches were taken. Two chattering men, one Gujarati, the other Parsi, had settled in on the bench next to me, blabbering away in Gujarati, each with a different accent. The Parsi spoke in only two notes – shrill and deep – alternating them. When they both talked rapidly at the same time, it sounded as if a parrot and a myna were having a duel.

Tired of their endless chatter, I got up and was about to head towards the Taj Mahal Hotel when I saw him coming my way. I didn't know his name so I couldn't call him. But when he saw me our eyes locked, as though he'd found what he'd been looking for.

There were no empty benches, so I proposed, "It's been a long time since we last met. Let's go over there to the restaurant. All the benches here are taken."

He said a few things by way of formality and came along. We walked a bit and then sat down in the large cane chairs in the restaurant. After I had ordered tea I offered him my cigarettes. Coincidentally, just that day I had gone to see Dr Karolkar and he had advised me to quit smoking altogether, or, if I couldn't do that, switch to smoking better quality cigarettes, like 555 for instance. So, following the doctor's advice I had bought this tin that very evening. He stared at the tin, then at me. He started to say something but then decided against it.

I broke into a laugh. "Don't think that I've started smoking these on your advice. Actually you might call it pure coincidence. Today I too ended up seeing Dr Karolkar because lately I've been feeling this pain in my chest. Anyway, he advised me to smoke these, but much less."

As I said this, I glanced at him and realized that my words had upset him. I took Dr Karolkar's prescription out of my pocket and put it on the table. "I can't read his handwriting but he seems to have crammed every vitamin on to this one prescription."

He glanced at the prescription with Dr Karolkar's name and address embossed in black letters along with the date. The earlier agitated look quickly faded from his face. He smiled and said, "Why is it that most writers suffer from vitamin deficiencies?"

I replied, "Certainly not because they don't get enough to eat. It's more likely because they work a lot and get paid a pittance."

Meanwhile the tea arrived and we started talking about other things.

An interval of a month, maybe a month and a half, fell between our first and second meetings. His face now looked paler than before and there were dark circles around his eyes. Apparently he was suffering from some spiritual ailment which troubled him constantly. Every now and then he would stop short in the middle

of a sentence and quite unconsciously, let out a sigh. Even when
he tried to laugh his lips didn't move.

Seeing him in this condition I asked abruptly, "You look sad ...
why?"

"Sad?" A faint smile, like the one on the face of a person who is
dying but wants to show that he isn't afraid, appeared on his face.
"I'm not sad. Could it be that you're in a sombre mood yourself?"

He finished his tea in a single gulp and quickly got up. "All
right," he said, "I've got to go. I have an important matter to take
care of."

I was certain that he didn't have "an important matter to ..."
Yet, I let him leave without trying to stop him. I again failed to
find out his name, but I did realize that something was bothering
him – mentally and spiritually. He was sad, or rather sadness had
completely permeated his being. But he didn't want anyone to
know. He wanted to live two lives – one that was real and another
that he was busy creating every minute and second. Both the lives
were a failure. Why? That I don't know.

It was again at Port Apollo that we ran into each other for the
third time. This time, however, I took him to my place. Although
we didn't say anything on the way, we did talk quite a bit once we
got home. The moment he entered the room, a gloomy look
appeared on his face and lingered there for a few seconds. He quickly
steadied himself and, unlike in the past, tried to appear unusually
cheerful and chatty. It made me feel even more sorry for him. He
seemed to be denying the reality of something as certain as death.
What was even worse, he sometimes seemed to be quite satisfied
with his self-deception.

As we talked, he noticed the framed photograph on my table.

Getting up and moving closer to the photograph he asked, "May I have a look, with your permission of course?"

"By all means!"

He gave the photograph a fleeting look and then sat down. "Quite a goodlooking woman. I guess she's your ..."

"No, no. It was a long time ago. I was attracted to her, rather, I almost fell in love with her. Unfortunately, she never knew about it, and I – no, she was married off to ... Anyway, this is a memento of my first love, which died even before it had a chance to be born."

"A memento of your first love! You must have had quite a few affairs since." He ran his tongue over his dry lips. "I mean you must've had many requited and unrequited loves in your life."

I was about to set him straight and tell him that this humble man was just as barren in the matter of love as he was. But, god knows why, I held back. Instead, I basically lied for no reason at all. "Yes, sure. Such affairs do come along, don't they? You must've had quite a few yourself."

He didn't say anything and became completely silent, as though he had plunged into deep waters. After he'd been submerged in his own thoughts for a long time and his silence began to weigh on me, I said, "Well, sir, where are you lost?"

He was startled. "I? Nowhere. I was just thinking about something."

"Were you reminded of something in the past?" I asked. "Stumbled on a lost dream? Some old wounds starting to hurt again?"

"Wounds? Old wounds? Well, not wounds. Just one – very deep and vicious. And I have no desire for more. One is enough." Saying that, he got up and attempted to pace inside my room.

Attempted, because my place was small and cluttered with chairs, a table, a cot and what all – there was really no room to pace. He could only go as far as the table and then had to stop. This time, though, he looked at the photograph closely and said, "How much she resembles her! Her face wasn't quite as playful though. She had big eyes, the kind which see as well as understand." He heaved a sigh and sat down in the chair. "Death is beyond comprehension, especially when it seizes someone in the prime of youth. I believe there's another power besides god, extremely jealous and begrudging anyone's happiness. Well, never mind."

"No, no, go on," I insisted, "if you don't mind. To tell you the truth, I thought you had probably never fallen in love."

"What made you think so? A few minutes ago you said that I must've had quite a few affairs myself, didn't you?"

He looked at me questioningly. "If I haven't loved, then why this sorrow which keeps gnawing at my heart? Why this affliction? This sadness? This state of being oblivious to myself? Why am I melting away like wax, day and night?"

Ostensibly he was asking me, but in fact he was asking himself.

I told him, "I lied when I said that you must've had quite a few affairs in your life. But you lied too, when you said you weren't sad and that nothing was bothering you. It's not easy to know what's inside another person's heart. There could be any number of reasons why you feel sad, and unless you choose to tell me yourself, I can't very well come to any conclusion, can I? That you're becoming frailer and frailer by the day is obvious. Surely you've suffered a big shock and I do sympathize with you."

"Sympathize!" Tears rushed to his eyes. "I don't need sympathy. Sympathy can't bring her back, can't pull the woman I loved out of the abyss of death and return her to me. You have never loved. No, you have not. I'm certain of that. For you're unscathed by its failure. Look at me," he looked at himself, "do you see any spot where love hasn't left its scars? My entire existence is nothing more than the rubble of love's crumbling abode? How can I relate this tale to you? And why should I? You wouldn't be able to understand. The words, My mother died, are not likely to affect a stranger as much as her own son. To you, indeed to anybody, my tale of love would seem commonplace. But the way it has affected me, how can anyone understand it! Only I have experienced this love and only I have borne its brunt."

He fell silent. His throat had become dry – obvious from his repeated attempts to swallow.

"Did she deceive you? Or was there something else?"

"Deceive? She could never deceive. For god's sake, don't use that word. She was not a woman, she was an angel. But woe to death that couldn't see us happy and gathered her up in its wings and took her away forever – ah! You've opened my wounds. So now listen. I'll tell you part of that distressing tale. She came from a distinguished, wealthy family. When we first met, I'd already squandered away the whole of my ancestral property on a life of debauchery. Nothing remained. I left my home and went to Lucknow. Since I used to own a car myself, the one skill I had was driving. So I decided to become a chauffeur. My first job was at the residence of Dipty Sahab and she was his only daughter."

He drifted off into his own thoughts and stopped talking. I too remained silent.

After a moment he snapped out of his reverie and said, "What was I saying?"

"That the Dipty Sahab hired you."

"Yes. She was the Dipty Sahab's only daughter. Every morning at nine I'd drive her, Zohra, to school. She observed purda, but how long can one remain hidden from one's chauffeur! I was able to see her face on the second day itself. She wasn't just beautiful ... she had something quite special about her. She was a serious and poised young woman. The straight parting in her hair gave her an unusual aura of dignity. She ... she ... how do I explain to you what she was really like. I don't have words to describe her inner and outer beauty."

He kept reciting his Zohra's accomplishments for a long time – making several attempts along the way to describe her in words, but failing repeatedly. It seemed, too many thoughts had crowded his head. Now and then his face would light up in the middle of a sentence, only to be quickly clouded over by a gloom which left him talking in sighs. He was telling his story extremely slowly, as if relishing it himself. His story, which he recounted one piece at a time, went something like this ...

He fell madly in love with Zohra. He spent the first few days looking for opportunities to steal a glance at her and working out all kinds of plans. But when some sense prevailed, he realized he and Zohra were miles apart. How can a chauffeur even think of falling in love with the daughter of his employer. That bitter realization clouded his days with unrelenting sadness. One day though, he dared to scribble a few lines to Zohra on a piece of paper. I remember those lines,

Zohra! I know I am your servant. Your father pays me a salary of thirty rupees a month. But ... I'm in love with you. What shall I do? I'm extremely confused.

He stuck the scrap of paper inside one of her books. The next morning when he drove her to school his hands shook and many times he very nearly lost control of the steering. But with god's grace no accident occurred. He spent the whole day in a strange state of mind. In the evening, when he was driving her back from school, she asked him to pull over. When he did so, in an extremely serious tone she said, "Look Naim, don't repeat this ever again. I haven't told my father about the letter you slipped inside my book. But if you ever do this sort of thing again, I'll be forced to report the matter to him. Understand? Okay. Now drive on."

After that, he tried hard to quit working for Dipty Sahab and extinguish his love for Zohra, but he couldn't succeed. This tug of war went on for a month. One day he picked up courage and wrote her another letter. He slipped it in her book and waited for the decree of his fate. He was sure that he'd be dismissed from his job the next morning, but nothing happened. On their way back from school that evening, Zohra once again spoke to him and admonished him. "If you don't care about your own honour, at least care about mine." She said all this with such gravity and firmness that Naim's hopes were completely dashed. Then and there he resolved to quit his job and leave Lucknow for good.

At the end of the month, he wrote one final letter to Zohra by the dim light of his lantern. With pain and anguish he told her,

Zohra! I've tried my best to act on your advice. Believe me I have. But I cannot control my heart. This is the last time I write to you. I'll leave Lucknow by tomorrow evening so you need not say anything to your father. Your silence will decide my fate. I'll live far away from you ... but don't think I can ever stop loving you. My heart will always be at your feet no matter where I live. I will always remember the days when I drove the car so carefully and slowly in order to save you from jolts. What else could I have done for you anyway?

This letter too he slipped into her book as soon as an opportunity presented itself. As they drove to her school in the morning, Zohra didn't say a word to him. Nor did she speak to him on their way back in the evening. He went to his room utterly dejected. He packed the few belongings he had and put the bundle away in a corner. Then he sat down on his cot and, in the pale light of the lantern, thought about the precipitous gulf that separated him from Zohra.

He was too despondent, extremely aware of his own insignificance. He was just a lowly servant after all! What right did he have to fall in love with his employer's daughter. But every now and then he would think – it wasn't his fault that he'd fallen in love with her. And besides, his love was not a deception. Around midnight, as he was mulling over these thoughts, he heard a knock on the door. His heart jumped to his throat, but then he thought it must be the gardener. It was possible someone had fallen sick at his home and he'd come for help. But when he opened the door, Zohra stood there, yes, Zohra, in the December chill, without even her shawl.

He was tongue tied. He didn't know what to say. There was a deathly silence for a few moments and then, finally, her lips moved and she said in a trembling voice, "Well, Naim, I'm here. Tell me what you'd like me to do. But before you tell me,

I have a few questions of my own."

Naim was silent. Zohra asked, "Do you really love me?"

Naim was hurt. His face flushed.

"Zohra," he said, "you're asking a question that would debase my love if I attempted to answer it. Instead, let me ask you, Don't I?"

Zohra didn't respond. After a brief silence she asked, "My father has a lot of money, but I don't have a single paisa to my name. Whatever is said to be mine is, in reality, not mine but his. Without wealth would you still love me as dearly?"

Being an overly sensitive man, Naim felt as if the question was an affront to his dignity. In a voice weighed down with sorrow, he said, "For god's sake, Zohra, please don't ask such questions, answers to these can be commonly found in even third rate romance novels."

Zohra stepped into the room and sat down on the cot. "I'm yours," she said, "and will always be."

She kept her word. After she and Naim had moved to Delhi, married, and set themselves up in a small house, Dipty Sahab came looking for them. As Naim had already found work, he wasn't home. Dipty Sahab scolded Zohra up and down, accusing her of sacrificing her honour. He wanted her to leave Naim and put all that had happened behind her. He was even willing to pay Naim two or three thousand rupees. But none of this had any effect, and, ultimately, he had to return home disappointed. Zohra wasn't ready to leave her husband at any cost. She said to her father, "Daddy! I am truly happy with Naim. You would never have found a better husband for me. We don't ask you for anything. But if you can, give us your blessings, we'll be grateful for that."

Dipty Sahab was incensed. He threatened to have Naim arrested. Zohra, however, asked him matter of factly, "But Daddy! What is Naim's crime? The truth is we're both innocent. We love each other and he's my husband. This isn't a crime. And I'm no longer a minor."

Dipty Sahab was a shrewd man. He immediately realized he wouldn't be able to prove Naim guilty when his own daughter was a willing partner. He left Zohra for good. Later on, he tried to put indirect pressure on Naim through other people and even tried to buy him off, but failed in that as well.

Zohra and Naim were living happily, even though Naim's salary was dreadfully small and Zohra, who'd been brought up in great comfort and luxury, now had to contend with homely clothes on her body and do all the chores with her own hands. But she was happy and found herself in a new world where she continually discovered fresh dimensions of Naim's love. She was contented, very contented, and so was Naim. But one day, as god had willed it, Zohra felt a severe pain in her chest and before Naim could do anything, she passed away, leaving his world dark forever.

It took him four hours to recount this story. He spoke haltingly, as if relishing every word he uttered. By the time he finished, his face no longer looked pale. It was flushed, as though blood had been injected into him slowly, but his eyes had tears in them and his throat was dry.

His tale told, he got up quickly as if in a terrible hurry, and said, "I made a big mistake. I shouldn't have told you the story of my love. I made a terrible mistake. All this about Zohra should have remained sealed inside my heart, but, but ..." His voice became hoarse. "I'm alive and she ... she ..." He couldn't say anything more. He shook my hand quickly and left the room.

I never saw him again. I went to Port Apollo many times purposely to look for him, but never found him there. I did receive a letter from him six or seven months later in which he wrote,

Sir!
You will recall, I told you the story of my love at your place. It was only a story, an untrue story, for there's no Zohra, nor a Naim. Although I do exist, I'm not the same Naim who was in love with Zohra. One day you said there were people who were truly barren of love. I am one of them, one who has spent his entire life merely deluding his heart. Naim's love for Zohra was a pastime and Zohra's death – I still don't understand why I killed her – it's quite possible that that too had something to do with my inner darkness.

I don't know if you believed my story to be true or false, but let me tell you something very strange. I, the creator of that false story, believed it to be true, based completely on reality. I felt that I had really loved Zohra and she had really died. It might surprise you even more to hear that the story became increasingly real to me as time passed. I could clearly hear Zohra's voice, even her laughter ring in my ears ... I could feel her warm breath on my body. Every little detail of the story came to life and so, in a manner of speaking, I dug my grave with my own hands.

Even if Zohra isn't fiction, I am. She's dead, so I must die too. This letter will reach you after my death. Farewell. I will find Zohra, I'm sure. But where? Of that I'm not so sure.

The only reason I've scribbled these lines to you is because you're a writer. If you can turn all of this into a story you may be able to sell it for seven or eight rupees, since you once said you can make that much from a story. That will be my gift to you. Goodbye.

Your acquaintance, Naim.

Naim created Zohra for himself and died. I created a story for myself and lived – that's my injustice.

---

"Barren" has been translated from "Baanjh," in *Manto ke Afsane*, and later in *Mantorama*, Sang-e Meel Publications, Lahore, 1990.

# Saha'e

Don't say that one lakh Hindus and one lakh Muslims died, say that two lakh human beings died. Two lakh human beings dying is not such a great tragedy after all. The tragedy, in truth, is that those who killed and those who were killed both have nothing to show for it. After killing a lakh of Hindus, the Muslims may have thought that they had finished off Hinduism. But it lives, and will live on. Likewise, after killing a lakh of Muslims, the Hindus may have exulted that this will have killed Islam. But the truth is before you – this hasn't managed to put even a scratch on Islam. They are foolish who think that guns can kill religions. Mazhab, din, iman, dharm, faith, belief – all these are found in our soul, not in body. How can they be annihilated by butcher's cleavers, knives and bullets?"

Mumtaz was unusually excited that day. Just the three of us had come to see him off at the ship. He was leaving us for an indeterminate period of time and was headed for Pakistan – a Pakistan we hadn't even in our dreams ever imagined coming into being.

The three of us were Hindus. Our relatives in West Punjab had incurred heavy losses in terms of both property and lives ... presumably why Mumtaz had decided to leave. Juggal had received a letter from Lahore informing him about his uncle's death in communal riots, affecting him badly. Still under the impact of the news, he casually said to Mumtaz one day, "I'm wondering what I would do if riots broke out in my neighbourhood."

"Yes, what would you do?" Mumtaz asked.

"I might kill you," Juggal said in all seriousness.

Mumtaz fell silent, dead silent. His silence continued for nearly eight days, and broke only when he suddenly announced that he was leaving for Karachi by ship, at quarter to four, that very afternoon.

None of us talked to him about his decision. Juggal was deeply conscious of the reason behind Mumtaz's departure. It was his comment, "I might kill you." Perhaps he was still wondering, whether in the throes of passion he could kill Mumtaz, his bosom buddy or not. That's why he was the silent one amongst us. But, strangely enough, Mumtaz had become unusually talkative, especially during the few hours before his departure.

He had been drinking since he got up in the morning. He had packed his baggage as though going on a vacation. He would talk to himself and laugh for no apparent reason. If a stranger saw him in this state, he would have thought that Mumtaz was overwhelmed with joy at the prospect of leaving Bombay. But we knew that he was trying hard to deceive both himself and us in order to hide his true feelings.

I tried many times to talk to him about his sudden departure. I even gestured to Juggal to bring up the subject, but Mumtaz never gave us a chance.

After downing three or four drinks, Juggal became even quieter and went to lie down in the other room. Braj Mohan and I stayed with Mumtaz. He had many bills to settle, give the doctor's fees, fetch his clothes from the cleaners – all these chores he completed lightheartedly and easily enough. But as he was taking a paan from the stall next to the restaurant on the farther end of the street, his eyes began to well up with tears. As we moved away from the stall, he put his hand on Braj Mohan's shoulder and said softly, "You remember, don't you, how Gobind lent us a rupee ten years ago, when we were down on our luck?"

All along Mumtaz remained silent. But once we returned home he broke into another endless stream of small talk – all totally unconnected, but nonetheless so full of feeling that Braj Mohan and I found ourselves fully participating in it. When the time for his departure drew near, Juggal came in and joined us too. But just as the cab started for the docks, a hush fell over everyone.

Mumtaz's eyes said goodbye to the wide sprawling bazaars of Bombay, until the cab pulled into the harbour. The place was terribly crowded. Thousands of refugees, a few of them affluent, most poor, were leaving – a crush of people. And yet Mumtaz alone seemed to be leaving, leaving us behind for a place he had never seen before, a place which, no matter how he tried to get used to, would still remain unfamiliar. This was my thinking at any rate. I couldn't tell what was going through Mumtaz's mind.

After his bags had been taken to the cabin, he took us out on to the deck. For a long time he gazed at the point where sky and sea came together. Then he took Juggal's hand in his and said, "How perfectly deceptive, this meeting of the sky and the sea, and yet so incredibly delightful!"

Juggal remained silent. Perhaps his earlier remark "I might kill you," was still stinging him inside.

Mumtaz ordered a brandy from the ship's bar. He had been drinking the same since the morning. Drinks in hand, we stood against the guardrail. There was a lot of noise and commotion as refugees piled into the ship. Sea birds hovered over the apparently still water.

Abruptly Juggal downed his glass in one huge gulp and said rather crudely, "Do forgive me Mumtaz. I think I hurt you the other day."

Mumtaz paused briefly and then asked, "When you uttered those words, I might kill you, were they exactly what you were thinking? You had come to this decision with a cool head?"

Juggal nodded his head and then said, "But I feel sorry."

"You'd have felt worse had you actually killed me," Mumtaz said philosophically. "But only if you had paused to reflect that you hadn't killed Mumtaz, a Muslim, a friend, but instead a human being. If he was a bad man, what you would have killed was not his badness, but the man himself. If he was a Muslim, you wouldn't have killed his Muslimness, but his being. If Muslims had gotten hold of his dead body, it would have added a grave to the cemetery, but the world would have come up one human short."

Stopping to think a bit, he resumed, "Likely, the people of my religion would have anointed me a martyr, but I swear I would've torn through my grave and cried that I wouldn't accept the title. I don't want this diploma without any exam. Some Muslim murdered your uncle in Lahore, you heard the news in Bombay and murdered me. Just tell me this, what medals do we deserve for this? What robes of honour do your uncle and his killer back in Lahore deserve?

"If you ask me, the victims died the miserable death of a pie-dog, and their killers killed in vain, utterly in vain."

Mumtaz got worked up as he spoke, but the emotional excess was matched by an equal measure of sincerity. His observation that mazhab, din, iman, dharm, faith, belief – all these were found in our soul, not in the body, and that they couldn't be annihilated by cleavers, knives, and bullets had made an especially deep impression on me. So I told him, "You are absolutely right."

This made Mumtaz think again. He said with some unease, "No, I wouldn't call it, Absolutely right. I mean, yes, sure, this is all okay. But perhaps I haven't been able to say it all clearly, the way I want to. By Religion, I don't mean this religion, nor this dharm, which afflicts ninety nine per cent of us. I rather mean that very special thing which sets one individual apart from all others, the special thing which shows that someone is truly a human being. But what is it? Unfortunately I can't put it on my palm and show it to you." A sudden gleam appeared in his eyes and he asked, as if to himself, "But what exactly was special in him? A staunch Hindu, who worked the most abominable profession, and yet his soul – it couldn't have been more luminous?"

"Whose soul?" I asked.

"A certain pimp's."

The three of us started. Mumtaz's tone was natural enough, so I asked him in perfect seriousness, "A pimp's?"

Mumtaz wagged his head in affirmation. "What a man! Amazing. And even more amazing is the fact that he was, as is commonly called, a pimp – a procurer of women – and yet had an absolutely clean conscience."

Mumtaz paused for a few moments, as if refreshing his memory of past events, and then said, "I don't remember his full name. Something Saha'e. He came from Benaras. He was very concerned about cleanliness. He lived in a small place, but had elegantly divided it into neat little sections. The customers' privacy was scrupulously maintained. There were no beds or cots, only mattresses and bolsters. The bed sheets and pillowcases were always clean and spotless. And even though he had a servant, he did all the cleaning and dusting himself. Not just cleaning, he did everything himself, always putting his heart to it. He was not given to cheating or deception. If it was late at night and only watered down liquor could be had in the neighbourhood, he would say straight out, "Sahab, don't waste your money." If he had a suspicion about one of the girls, he'd let you know up front. He even told me that he had earned twenty thousand rupees within a period of three years, taking two and a half rupees as commission from every ten. He only wanted to make another ten thousand. Why only ten? Why not more? He said that after he has made thirty thousand rupees he would return to Benaras and open a fabric shop. I don't know why he was so keen on opening a fabric shop, of all things."

At this point in the narration I couldn't hold back my surprise, "Really, a strange man!"

Mumtaz continued. "I used to think he was a fake right down to his toe. A big fraud. Who could believe that he called all the girls who worked for him his daughters. Back then it was beyond my comprehension that he had opened saving accounts at the post office for all the girls. Every month, he'd deposit all their income for them. It was just unbelievable that he actually paid out of his own pocket for the expenses of some ten to twelve girls. Everything he did seemed to me a bit too contrived.

"One day when I went to his place he told me that it was Amina and Sakina's day off. He said, I let them go out one day every week

173

so that they could go to some restaurant and satisfy their craving for meat. Here, as you know, everyone else is a vaishnava. I smiled in my heart thinking he was taking me for a ride. Another day he told me that the Hindu girl from Ahmedabad, whom he had married off to a Muslim customer, had written him a letter from Lahore saying that she had made a votive request at the tomb of Data Sahab which had been granted. So now she had made another such petition on behalf of Saha'e – that he may earn his thirty thousand soon and return to Benaras to open his fabric shop. I broke out laughing. I thought, since I'm a Muslim, he is just trying to please me."

"Were you wrong about him?" I asked.

"Absolutely! There was no difference in his word and deed. It is possible that he had some weaknesses, he may have slipped several times in his life, but on the whole, he was a very fine person."

"And just how did you come to know this?" Juggal asked.

"At his death." Mumtaz fell silent for a while. After some time he peered into the space where the sky and sun had gathered in a foggy embrace.

"The rioting had begun. Early in the morning one day, I was passing through Bhindi Bazaar. There were only a few people around due to the curfew. The streetcar was also not running. I walked along looking for a taxi. When I neared the JJ Hospital, I saw a man rolled into a bundle by the large bin on the sidewalk. I thought it must be some day labourer sleeping, but when I saw the blood and gore splattered on the cobblestones, I stopped. It was clearly murder. I thought it best to get out of there, but then I perceived a slight movement in the body. I stopped again. Not a soul was around. I bent over and peered down at the body. It was the familiar face of Saha'e, but stained all over with blood. I sat down beside him on the sidewalk and looked closely. His twill shirt, which always looked spotless, was soaked in blood. The wound was perhaps near the ribs. He started to moan faintly. I carefully shook his shoulder, as one does to wake up somebody sleeping. One or two times I even called him by the only name I knew. I was about to get up and leave when his eyes opened. For a long time he stared at me with those half-opened eyes. Then his entire body started twitching, and recognizing me he said, You? You?"

"One after another I asked him all kinds of questions – Why had he come to that area? Who had wounded him? How long had he been lying on the sidewalk? The hospital was right across from us, should I let them know?

"He was too weak to talk. After I'd fired off all my questions, he groaned out these words with the greatest difficulty – My time was up. This is how bhagwan willed it!

"Who knows what bhagwan wanted, but being a Muslim, I didn't want to see a man I knew to be a Hindu die in a Muslim neighbourhood, feeling that his murderer was a Muslim, as was the man who now stood watching his life ebb away. I'm not a coward, but at that time I felt worse than a coward. On the one hand, I was afraid of being arrested for the murder, and on the other I was scared that even if I weren't arrested, I could still be detained for interrogation. It also occurred to me that if I took him to the hospital he might implicate me to avenge himself. After all, he was dying, why not take me along too? Assailed by such thoughts I was about to flee when Saha'e called my name. I stopped. I didn't want to, but my feet simply froze. I looked at him as though telling him, Get on with it, mister, I have to go.

"Doubling over with pain he unbuttoned his shirtfront with great difficulty, but as he put his hand inside his strength gave way. At that point he said to me, "In the waistcoat's side pocket under the shirt, there's some jewellery and twelve hundred rupees. It is Sultana's property. I'd left it with a friend for safekeeping. Today ... I was going to send it to her – you know it's getting ever more dangerous these days. Please give it to her and tell her to leave right away. But be careful yourself!"

Mumtaz fell silent, but I felt as though somewhere far away, where the sky and the sea were curled up in a foggy embrace, his voice was slowly dissolving into the voice of Saha'e, as it rose on the sidewalk near the JJ Hospital.

The ship whistled. Mumtaz said, "I did go and see Sultana. When I gave her the jewellery and money, she broke into tears."

We said goodbye to Mumtaz and left the ship. He was standing on the deck by the guardrail, waving his right hand. I said to Juggal, "Don't you feel as though Mumtaz is calling out to Saha'e's spirit to make it his mate on his trip?"

Juggal only said, "How I wish I were Saha'e's spirit!"

---

"Saha'e" has been translated from "Saha'e," in *Khali Botalen Khali Dibbe*, and later in *Mantorama*, Sang-e Meel Publications, Lahore, 1990.

# Black Margins

## Wages of Labour

Looting and plundering went on.
   Fire blazed all around.
   The temperature rose.

   A man passed by, gleefully singing to the accompaniment of his harmonium,

   *Jab tum hi gayé pardes*
   *Laga kar thes*
   *O pritam pyaré*
   *Duniya mé kaun hamara ...*

   (Now that even you've deserted me, to live in a foreign land whom can I call my own, O my beloved.)

   A boy hurried past with a bag stuffed with papads. He stumbled and a packet of papads falling out of his bag scattered all around. As he bent to pick them up, a man running away with a sewing machine said to him, "Let them be, beté. They will turn crisp on their own."

Thud! A heavy gunnysack landed smack in the middle of the marketplace. A man rushed forward and plunged his dagger into it. Instead of human entrails, came out sugar – snowwhite granules of sugar. People flocked there and began to fill up their shirtfronts. One man had no shirt on. He promptly took off his tehmad and began to fill it with fistfuls of sugar.

"Make way! Make way!" A tanga loaded with freshly painted almirahs sped along.

A bolt of muslin fluttered down from the window of a tall building overlooking the street. The flame licked it gently. The muslin was reduced to ashes before it touched the ground.

"Pon, Pon," the shrill horn of a car mingled with the screams of two women.

Ten or fifteen people had pulled a safe out of a house and were breaking it open with clubs.

Another man darted out of a house with a load of Cow and Gate milk tins propped under his chin and started walking up the street slowly.

A loud cry was heard – "Lemonade, come, come, have a bottle of lemonade. It's summertime."

A man with a tyre around his neck took two bottles of lemonade and hurried off without a word of thanks.

Another cry went up – "Fire! Someone call the fire department! Or everything will burn down." No one paid attention.

The looting and pillaging proceeded at a brisker pace now as the fire blazed all around. After some time gunshots were heard.

The police found the bazaar deserted. In the distance, near a car engulfed in smoke, they spotted the shadow of a man, and blowing their whistles, they headed in that direction. The shadowy figure quickly disappeared into the smoke, with the police in hot pursuit.

When the police emerged from the smoke, they saw a Kashmiri labourer sprinting off with a heavy gunnysack on his back.

The police made themselves hoarse whistling, but the man didn't stop. He had a load on his back – not a light load either, a gunnysack stuffed full. Yet he was speeding along so effortlessly as if there was nothing on his back.

The policemen were gasping for breath. In exasperation one of them took out his pistol and fired. The bullet hit the Kashmiri labourer in his calf. The gunnysack rolled off his back.

Panicked, he turned to look at the police slowly coming up behind him. He also looked at his bleeding calf. Then with a sudden burst of energy he hoisted up the sack and limped off as quickly as he could.

"To hell with him," said the policemen, exhausted.

But just at that moment the Kashmiri tottered and fell face down. The sack landed right on top of him.

The policemen grabbed him and whisked him and his sack away to the station. On the way the Kashmiri said, "Hazrat, why arrest me? I'm poor. I only took a sack of rice. Something I eat, to keep myself alive. You've unfairly shot me."

But they couldn't have cared less.

At the station, the Kashmiri kept blabbering in his own defence. "Sir, other people were after bigger game. I only took a sack of rice. Hazrat, I'm very poor ... I just eat rice every day."

Tired of pleading, the Kashmiri eventually gave up. He took off his dirty cap and wiped the sweat from his forehead. Then he looked wistfully at the bag of rice and held out his hand before the Police Inspector. "All right, sir. Keep the sack ... Just give me my wage ... Four annas!"

## Sharing the Loot

An unruly crowd of forty or fifty lathi wielding men began moving towards a house to loot and plunder.

Suddenly, a frail middle aged man tore through the crowd, turned around and spurred on the rioters like some kind of a leader, "Brothers, this house is filled with wealth, innumerable priceless objects. Come on, let's take it over and divide up the booty."

Several lathis were thrown in the air. Fists went up and the sky rent with a burst of loud cries.

The mob, led by the frail looking, middle aged man, converged on the house "filled with wealth, innumerable priceless objects."

Coming to the door, the frail man stopped and again exhorted the rioters, "Brothers, everything inside the house is yours. But remember, don't rush around and no fighting either. Come on."

"The door has a lock on it," somebody shouted.

"Break it," shouted someone else.

"Yes, yes, let's break it."

Several lathis were thrown in the air. Fists were made and the sky rent with a burst of loud cries.

The frail man gestured them to stop. He smiled and said, "Brothers, wait a minute. Let me open the lock with a key."

And saying this, he took out a keychain from his pocket, selected a key and opened the lock. The heavy sheesham door creaked loudly and opened. The rioters jostled each other, frantically trying to enter.

The frail man wiped the sweat off his forehead with his sleeve and said, "Easy, brothers, easy. Everything in the house is yours. Why this scrambling?"

Order swept through the rioters immediately. They began to enter the house one at a time. But the moment the plundering began, it was back to the same frenzied scrambling. They looted without mercy.

When the frail man saw this, he said in a pained voice, "Brothers, easy. There's no need to fight amongst yourselves. Don't grab and yank at things. Cooperate with each other. Don't be jealous if someone has found something valuable. This is a big house. Find something precious for yourself too. Don't act like savages. If you scramble, things will probably get broken and that will be your loss."

The rioters once again came to order. Slowly the house was emptied of its valuables.

All the while the frail man was offering advice, "Look brother, a radio. Handle it carefully, it might break otherwise. Take the cord too."

"Fold it up, brother, fold it up. It's a walnut tea table with delicate ivory work. It's very fragile. Well, it's all right now."

"No, no, don't drink here. You'll get tipsy. Take it home."

"Wait, wait, let me turn off the main switch, otherwise you will get a shock."

Just then loud noises came from a corner. Four looters were grabbing at a rolled-up length of silk.

The frail man rushed over and reproached them, "How silly can you be? You'll tear this priceless fabric to shreds. This house has everything. There must be a yardstick lying somewhere ...

Find it so you can measure the cloth and divide it amongst yourselves."

Suddenly a dog barked, woof, woof, woof. A big Alsatian rushed in and mauled several of the rioters in no time at all.

"Tiger! Tiger!" the frail man shouted.

Tiger, who was holding the collar of one of the raiders in his mouth, wagged his tail, lowered his head and started to move towards the frail man.

With Tiger's arrival, the intruders vanished from the scene, except for the man whose collar was still stuck in the dog's mouth.

He looked at the frail man and asked. "Who are you?"

The frail man smiled and said, "The owner of the house. Ai! Look out! That crystal vase is slipping out of your hands!"

## Fifty-Fifty

A man picked out a large wooden chest for himself. But when he tried to lift it, it did not move an inch.

Another man, who had failed to find anything useful for himself, said to the first one, "May I help?"

The first man accepted the offer. The other man gave the chest a mighty push with his strong hands, lifting it on to his back. The other one supported him. The two began to walk.

It was indeed very heavy. The man carrying the chest thought his back would break any minute under its weight. But the prospect of reward lessened the physical discomfort.

In comparison, the man who had spotted the chest was weak. Placing one of his hands on it, he walked alongside, keeping his right to ownership intact.

When the two reached a safe spot, the man who had done all the work of carrying it put the chest down and said, "So, what's my share?"

"One fourth."

"That's not enough."

"I think it is. I think it's too much. I was the one who found the chest."

"Right. But who carried that heavy load all this way?"

"Do you agree to fifty-fifty?"

"Very well. Open it."

The chest was opened. Out came a man with a sword in his hand. He turned the two claimants into four.

## Appropriate Action

When the mohalla was raided, some members of the minority community were murdered. The survivors fled. However, one couple took refuge in the basement of their house.

The husband and wife spent two entire days and nights expecting marauders to barge in any second.

No one came.

Two more days passed. Their fear of death lessened. Their need for food and water became more pressing.

Four more days passed. By then the couple no longer cared whether they lived or died. They came out of their hideout.

In a feeble voice, the husband tried to attract people's attention, "We've come to surrender, please kill us."

His interlocutors were thinking, "Killing is a sin in our religion."

They were all Jains.

They consulted among themselves and then handed the couple over to the people of another mohalla for "appropriate action."

## Correction

"Who are you?"

"And you?"

"Har Har Mahadev! Har Har Mahadev!"

"Har Har Mahadev!"

"What's the proof?"

"Proof ...? My name is Dharamchand."

"This is no proof."

"You may ask me anything from the four vedas."

"We don't know the vedas ... We want proof."

"What proof?"

"Loosen the waist cords of your pyjama."

A cry went up as the pyjama was lowered. "Kill him! Kill him!"

"Wait, wait, I'm one of you. I'm your brother. I swear by bhagwan, I'm your brother."

"Then what's the meaning of this?"

"Our enemies control the place I come from. So I had to do it to save my life. This has been my only mistake. The rest of me is fine."

"Chop off his mistake!"

The mistake was chopped off. So was Dharamchand.

## An Enterprise

Fire broke out. The entire mohalla went up in flames.
Only one shop escaped.

The signboard on the shop read,
"A complete range of building materials sold here."

## A Raw Deal

Two friends pooled their resources. They selected a girl from a group of ten or twenty and bought her for forty rupees.

After having spent the night with her, one of them asked, "What's your name?"

The man was furious when he heard the girl's name.

"We were told that you belong to the other religious community!"

"You were told a lie," the girl replied.

The man ran to his friend and said, "That bastard doublecrossed us. He palmed off one of our own girls! Come on, let's take her back."

## Beastliness

With great difficulty the couple had managed to save some household possessions.

But their young daughter was missing.

There was a baby girl, the mother clasped her to her breast.

They had a brown buffalo. The rioters took it away. The cow somehow escaped their notice, but its calf could not be found.

The husband, the wife, the baby girl, and the cow were hiding in one place. The night was pitch-dark. When the little girl, overwhelmed by fear, started crying, it sounded like someone beating drums in the stillness of the night. The mother got nervous. She covered the girl's mouth with her hand so that the enemy would not hear her. The sound was muffled. As a further precaution, the father covered the girl with a thick, coarse sheet.

After some time, the sound of a calf was heard mooing in the distance. The cow pricked up her ears. She became restless and began to run up and down mooing loudly in response. They tried in vain to calm the cow down.

Having heard all the noise, the enemies closed in. Light from their burning torches flashed in the distance.

The wife snapped at her husband, "Damn it! Who asked you to bring this wretched beast along?"

## Humility

The moving train was forcibly brought to a halt. Those who belonged to the other religion were dragged out and killed with swords or bullets. The rest of the passengers were treated to halva, fruits and milk.

Before the train continued on, the chief organizer of the hospitality addressed the passengers, "Bhaiyon aur Behnon! We found out about this train's arrival rather late. That's why, even though we wanted to, we weren't able to treat you in a more befitting manner."

## Sorry

The knife slashed his stomach all the way to his navel.

His pyjama cord was severed.

Words of regret escaped the knifewielder's tongue, "Tsch, tsch, tsch ... I've made a mistake!"

## Jelly

At six in the morning the vendor who sold ice on a pushcart was stabbed to death near the petrol pump.

His corpse lay on the road till seven. Drops of water from the melting ice trickled down on it.

At quarter past seven, the police hauled the corpse away. The ice and blood remained on the road.

A tanga passed by. The child noticed the patch of fresh, congealed blood glistening on the road. His mouth began to water. He tugged at his mother's sleeve and pointed at it, "Look Mummy, jelly!"

## What's the Difference

I placed my knife on his jugular vein and ran it slowly across his neck, slaughtering him in the halal manner prescribed by Islam.

"What have you done?"

"Why?"

"Why did you kill him that way?"

"I enjoy it that way."

"To hell with your enjoyment. You should have just hacked his neck off with a single blow, the way they do in jhatka. Like this."

And the one who had slaughtered in the prescribed manner was himself slaughtered in the jhatka way.

---

"Black Margins" has been translated from "Siyah Hashiyé," originally published by Maktaba Jadeed, Lahore, 1952.

# The Dog of Tetwal

The two sides had not budged from their positions for several days now. Occasional bursts of firing – about ten or twelve rounds in a day – were to be heard, but never the sound of human shrieks.

The weather was pleasant – the wind wafted across, spreading the scent of wild flowers. Oblivious to the battle on the peaks and slopes, nature was immersed in its necessary work – the birds chirped as before, the flowers continued to bloom, and lazy honeybearing bees sleepily sipped nectar in the old, time honoured way.

Each time a shot echoed in the hills, the chirping birds would cry out in alarm and fly up, as though someone had struck a wrong note on an instrument, and shocked their hearing.

September-end was meeting the beginning of October in roseate hue. It seemed that winter and summer were negotiating peace with one another. Thin light clouds like fluffed-up cotton sailed in the blue sky, as if out on an excursion in their white shikaras.

For several days now, the soldiers on both sides of the mountain posts had been restless, as no decisive action was taking place. Lying in their positions, they would get bored, and then attempt to recite sh'ers to one another. If no one listened, they would hum to themselves. They remained lying down on their stomachs or backs on the rocky ground, and when the order came, let off a round or two.

The two sides were entrenched in rather safe positions. The high velocity bullets crashed against the shields of stone and fell to the ground. The two mountains on which the forces were ranged were of about the same height. Between them was a green valley – a rivulet wriggling like a fat snake on its chest.

There was no danger of air raids. Neither side possessed artillery. Therefore fires would be lit without fear or danger, and smoke from fires on both sides would rise and mingle in the air. At night, it was absolutely quiet. The soldiers on both sides could hear bursts of laughter from the other. Once in a while, entering into this spirit, a soldier would begin to sing, and his voice would awaken the silence of the night. The echoes would then reverberate, and it would seem that the mountains were repeating what they had just heard.

One round of tea had just been taken. The pine coals in the stone chulhas had grown cold. The sky was clear. There was a chill in the air. The wind had ceased to carry the scent of flowers, as though they had shut their vial of perfume for the night. However, the sweat of the pines, their resin, left an odour in the air which was not wholly unpleasant.

Everybody slept wrapped in their blankets, but in such a way, that in a single movement they could arise, ready for battle.

Jamadar Harnam Singh was on guard. When his Rascope watch showed that it was two o'clock, he woke Ganda Singh and told him to take station. He wanted to sleep, but when he lay down he found sleep a distant proposition, as distant as the stars in the sky. Jamadar

Harnam Singh lay on his back, and gazing up at the stars, began to hum,

> *Bring me a pair of shoes, studded with stars*
> *Studded with stars*
> *O Harnam Singh*
> *O Yaara*
> *Even if you have to sell your buffalo.*

Harnam Singh saw star-studded shoes scattered all over the sky, all a-twinkle.

> *I will bring you shoes, studded with stars*
> *Studded with stars O Harnam Kaur*
> *O Lady, even if I have to sell my buffalo.*

He smiled as the song came to an end, and realizing that he would not be able to sleep, he rose and woke up everybody else. The thought of his beloved had made him restless. He wished for some nonsensical chatter that would recreate the mood of the beloved in the song.

They did begin to talk, but in a desultory fashion. Banta Singh, the youngest, and the one with the best voice, went and sat on one side. The rest, though yawning all the while, kept gossiping about trivial but entertaining matters. After a while, suddenly, Banta Singh began singing "Heer" in a melancholic voice,

> *Heer said, the jogi lied, no one placates a hurt*
> *lover. I have found no one, grown weary, looking*
> *for the one who calls back the departed lover.*
> *A falcon has lost the kunj to the crow — see, does it*
> *remain silent or weep?*

*Happy talk and stories to entertain the world are*
*not for the suffering one.*

After a pause he began singing Ranjha's reply to Heer's words,

*The falcon that lost the kunj to the crow has,*
*thank god, been annihilated.*
*His condition is like the fakir who gave away his*
*all, and was left with nothing.*
*Be contented, feel the pain less and god will be*
*your witness.*
*Renouncing the world and donning the garb of*
*sorrow, Syed Waris has become Waris Shah.*

Just as abruptly as Banta Singh had begun to sing, he fell silent. It appeared as if the soil tinted mountains too had taken on the mantle of grief.

After a while, Jamadar Harnam Singh let out a mighty oath at an imaginary object, then lay down. Suddenly, in the melancholy stillness of the last quarter of the night, the barking of a dog began to resound. Everyone was startled. The sound did not come from too far off. Jamadar Harnam Singh sat up and said, "From where has this barking one come?"

The dog barked again. Now the sound was much closer. After a few moments there was a rustling in the bushes.

Banta Singh rose and moved towards the bushes. When he returned, he had with him a stray dog, its tail wagging.

He smiled, "Jamadar sahab, when I asked him, he said, I am Chapad Jhunjhun."

Everyone laughed. Jamadar Harnam Singh addressed the dog affectionately, "Come here, Chapad Jhunjhun."

The dog approached Harnam Singh, wagging its tail. It began sniffing the stones on the ground, in the belief that some food had been thrown there.

Jamadar Harnam Singh reached into his bag, took out a biscuit and threw it in his direction. The dog sniffed at the biscuit and opened its mouth. But Harnam Singh leapt at it and picked it up, "Wait ... He could be a Pakistani."

Everybody laughed at this. Banta Singh came forward, stroked the dog on its back, and said to Jamadar Harnam Singh, "No, Jamadar sahab, Chapad Jhunjhun is a Hindustani."

Jamadar Harnam Singh laughed, and looking at the dog, said, "Oye, show me the identification!"

The dog wagged its tail.

Harnam Singh laughed heartily, "This is no identification ... All dogs wag their tails."

Banta Singh caught the dog's trembling tail. "The poor thing is a refugee!"

Jamadar Harnam Singh threw down the biscuit, and the dog immediately pounced on it.

Digging up the ground with the heel of his boot, one of the soldiers said, "Now, even dogs will have to be either Hindustani or Pakistani!"

The Jamadar took out another biscuit from his bag and threw it towards the dog, "Like the Pakistanis, Pakistani dogs too will be shot."

"Hindustan Zindabad!" Another soldier loudly raised the slogan.

The dog, which had just begun to move forward to pick up the biscuit, suddenly frightened, backed off with its tail between its legs.

Harnam Singh laughed, "Why do you fear our slogan, Chapad Jhunjhun ... Eat ... Here, take another biscuit!" And saying so he took another biscuit out and threw it.

The soldiers talked on and soon it was morning.

In the blink of an eye, just as when one presses a button and the electricity generates light, the sun's rays flooded the mountainous region of Tetwal.

The battle had been raging in that area for some time. Dozens of lives of soldiers would be lost for each mountain, and even then the hold of either side was tenuous. If they held the range today, tomorrow their enemies did, the following day they captured it back, and the day after that, their enemies did so.

Jamadar Harnam Singh picked up his binoculars and surveyed the surrounding area – smoke was rising from the mountain in front. This meant that a fire was being stoked there too, tea was being readied, and the thought of breakfast was on the mind. Undoubtedly, the other side too could see smoke rising from their camp.

At breakfast, each soldier gave a little to the dog, which it ate with gusto. Everyone was taking a keen interest in the dog, as if they wanted to make it a friend. Its arrival had brought with it an element of cheerfulness. From time to time, each one would affectionately address it as Chapad Jhunjhun and cuddle it.

On the other side, in the Pakistani camp, Subedar Himmat Khan was twirling his impressive moustaches – which had many a story in its past – and was carefully studying the map of Tetwal. With him sat the wireless operator, who was taking orders from the Platoon Commander for Subedar Himmat Khan. At some distance, Bashir, leaning against a rock, was holding his gun and softly humming,

*Where did you spend the night,*
*my love. Where did you spend ...*

As Bashir swung into the mood and raised his pitch, he heard Subedar Himmat Khan's stern admonition, "Oye, where were you last night?"

When Bashir's enquiring gaze shifted towards Himmat Khan, he saw him looking elsewhere, "Tell me, oye ...!"

Bashir turned to see what Himmat was looking at.

The same stray dog, which, a few days earlier, had come to their camp like an uninvited guest and stayed on, was back, sitting a little distance away.

Bashir smiled, and turning to the dog, began,

> *Where did you spend the night,*
> *my love. Where did you ...*

The dog began wagging its tail vigorously, sweeping the rocky ground around him.

Subedar Himmat Khan picked up a pebble and threw it at the dog, "Saala knows nothing except how to wag his tail."

All of a sudden Bashir looked carefully at the dog. "What's this around his neck?" He started walking towards the dog, but even before he reached it, another soldier took off the rope tied around its neck. A piece of cardboard with something written on it was strung to it. Subedar Himmat Khan took the piece of cardboard and asked the soldiers, "Does any one of you know how to read this?"

Bashir came forward and picked up the cardboard piece and said, "Yes I can read a bit." With great difficulty he spelled out "Cha-p-Chapad-Jhun-Jhun ... Chapad Jhunjhun ... What's this?"

Subedar Himmat Khan twirled his legendary long moustaches vigorously, "It must be some word, some ..." Then he asked, "Bashir, is there anything else written there ...?"

Bashir, immersed in deciphering the writing, replied, "Yes, there is. This is a Hindustani dog."

Subedar Himmat Khan began thinking aloud, "What does this mean? What was it you read? ... Chapad ...?"

Bashir then answered, "Chapad Jhunjhun!"

One soldier spoke as if with great knowledge, "Whatever the matter is, it lies here."

Subedar Himmat Khan thought this appropriate. "Yes, it does seem so!"

Bashir read the text inscribed on the cardboard once more, "Chapad Jhunjhun. This is a Hindustani dog."

Subedar Himmat Khan took up the wireless set and placing the headphones firmly over his ears, personally spoke to the Platoon Commander about the dog – how it had first come to them and stayed for several days, and how one night, it disappeared from their midst. Now that it had returned, there was a rope tied around its neck with a cardboard piece strung on it, on which was written ... and this message he repeated three or four times to the Platoon Commander, "Chapad Jhunjhun. This is a Hindustani dog." But they too could not come to any conclusion.

Bashir sat on one side with the dog, speaking lovingly and harshly by turns, and asked it where it had disappeared for the night, who had tied the rope and the cardboard around its neck. But, he did not get the answer he desired. When questioned, the dog would just wag its tail in answer. Finally, in anger, Bashir caught it and gave it a violent shake. The dog whined in pain.

Having spoken on the wireless set, Subedar Himmat Khan contemplated the map of Tetwal for some time. He then rose in a decisive manner. Tearing off the top of a cigarette packet, he handed it over to Bashir, "Here, Bashir, scribble on this in the same creepy-crawly Gurmukhi, as they have."

Bashir took the piece of the cigarette packet and asked, "What should I write, Subedar Sahab?"

Subedar Himmat Khan twirled his moustaches and reflected, "Write ... just write." He took out a pencil from his pocket. Giving it to Bashir, he asked, "What should we write?"

Bashir passed the pencil tip between his lips and began thinking. Suddenly, in a contemplative, questioning tone he asked "Sapar Sunsun ...?" Then, satisfied, said in a determined way, "Okay, the answer to Chapad Jhunjhun can only be Sapar Sunsun. They will remember their mothers, these Sikhras!" Bashir put the pencil to the top of the cigarette pack, "Sapar Sunsun."

"One hundred per cent ... write Sa-pa-r-Sunsun!" Subedar Khan laughed loudly. "And write further ... This is a Pakistani dog!"

Subedar Himmat Khan took the cardboard piece from Bashir's hand, made a hole in it with the pencil, and after stringing the rope through it, moved towards the dog, "Take this to your offspring!"

All the soldiers laughed at this.

Subedar Himmat Khan tied the rope around the dog's neck. The dog kept wagging its tail all the while. The Subedar then gave it something to eat, and in a didactic manner, said, "Look friend, don't commit treachery... Remember, the punishment for a traitor is death."

The dog kept wagging its tail ... After it had eaten its fill, Subedar Himmat Khan picked up the rope and led it towards the sole trail on the hill and said, "Go, deliver our letter to our enemies ... But make sure you come back. This is the command of your officer, understand?"

The dog, still wagging its tail, began walking ever so slowly, along the trail that took a winding route into the lap of the mountains.

Subedar Himmat Khan took up his gun, and fired once in the air.

The shot and its echo were heard on the other side, at the Hindustani camp, but they could not fathom its meaning.

For some reason, Jamadar Harnam Singh had been grumpy that day, and the sound of the shot made him even more irritable. He gave the order to fire. Consequently, for the next half hour a futile rain of bullets poured from either side. Eventually sated of the diversion, Jamadar Harnam Singh called a halt to the firing and began combing his beard with greater ferocity. Having done that, he methodically bundled his hair into the net and asked Banta Singh, "Oye, Banta Singh, tell me, where has Chapad Jhunjhun gone? The ghee didn't go down well with the dog."

Banta Singh missed the implication of the idiom and said, "But we didn't feed him any ghee."

Jamadar Harnam Singh laughed boisterously, "Oye, ill read lout, there's no use talking to you."

Meanwhile, the soldier on watch, who was scanning the horizon with his binoculars, suddenly shouted, "There, he's coming ..."

Everybody looked up.

Jamadar Harnam Singh asked, "What was the name again?"

The soldier on duty said, "Chapad Jhunjhun ... Who else!"

"Chapad Jhunjhun?" Jamadar Harnam Singh got up. "What is he doing?"

The soldier answered, "He's coming."

Jamadar Harnam Singh took the binoculars from the soldier and began looking around. "He's coming our way. The rope is tied around his neck ... but he's coming from there ... the enemy camp ..." He let out an oath at the dog's mother, raised the gun, aimed and fired.

The shot was off its mark. The bullet hit a short distance away from the dog, causing the stones to fly up, and buried itself in the ground. The dog, fearful, stopped.

On the other side, Subedar Himmat Khan saw through the binoculars that the dog was standing on the path. Another shot and the dog started running the opposite way. It ran, with its tail between its legs, towards Subedar Himmat Khan's camp.

Himmat Khan called out loudly, "The brave are never afraid ... Go back!" And he fired a shot to scare the dog.

The dog stopped again.

From the other side, Jamadar Harnam Singh fired his gun. The bullet whizzed by, past the dog's ear.

The dog jumped and flapped its ears violently.

From his position, Subedar Himmat Khan fired his second shot that buried itself near the front paws of the dog.

Frightened out of its wits, it ran about – sometimes in one direction, sometimes the other.

Its fear gave both Subedar Himmat Khan and Jamadar Harnam Singh, in their respective places, a great deal of pleasure and they began guffawing.

When the dog began running in his direction, Jamadar Harnam Singh, in a state of great fury, uttered a terrible oath, took careful aim and fired.

The bullet struck the dog in the leg and its cry pierced the sky.

The dog changed its direction and limping, began running towards Subedar Himmat Khan's camp.

Now the shot came from this side – just to scare it. While firing Himmat Khan shouted, "The brave pay no attention to wounds. Put your life on the line ... go back ..."

Terrified, the dog turned the other way – one of its legs had become useless. It had just about managed to drag itself a few steps in the other direction on three legs, when Jamadar Harnam Singh aimed and fired. The dog fell dead on the spot.

Subedar Himmat Khan expressed regret, "Tsch tsch ... the poor thing became a martyr!"

Jamadar Harnam Singh took the warm barrel of the gun in his hand and said, "He died a dog's death."

"The Dog of Tetwal" has been translated from "Tetwal ka Kutta," the Devnagari version, published in *Sa'adat Hasan Manto: Dastavez*, vol. 2, Rajkamal, Delhi.

# Open It!

The special train, which left Amritsar at two in the afternoon, reached Mughalpura after eight hours. Several people were killed along the way, a good many injured, and some fled in different directions.

At ten in the morning, when Sirajuddin opened his eyes in the camp and saw the tumultuous crowds of men and boys around him, he almost lost his wits. For a long time he kept staring at the sky. The noise filled the camp but old Sirajuddin's ears were as if sealed. He couldn't hear anything. Anyone seeing him would have assumed that he was deep in thought. But he had become senseless. It was as though he was suspended in space.

As he kept staring vacantly at the sky, his eyes suddenly caught the sun. Its rays coursed through every pore of his body and he got up. A collage of images flitted across his mind – plunder, fire, escape, gunshots, night ... and Sakina.

Sirajuddin stood up instantly and began to comb the sea of humanity around him like one possessed. He desperately searched for Sakina in the camp for full three hours, shouting her name all the time. But there was no trace of his only daughter. Chaos reigned all around. While some were looking for their missing children, others looked for their missing mothers, wives and daughters.

Tired and exhausted, Sirajuddin found a spot to sit down and tried to recall where and when Sakina got separated from him. However, all he could remember at that moment was the sight of his wife's corpse with all her entrails spilled out. He had no memory of anything after that.

He and Sakina were running bare feet. Her dupatta had slipped. When he stopped to pick it up Sakina had shouted, "Abbaji, leave it." But he had picked it up. At this thought his hand involuntarily went to the bulge in his pocket. It was indeed Sakina's dupatta. But where was she?

Sirajuddin tried hard to remember. Did he and Sakina reach the station? Did she get on the train with him? When the train had stopped along the way and the rioters had come aboard, was it then that he had lost his senses and they had taken her away? He could not decide.

Sirajuddin's mind was bristling with questions, which had no answers. He needed sympathy. So did the mass of humanity around him. He tried to weep but couldn't. All his tears had dried up.

After six days, when Sirajuddin had recovered a little from his shock, he met some young men ready to help. Eight in number, they were equipped with a lorry and guns. He blessed them.

Sirajuddin gave them a description of his daughter, "She's fair and very beautiful like her mother, not me. She's about fourteen, has dark hair, and a big mole on her right cheek. She's my only daughter. Please try to find her, god will bless you."

Those young volunteers reassured Sirajuddin. If his daughter was alive she would be with him in a few days.

They had tried. At great risk to their lives they went to Amritsar. They rescued many men, women and children and took them to safety. But even after ten days they could not find Sakina.

However, one day when they were going to Amritsar on the same mission, they saw a girl by the roadside near Chuhrat. The sound of the lorry startled the girl and she began to run away. The volunteers stopped the lorry, ran after her and caught her in the field. She was beautiful and had a big mole on her right cheek.

One of the young men said to her, "Don't be afraid. Is your name Sakina?"

The girl went pale. She didn't answer. When the youths reassured her, her fear lessened. She told them that she was indeed Sakina, Sirajuddin's daughter.

They were kind to her. They fed her, gave her milk to drink and helped her up on to the lorry. Feeling awkward without her dupatta, she vainly tried to cover her breasts with her hands. One of the young men handed his jacket to her.

Several days passed. Sirajuddin didn't receive any news of Sakina. He would make the rounds of camps and offices throughout the day but could not find any clue of his daughter's whereabouts. At night he would pray for the success of the volunteer youths.

One day Sirajuddin spotted those young men in the camp. They were sitting on the lorry. He went running up to them. The lorry was about to start. He asked one of them, "Beta, did you find my Sakina?"

"We will, we will," all said in one voice. The lorry started. Once again he prayed to god for their success. It made him feel good.

That evening, Sirajuddin was sitting in the camp when he noticed some commotion. Four men were carrying a girl on a stretcher.

When he enquired he was told that the girl was found unconscious near the railway lines. He followed them.

The men brought her to the hospital and went away. He stood outside for some time, leaning against a wooden pole. Then slowly he went in. In a solitary room he saw a stretcher with a lifeless body lying on it. Taking small steps, he advanced towards it.

Somebody switched on the light.

He saw a mole glinting on the pale face of the corpse and screamed, "Sakina!"

The doctor who had switched on the light asked him, "What is it?"

"I ... I'm her father," he managed to blurt out from his parched throat.

The doctor looked at the body lying on the stretcher and felt its pulse. Then he pointed to the window and said to him, "Open it."

The body stirred slightly on the stretcher.

The lifeless hands untied the waistband.

And lowered the shalwar.

"She's alive! My daughter's alive!" Old Sirajuddin shouted with joy.

The doctor broke into a cold sweat.

---

"Open It" has been translated from "Khol Do," in *Sau Kendil Power ka Bulb: Sa'adat Hasan Manto ke Ikkis Muntakhab Afsane,* Modern Publishing House, New Delhi, 1980.

# Cold Meat

Kulwant Kaur rose from her bed as Ishar Singh entered the hotel room. She peered at him with her sharp eyes and bolted the door. It was past midnight. A strange, mysterious silence had swept over the suburbs of the city.

Kulwant Kaur came and sat cross-legged on the bed. Ishar Singh was probably trying to untie the knot of his jumbled thoughts. He stood in a corner with his kirpan in hand. A few moments passed in silence. Then, dissatisfied with the way she was sitting, Kulwant Kaur moved to the edge of the bed, lowered her legs and began swinging them. Ishar Singh was still silent.

Kulwant Kaur was a well-endowed woman with strong limbs. She had wide, rounded hips, unusually high breasts and sharp eyes. There was a slight trace of bluish down on her upper lip. The profile of her chin suggested that she was a woman to be reckoned with.

Ishar Singh was still standing in the corner with his head lowered. The tightly wrapped turban on his head was coming loose. The hand holding the kirpan was shaking. However, his physique and awesome stature made it evident that he was just the right man for Kulwant Kaur.

A few more moments passed in ominous silence before Kulwant Kaur lost her patience. Her eyes rolled, but she could only exclaim, "Ishar Siyan!"

Ishar Singh lifted his head to look at her, but he could not bear Kulwant Kaur's glare and turned his eyes away.

Kulwant Kaur screamed, "Ishar Siyan." But immediately she controlled her voice, went over to him and asked, "Where have you been all these days?"

Licking his parched lips, Ishar Singh said, "I have no idea."

Kulwant Kaur was furious. "What kind of fucking answer is that?"

Ishar Singh flung his kirpan aside and slumped down on the bed.

It looked as if he had been sick for the last few days. Kulwant Kaur looked at Ishar Singh stretched out on the bed. Her heart went out to him. Putting her hand on his forehead she asked, "Jaani, what's wrong?"

Ishar Singh, who had been staring at the ceiling, turned his gaze on Kulwant Kaur, looking for some pity in that familiar face. "Kulwant."

There was pain in his voice. All of Kulwant Kaur gathered into her upper lip. She bit it and said, "Yes, Jaani."

Ishar Singh removed his turban and looked at her again – his eyes searching for understanding and help. Then, slapping her fleshy buttocks, he jerked his head and said, as if to himself, "I'm going crazy."

His hair came down with the jerk. Kulwant Kaur began to run her fingers through it and asked lovingly, "Ishar Siyan, where have you been all these days?"

"In bed, with my enemy's mother."

He looked at her intently and suddenly began to vigorously massage her upturned breasts. "Kasam Wahé Guru ki, you are indeed quite a woman."

Kulwant Kaur brushed his hands away with a flirtatious air and asked, "Tumhé meri kasam, tell me, where have you been? In the city?"

He tucked his hair into a bun and replied, "No."

Kulwant Kaur was incensed. "You must have been to the city. And you have surely looted a lot of money which you're hiding from me."

"I'm not my father's son if I've lied to you."

That silenced Kulwant Kaur for a while. Before long she flared up again, "What I don't understand is what happened to you that night. You were lying beside me in bed as usual. You had made me put on all the jewellery you'd looted in the city. You were kissing me, when all of a sudden something got into your head. God alone knows what! You stood up, put on your clothes, and simply dashed out."

Ishar Singh turned pale. And the minute she noticed it she blurted out, "See how you blanch ... Ishar Siyan. Something has been going on, I swear by Wahé Guru."

"Nothing's been going on, I swear by your life."

But his tone had no life in it, which only strengthened her suspicion. Biting her upper lip she said, "Ishar Siyan, you're not the man you were eight days ago. Why's that?"

Ishar Singh got up with a start as though someone had attacked him. He gathered Kulwant Kaur into his strong arms and began to squeeze and kiss her relentlessly. "Jaani, I'm the same. Press hard, it will cool the heat in your bones."

Kulwant Kaur didn't resist him. Nonetheless she kept returning to her earlier complaint, "What happened to you that night? Really?"

"My enemy – his mother got screwed."

"What? Aren't you going to tell me?"

"Tell you what? As if there was something to tell."

"May you cremate me with your own hands if you're lying." Ishar Singh wrapped his arms around her shoulders and dug his lips into hers. His moustache crept into her nostrils and made her sneeze. They broke into laughter.

Ishar Singh took his vest off, all the while eyeing Kulwant Kaur lustfully. "Come, let's have a game of cards."

Tiny beads of perspiration appeared on her upper lip. She rolled her eyes and cooed flirtatiously, "Get lost."

Ishar Singh pinched her wide, rounded bottom and she leapt to one side. "Don't, Ishar Siyan, that hurts."

He moved closer and began to chew Kulwant Kaur's lips. She crumbled immediately. He threw aside his shirt and said, "Well then, let's get to the trump card."

Kulwant Kaur's upper lip began to quiver. He peeled off her shirt and put it aside, eyeing her naked body lewdly. Pinching her on her arm he said, "Kasam Wahé Guru ki, Kulwant, you're some woman."

Kulwant Kaur looked at the red blotch on her arm and said, "Ishar Siyan, you're a brutal tyrant."

Ishar Singh's lips smiled behind his dark, bushy moustache. "Let there be tyranny today!" And he unleashed more tyranny – he bit her upper lip and earlobes, ravaged her large bosom and slapped her bottom resoundingly. He planted forceful kisses on her cheeks and sucked her breasts vigorously, wetting them with his drool. Kulwant Kaur was burning with desire — a kettle of water come to boil. But all this foreplay could not light the fire of his own passion. Like a beaten wrestler, he used all the tricks known to him, but in vain. Every nerve in Kulwant Kaur's body was already reverberating, and frustrated by all the unnecessary teasing and beating about the bush, she murmured, "Ishar Siyan, you've shuffled enough. Now throw the trump."

Hearing this, Ishar Singh felt as though the entire deck of cards had slipped from his hands on to the floor. He lay beside Kulwant Kaur, huffing and puffing, a layer of cold sweat covering his forehead. Kulwant Kaur tried every means she knew to arouse him, but in vain. When all these silent efforts failed and Kulwant Kaur's taut body was left unsatiated, she was disgusted. She picked up a sheet to cover herself quickly and said with cold fury, "Ishar Siyan, who's the bitch you've spent the last few days with? Who has sucked you dry?"

Ishar Singh just lay there on the bed, mute and panting.

Kulwant Kaur was boiling with rage, "Just tell me who the bitch is ... your lover, your trump card?"

Ishar Singh could only reply feebly, "There's no one, Kulwant. Really, there's no one."

Kulwant Kaur placed her hands on her wide hips. "Ishar Siyan, I must know the truth today. Take an oath on Wahé Guru and tell me — Is there another woman?"

Ishar Singh wanted to say something, but Kulwant Kaur silenced him, "And before taking the oath keep in mind that I'm the daughter of Sardar Nihal Singh. I'll make mincemeat of you if you lie to me. Now, come on, take the oath and then tell me there's no woman behind all this."

Ishar Singh nodded his head sadly. Kulwant Kaur went absolutely mad. She leaped to pick up the kirpan, peeled off its sheath as if peeling the skin off a banana and pounced on Ishar Singh.

The next moment blood gushed out. But still Kulwant Kaur was not pacified. She pulled at his hair like a wild cat, hurling obscenities at his other woman. After a while, Ishar Singh implored faintly, "Let go now Kulwant, let go." His tone was heartrending. Kulwant Kaur stepped back.

Blood trickled from the wounds on his cheeks and saturated his moustache. He opened his trembling lips and cast a baleful, poignant look at Kulwant Kaur. "Meri jaan, you've been very hasty. But never mind."

Kulwant Kaur's jealousy flared up again. "Who's that bitch, I am asking you?"

The stream of blood reached Ishar Singh's mouth. As he tasted his own blood he felt a cold shiver run through his body. "I? I've killed six men with that kirpan. The same one with which you ..."

Kulwant Kaur's head was filled with the other woman. "I'm asking you again – *who* is the bitch?"

Ishar Singh's eyes were starting to blur. But there was a sudden spark in them as he said to Kulwant Kaur, "Don't call her a bitch."

Kulwant Kaur screamed, "Who is she?"

Ishar Singh was choking. "I'm telling you," he said, running his hand over his shoulder and smiling as he touched his warm blood, "Man is a damned motherfucking creature."

Kulwant Kaur was waiting for his reply. "Ishar Siyan, get to the point."

Ishar Singh's smile grew bigger behind his moustache. "I'm coming to the point. You've slit my throat. I'll tell you the whole story, but slowly."

His head drenched in cold sweat, he began, "Kulwant, my life, I can't tell you what happened to me. Man is a strange motherfucking creature. When the looting was going on in the city, I joined in along with the others. I handed over to you all the money and jewellery that I could lay my hands on. But there's one thing I did not tell you about."

Ishar Singh felt a sharp pain in his wound and began to groan. Kulwant Kaur showed no concern and asked him pitilessly, "What's that?"

Ishar Singh blew some drops of blood off his moustache. "The house we broke into ... there were ... seven people ... I ... I killed six of them ... with that kirpan with which you've ... Forget it ... listen ... there was a girl ... very beautiful ... I picked her up ..."

Kulwant Kaur was listening with rapt attention. He blew the blood drops from his moustache again. "Jaani, how can I say this to you ... she was so beautiful. I could've hacked her up but ... I said to myself, Ishar Siyan, you enjoy Kulwant Kaur every day ... why not try this new dish today?"

Kulwant Kaur could only grumble, "I see!"

"I put her over my shoulder and left the place. On the way ... what was I saying? Yes, on my way, beside the canal I laid her under the shade of some shrubs ... first I thought ... I'll shuffle her a bit ... but then ... I decided to ..." His tongue was parched.

Kulwant Kaur moistened her own throat with her spit, "Go on ..."

Ishar Singh could barely get the words out of his mouth, "I ... I threw the trump, but ..." His voice sank.

Kulwant Kaur shook him violently, "What happened?"

Ishar Singh strained to open his eyes and gazed at Kulwant Kaur shaking with rage.

"She ... she was dead ... a corpse ... a lump of cold flesh. Jaani, give me your hand."

Kulwant Kaur placed her hand on his. It was colder than ice.

---

"Cold Meat" has been translated from "Thanda Gosht," in *Sau Kendil Power ka Bulb: Sa'adat Hasan Manto ke Ikkis Muntakhab Afsane,* Modern Publishing House, New Delhi, 1980.

# Toba Tek Singh

Two or three years after the Partition, it occurred to the governments of Hindustan and Pakistan that, just as they had exchanged civilian prisoners, they should exchange the lunatics confined in the asylums as well. In other words, Muslim lunatics interred in the asylums of Hindustan should be sent to Pakistan, and the Hindu and Sikh lunatics confined in the asylums of Pakistan should be handed over to Hindustan.

It is difficult to say if this was the right thing to do. Anyway, the decision was made by the wise, and accordingly, several high level conferences were held on either side, and a date set for the exchange. A thorough investigation followed. The Muslim lunatics whose families were still living in Hindustan were allowed to stay on. The rest were dispatched to the border. In Pakistan, where most of the Hindus and Sikhs had already migrated, the question of retaining anyone did not arise. All the Hindu and Sikh lunatics were sent to the border under police escort.

It is not known what transpired there, but when the news of the exchange reached here, in Lahore, it evoked some very interesting and intriguing responses. A Muslim lunatic who had been reading *The Zamindar* regularly for the last twelve years, was asked by his friend, "Maulvi Sahab, what is this Pakistan?"

"It's a place in Hindustan where they make cut throat razors," he answered after profound reflection.

His friend looked satisfied with the answer.

In the same vein, a Sikh lunatic asked another Sikh, "Sardarji, why are we being sent to Hindustan? We don't even know the language they speak there."

The other one smiled, "I know the language of the Hindustooras. These Hindustanis are devils and strut about haughtily ..."

A Muslim lunatic, while taking his bath, raised the slogan "Pakistan Zindabad" with such gusto, that he slipped on the floor and passed out. There were some lunatics who were not really insane. Most of them were murderers, whose relatives had bribed the officials to have them sent to the mental asylum, to save them from the hangman's noose. These men had some vague notions about why Hindustan had been partitioned and what Pakistan was, but they did not know the whole story. The newspapers were no help. The policemen on guard were ignorant and illiterate – one could make out precious little from their conversations. All they knew was that there was a man named Mohammad Ali Jinnah whom people called Qaed-e-a'zam, the great leader. And he had created a new land for the Muslims called Pakistan.

However, they did not know a thing about its actual location and its boundaries. That is why all the inmates of the asylum who weren't completely insane were thoroughly confused about whether they were in Hindustan or Pakistan. If they were in Hindustan, then where was Pakistan? And if they were in Pakistan, then how was it possible since only a short while ago they had been in Hindustan, and they had not moved from the place at all?

One lunatic got so embroiled in this Hindustan-Pakistan rigmarole that he became all the more insane. One day, as he was sweeping the floor, he suddenly climbed up a tree. Perched on a branch, he delivered a two hour long speech on the delicate Hindustan-Pakistan issue. When the guards asked him to come down, he climbed up even higher. When they threatened him, he said, "I want to live in neither Hindustan nor Pakistan ... I'd rather live on this tree."

After much fuss, when his fits ebbed, he climbed down, and hugging his Hindu and Sikh friends, began to cry. He was saddened by the thought that they would go over to Hindustan, leaving him here.

A Muslim radio engineer, who held an MSc degree, usually stayed aloof from the other lunatics and wandered about silently on a particular garden path all day long. A sudden change in him was manifested by the fact that he took off all his clothes, handed them over to the guards, and began to race around stark naked.

A fat Muslim lunatic from Chiniot, who had been an energetic member of the Muslim League and bathed some fifteen or sixteen times a day, abruptly gave up this habit. His name was Muhammad Ali. One day, he declared in his enclosure that he was Mohammad Ali Jinnah, the Qaed-e-a'zam. Following him, a Sikh lunatic styled himself Master Tara Singh. The imminent bloodshed in the enclosure was, however, avoided by declaring both of them dangerous and confining them in separate cells.

There was a young, Hindu lawyer from Lahore who had turned insane after a failed love affair. He was heartbroken when he learnt that Amritsar had gone to Hindustan. The Hindu girl he was in love with, lived in that city. Though rejected by her, the lawyer could not forget her even in his madness. So he would abuse all the Hindu and Muslim leaders who had got together to split Hindustan into two – turning his beloved into a Hindustani, and him into a Pakistani.

When the talk about the exchange began, a few lunatics consoled the lawyer, telling him not to lose heart. He would now be sent to Hindustan, where his beloved was. But he did not want to leave Lahore because he thought that his practice would not flourish in Amritsar.

In the European Ward there were two Anglo-Indian lunatics. When they learnt that the English had left after granting independence to India, they were deeply shocked. They would now spend hours in secret confabulation about their changed status in the asylum. Would the European Ward be there or done away with? Would they be served breakfast anymore? And, instead of Western style bread, would they be forced to swallow the "bloody Indian chapatti?"

There was a Sikh in the asylum who had been there for the past fifteen years. He would often be heard blurting out a string of strange, unintelligible phrases like "Opar di gurgur di annexe di bay dhiana di mung di daal of the laltain." He slept neither at night, nor during the day. The guards said that he had not slept a wink in the long period of fifteen years. He did not even care to lie down, though he would lean against a wall and take a "tek" now and then.

His feet and ankles were swollen from standing all the time. But despite his physical discomfort, he would not lie down to rest. He would listen intently whenever there was a discussion in the asylum about Hindustan, Pakistan, and the exchange of lunatics. If anyone asked him about his opinion, he would reply in all seriousness, "Opar di gurgur di annexe di bay dhiana di mung di daal of the government of Pakistan."

Later on, however, "of the government of Pakistan" was replaced by "of the government of Toba Tek Singh" and he began to ask other lunatics where Toba Tek Singh, the place he came from, was. But no one knew whether it was in Pakistan or Hindustan. Those who attempted to explain got entangled in the confusion that

Sialkot, which earlier had been in Hindustan, was now reported to be in Pakistan. Who knew whether Lahore, which was now in Pakistan, would not go over to Hindustan the following day, or the whole of Hindustan would not turn into Pakistan? And who could say with certainty that some day, both Hindustan and Pakistan would not vanish from the face of the earth altogether!

The lunatic's kesh had become sparse and straggly. As he seldom took a bath, the hair on his head was entangled with his beard, giving him a fearsome look. But he was a harmless fellow, and had never got into a brawl with anyone during the last fifteen years. The older staff in the asylum knew that he was a fairly well to do landlord from Toba Tek Singh, where he had considerable landed property. One day, without any warning, his brain had gone awry. His relatives had brought him here, bound in heavy chains, and had him admitted to the asylum.

Once a month, his people would come to enquire after his well being, and then go back. This arrangement continued for a long time. But as the disturbances concerning Hindustan and Pakistan began to mount, these visits stopped.

His name was Bishen Singh, but everyone called him Toba Tek Singh. He had no notion of the passage of time – what day or month it was, or how many years had passed. But every month, when it was time for his relatives and friends to come, he would somehow come to know of it. He would tell the guard that his "visit" was on its way. He would give himself a good bath, scrub his body with soap, oil his hair and comb it. He would call for his clothes, which he never wore on any other occasion. Thus spruced up, he would go to meet his visitors. If they asked him anything, he would either stay silent, or sometimes blurt out, "Opar di gurgur di annexe di bay dhiana di mung di daal of the laltain."

He had a daughter who had grown up a little, every passing month, during these fifteen years, and was now a young woman. Bishen Singh could not recognize her. She used to cry at the sight of her father when she was an infant. Now, a grown woman, tears still flowed from her eyes, seeing her father.

When the Hindustan-Pakistan controversy started, he began asking other inmates where Toba Tek Singh was. As he did not get any satisfactory answer, his curiosity deepened. Now no one came to visit him. Earlier, he would always know beforehand when the "visit" was due. But now, it seemed as though the voice of his heart, which would foretell him about their arrival, had stilled.

He longed for his people, who used to give him solace and bring fruits, sweets and clothes. If he had asked them where Toba Tek Singh was, they would have certainly told him whether it was in Pakistan or Hindustan, for he believed that they came from Toba Tek Singh where he had his lands.

In the asylum there was a lunatic who called himself Khuda. When Bishen Singh asked him one day if Toba Tek Singh was in Pakistan or Hindustan, he, as usual, guffawed heartily, and said, "It's neither in Pakistan nor in Hindustan, for we haven't yet passed the orders."

Bishen Singh begged this "god" to pass the orders, so that the knotty issue was resolved once and for all. But he was very busy, as he had to pass numerous other orders. One day Bishen Singh lost his patience and burst out, "Opar di gurgur di annexe di bay dhiana di mung di daal of Wahé Guruji da Khalsa and Wahé Guruji ki Fateh ... jo bolé so nihaal sat sri akaal."

He probably wanted to say that he was, after all, a Muslim god ... He would have surely listened if he had been the god of the Sikhs.

A few days before the exchange, Fazal Deen, a Muslim friend of Toba Tek Singh, came to visit him. He had never come before. When Bishen Singh saw him, he turned away and made to leave, when the guards stopped him.

"This is your friend Fazal Deen. He has come to see you."

Bishen Singh looked at Fazal Deen, and then began to mutter something to himself. Fazal Deen came forward and put his hands on his shoulders. "I've been thinking of coming here to meet you for a long time, but just couldn't find time. Your people have reached Hindustan safely ... I did whatever I could for them. Our daughter Roop Kaur ..." He stopped mid sentence.

"Daughter Roop Kaur?" Bishen Singh tried to recall something.

Fazal Deen went on haltingly, "Yes, she too ... is quite well. She too has gone away with them."

Bishen Singh said nothing. Fazal Deen resumed, "Give my salaam to Bhai Balbeer Singh and Bhai Vadhwa Singh ... to Behn Amrit Kaur, too. Tell Bhai Balbeer Singh that Fazal Deen is happy ... The two brown buffaloes that he had left here have both calved ... one a male calf and the other a female one that died six days after its birth. And tell me if there is anything more that I can do for you. I'm always at your service. And here, I've brought some homemade sweets for you."

Bishen Singh picked up the packet of sweets and handed it over to the guards standing near by. Then he asked Fazal Deen, "Where is Toba Tek Singh?"

Fazal Deen replied with alacrity, "What do you mean? It's where it always was."

Bishen Singh was persistent. "In Pakistan or in Hindustan?"

"In Hindustan ... No, no, it's in Pakistan." Fazal Deen was flummoxed.

Bishen Singh walked away from there muttering, "Opar di gurgur di annexe di bay dhiana di mung di daal of the Pakistan and Hindustan of the dur fité munh."

Preparations for the exchange were complete. The lists of lunatics to be sent across had reached from both sides, and the day of the exchange had been fixed.

On a severely cold day, police lorries packed with Hindu and Sikh lunatics proceeded towards the border under police escort. The concerned officials also accompanied them. On the Wagah border the superintendents of the two sides met, and after the preliminaries were taken care of, the exchange began and continued the whole night.

It was indeed a hard job getting the men out of the lorries and handing them over to the officials on the other side. Some just refused to budge from their place. Those who agreed to come out were difficult to manage, as they ran off in all directions. The naked ones among them tore off their clothes as soon as they were made to put them on. If one called names, another burst into a song. While some fought, others cried and wailed. It was difficult to hear anything in the fracas. Female lunatics made their own noises. And the cold was so severe that it made one's teeth chatter.

The majority of the lunatics were against this exchange. This is because they could not make out why they were being uprooted from their homes. Those who could still reason and think, raised the slogan, "Pakistan Zindabad" and "Pakistan Murdabad." They almost came to blows because the slogan incited both the Muslims and the Sikhs.

When Bishen Singh's turn came and the concerned official on the other side of the border began to enter his name in the register, he asked, "Where is Toba Tek Singh? ... In Pakistan or in Hindustan?"

The official laughed, "In Pakistan."

At this, Bishen Singh leaped to one side and ran back to his companions who were still there. The Pakistani soldiers caught hold of him and tried to push him towards the other side, but he refused to move. "Toba Tek Singh is here!" And then he raised his voice, "Opar di gurgur di annexe di bay dhiana di mung di daal of Toba Tek Singh and Pakistan."

They tried their best to persuade him that Toba Tek Singh had already gone to Hindustan, or would be sent there immediately. But he was resolute. When they tried to move him forcibly to the other side, he stood on his swollen legs at a spot in the middle, in a posture that seemed to suggest that no power on earth could move him from there.

Because he was a harmless fellow, they did not use force anymore. He was allowed to stand right there, while the exchange proceedings continued.

Just before sunrise, a sky rending cry emerged from the gullet of Bishen Singh, who till then had stood still and unmoving. Several officials came running to the spot and found that the man who had stood on his legs, day and night for fifteen years, was lying on his face. Over there, behind the barbed wires, was Hindustan. Over here, behind identical wires lay Pakistan. In between, on a bit of land that had no name, lay Toba Tek Singh.

---

"Toba Tek Singh" has been translated from "Toba Tek Singh," in *Savera*, 1953.

# Ismat Chughtai

About one and a half years ago when I was in Bombay I received a postcard from a gentleman in Hyderabad. The message read somewhat like this –

How is it that Ismat Chughtai and you didn't marry? It would have been wonderful if the two personalities, Manto and Ismat, had come together. What a shame! Ismat married Shahid Latif and Manto ...

It was about this time, a conference of Progressive Writers was held in Hyderabad. Though I did not attend the conference I read accounts of its proceedings in a journal published from Hyderabad. It was mentioned that many girls had approached Ismat Chughtai there and asked her why she did not marry Manto.

I do not know whether the report was true or false. But when Ismat returned to Bombay, she told my wife that when a lady in Hyderabad had asked her whether Manto was a bachelor she had replied sharply, "Indeed, no." Hearing this the lady was sorely disappointed and became quiet. Whatever the truth, it is curious that in all of India, only the men and women of Hyderabad have been so concerned about Ismat's marriage and mine.

Though I did not reflect on it at that time, I wonder now. If Ismat and I had really become man and wife, then ...? It is a big speculative "if" of history that is a little like asking – if Cleopatra's nose had been longer by one eighteenth of an inch, what consequences would it have had on the history of the Nile valley? However, in the present case, Ismat is no Cleopatra, nor Manto, Mark Antony. It is certain though, that if Manto and Ismat had married, it would have had an atom bomb effect on the history of contemporary fiction. Short stories would have become a thing of the past and tales would have been reduced to riddles. The milk of diction would have dried into some rare powder or burnt to ashes. Maybe their signatures on the marriage contract would have been their last compositions. Well, who could say with certainty that there would have been a marriage contract at all! It seems more probable that both would have written stories on the marriage contract and put their signatures on the officiating Qazi's forehead as a proof of the marriage. During the marriage ceremony, a dialogue like the following might have ensued,

"Ismat, Qazi Sahab's forehead looks like a writing board, doesn't it?"

"I beg your pardon?"

"What's wrong with your ears?"

"Nothing. It's your feeble voice that refuses to come out of your throat."

"Don't be silly. Well, I said Qazi Sahab's forehead looks exactly like a writing board."

"A writing board is absolutely flat."

"Don't you think his forehead is flat?"

"Do you even know what Flat means?"

"No!"

"Flat is what your forehead is. Qazi Sahab's is ..."

"Very beautiful!"

"That it is."

"*You're* teasing *me*."

"It's *you* who's teasing me."

"On the contrary, you're teasing me."

"And I say, you're teasing me!"

"You must admit that you're teasing me."

"Come on, you're behaving like a husband already."

"Qazi Sahab, I shan't marry this woman. If your daughter's forehead is as flat as yours, then please marry me to her."

"Qazi Sahab, I won't marry this fellow. Please make me your wife, if you don't have four already. I like your forehead very much."

In the Preface of *Chotein*, Krishan Chander writes,

Ismat and Manto could not be more similar in their fictional art. Few Urdu writers can match them in their ability to leave a reader entirely clueless, to arouse his wonderment and suspense and then, in the end, suddenly change this wonderment and suspense into joy.

Had we thought of getting married, then instead of drowning others in wonder and agitation we ourselves would have been drowned in it. And when we would have come to our senses after the initial shock, then our wonderment and agitation would have changed into sorrow, not joy. Ismat and Manto, nikah, marriage – what a ludicrous idea!

Ismat writes,

How many Shaukats, Mahmoods, Abbases, Askaris, and Yunuses are dispersed in the small world of love; like cards they're shuffled and dealt out of the deck. Someone tell me who is the Jack among them. Shaukat's roving, hungry eyes, Mahmood's limbs that crawl like a serpent, Askari's ruthless hands, Yunus' black mole under his lower lip, Abbas's vacuous smile; then so many others endowed with broad chests, broad foreheads, luxuriant hair, shapely calves, strong hands. All these are jumbled together like a skein of tangled twine. Puzzled, I stare at the skein not knowing which end I should pull so that one strand comes out untangled, and with its help I could fly beyond the horizon, reaching out like a kite. [*Chhoti Aapa*]

Manto writes,

I know this much, that to love a woman and to buy land are the same to you. So, instead of falling in love, you had better buy one or two bighas of land and occupy them for your whole life. Only one woman in a lifetime? And the world is so full of them! Why does it (the world) hold so many attractions? Why didn't Allah stop Himself right after creating gandum? Listen to me, enjoy the life that you have been blessed with. You are the kind of shopper who would amass wealth his whole life to find a suitable woman but would always consider the wealth inadequate. I am the kind of customer who will conclude deals with many women in his life. You want to fall in love so that some second-rate writer has the opportunity to recount it as pulp fiction. This will be published by Narain Dutt Sahgal on yellow paper and sold as junk in the flea market. I want to eat up, like termites, all the pages of my life so that no vestige of it remains. You want life in love. I want love in life. [*Takleef*]

If Ismat had found the end of a string in that skein of tangled twine which would have made it possible for her to soar beyond the horizon like a kite, and if Manto had been able to turn himself into a termite swallowing up even half the pages of the book of his life, they would not have left such a deep mark on literature. Ismat would have remained in the high heavens, beating her wings, and Manto's admirers would have stuffed the rest of the book of his life into his belly and enclosed him in a glass case.

Krishan Chander also says this in his Preface to *Chotein*,

As soon as Ismat's name is mentioned, the male fiction writers begin to have fits. They are embarrassed. They cringe and are overwhelmed by a sense of shame. This preface is also the result of a desire to blot out this sense of shame.

Whatever I am writing about Ismat is not out of shame. In fact, I owe her a debt – a debt I intend to pay back with a small interest.

I do not remember which of her stories I read first. As I was writing these lines I delved deep into my memory but it didn't help. It seems I had read them all even before they were written down. That is why I didn't have any fits. However, when I saw her I was sorely disappointed.

The office of the weekly *Musawwir* was situated at Adelfi Chambers, flat number 17, Clair Road, Bombay. Shahid entered the office with his wife. It was August 1942. All the Congress leaders, including Mahatma Gandhi, had been arrested. The city was in chaos. The air reeked of politics. For some time we talked about the Independence Movement, then changed the topic and began talking about short stories.

About a month earlier, Ismat's short story "Lihaf" had been published in *Adab-e-Lateef*. I was working at All India Radio, Delhi then. After reading it, I had told Krishan Chander, "The story is very good, but the last line betrays a lack of craft." Had I been the editor in place of Ahmad Nadeem Qasimi, I would have certainly deleted it. So, when our talk veered towards short stories, I told Ismat,

I liked your story "Lihaf." Your special merit lies in using your words with utmost economy. But I'm surprised that you've added the rather pointless line, "Even if someone gives me a lakh of rupees, I won't tell anyone what I saw when the quilt was lifted by an inch."

"What's wrong with that sentence?" Ismat had retorted.

I was going to say something but just then I looked at her face. There I saw the kind of embarrassment that overwhelms common, homely girls when they hear something unspeakable. I felt greatly disappointed because I wanted to have a detailed discussion with her about "Lihaf." As she left, I told myself, "The wretch turned out to be a mere woman after all!"

I still remember, I had written a letter to my wife in Delhi the following day –

I met Ismat. You'll be surprised to know that as a woman she is exactly like you. I was bitterly disappointed. But you'll certainly like her. When I alluded to the last line of her story she was embarrassed.

After a long time, when I reflected seriously on my extreme reaction, I strongly felt, it is imperative in art to stay within one's natural limits in order to create something enduring. Where is the art practised by Dr Rasheed Jahan now? Some of it got lost along with her long tresses, and some of it must have taken shelter in the pockets of her pantaloons. In France, George Sand had taken off the cloak of femininity and embraced a life of affectation. She may have been instrumental in making Chopin, the Polish composer, create some gems of music despite his blood spitting, but her own creations died a stifling death in her own country.

I reflected, let the women fight head and shoulders with men on the battlefields, let them excavate mountains, let them become story writers like Ismat Chughtai, but their palms should be adorned with henna. Bangles should tinkle on their wrists. I regret having made that remark about Ismat Chughtai at that time.

If she had not been "a mere woman, after all!" then we would

---

George Sand: pen name of Amandine Aurore Lucie Duderant (née Dupin) (1804-76), French novelist and author of such works as *La Mare au Diable* (1846). She was a champion of women's rights.

not have found such fine and sensitive stories like "Bhulbhulaiyaan," "Til," "Lihaf" and "Gainda" in her collections. They portray different facets of a woman, neat and transparent, purged of all artifice. These are not flirtations or coquetry designed to conquer men. They have nothing to do with the coarse gestures of the body. The objective of these spiritual gestures is man's conscience which encompasses the unknown and unintelligible, yet tender nature of a woman.

His complexion changed. "Poor child. Perhaps he has lost his father."

"God forbid!" I clasped the child to my breasts.

"Tain!" The child fired the gun.

"Hey, firing at your Abba!" I snatched his gun. [*Bhulbhulaiyaan*]

People say, Ismat is a bad woman, a witch. Asses! She has distilled the essence of a woman's soul in these four lines. And these people judge her on the basis of their abominable morality. They should be made to stand before a cannon and shot through the head.

When "Dozakhi" was published in *Saqi*, my sister read it and told me, "Sa'adat, how shameless can this Ismat be. She didn't even spare her dead brother! How can she write such things about him?"

I said, "Iqbal, if you promise to write a sketch like this after my death, by god, I'm ready to die this very day."

Emperor Shah Jahan had the Taj Mahal built to commemorate his love for his beloved. Ismat wrote "Dozakhi" in memory of her beloved brother. Shah Jahan made others carry the stones, carve them and then build the grand mausoleum for the mortal remains of his beloved. Ismat gathered a multitude of sisterly emotions, erected a high scaffolding with them, and then gently put her brother's body on top of it. The Taj looks like a brazen marble exhibit of Shah Jahan's love – "Dozakhi," on the other hand, is an exceedingly subtle and exquisite gesture of Ismat's love. The title is not a screaming advertisement for the paradise that has been created in it through its content.

After reading the sketch, my wife had asked Ismat, "What is this nonsense you've written?"

"Don't chatter. Just get me some ice."

Ismat had the habit of chewing ice. She would hold a piece in her hand and crunch on it noisily. She wrote several of her short stories in this fashion. She would lie face down on the charpai supported by her elbow, with a notebook open before her on the pillow. She would hold a fountain pen in one hand and a chunk of ice in the other. The radio would be blaring, but Ismat's pen would race along the paper with a gentle rustle as her teeth crunched the ice into pieces.

Ismat writes in fits and starts. She may have had a lean period when for months she wrote nothing, but when she was taken over by the fits, hundreds of pages came out of her pen in a steady flow. And then she became supremely indifferent to eating, drinking or a bath. She just lay there, face down on the charpai, resting on her elbow and committing her ideas to ink, not caring about her spellings or the use of diacritical marks. She finished a long novel like *Terhi Lakeer*, as far as I know, in seven or eight sittings.

Krishan Chander writes about the pace of her narration,

The stories remind one of a horse race. That is, speed, movement, briskness (I think Krishan Chander meant, lightning speed) and acceleration. It is not only that the stories seem to be on the run but the sentences, images, metaphors, the sounds and the sensibilities of the characters and their feelings all seem to be moving along in a cluster with the force of a storm.

Ismat's pen and tongue both run fast. When she starts writing, her ideas race ahead and the words cannot catch up with them. When she speaks, her words seem to tumble over one another. If she enters the kitchen to show her culinary skill, everything will be in a mess. Being hasty by nature, she would conjure up the cooked roti in her mind even before she had finished kneading the dough. The potatoes would not yet be peeled although she would have already finished making the curry in her imagination. I feel sometimes she may just go into the kitchen and come out again after being satiated by her imagination. However, in contrast to this haste, I have seen her perfectly relaxed when stitching clothing for her baby daughter. She may make spelling mistakes while writing but her needle does not shake even a bit while stitching. Each stitch in its own place without any loose ends anywhere!

Ismat writes in *Uff, Ye Bachché* (Oh! These Children!),

To call it a house is a misnomer. It is a veritable mohalla. There may be epidemics or plagues, children elsewhere may die, but none here will kick the bucket! Every year, by the grace of god, the house turns into a hospital. People say children also die. . Well, they just may. How do I know?

And just a few days ago in Bombay, when her daughter Seema was down with whooping cough, Ismat stayed awake through the night. She was deeply upset and looked lost the whole time. One knows the real nature of love only when one becomes a mother.

Ismat is very stubborn. Obstinacy is her second nature, almost like a child – she will never accept any view or even a natural law without a show of resistance. First, she refused to get married, when she somehow agreed to that, she refused to become a mother. She will suffer and face troubles but will not give up her stubbornness. I think this is her strategy – to test life's truths through her conflicts with them. She has her own ways, which are always different.

One finds the same traits of obstinacy and refusal in her male and female protagonists. A couple may be deeply in love – but they will go on denying it, longing to kiss – one will prick the other's cheek with a needle, wanting to caress the other – one will instead strike the other so violently as to make him/her wince. This kind of violent or negative love that begins much like a sport, ends in tragedy in her stories.

If I live to see Ismat meeting the same fate, I will not be surprised.

I have known Ismat for five or six years. Given our fiery and volatile temperaments, it is only natural that we should have many fights. Yet, surprisingly, we do not fight, except for once when we had just a minor tiff.

Shahid and Ismat had invited us to their house at Malad. When we were through with the dinner, Shahid said, "Manto, you still make mistakes in your usage." I rejected the contention out of hand. The argument started and raged on through the night.

When the clock struck half past one, Shahid declared that he was exhausted. But Ismat kept on arguing in support of her husband. The clock struck two. I was not ready to give in. It was then that Ismat used the phrase "dast darazi." I cut her off immediately, pointing out that the right expression is "daraz dasti." The clock struck three. Ismat did not admit to her mistake. My wife had already gone off to sleep. To put an end to the hair-splitting, Shahid fetched the dictionary from the adjacent room. "Dast darazi" could not be found in the list of items under "D," even though "daraz dasti" and its meanings were listed there. Shahid said, "Ismat, you have to accept defeat." Now husband and wife began quibbling. The roosters began to crow. Ismat flung the dictionary to one side and said, "When I compile a dictionary, the right expression there will be dast darazi. What's this nonsense? Daraz dasti!"

Eventually the arguments came to an end. We did not fight after that, rather we do not allow things to come to such a pass. Whenever our conversation reaches a flashpoint, either Ismat changes track or I turn to safer turf.

I like Ismat and she likes me. But if someone asked suddenly, "What exactly is it that you like in each other?" then I am sure both of us would go blank in our minds for a few moments.

Ismat's appearance may not be irresistible, but she is certainly attractive. I still remember our first meeting. She wore a simple dress – a white sari with a small border, a tightfitting blouse with black stripes on a white background. She held a small purse in her hand and wore flat brown sandals. Her small but sharp and inquisitive eyes gleamed behind thick glasses. Her short curly hair had a crooked parting. The merest trace of a smile brought dimples to her cheeks.

I did not fall in love with her, instead, my wife fell for her. However, if Safiya dares to express her love for her, Ismat is sure to say, "The cheek you have! Men of your father's age have fallen for me!"

I know a fellow writer, an old man, who had a crush on her. He had expressed his love for her through his letters. Ismat encouraged him in the beginning, but eventually gave him such a drubbing that the poor man began to see stars. He may never write this "true" story.

To avoid the risk of a fight, Ismat and I talk very little. Whenever a story of mine is published, she praises it. After "Nilam" was published she was very enthusiastic in her appreciation. "Really, what's this nonsense about addressing a woman as Behn? You're right. For a woman, to be addressed as a sister by a man is an insult."

It made me wonder because she calls me "Manto Bhai" and I call her "Ismat Behn." God help us!

In the course of our five, six year friendship, I cannot recall any extraordinary event. Once, both of us were arrested for obscenity. This charge had been brought against me twice before. But for Ismat it was something new. So she was very upset. Luckily it turned out to be illegal because the Punjab Police had arrested us without a warrant. Ismat was happy. But how long can one destined for trouble remain secure? Eventually, she had to present herself before the Lahore court.

It is a long journey from Bombay to Lahore. But Shahid and my wife accompanied us. We had great fun. Safiya and Shahid teamed up and began to tease us about the obscenity charge. They kept harping on the hard life to come after the arrest and described scenes of prison life in frightening detail. Finally, Ismat flared up and said, "Let them send us to the gallows, we'll stand by the truth."

We had to go to Lahore twice in connection with this lawsuit. On both occasions, students from nearby colleges came in large numbers to see us in the court. Noticing this, Ismat said to me, "Manto Bhai, tell Choudhry Nazeer to collect a fee from those who want to see us. At least we can pay our fares with it."

As said, we went to Lahore twice and on both occasions we bought ten or twelve pairs of sandals and shoes from the Karnal Boot Shop. Someone had asked Ismat in Bombay, "Did you go to Lahore in connection with the lawsuit?"

"No. We went to buy shoes."

This was about three and a half years ago. It was Holi. Shahid and I were sitting on the balcony of their flat at Malad, drinking. Ismat began to incite my wife, "Look Safiya, these fellows are squandering so much money, why don't we join in?" They tried to pick up courage for a whole hour. Suddenly, there was a commotion. In walked Mukherjee, the Filmistan producer, with his portly wife and a few others in tow, and they literally assaulted us. In just a few seconds their [Safiya and Ismat's] faces had become unrecognizable.

Ismat's gaze shifted from the whisky to coloured powders and dyes, "Come on Safiya," she said, "let's spray them with colours."

All of us went out to the bazaar and Holi started in earnest on G B Road. Blue, yellow, green, black – colours were being sprayed all around. Ismat was in the vanguard. She smeared a large Bengali woman with tar. At that moment I was reminded of her brother Azim Baig Chughtai. Ismat's voice boomed like that of a military commander, "Let's invade the house of the fairy faced."

Everyone liked her idea. In those days, Naseem Bano was

working for our film *Chal Chal re Naujawan*. Her bungalow was also on G B Road. Within minutes we were all inside her house. Naseem, as usual, was in full make-up. She wore a fine georgette sari. Hearing our noise, she and her husband came out. Ismat, drenched in colours, looked like a goblin. My wife had so much colour on her face that another coating wouldn't have made any difference. Ismat told her, "Safiya, Naseem is really beautiful."

I looked at Naseem and said, "Beautiful, but cold."

Ismat's small eyes rolled behind her eyeglasses stained with colours. "Cold things," she said, "sit well with hot tempered people."

Saying this she marched past and in a second the fairy faced Naseem was looking like a circus clown.

Ismat and I often pondered over strange things. "Manto Bhai, I feel like writing about the romance between roosters and hens" or she would say, "I'll join the Defence Services and learn to fly planes."

A few months ago, Ismat and I were returning from Bombay Talkies by electric train. During the conversation, I said, "In Krishan Chander's writings I find two frequently occurring motifs – rape and the rainbow."

Ismat looked interested. "That's right," she agreed.

"I'm thinking of writing an essay on him with the title, Krishan Chander, The Rainbow, and Violent Rape. I wonder what the underlying relationship between rape and rainbow could be?"

Ismat pondered over this for a while. "From an aesthetic point of view, the different colours of the rainbow are very attractive and beautiful. But you're looking at it from another angle."

I said, "Oh yes, red is the colour of fire and blood. In mythological iconography this colour is associated with the planet

Mars, the executioner in the sky. Maybe this colour is the common link between rape and the rainbow."

"Maybe. But do write your essay."

"In Christian paintings the red colour is the symbol of divine love. No, no." An idea flashed through my mind. "This colour is associated with the intense desire for crucifixion. The Virgin Mary is also portrayed wearing red clothes which is a sign of chastity." As I said this, my eyes fell on Ismat's white dress.

She broke into a smile. "Manto Bhai, you must write this essay. It'll be very interesting, but get rid of the word Violent in the title."

"Krishan will object. He deplores the act because of its violence."

"His complaint is useless. How would he know – his heroines might have thoroughly enjoyed this violence!"

"God knows better."

Many articles have been written about Ismat's fictional art – less for, more against. If some of them are far fetched, others defy all comprehension.

Even Patras Sahab, who had been held in check until then by Lahore's middlemen, took off his gloves and wrote down an article on her. He is brilliant and witty, so the article is coherent and interesting. Talking about the label "woman," he writes,

It seems that a powerful and seasoned editor (this reference is to Salahuddin Sahab) also wants to keep men and women separate in the realm of literature. He says that as far as women writers are concerned Ismat Chughtai has the same stature among them that George Eliot had in English literature at one time. As though literature is like a tennis tournament where men and women play matches separately.

George Eliot's stature is assured, but merely dropping her name is hardly relevant in the context. What should be investigated is whether there is any essential distinction, not in the external circumstances but in something that is inherent, fundamental, natural, that makes literature produced by women different from that produced by men. If there is some such distinction, then what is it? Whatever the answers to these questions, they cannot justify the division of writers on the basis of their sex.

It is entirely probable that the answers to the above questions will not justify putting writers in separate compartments. But, before giving their reply, people will certainly want to know the sex of the person who asked the question – male or female? Once that is clear, the questioner's natural expectations will be evident to a great extent.

Patras Sahab's sentence, "As though literature is like a tennis tournament" is typical of his penchant for fiqre-bazi, or witticism. Literature is not a tennis tournament. It is not indecent for men and women to play matches separately. When Patras Sahab delivers a lecture in the classroom, the content of the lecture does not differ on the basis of the sex of the students. But when he has to think about their mental development, he will not ignore their gender.

Let a woman become George Eliot or Ismat Chughtai, that does not mean that one should ignore the impact of gender on the literature produced by her. Will Patras Sahab offer the same insight in the case of literature produced by transvestites? Is there any distinction – natural, internal, fundamental – that differentiates the literature produced by ordinary men and women from that produced by transvestites?

I consider it vulgar to label people as "man" or "woman." It is ridiculous to put up signboards on mosques and temples declaring that they are houses of worship. But from an architectural point of view, when we compare them with residential dwellings, we do not ignore their sacred character.

Ismat's identity as a woman has left its deep imprint on all branches of her writing, which guides us at every step in our appreciation of her art. Her merits and inadequacies as a writer, of which Patras Sahab has made an objective assessment in his article, cannot be viewed in isolation from her gender. And there is no way – critical, literary or chemical – to do that.

There is one Aziz Ahmad who, in a critique of Ismat Chughtai's *Terhi Lakeer* in *Naya Daur*, writes,

Ismat has just one way of experiencing the body and that is through fondling. All the men who figure in her novel, from Rasheed to Taylor, have been judged by their physical or mental sexual activity. Most of the time it is passive. This is her only means to know men, life and the universe: "Abbas' hands flashed like lightning under heaps of quilts and small vibrations spread among the group of girls." Rasul Fatima's tiny hands are an indication of a dark sexuality. And a somewhat less obscure version of it is the revulsion and love felt by the matron. She was surprised that the girls did not feel the probing eyes of the rakes crawling along their thighs. In this regard, Shamman's feminine sensibility (attention Patras Sahab) feels the touch of fingers on her thighs.

Aziz Ahmad Sahab is wrong in asserting that in Ismat the only way of perceiving is through fondling. First of all, it is wrong to call it fondling, because that is an act which goes on for some time. Ismat is extremely sensitive. A gentle caress is enough for her. In her, the other senses seem to be equally active. For instance, the auditory sense and the sense of smell. As far as I can see, the sense of hearing has a greater role in her writings –

Gharrrr, phat, shoon, phash. The car was groaning outside in the carport. He kept on turning the tuning knob on the radio, kharr, khaan, shauh, shash, gharum. Tears welled up in my eyes.
Tanan, Tanan. The cycle bell rang. I realized Edna had come. ["Puncture"]

Then, as she tried to doze off, loud bangs and peals of laughter came from the roof.

The bahu came down the stairs banging her feet, while her anklets tinkled.
Ghan ... ghan ... ghan – the bahu mumbled. ["Saas"]

The baby will croon – koon, koon – and then begin to slurp – chapar ... chapar ... ["Safar Mein"]

It was like a cat licking a plate – sapar ... sapar ... ["Lihaf"]

Tick tock, tick tock, his heart began to beat like a clock.
Mosquitoes breaking out into loud guffaws. ["Til"]

A mysterious, graveyard-like sob vibrated in the wind. ["Jhurri Mein Se"]

The tinkling of ghungroo and the sound of clapping crept into my body and began to dance in my veins. ["Pesha"]

The sense of smell is also active at places –

Just smell the stench of that rotten hookah. Oh god, thu ...
The odour of syrup was so strong that it was difficult to sleep. ["Da'in"]

The mustard oil would begin to give off a stench on the eighth day. ["Neera"]

Her body exuded a strange, sickening odour.
The warm scent of attar had made her all the more attractive.
Flaring my nostrils, I sniffed the air. There was only the warm scent of attar, sandalwood and henna, nothing else. ["Lihaf"]

He had drawn even the deep sighs and soft fragrance in colour. ["Til"]

A man's shirt, pervaded by the odour of cigarettes? ["Hero"]

She picked up tiny leaves of coriander and began to sniff them. ["Mera Bachcha"]

All her senses work at appropriate places and work properly. Aziz Sahab's view that sex is omnipresent in her writing like a disease may be correct in the way he looks at it. But let him not suggest prescriptions to remedy it. In any case, even writing itself is a disease. A perfectly healthy man whose temperature never fluctuates from 98.6 will forever remain barren, his life's slate absolutely cool and clean.

Aziz Ahmad Sahab further writes,

The greatest tragedy of her heroines is that no man has ever loved them deeply, nor they any man. Love bears the same relationship to the body as electricity bears to a wire. Just press the switch and love lights up the world like a thousand candles. It makes the fan move in the scorching heat of the noon. With the strength of a thousand demons it turns the wheels of the great machines of life. And sometimes it does up the hair or irons the clothes. As a writer, Ismat Chughtai has no conception of such love.

It is clear that Aziz Ahmad Sahab regrets this. But this love, of which he seems to have some knowledge, appears to have been created by him according to a five year plan and now he wants to impose it on everyone. To go along with him, let me imagine that Ismat's heroines were unaware of both the AC and DC currents of love. Even then, how does it follow that they neither loved anyone deeply, nor anyone loved them?

Ismat, of course, knows nothing of the kind of love which Aziz Ahmad Sahab has manufactured. It is precisely this ignorance which makes her writing possible. Today, if the wires of her life were connected to this love and if the switch were flicked, it is quite possible that another Aziz Ahmad would be born, but Ismat, who has produced "Til," "Gainda," "Bhulbhulaiyaan" and "Jaal" would certainly die.

There are as many opinions as there are critics —

Ismat's plays are weak. There are loose ends here and there. Her plots are not well-knit. The scenes do not dovetail into one another, but remain a jumble of patches. She feels like a stranger at parties. She is obsessed with sex, so much so that it seems to be a disease. Ismat's childhood was not conducive to her mental development. She excels in describing what goes on behind the curtain. Ismat is not interested in society but in people. Not in people but in individuals. Ismat has just one way of perceiving the body and it is through fondling. Her stories have no direction. Ismat's acute power of observation is extraordinary. Ismat is an obscene writer. She is a genial humourist and a satirist, and her style is characterized by these salient features. Ismat walks on the edge of a sword. And so on ...

A lot has been said about Ismat and continues to be said. Some will like her, some won't. But her creativity stands much above people's liking or disliking. Good, bad, naked, covered – whatever, it must endure. Literature has no geographical limits. It should be saved, as far as possible, from the stranglehold of cliché and repetitiveness.

A long time ago, a gentleman called Desh from Delhi did a strange thing. He published a book with a title running something like "Others' Stories, Told by Me," or "Many Will be Benefited by Reading This." The volume included one story each by Ismat, Mufti, Premchand, Khwaja Mohammad Shafi, Azim Baig Chughtai and myself. The "Introduction" consisted of a desultory critical write-up on Progressive literature. The book was dedicated to the editor's two tiny children. He sent Ismat and me each a copy of the book. Ismat did not take kindly to this crude and improper act on his part. In a rage she wrote to me,

Manto Bhai, did you see the book published by Desh? Give the fellow a good rattling, serve him a legal notice asking him to pay two hundred rupees for each composition or we will file a lawsuit. Something must be done, don't you agree? Anyone and everyone drags us down into the muck and we don't say anything. Give this fellow a good rubbing in, it will be fun. Just look at his cheek – he puts himself up as a great champion of forbidden literature, publishing our stories just to ensure the sale of the book. It's an insult that every other fellow tries to preach to us. Please write an article that includes everything I've written here. You may say, why don't *I* write it? My reply is – after you.

When I saw Ismat I told her, "First of all, there is Chaudhry Muhammad Husain of Lahore. If we ask him, he'll certainly file a lawsuit against Mr Desh."

Ismat smiled. "The idea is all right. But the truth is, we will also be rounded up with him."

I said, "So what? The court might not be an interesting place but the Karnal Boot Shop certainly is. We'll take him there and ..."

The dimples on Ismat's cheeks became deeper.

---

"Ismat Chughtai" has been translated from "Ismat Chughtai," in *Mukalmaat,* Ismat Special Number, Delhi, 1991.

# Ashok Kumar

Chaos reigned at Bombay Talkies when Najmul Hasan made off with Devika Rani. Filming had started, a few scenes had even been finished when Najmul Hasan pulled his heroine from the world of celluloid into the real world. But the person who was most distressed and worried at the Talkies was Himanshu Roy, Devika Rani's husband and the behind-the-scenes brains of the company.

In those days S Mukherjee, brother-in-law of Ashok Kumar and well-known filmmaker, was an assistant to Mr Savak Vacha, the sound engineer at the Talkies. Being a Bengali himself, he naturally felt for Himanshu Roy. Somehow or the other he wanted Devika Rani to come back. So, without consulting Himanshu Roy, he made some efforts on his own and, by using his exceptional tact, he persuaded Devika Rani to fly from the arms of her lover back into the arms of the Talkies, which offered her talent more room to grow.

And she did fly back. Then S Mukherjee used his tact once again and prevailed upon his distraught mentor, Roy, to take her back. Poor Najmul Hasan joined the list of lovers separated from their beloveds by political, religious and capitalist intrigues. He was cut off, with a pair of scissors as it were, from the film and dumped into the wastebasket. This created a problem – Who should now be cast opposite the already smitten Devika Rani as her lover on the screen?

Himanshu Roy, an exceedingly hardworking filmmaker, pretty much kept to himself and remained quietly absorbed in his work. He had wanted Bombay Talkies to resemble a dignified academic institution and had established it accordingly. This was the reason he had chosen Malad, a village quite far from the city of Bombay, as the site for his film company. He didn't want an outsider for the role because he didn't hold a good opinion of them. Also, Najmul Hasan was an outsider.

Here again S Mukherjee came to his mentor's assistance. His brother-in-law, Ashok Kumar, who had finished a Bachelor of Science degree and studied law for a year in Calcutta, was working as an apprentice in the laboratory at Bombay Talkies. He had a good face and could also sing and play a little. In the course of discussions, Mukherjee mentioned him for the role of the hero. Himanshu Roy had been taking chances all his life. "Well, why not?" he said. "Let's give it a try."

Darsching, the Talkies' German cameraman, gave Ashok a screen test. Himanshu Roy saw the results and approved him for the role. The German film director, Franz Osten, had a different opinion but who at the Talkies could dare to go against Himanshu Roy. So Ashok Kumar Ganguly, barely twenty two years old, was selected as Devika Rani's leading man.

A succession of films followed. Devika Rani and Ashok Kumar became an inseparable screen couple. Most of their films were great hits. Whenever Devika Rani, a veritable doll, appeared on screen in perfect harmony with the incredibly innocent looking Ashok Kumar, they elicited feelings of endearment from the audience. Harmless guile, coltish antics, incredibly hilarious romance – even people who normally liked bold, passionate love, both in life and on screen, couldn't help being attracted to this soft, supple and gentle love, and became particularly fond of the pair. Back then, Ashok Kumar was the ideal hero of school and college going girls and boys, sporting loose, long sleeved kurtas, roaming around singing – *Tu ban ki chidiya, main ban ka panchhi, ban-ban boloon re.*

I saw a few of Ashok Kumar's films. Clearly, Devika Rani was way ahead of him in terms of acting skills. As a leading man he looked like a chocolate doll. But little by little the fledgling began to grow feathers and shake off the effects of the intoxicated ideal of Bengali love.

When Ashok came out from behind the laboratory blinds on to the silver screen, his salary was fixed at seventy five rupees a month. This made him very happy. In those days the amount was more than enough for someone living alone and that too so far away from the city. When his salary was suddenly doubled to one hundred and fifty rupees it made him even happier. But when it shot up to two hundred and fifty rupees, he began to get nervous. Recalling the way he felt at that moment he said to me, "By god, I felt a strange sensation. Two hundred and fifty rupees! When I received the notes from the cashier, my hands began to shake. I had no idea where I'd put all that money. My house? Well, it was just a small place – a bed and two or three chairs, surrounded by a forest. What if a thief broke in during the night? What if he knew I had two hundred and fifty rupees? I didn't know what to do. I was in a fix. Theft and robbery gave me the shivers. After I returned home I made many plans. Finally I hid the notes in a rug under the bed. But all night long, I was assaulted by terrible dreams. The first thing I did the next morning was to take the money to the post office and deposit it there."

While Ashok was telling me this at his house, a Calcutta filmmaker arrived with a contract ready to be signed. But Ashok wouldn't sign it. The filmmaker was offering eighty thousand rupees, but Ashok was demanding one hundred thousand and no less. A far cry from two hundred and fifty!

Ashok's brother-in-law, S Mukherjee, also became quite a success at Bombay Talkies. Mukherjee was an intelligent man, a shrewd observer of everything happening around him. In time, he became a producer – not just any ordinary producer, a really big one. He made several silver and golden jubilee films under the banner of Bombay Talkies, and also laid the foundation of a particular school of screenwriting. The present writer considers him his teacher in this regard.

Ashok's popularity increased with each passing day. Since he didn't go out much and kept to himself, whenever people did catch a glimpse of him, riots followed. Traffic came to a halt, fans crowded around him, and eventually the police would be forced to use their batons to save him from his admirers' extreme adulation.

Ashok was insufferably churlish when it came to dealing with his fans' passionate devotion. He would become testy in no time at all, as if somebody had sworn at him. I told him many times, "Dadamuni, this behaviour of yours is absolutely shameful. Instead of feeling happy, you become angry. Don't you even understand that they love you?" But perhaps he didn't understand.

He was a complete stranger to love. At least he was before Partition. What changes may have occurred in him since, I can't say. Many beautiful girls came into his life, but he behaved very rudely with all of them. He is a typical jat by nature, strangely coarse in his table manners and living style.

Devika Rani tried charming him, but he spurned her artlessly. Another actress boldly called him home. She expressed her love for him in the gentlest and most tender words, but when Ashok broke her heart with his characteristic rudeness, she changed track and said, "Oh, I was just testing you. Why, you're like a brother to me."

He did like her figure though and also the way she always looked freshly bathed and glowing. So when she did a quick about face and called him her brother, he felt crushed.

Although Ashok was not interested in love, like any ordinary man he did look at women leeringly. He examined their alluring attributes closely and even talked to his friends about them. Sometimes, he also felt the desire to be physically close to a woman, but, as he said, "Manto yaar, I don't have the nerve."

In such matters he is really very timid, which has proved a boon for his married life. If one were to tell his wife Shobha about his lack of courage in this matter, she would certainly say, "Thank god Ganguly does not have this courage, and I pray to god that he never finds it."

I am puzzled why. Especially when hundreds of women openly tempted him to plunge into the blaze of love. Without exaggeration he must have received thousands of letters from women in his personal mail – letters filled with expressions of love. But from this huge pile, as far as I know, he probably never read more than a hundred himself. Such letters keep coming. D'Souza, his skinny, half-dead secretary, reads them with great relish, becoming skinnier and even more lifeless.

A few months before Partition, Ashok was in Calcutta in connection with the film *Chandrashekhar*. Returning to his place from the residence of Shahid Suhrawardy, then prime minister of Bengal, where he had watched some 16 mm film, his car was stopped by two beautiful Anglo-Indian girls who wanted a lift. Ashok indulged in this fun for a few moments, but lost his new cigarette case in the bargain. When the bolder of the two girls took a cigarette she also impudently took the cigarette case. Later, he thought of striking up a relationship with them many times. It was a simple thing, but he never dared.

An absolutely insipid film, full of swords and shields, maces and bang-bang, was being made in Kolhapur. Ashok had a little work left to do in it. They called him for it many times but he didn't go – he detested his role in that film. But he had contracted to do it, so eventually he had to go. He took me along. I was writing the film script of *Ath Din* for Filmistan at that time. Since Ashok was going to produce and direct that film he said, "Come along yaar, we'll work there in peace."

What peace? People soon found out that Ashok Kumar had come to Kolhapur. Fans started to gather around the hotel where we were staying. The owner of the hotel was a clever man and he'd find various ways to disperse them. But still some of the persistent ones hung around, moving from place to place in order to catch a glimpse of their beloved actor. As I mentioned earlier, Ashok treated his fans discourteously. I don't know how they felt about his rebuffs, but I certainly didn't like his behaviour at all.

Both of us went for a stroll one evening. Ashok was in disguise – big, dark sunglasses, a stick in one hand, and the other hand grabbing on to my shoulder to use me as a shield, if the situation so called. In this way, we reached a store. Ashok wanted to buy something to protect himself against the harmful effects of the dust in the Kolhapur studios. When he asked for it, the proprietor gave him a fleeting look before taking a few steps towards the cabinet. Then abruptly, he turned around and exploded like a delayed-action bomb, "Who the hell are you?"

"Who am I?" Ashok replied. "I am who I am."

The proprietor looked closely at the face hidden behind the huge sunglasses. "My – you're Ashok Kumar!"

"Not a chance. He must be somebody else," he retorted in an exceedingly gruff manner. And then saying, "Let's go, Manto," he put his hand on my shoulder and the two of us walked out without buying the medicine.

As we were turning the corner of the hotel, three Marathi girls appeared in front of us – very clean looking, fair, wearing kumkum on their foreheads, flower strings in their hair, and light, delicate sandals on their feet. One of them, holding oranges in her hands, shuddered with excitement the instant she saw Ashok. "Ashok!" she cried to her friends in a muffled voice as the oranges, all of them, dropped from her hands and scattered on the road. Ashok let go of my shoulder and sprinted off.

After S Mukherjee and his entire team walked out of Bombay Talkies and set up their own studio, Filmistan, I caught a glimpse of Ashok now and then. My first real meeting with him, however, had to wait until I started working there myself.

As things go with film personalities, they seem to be one thing on the screen and something entirely different in real life. So was the case with Ashok. The real Ashok was dark, had plump, rough hands and a strong, well-toned body. He had a rustic way of talking and rather abrupt, unnatural manners. When we were introduced, I said, "I am very pleased to meet you."

He parroted out a reply in stock phrases.

Once, when someone came to visit Filmistan he said to Ashok in an exceedingly polite manner, "I feel I've also had the honour of meeting you before." Ashok replied in a dubious tone, "Ji ... ji mujhé kabhi muqabla nahin huva," ("Well, I don't think I've encountered you before") articulating the "qaaf of muqabla" from his throat. He immediately realized that he had used the word incorrectly, but he glossed over it.

Ashok is very fond of Urdu. He tried to learn it but couldn't get past the primer. He still has a smattering of it. He can even write a sentence or two in Urdu. At the time of Partition, when I parted from him after leaving Bombay Talkies, he wrote a letter to me in Urdu asking me to come back. But regretfully, I couldn't respond to him for a number of reasons.

Like other women, my wife was a great admirer of Ashok Kumar. One day, I brought him home. The moment we entered I called out loudly, "Safiya, come! Ashok Kumar is here."

Safiya was busy inside making rotis. After my repeated calls she finally came out. I introduced her to Ashok, "She is my wife, Dadamuni. Shake hands with her."

Safiya and Ashok were both embarrassed. I grabbed Ashok's hand. "Come on, Dadamuni, shake hands. Why be so shy?"

Eventually he had to shake hands.

As it happened keema-filled rotis were being prepared that day. Although Ashok had already had his meal, when he sat down to eat, he wolfed down three.

It is absolutely mindboggling that afterwards, whenever this dish was made in our house in Bombay, Ashok would invariably show up. Neither I nor Ashok can explain it. Maybe it has something to do with the old saying – On each grain is inscribed the name of its consumer.

I have just now called Ashok, "Dadamuni." This means "elder brother" in Bengali. After I became friendlier and more informal with him he forced me to call him that. "Whatever for?" I asked him. "You're not older to me. In fact, I'm older. Calculate it if you like."

On calculation, it turned out that he was two months and a few days older. So instead of Ashok or Mister Ganguly I had to call him Dadamuni. I liked it because it had a touch of the sweetness and roundness of rasgulla, the favourite sweetmeat of Bengalis.

In the beginning, he addressed me as Mr Manto. Later, after I agreed to call him Dadamuni, he started calling me simply Manto, which I didn't like at all.

On screen he seemed like a chocolate hero to me, but in real life he was quite athletic. His punch was so hard that it could easily crack a wooden door. He practised boxing every day at home and liked hunting. He could do the most strenuous jobs. What I regretted was his lack of aesthetic sense. His house could have had the loveliest furnishings if he had wanted them. But he never cared about such things. And when he did pay attention to them, the result was never pleasing. He would pick up a brush and paint all the furniture dark blue, or break the back of the sofa and turn it into some odd shaped divan.

His house by the seashore is in a particularly filthy area. Salt water splashes against the outer windows corroding their iron grillwork. A gloomy smell drifts from the layers of rust. But Ashok is entirely oblivious to it. His refrigerator would be rotting in the corridor with his big Alsatian dozing right beside it. In a room near by, his children would raise a rumpus, while Ashok Kumar, perched on his toilet seat, would be busy making all kinds of calculations on the bathroom wall about the horse likely to win at the races, or he would be holding a paper with dialogues, thinking up the best way to deliver them. Ashok is particularly fond of palmistry and astrology. He learned the latter from his father and has also studied numerous books on the subject. In his free time, he reads horoscopes of his friends. After looking over my horoscope one day, he asked, "Are you married?"

"Don't you know?" I said.

After a brief silence he said, "I know. But look Manto ... Tell me one thing ... You haven't had a child yet?"

"What's the matter?" I asked. "Come on, tell me."

He told me hesitatingly, "It's nothing ... just that people with your astral signs always have a son as their first child but that child doesn't live."

Ashok didn't know that my son had died after living only a year.

He later told me that his own first child was a stillborn son. "The position of your stars and mine is nearly the same," he said. "It isn't possible for someone with that alignment of stars to not have a son for his first born, or for that son not to die."

Ashok trusts astrology completely, provided the calculations are done correctly. He often says, "Just as the addition or subtraction of even a single pie in accounting can hopelessly mess up the total, so can a slight miscalculation about the position of the stars lead us astray. That's as good a reason to not trust any conclusion one hundred percent. It's entirely possible that one may have made a mistake."

For the horse races too, he generally sought help from astrology. For hours he would sit in the bathroom making calculations, but he would never place a bet higher than a hundred rupees on any race. And strange as it may sound, he has always won. The hundred might become a hundred and ten or remain just a hundred, but it never shrank, not even by a paisa. He didn't bet to win, but simply to entertain himself. His beautiful wife Shobha, mother of three, always accompanied him to the races. After entering the members' enclosure he would sit alone in a corner. A few moments before the start of a race, he would give his wife the money to buy tickets for particular numbers. At the end of a race it was again his wife who went to the window to cash in the winning tickets.

Shobha is a housewife. She has some education but Ashok jokingly calls her "illiterate." Ashok has a very successful married life. Despite their wealth, Shobha does all the housework herself, wearing a cotton sari, like a typical Bengali woman, with a huge bunch of keys tied to one of its ends. I've always found her busy working. Whenever there is a round of whisky in the evening, she is the one who prepares delicacies like gazak to go with it, or different snacks such as namakparas, roasted dal, or fried potatoes.

Since I drank too much she often admonished Ashok, "Look Ganguly, don't give Mr Manto any more to drink, otherwise Mrs Manto will complain to me again."

Mrs Manto and Mrs Ganguly were friends and we put them to good use. Good quality cigarettes had become scarce due to war. Whenever some arrived from abroad they were promptly whisked away to the black market. We routinely bought them from the black market. But now and then, when we could get them, or anything at all for that matter, at the regular price, we found a strange pleasure in it.

Sometimes, Mrs Ganguly took my wife shopping. More or less every major shop owner knew that Mrs Ganguly was Ashok Kumar's wife. So all she had to do was ask for something and the item rolled out from the darkest regions of the black market. Then again, Bombay men tended to be quite courteous and kindhearted to women. Whether you had to withdraw money from the bank, post a registered letter, or buy a ticket for the train or cinema – if a man went he'd have to waste hours, but for a woman it took no more than a minute.

Ashok hardly ever took advantage of his fame and popularity, but sometimes others used their acquaintance with him for their own benefit without his knowledge. Raja Mehdi Ali Khan once did just that, in a rather interesting manner. Raja was working in Filmistan after I had left. He was writing a story for Wali Sahab. One day Ashok's secretary phoned me to say that Raja Mehdi Ali Khan was ill. I visited him and found him in a terrible shape. His throat was so inflamed and swollen that he could hardly talk and felt very weak to get up even with the help of others. And what was he doing about it – gargling with lukewarm salt water and applying Oriental Balm.

I suspected diphtheria. Without further thought I put him into a car and phoned Ashok. He gave me the name of a doctor he knew and told me to take him there. And so I did. The diagnosis revealed that Raja was indeed suffering from that often fatal disease. Following the doctor's advice, I immediately had him admitted to the hospital for contagious diseases, where he was duly inoculated. The next day I phoned Ashok and informed him about the nature of Raja's illness. When he did not express any concern, I became furious, "What kind of a person are you? A man is suffering from such a dreadful disease – the poor fellow has no one here to look after him and you show no concern at all!"

In reply he only said, "We'll go see him this evening."

I put the phone down and went to the hospital. Raja was feeling a little better that day. I had with me the vaccines the doctor had asked for. I gave them to Raja, comforted him, and went off to my work.

In the evening, Ashok got hold of me in Wali's office. I was still angry with him but he persuaded me to forgive him. We got in his car and drove to the hospital. Ashok told Raja that he had been terribly busy so he couldn't come earlier, and asked to be forgiven. We talked about this and that for a while and then left. Ashok dropped me off at my place and continued on to his home.

The next day when I visited Raja, what did I see? Raja was sitting there with the pomp and majesty of a real raja – crisp, clean sheets, his pillowcase freshly laundered and sparkling, a pack of cigarettes in his hand, a flowerpot on the window sill, one leg stretched over the other, wearing spotless hospital clothes, ensconced in luxury and reading a newspaper. I was absolutely amazed. I asked, "Well, Raja, how did this come about?"

He smiled. His huge mop of a moustache shook. "This is nothing. You just wait and see."

"What?" I asked.

"Comforts, pleasures. If I stayed here for a few more days, you'd see the adjoining room turn into a veritable harem. May Ashok live long, my Ashok Kumar! Tell me, why didn't he come along?"

After a short while he told me that all this was thanks to Ashok. When the hospital staff found out that Ashok had come to enquire after him, everyone, young and old, barged in asking the same questions, What – had Ashok really come to enquire after him? What was his relationship with Ashok? Would Ashok come again? When and at what time?

Raja told them that Ashok was a very close friend. Always ready to give his life for him, if it came to that. He even wanted to stay at the hospital with him but the doctors wouldn't allow it. If it weren't for his contractual obligations he would come every morning and evening. He will certainly come this evening. And the result of all this? Every imaginable comfort piled on Raja in what was basically a free room in a charity hospital.

Visiting hours over, I was about to leave when a throng of female medical students walked in. Raja smiled and then said, "Khwaja, I think the adjoining room's going to be too small for my seraglio after all."

Although he is quite a good actor, Ashok can only perform well when he's working with people he knows and can be informal with. That's the reason he hasn't discharged himself satisfactorily in films that weren't produced by his normal team. Among his own people, he's able to work openly and freely. He can give advice to technicians and listen to what they have to say. He can also consult others about his acting and solicit their opinions about the various ways he has rehearsed a scene. If suddenly, he is taken out of this familiar territory, he feels quite lost.

Since he is educated and has been associated with a reputable film company like Bombay Talkies for many years, he has acquired competence in nearly all segments of the industry. He knows the finer points of camera work, understands the intricate problems of the laboratory, has practical experience in editing, and has also studied the complexities of directing. So when Rai Bahadur Chunni Lal of Filmistan invited him to produce a film, he accepted the offer immediately.

At about this time, Filmistan's propaganda movie, *Shikari*, had just been completed. I was enjoying some leisure and was relaxing following a very hectic work schedule that had lasted several months. One day, Savak Vacha showed up. After making small talk for a while he suddenly said, "Sa'adat, write me a story for Ganguly."

I didn't understand what Savak meant. I was an employee of Filmistan and my job was to write stories. Writing one for Ganguly didn't require a special request from Savak. Anybody responsible enough at the studio could have asked me to do it and I would have complied. I later learned that since Ashok was going to produce the film himself, he wanted me to write a story – an unusual story. The reason he didn't ask for it personally was that he already had quite a few stories which others had written.

Anyway, an appointment was made with Savak and all of us gathered at his clean, tidy flat. Ashok himself had no idea what kind of story he wanted. "Well, Manto," he said, "write something that's truly entertaining. And don't forget that this will be my first production."

Together we racked our brains for hours but couldn't come up with a suitable idea for a story. The Aga Khan's diamond jubilee was underway and a colossal tent had been set up in Brabourne Stadium next door to Savak's flat. I tried to get some inspiration from that. Savak also had a fine piece of sculpture in his sitting room. I explored that for possibilities too. I even thought about my earlier writings. Nothing helped. It seemed I'd run into a dead end.

To wash away the accumulated frustration of a completely

fruitless day, we gathered on the terrace for a round of brandy in the evening. I must say, when it comes to choosing liquor, Savak Vacha's taste is the best. The brandy had both flavour and body. The minute it went down our throats we could feel a blossoming sense of pleasure. The Churchgate station was directly across from us. The market below was bustling, at its farthest end the sea lay face down, perfectly calm as if resting. Big, expensive cars glided by smoothly on the shimmering surface of the road. A steamroller came into view, huffing and puffing. A thought drifted into my mind – suppose a beautiful girl dropped a letter from the terrace with the intention of marrying whoever picked it up, what then? It was possible that the letter might fall on a Packard. Then again, it was equally possible that it might blow over to the man driving the steamroller. The possibilities were endless, and interesting too.

I mentioned my thought to Savak and Ashok. They liked it. To enjoy it even more we poured another round of brandy and indulged in unrestrained fantasies. By the time the party broke up, we had decided to build the story around this idea.

The story was prepared but it metamorphosed into something entirely different. There was neither a letter written by a beautiful girl, nor a steamroller. At first we had wanted it to be a tragedy, but Ashok favoured a comedy, and a fast-paced comedy at that, so we exercised the balance of our mental resources towards that end. The story was finalized. Ashok liked it, and filming got underway. Every single frame was prepared according to Ashok's direction. Very few people know that Ashok Kumar directed *Ath Din* in its entirety. Although D N Pai's name appears in the film's credits as its director, not even an inch was actually directed by him. The "director" didn't have much importance in the Bombay Talkies' organization. Everybody worked as a team. At a film's release, the name of one of the team members was listed as its director. The same procedure was followed at Filmistan. Since D N Pai was the film editor and very skilled at his job, it was collectively decided to put his name in the credits.

Ashok is as good a director as he is a character artist. I found that out during the shooting of *Ath Din*. No matter how ordinary the scene, he worked very hard on it. A day before the shooting he would ask me for the revised scene and then sit in his bathroom for hours contemplating its minutiae. It may sound odd but the bathroom was the only place where Ashok could concentrate fully on matters requiring his attention.

This film featured four new actors – Raja Mehdi Ali Khan, Upendranath Ashk, Mohsin Abdullah, former husband of the "mysterious" Neena, and the present writer. S Mukherjee was to be given a role but when the time came, he backed out, using my refusal to work in his film *Chal Chal re Naujawan*, (because of camera fright) as a convenient excuse. The fact is he was himself scared of the camera.

Mukherjee was to be cast in the role of a shell-shocked soldier. The uniform and the rest of the paraphernalia were ready. Ashok was baffled when he backed out. He had no idea who else to pick for the role. Shooting had to be suspended for several days. When Rai Bahadur Chunni Lal started to get testy, Ashok came to me. I was rewriting some of the scenes. He took the papers from my table, put them aside and said, "Let's go, Manto."

I went out with him. I thought he was taking me to listen to the tune of a new song. Instead he brought me straight to the set and said, "Here, you play the role of the madman."

I knew that Mukherjee had turned down the role and that Ashok was having a difficult time finding someone to do it. What I didn't even suspect was that he'd ask me to do it. So I said, "You haven't gone mad, have you?"

He became serious and said, "No Manto, you'll have to."

Raja Mehdi Ali Khan and Upendranath Ashk chimed in. Raja said, "You've cast me as Ashok's brother-in-law even though I'm a nice person and I was most unwilling to play that part because I respect him a lot. So I'm sure if you play a madman the sky won't cave in, will it?"

We started to joke around. But what started as a joke ended with Sa'adat Hasan Manto being cast as the mad Flight Lieutenant Kripa Ram. God alone knows what I had to go through in front of that camera.

The film was finished. When it was released it turned out to be quite a success – critics called it the best comedy. Ashok and I were especially happy. We decided that our next film would be an entirely new kind, but this was not to be.

Shortly after the filming of *Ath Din* began, Savak left for London seeking medical treatment for his ailing mother. By the time he returned, the film industry had gone through a revolution. Many companies had gone bankrupt. Bombay Talkies was in a very bad shape. After the mourning period for the deceased Himanshu Roy, Devika Rani left the industry to tie the knot with the artist son of an exiled Russian nobleman. After that many foreigners took over the running of Bombay Talkies but couldn't improve its condition. Eventually Savak Vacha returned from London and with Ashok's help, he boldly took the reins into his own hands.

Ashok had to leave Filmistan. In the meantime, I too received an offer of one thousand rupees a month from the Lahore based Mr Moti B Gidwani. I would have accepted it but I was waiting for Savak. When he and Ashok got together at Bombay Talkies, I joined them. It was the period when the British were drawing up rough sketches for the partition of India, in other words, when they were standing on the sidelines gleefully watching the conflagration they had themselves started.

By the time I stepped into Bombay Talkies, Hindu-Muslim riots had already begun. In these riots, people's heads were being knocked off and big fires being set, the way wickets are knocked down and boundaries hit in cricket.

After taking over, Savak Vacha took stock of the poor condition of Bombay Talkies, and had to face many difficulties. He removed an undesirable person, who happened to be a Hindu, which eventually created many problems. But when his position was filled, I realized that Muslims held the key positions. I was there, as were Shahid Latif, Ismat Chughtai, Kamal Amrohi, Hasrat Lukhnawi, Nazir Ajmeri, Nazim Panipati and the music director Ghulam Haider. When all of them came together, the Hindu employees felt hatred for Savak Vacha and Ashok. When I mentioned this to Ashok, he burst out laughing, "I will tell Vacha and he will give them a dressing down."

The dressing down produced exactly the opposite result. Vacha started getting anonymous threatening letters – if he didn't throw out the Muslims, his studio would be torched. Vacha would read those letters and fly into a rage. "Those bastards, they're telling me I'm at fault. So what if I am? Why do they care? They'll torch the studio? Let them. I'll throw them smack in the middle of the fire."

Ashok's mind and heart are blissfully free of communal prejudice. He could never think along the lines of those people who sent such threats. He always told me, "Manto, this is just madness. It will pass."

But, instead, the madness continued to grow. I was beginning to feel guilty. Ashok and Vacha were my friends – they took my advice, trusted me. But I was no longer sure of my own feelings. What if something adverse did happen to the Talkies, how would I face Ashok, how would I face Vacha?

The riots were at their peak. One day, on our way home from the Talkies we stopped for quite a while at Ashok's place. In the evening he offered to drive me home. To take a shortcut, he drove through a belligerent Muslim neighbourhood. A wedding procession was coming from up ahead. The minute I heard the band playing, I lost my wits. I clutched at Ashok's hand and shouted, "Dadamuni, where have you brought us?" Ashok understood my anxiety, smiled and said, "Don't worry."

How could I not worry? The car was passing through a fanatically Muslim neighbourhood where no Hindu dared set foot. To top it all, just about everyone recognized Ashok and knew that he was a Hindu, a famous Hindu whose murder would put quite a feather in their caps. I didn't know any prayers in Arabic, nor even a single verse from the Quran suitable for the situation. I was cursing myself and praying incoherently in my own words with my heart pounding away, "Dear god, don't let me down. Please don't let any Muslim kill Ashok or I'll have to keep my face bowed out of shame and guilt for the rest of my life." This wasn't the face of my community, but my own, and yet I didn't want it to be lowered before another community because of such a heinous act.

When the car came near the wedding procession, people started to shout, "Ashok Kumar, Ashok Kumar." I froze. But Ashok kept his hands on the steering wheel and remained quiet. I was about to shake off the numbing sense of fear and tell the mob to be sensible – that I was a Muslim and that he was escorting me back to my place – when two young men stepped forward and said calmly, "Ashok Bhai, you won't find a way through up ahead. Here, drive through this side street."

Ashok Bhai? Ashok was their brother. Then who was I?

I took a quick look at my clothes – khadi. God knows who they thought I was. Then again, it was quite likely that in Ashok's presence they hadn't noticed me at all.

When our car pulled out of that neighbourhood ... did I breathe a sigh of relief! Just as I was thanking god, Ashok laughed and said, "You panicked for no reason at all. These people don't bother artists."

A few days later at the Talkies, when I literally cut up Nazir Ajmeri's story – which was filmed as *Majbur* – and tried to make some changes in it, Nazir Ajmeri admonished both Ashok and Vacha, "Don't involve Manto in such discussions. He's a storywriter himself, he can't remain impartial."

I thought about that quite a lot but couldn't understand it at all. In the end I told myself, "Manto Bhai, you won't find a way through up ahead. Stop the car and drive through a side street." Quietly I took a side street and came to Pakistan where my short story "Thanda Gosht" was put on trial.

---

"Ashok Kumar" has been translated from "Ashok Kumar," in *Meena Bazaar,* Maktaba-e Shahraah, Delhi, 1953.

# Sa'adat Hasan Manto

By now a lot has been written and spoken about Manto. More against and less for. It would be difficult for a discerning person to arrive at a definitive view on the basis of these writings. As I sit down to write this essay, I find it difficult to convey my own impressions about Manto. In a sense it should be easy for me because I have been very close to him. To speak the truth, I am his persona.

I have no objection to whatever has been written so far about this man. But I do feel that the views expressed in such writings are far from the actual truth. Some call him a devil, others characterize him as a bald angel. Hold on for a minute, let me see if he is overhearing us. No, it's all right. Now I remember, this is his hour of booze. He is accustomed to taking strong drinks after six in the evening.

We were born together and I hope, will die together. However, it is quite possible that Sa'adat Hasan will die and Manto will continue to live. This thought worries me often. That is why I have done everything I can to keep him in good humour. If he remains alive and I die, it will be like having the eggshell without the white and the yolk inside it.

Without further ado let me tell you right away that, up till now, I haven't seen another fellow as devious as Manto. He is a host in himself. He is quite familiar with the idea of the triangle but I know that he has not yet become a trinity. These hints are of a kind that can only be understood by discerning readers.

I've known him from birth. We were born together at the same hour on 11 May, 1912. But he always tried to turn himself into a tortoise whose head and shoulders could not be traced once he drew them inside his body. But I am, after all, his alter ego and have studied each of his gestures.

Now let me tell you how this donkey of a fellow became a storywriter. Critics wax eloquent in their long essays about him in order to exhibit their own erudition and allude to Schopenhauer, Freud, Hegel, Nietzsche, Marx and so on. But the reality eludes them by a long chalk.

Manto's fictional art is the result of contradictory elements in his makeup. His father, may god forgive him, was authoritarian, while his mother was tender hearted. You can very well imagine what form this grain of wheat took, grinded as it was between these two contradictory forces.

Next I come to his school life. He was an intelligent boy but very mischievous. At that time he would have been 3.5 feet tall at the most. He was the last child of his parents and was loved by them. However, he did not get an opportunity to meet his three elder brothers who were all much older and were away studying in Europe. They were his stepbrothers. How he wished they would come home and treat him as their younger brother! This wish of his was fulfilled only after the literary world had already recognized him as a great storywriter.

Let us turn to his storytelling art. He is a fraud of the first order. The first story he wrote was "Tamaasha," based on the bloody incident at the Jallianwala Bagh. He did not publish this story under his real name, and escaped the long arm of the police. Then his restive temperament developed an urge to acquire higher education. It will be interesting to mention here that he failed the matriculation exam twice. He could only pass on his third attempt and that too, in the third division. And you may be surprised to know that he failed in the Urdu paper!

Now people say that he is a great writer in Urdu. When I hear this I laugh because even now he doesn't know Urdu well enough. He hunts for words in the way a flycatcher hunts for butterflies with his net. He cannot lay his hands on them. That's the reason there is a dearth of beautiful words in his writings. He is a club wielder, and he happily bears the blows that fall on his shoulders.

Manto is adept at club fighting. His skill at it, to use the common idiom, is not like the jat method of club fighting. On the contrary, he is adept in the strategic moves of the fight. He is one of those who do not tread the beaten path but prefer to walk a tightrope. People expect him to fall any moment, but so far, the shameless fellow has not fallen even once. Maybe he will fall on his face one day and not be able to rise again. But I know that even at the hour of death he will tell people that he fell to experience the pleasure of it!

I have already stated that Manto is a fraud of the first order. A further proof of this fact is that he says that he doesn't write the stories, the stories write him. This is also a fraud. As a matter of fact, I know that when he wants to write a story he feels exactly the way a hen feels when it has to lay an egg. But he doesn't lay his eggs in privacy. He lays them in full view of the public. With his friends assembled and his three daughters raising a racket, he sits, doubled up on his special chair, laying his eggs. In no time these eggs turn into chicks in the form of stories.

His wife does not like his being a writer. She asks him to give up storywriting and open a shop somewhere. But the shop that is always open in the world of Manto's imagination contains more goods than any grocer's shop ever could. That's why he often wonders if he ever does open a store, will he himself turn into cold storage with all his ideas and thoughts frozen inside.

As I am writing this I am afraid, lest Manto should get angry. One can put up with his strange ways, but not when he is angry. Then he becomes a devil. Of course, only for a few minutes. But for those few minutes, only god can help you.

As to the art of his storywriting, he brags a lot. But I know, since I am his alter ego, that such pretensions are also a fraud. Once he wrote somewhere that his pockets are always filled with sheaves of stories. But the truth is just the opposite. When he wants to write a story he thinks about it at night, but nothing comes of it. He gets up at five in the morning and tries to find an idea for a story in the newspapers, but fails to do so. Then he goes into the bathroom and tries to cool off his frenzied head so that he can think. But all this is in vain. Irritated, he picks up a fight with his wife about nothing. Failing there as well, he goes out to buy a paan. But the paan just sits on his table and the subject matter for a story still eludes him. Finally, in desperation, he picks up his pen or pencil, writes 786 and begins the story by scribbling whatever comes to his mind on the first line. "Babu Gopinath," "Toba Tek Singh," "Hatak," "Mummy," and "Mozel"

---

786: Numerical value of the letters that form the phrase "In the name of Allah, the most merciful, ever benevolent," spoken by Muslims before commencing an act.

have all been written in this fraudulent manner.

It is strange that people regard him as irreligious and obscene. I also feel that he comes within the purview of such terms. This is because he often deals with themes that are indecent and uses words in his writings that might be considered objectionable. However, I know that whenever he has written anything he has begun by putting 786 on the top of the first page, which stands for Bismillah. And this fellow, who often appears to be a non-believer, becomes a momin, a believer, on paper. This is the thin skinned Manto. You can break him with the help of your fingers just as you break soft shelled nuts. Otherwise he is a man who can withstand an iron hammer and still not break.

I now turn to Manto's personality, which can be described in a couple of words – a thief, liar, cheat and a crowd pleaser. He has often taken advantage of his wife's laxity to make short work of hundreds of rupees. He would give her eight hundred rupees at the beginning of the month and keep a stealthy eye on the place she put it. The very next day, he would filch a hundred rupees from there. When the poor woman discovered the loss, she would begin chiding and chastising the servants.

Manto is generally regarded as a straight talker. But I don't quite agree with this view. He is false through and through. In the beginning he could get away with his false claims around the house because there was a special Manto flavour in them. Later, his wife discovered that whatever she was told about "some special matter," was false. Manto uses lies sparingly, but it is a shame that now the members of his family think that whatever he says is a lie. It is like the mole that a woman paints on her cheek with kohl.

Manto is an ignoramus. He never studied Marx, nor did he set eyes on any work by Freud. He knows Hegel and Havelock only by name. However, it is amusing that people, I mean critics, say that he has been influenced by all these thinkers. As far as I know, Manto is never influenced by anyone's ideas. He considers interpreters of the world stupid. One cannot explain the world to others ... one has to understand it for oneself.

His efforts to make himself understood have turned him into an entity that is beyond comprehension. At times he talks such nonsense that it makes me laugh.

I can tell you with full conviction that this Manto who has been taken to court several times on charges of obscenity, is a lover of purity. I must also tell you that he is so fastidious about purity that he keeps on tidying himself up.

---

"Sa'adat Hasan Manto" has been translated from "Sa'adat Hasan Manto," in *Sarkandon ke Peeché,* Hali Publication House, Delhi.

# Pandit Manto's First Letter to Pandit Nehru

Panditji, assalam alaikum!

This is the first letter that I am sending you. By the grace of god, you are considered very handsome by the Americans. Well, my features are not exactly bad either. If I go to America, perhaps I will be accorded the same status. But you are the prime minister of India, and I am the famed storywriter of Pakistan. Quite a deep gulf separates us. However, what is common between us is, that we are both Kashmiris. You are a Nehru, I am a Manto. To be a Kashmiri is to be handsome, and to be handsome ... I don't know.

I have a long cherished desire to meet you. (We might yet meet during our lifetime.) The older people from my side often meet those from yours. But so far I have not had any opportunity to meet you. What a great pity that I have not even seen you. Of course, I have once heard you on the radio.

As I said, I have long harboured this desire to meet you. Being Kashmiris, we have a common bond. But now I wonder if there is any need for it. One Kashmiri does run into another in bylanes, or at crossroads.

You settled on the bank of a nahr, a river, and came to be known as Nehru. I ponder how I became a Manto. You may have visited Kashmir a million times. I could just go up to Banihal. My Kashmiri friends who know the Kashmiri language tell me that Manto means "Munt," that is, a measuring stone weighing one and a half seer! I am sure you know Kashmiri. If you take the trouble to write a reply to this letter, do write to me about the origin of the word "Manto."

If I am just one and a half seer, then there cannot be any comparison between us. You are the whole stream while I am just one and a half seer! How can I take you on? But we are both the kind of guns that ... as the well-known proverb about Kashmiris goes ... "Take a shot in the dark." Please do not take it amiss. When I heard this so-called proverb, I felt terrible. But I mention it light heartedly, because it sounds interesting. Otherwise, we both know that we Kashmiris have never accepted defeat in any field.

In politics, I can mention your name with pride, because you know well the art of contradicting yourself. To this very day, who could beat us Kashmiris in wrestling? Who can outshine us in poetry? But I was surprised to learn that you want to stop the rivers from flowing through our land. Panditji, you are only a Nehru. I regret that I am just a measuring stone weighing one and a half seer. If I were a rock of thirty or forty thousand maunds, I would have thrown myself into the river, so that you would have to spend some time consulting with your engineers on how to pull it out.

Panditji, there is no doubt that you are a great personality. You are the prime minister of India. You are the ruler of the country that was formerly mine. You are everything. But pardon me for saying that you have never cared for this humble one.

I would like to tell you an interesting anecdote. Whenever my late father – who was, obviously, a Kashmiri – ran into a hato, he would bring him home, seat him in the lobby, and treat him to Kashmiri salty tea and kulchas. Then he would tell the hato proudly, "I'm also a koshar." Panditji, you are a koshar too. By god, if you want my life, it is yours for the asking. I know and believe that you have clung to Kashmir because, being a Kashmiri, you feel a sort of magnetic love for that land. Every Kashmiri, even if he has not seen Kashmir, should feel this way.

As I already mentioned, I have only been up to Banihal. I have seen places like Kud, Bataut and Kashtwar. I have seen their poverty along with their beauty. If you have removed this poverty, then keep Kashmir to yourself. But I am sure you cannot do it, despite being a Kashmiri, because you have no time.

Between us Pandit brothers, do this – call me back to India. First I will help myself to shaljam shabdegh at your place, and then take over the responsibility of Kashmiri affairs. The Bakshis and the rest of them deserve to be sacked right away. Cheats of the first order! You have no reason to bestow such honours on them. Is this because it suits you? But why at all ...? I know you are a politician, which I am not. But that does not mean I do not understand anything.

The country was partitioned. Radcliffe employed Patel to do the dirty work. You have illegally occupied Junagarh, which a Kashmiri could do only under the influence of a Maratha. I mean Patel (god forgive him!).

You are a writer in English. Over here, I write short stories in Urdu, a language that is being wiped out in your country. Panditji, I often read your statements that indicate you hold Urdu dear. I heard one of your speeches on the radio at the time the country was divided.

---

**Hato:** a derogatory term for a daily labourer who carries goods in the hilly areas. It is a usage that has currency mainly in Kashmir.
**Koshar:** a colloquial term for Kashmiris.
**Shaljam shabdegh:** turnip and meat preparation cooked overnight in a wok.
**Bakshi:** Ghulam Muhammad Bakshi, then chief minister of Jammu & Kashmir.

Everyone admired your English. But when you broke into so-called Urdu, it seemed as though some rabid Hindu Mahasabha member had translated your English speech, which was obviously not to your liking. You were stumbling over every sentence. I cannot imagine how you agreed to read it aloud.

It was the time when Radcliffe had turned India into two slices of a single loaf of bread. It is regrettable that they have not been toasted yet. You are toasting it from that side and we, from this. But the flames in our braziers are coming from outside.

Panditji, this is the season for babbogoshas. What injustice, that you have given Bakshi all the rights over them, and he does not send me even a few as a gift! Well, let the gift go to hell, babbogoshas too ... No, on second thoughts, let them be. Actually, I wanted to ask you, why you don't read my books? If you have read them, I am sorry to say that there was no appreciation from you. However, it is more regrettable if you have not read them at all, because you are a writer yourself.

I have one more grievance against you. You are stopping water from flowing into our rivers, and taking a cue from you, publishers in your capital are hurriedly publishing my books without my permission. Is this proper? I thought that no such unseemly act could be perpetrated under your regime. You can find out right away how many publishers in Delhi, Lucknow, and Jalandhar have pirated my books.

Several lawsuits have already been filed against me on charges of obscenity. But look at the injustice of things, that in Delhi, right under your nose, a publisher brings out the collection of my stories and calls it, *The Obscene Stories of Manto*. I wrote the book *Ganjé Farishté*. An Indian publisher has published it as *Pardé ké*

*Peeché* ... Now tell me, what should I do?

I have written a new book. This letter addressed to you is the preface to it. If this book is pirated too, then by god, I'll reach Delhi some day, catch you by the throat and will not let go ... I will latch on to you and make your life hell. Every morning you will have to treat me to salty tea along with a kulcha. Shaljam shabdegh, in any case, will have to be there every week.

As soon as the book is out, I will send you a copy. I hope you will acknowledge receipt of it, and let me know your opinion of it.

You may get the scent of burnt meat in this letter of mine. You know there was a poet in our Kashmir, Ghani, who was well known as "Ghani Kashmiri." A poet from Iran had come to visit him. The doors of his house were always open. He used to say, "What is there in my house that I should keep the doors locked? I keep the doors locked when I am inside the house because I am its only asset." The poet from Iran left his poetry notebook in the vacant house. One couplet in that notebook was incomplete. He had composed the second line, but could not do the first one. The second line ran thus, "The smell of kebab is wafting from your clothes." When the Iranian poet returned and looked in his notebook, he found the first line written there, "Has the hand of a blighted soul touched your daaman?"

Panditji, I am also a blighted soul. I've taken issue with you, because I am dedicating this book to you.

27 August, 1954                                    Sa'adat Hasan Manto

---

"Pandit Manto's Letter to Pandit Nehru" has been translated from "Dibacha" first published as a Foreword to Sa'adat Hasan Manto's novelette, *Beghair Unwaan ke*, Maktaba Jadeed, Lahore, 1954, but later dropped from subsequent editions.

# Tassels

Behind the bushes in the sprawling garden beside the kothi, a cat's newborn kittens were devoured by a tomcat. Then a bitch gave birth to pups, which grew up and roamed in and out of the kothi, barking and defecating day and night. They were poisoned – they died, one by one and so did their mother. Nobody knew where the father was. If he had been there he would have met a certain death.

Countless years passed.

The bushes in the garden beside the kothi had been pruned and trimmed thousands of times. Behind them, many cats and bitches had given birth to their young ones ... there was no trace of them. Her hens had the bad habit of laying eggs there, which she carried inside every morning.

In the same garden, a man had mercilessly murdered the young maidservant. Her tasselled red silk drawstring, which she had bought for eight annas just two days before, was coiled around her neck. The murderer had twisted it so hard that her eyeballs had popped out. Seeing her, she nearly passed out with high fever – perhaps has still not come to. But no, how could that be, because a long time after that murder, the hens had laid eggs ... no, the cats had given birth to kittens ... and there had been a wedding. There was a bitch with a sparkling red dupatta with tinselled fringes around her neck. Her eyes did not protrude ... but were sunk in their hollows.

A band had played in the garden – musicians in red uniforms had come carrying coloured bagpipes under their arms, producing strange sounds. From their uniforms dangled many tassels, which kept dropping and being picked up by people who tied them to their drawstrings. But in the morning there was no sign of them, all of them had been poisoned.

The bride acted strangely – the wretched woman gave birth to a child on her bed, not behind the bushes ... it was a large red tassel. Her mother died, as did her father – both were killed by the child. Nobody knew where her father was ... if he had been there, he would have died along with them.

The red uniformed band members with big tassels vanished, never to appear again. Tomcats prowled in the garden, ogling at her – they took her to be a basketful of meat scraps, although the basket contained small oranges.

One day she took out her two small oranges and placed them before the mirror. Stepping back, she tried to look at them from a distance, but they did not come into view. She thought they were too small but even as she was thinking this they grew bigger, and then she wrapped them in a silk cloth and put them on the mantel of the fireplace.

Now the dogs started to bark ... and the small oranges started to roll on the floor. They bounced on each floor of the kothi, hopped in each room, and skipping and hopping thus, started to race and run into the bigger gardens. The dogs played with them and also fought over them.

Nobody knows what happened – two of the dogs swallowed poison and died, the rest were eaten up by their sturdy maidservant. She had replaced the young maidservant who was murdered by some man by tightening the noose of a tasselled drawstring around her neck.

She had a mother, six or seven years older than her middle aged maidservant. She was not as sturdy as the maidservant. Every morning and evening, she went for a ride in the car and, like her hens with bad habits, she would lay eggs behind the bushes in distant gardens, but neither she nor her driver ever brought them back home.

She made omelettes and stained her clothes. When they dried up she threw them away behind the bushes in the garden, from where the buzzards picked them up.

One day her friend arrived – Pakistan Mail, car number 9612, PL.

It was very hot. Daddy had gone to a hill station, Mummy had gone for an outing. Everybody was sweating profusely.

The moment she entered the room, she took off her blouse and stood under the fan. Her breasts were hot and gradually grew colder ... her breasts were cold and gradually began to get hotter ... eventually, both breasts began to shake, turned lukewarm, and sour lassi was made.

A band played for her friend. The uniformed pipers with dangling tassels did not come. Instead there were small and large brass pots and pans, sounds coming out of them – thunderous and soft, soft and thunderous.

When her friend met her again, she told her that a change had come over her. She had actually changed, now she had two bellies, one old and one new, piled over each other. Her breasts were unappealing.

Then a band played for her brother. The sturdy middle aged maidservant cried a lot. Her brother comforted her. The poor thing was reminded of her own wedding.

All night long her brother and his bride grappled with each other – he kept laughing, she kept crying.

At daybreak, the sturdy middle aged maidservant took her brother away to console him.

The bride was given a bath first thing in the morning. Her shalwar had a red tasselled drawstring – nobody knows why that had not been tied around the bride's neck. She had very big eyes. If her throat had been strangled hard, they would have popped out of their sockets like the eyes of a slaughtered goat ... and she would have caught another fever. But the earlier fevers had not yet come down. Maybe they had ... and this was a new fever, which was rising gradually and she hadn't yet come to.

Their sturdy middle aged maidservant would comfort her brother. Her mother was learning how to drive. Her father lived in a hotel. He came for a visit sometimes and left after meeting his son.

Her brother would sometimes call his bride home. Every second or third day the sturdy middle aged maidservant would remember something that made her cry.

Her brother would console her, she would comfort him – the bride would go away.

Then she and her dulhan bhabhi both set off on an outing along with her friend – Pakistan Mail, car number 9612, PL.

Their outing took them as far as Ajanta, where painting was

taught. As they watched the paintings they were themselves transformed into pictures. There were colours all around – red, yellow, green, blue – all loud colours. They were silenced by the creator of those very colours. He had long hair and wore an overcoat in both winters and summers. He was goodlooking and always wore wooden sandals whether indoors or outdoors. After silencing the colours, he himself would start screaming – the three would quieten him. As he would quieten down, they would begin to scream.

The three painted countless works of abstract art in Ajanta.

In the paintings of the first one, there were always two bellies of different colours.

In the paintings of the second one, there was always the same woman, sturdy and middle aged.

In the paintings of the third one, there were only tassels and nothing else ... only the tassels of drawstrings.

Abstract paintings were being created but the breasts of the three kept drying up.

It was very hot, so hot that the three were drenched in sweat.

The instant they entered the room with khas blinds, they took off their blouses and stood under the fan ... the fan kept rotating but their breasts did not get colder or warmer.

Her mummy was in the other room. The driver was wiping mobil oil from her body.

Her daddy was in the hotel. The lady stenographer was rubbing eau-de-cologne on his forehead.

She was standing under the fan with her dulhan bhabhi and her friend – her breasts were getting neither colder nor warmer.

One day a band also played for her.

The deserted garden brightened up again. The creator of Ajanta colours decorated the flowerpots and doors. Extremely dark lipsticks paled on seeing his loud colours – one paled so much that she dropped there and became his disciple. He also designed her wedding dress. He created many facets on it. Viewed from the front, it showed bunches of multicoloured drawstrings. From another angle, it looked like a basket of fruits. From yet another vantage, a floral curtain draping the window. From behind, a heap of crushed watermelons, and from yet another angle, a jar full of tomato sauce. From above, it seemed like an example of incomparable art and from below, the vague poetry of Miraji.

Discerning eyes saw her in her wedding dress and were all praises for her.

The bridegroom was so impressed that the very next day he decided to become an abstract artist himself. He went with his bride to Ajanta and began to live there. It was there that they learnt that he was going to be married and that he had been living at his bride's for the past several days now.

His bride was the same dark coloured lipstick which was redder than the other lipsticks. At first, for a few months, she and the abstract art held his interest. But when in the jumble of lipsticks, Ajanta got lost and there was no news of the creator of colours, her bridegroom started a salt business, which proved very profitable.

In the colourful salt trade, her bridegroom met a brown crystal of salt – her breasts had not dried up and he liked them. No band played, but a wedding did take place.

She picked up her brushes and returned to the kothi.

The bitterness caused by their differences later changed into a strange sweetness. Her friend – Pakistan Mail, car number 9612, PL – who, after changing her husband, had travelled all over Europe and was now afflicted with tuberculosis, painted this sweetness in cubic art form – clear and transparent cubes of sugar placed over each other amidst cacti plants in such a way that there emerged two faces with bees sitting on them sipping nectar.

Then her friend swallowed poison and committed suicide. When she heard this tragic news she caught another fever. Nobody knows whether it was a fresh fever or the same earlier one, which had not come down.

Her father was in eau-de-cologne, in his hotel, massaging his lady stenographer's scalp.

Her mummy had handed over the management of the kothi to the sturdy middle aged maidservant. Now she could drive, but she had taken seriously ill. Still she cared a lot for the driver's motherless pup – she made it drink her mobil oil.

Her dulhan bhabhi and brother's life together had become mature and robust. They met each other with great love. One night, when her brother and the sturdy middle aged maidservant were together taking account of things, her dulhan bhabhi suddenly appeared. She was all alone. She had neither pen nor brush in her hands, but she accounted for both of them.

In the morning two big tassels of congealed blood were found in the room, tied around the neck of her dulhan bhabhi.

She felt her fever going down a little. Her life witnessed a strange sweetness after the bitterness caused by her differences with her bridegroom. This had been painted by her Pakistan Mail friend in cubic art form. She tried to change that sweetness back into bitterness. She took to drinking, but the bitterness barely touched her. Maybe she did not drink enough. She started drinking more, so much so that she started to swim in it. People started thinking that she would drown in it any moment, but she always rose to the surface, wiping the wine off her mouth and laughing loudly.

When she got up in the morning, she felt as if every inch of her body had cried out loudly during the night. From the graves that had not yet been dug, her unborn children were crying out for the milk that could have been theirs. But where was her milk ... it had been sucked dry by wild tomcats.

She started drinking more to drown herself in the bottomless sea, but her desire was not sated. She was intelligent and educated. She discussed sex frankly, without any pretensions. She did not think it wrong to sleep around. But still sometimes in the solitude of the night she had a desire to steal behind the bush, like one of her hens with bad habits and lay an egg.

When she was completely drained and had become a bony skeleton, people started to run away from her. She understood everything. She did not run after anybody and started living all alone, smoking cigarette after cigarette, emptying bottle after bottle and thinking about who knows what. At night she slept very little ... kept roaming around the kothi.

In the servant's quarters opposite, the driver's motherless child would cry for mobil oil, which had dried up with her mother.

The driver had crashed the car. The car was in the garage, the driver in the mortuary and her mother was lying in the hospital, where one of her legs had been amputated and the other was soon going to be.

Sometimes she would peep in the servant's quarters and feel a tremor in the depths of her breasts, but the lips of the constantly crying child could hardly be wetted with the tasteless dregs moving around at the bottom of her breasts.

Her brother had been living abroad for some time now. Finally one day his letter came from Switzerland saying that he was undergoing medical treatment there. The nurse was very nice and he was going to marry her right at the hospital.

The sturdy middle aged maidservant stole some jewellery, a little money, and a lot of her mother's clothes. After a few days she disappeared. Subsequently, her mother's operation was not successful and she died in the hospital.

Her father took part in the funeral procession. After that she did not see him again.

In the quarters, the child dried up. The mother of the motherless child had already died in the hospital.

Now she was all alone. She did away with all the servants, even the driver. She kept an ayah to look after his child. No burden, except of her thoughts, remained.

She wanted to gradually rid herself of thoughts also.

Occasionally, when she heard a knock on the door, she shouted from inside, "Go away, whoever you are, go away. I don't want to meet anybody."

In the safe, she found a lot of her mother's precious jewellery. She also had her own, which she was hardly fond of. Now she sat naked in front of the mirror for long hours, decorating her body with all the jewellery, drinking and singing obscene songs in a rough voice. There wasn't any other kothi near by, hence she had total freedom.

She had bared her body in many ways. Now she wanted to lay bare even her soul. But she felt an extraordinary hesitation and saw only one way to overcome it – drink, drink a lot, and make use of her naked body. The tragedy was – her body had been stripped to such an extent that it now seemed clothed.

In a small trunk, she found the painting paraphernalia, untouched for years. She used to paint a lot and got tired a long time ago. Now she took out all the paints, washed each brush, put them on one side and stood naked before the mirror. She started drawing figures on her bare body. This was her attempt to lay bare her being.

She could only paint the front of her body. All day her naked body was her canvas – she stood before the mirror, without food or water, daubing different colours on her body, making crooked lines. She wielded her brush with confidence. Around midnight she stepped back a little, examined herself carefully in the mirror and gave a sigh of satisfaction. After this she decorated all the pieces of jewellery on her bedaubed body one by one and gazed carefully at the mirror again.

She had hardly given a thought to the jewellery on her paint smeared body, when she heard a sound.

She turned.

At first she saw a man standing there, masked, with a knife in hand, as if about to attack.

The next instant she heard and saw him scream behind his mask. The knife dropped from his hand and he began to run erratically in different directions and fled through the first opening he found.

Then a strange thing happened. She ran after him, screaming, calling, "Wait, wait, I won't say anything to you, wait."

But he, who had come to steal who knows what, did not heed her, bounded over the wall and disappeared.

Disappointed, she came back.

His knife was lying near the threshold.

She picked up the knife and went back to her room.

Suddenly she saw herself in the mirror. Over her heart she had painted a leather coloured case, shaped like a scabbard.

She placed the dagger on it ... the case was a little too small.

She threw the dagger away and started to walk around, after gulping down four or five big draughts of liquor from the bottle. She had finished many bottles of liquor ... and had eaten nothing at all.

After moving around for some time she came and stood before the mirror again. Around her neck, under the jewellery, there was a drawstring-like scarf that had big tassels, which she had painted with a brush.

Suddenly she felt the scarf tightening and slowly digging into her neck.

She stood silently all the while, her eyes fixed on the mirror, as they started to come out.

After a while all the veins of her face began to swell up.

Then all of a sudden she let out a scream and fell face down on the floor.

---

"Tassels" has been translated from "Phunde," in *Sau Kendil Power ka Bulb: Sa'adat Hasan Manto ke Ikkis Muntakhab Afsane,* Modern Publishing House, New Delhi, 1980.

# By the Roadside

The days were similar. The sky was washed, clear and blue like her eyes, just like today. The sunlight was as strong, like a beautiful dream. The smell of the earth was also the same. The same kind of smell is filling my heart and mind right now ... and I, lying down as I am today, had handed over my fluttering soul to him.

He had said to me, Believe me, my life was empty without these moments which you gave me ... the vacant spaces in my being that have been filled are grateful to you. If you had not come into my life they would have remained unfulfilled forever. I don't know what more I can say to you. I have been so completely fulfilled that I feel I don't need you any longer.

And he went away, never to return.

My eyes shed tears, my heart cried out. I implored him. I asked him countless times why he didn't need me any longer. I now needed him all the more intensely after those moments which, as he said, filled the void of his being.

He said, The parts of your being that I needed to build and complete my own being were chosen and handed over to me in these very moments. Now that my fulfilment has been achieved, our relationship has to end.

Such cruel words ... I could not endure this stoning. I started to wail, but it didn't move him even one bit. I said, Those parts that have completed your being were a part of my being. Don't those parts have any relationship with me? Can the remaining part of my being sever its relationship with those parts? You have become complete by rendering me incomplete. Did I make you my Lord for this?

He said, Bees make honey by sucking nectar from flowers and buds, but even the last vestige of honey never comes near the lips of these flowers and buds. God makes us worship him, but he never worships himself. After spending some moments in isolation with non-being, he brought forth being. But where is non-being now? What need does being have for it now? The non-being was like a mother who the minute gave birth to being perished on the bed itself.

A woman can cry, she can't present arguments. A woman's most convincing argument is the tear that falls from her eye. I said to him, Look, I'm crying, my eyes are shedding tears. You may go if you so desire, but at least take along a few of my tears wrapped in the shroud of your handkerchief. I'll keep crying my whole life, but at least I'll remember that you took funereal care of a few of my tears, just to make me happy.

He said, I have made you happy. I have made you experience that tangible happiness which you could only dream of. Isn't that pleasure, that bliss, going to be the mainstay of your life's remaining moments? You say that my fulfilment has rendered you unfulfilled, but isn't this incompleteness enough to keep your life moving? I'm a man. Today you have completed me, tomorrow someone else will. The kind of elements my being is made up of foreordain that in my life, many such moments will come when I'll find myself feeling unfulfilled, and many women like you will enter my life to fill the void created by such moments.

I kept crying and fretting.

I thought, Those few moments were in my grip just now ... No, no, I was in their grip. Why did I hand myself over to those moments, why did I thrust my fluttering soul into the gaping cage of those moments. There was some joy, even pleasure, ecstasy ... yes, it was certainly there. It was in our conflict, but how did it happen that he remained intact and unbroken, while cracks have appeared in me. How strange that he does not require me now, but I feel I require him all the more intensely. He has become stronger, I have grown feebler. How strange that two clouds embrace in the sky – one dissolves into tears and begins to rain, the other becomes a flash of lightning, plays with rain and then bounds off in a rush. Whose law is this? Earth's? Sky's? Or of Him, who created them?

I kept wondering and fretting.

Two souls merge into one and after uniting, spread out into a passionate expanse. Is it all poetry? No, two souls contract into those tiny points, and then expand into a cosmos. But why is a soul sometimes abandoned in this universe to writhe in agony? Because of its crime of helping the other soul reach that tiny point?

What kind of universe is this?

The days were similar. The sky was blue like the colour of his eyes, just like today. The sunlight was as strong, and lying down as I am today, I had handed over my fluttering soul to him.

He isn't here now. Who knows after becoming a bolt of lightning what laments of small clouds he is playing with now. He completed himself and left. He was a snake that pulled away after coiling around me, leaving behind his trail to twist and turn inside my womb. Is this the process of my fulfilment?

No, no, how can it be my fulfilment ... this is destruction.

But why are the empty places in my body filling up?

What debris is filling in the hollows of my body? What sounds slither in my veins? Why am I folding into myself and writhing to reach the tiny point in my womb? After drowning, in what seas is my boat surfacing?

For which guest is milk being warmed on the fire blazing inside me? Why is this heart of mine carding my blood to fashion soft, tender quilts? And for whom is my mind knitting small and tiny dresses with the multicoloured threads of my thoughts?

For whom is my complexion beginning to glow? Why are the hiccups trapped in each part and each pore of my body beginning to sing lullabies?

The days were similar. The sky was blue like his eyes, just like today. But why has this sky come down from its heights and planted itself in my stomach. Why do his eyes scurry about in my veins?

Why is the roundness of my breasts acquiring the sacredness of mosques' arches? No, no, this is not holiness. I'll raze these arches to the ground. I'll smother this fire raging inside me so that no feast awaits the uninvited guest. I'll ravel all the multicoloured threads of my thoughts.

The days were similar. The sky was blue like his eyes, just like today.

But why do I remember those days from which he has removed the last trace of his footprints?

But whose footprint is squirming in the depths of my womb? Don't I know it? I'll scrape it out. I'll erase it. It's not a footprint, it's a boil, a very terrible boil. But why do I feel as if it is cotton wool ... if it's cotton wool, then for what wound – for the wound inflicted by him? No, no ... it seems it's cotton wool for a wound I have carried since birth, a wound that I have never seen ... which has been sleeping in my womb for ages.

What is this womb? A useless pot of clay, a plaything for children. I'll smash it and break it up.

But who is whispering in my ear? This world is a crossroads. Why are you giving away your secret to everybody? Remember, fingers will be pointed at you.

Fingers ... why wouldn't they be pointed in the direction he has gone, he who completed his being and left? Don't these fingers know that direction? This world is a crossroads. But he has abandoned me at the fork in the road. There was unfulfilment for me on this side, only tears ...

But whose tear is changing into a pearl in my shell?

Where will it be strung?

Fingers will be pointed. When the mouth of the shell opens and the pearl slips out and falls on the crossroads, fingers will be pointed ... towards the shell, and towards the pearl. The fingers will change into small snakes and coil around them, turning them blue with their poison.

The sky was blue like his eyes, just like today. Why doesn't the sky fall down? What kind of pillars are holding it up? Wasn't the earthquake that day enough to shake the foundation of the pillars? Why does it still stretch out over me as before?

My soul is drenched in sweat ... each of its pores is open. Fire is blazing from all directions, gold is melting in the cauldron inside me. The bellows are working, tongues of fire are leaping up, the gold is boiling like the lava of a volcano, blue eyes are scurrying around in my veins, the bells are ringing ... he is coming.

Close, close the doors.

The cauldron has been turned over. The molten gold is flowing. The bells are ringing. My eyelids are beginning to droop ... The blue sky is hazing over and coming down.

Whose sound of cry is this? Calm it down. Its screams are hammering at my heart. Quieten it ... Quieten it.

I am changing into a lap. Why am I becoming a lap?

My arms are opening up, the milk is boiling on the fires, the spheres of my breasts are becoming cups.

Here, bring this lump of flesh and lay it down on the soft, warm swaddling of the carded blood of my heart.

Don't seize it, don't take it away, don't separate it from me ... For god's sake, don't separate it from me.

Fingers ... fingers ... let fingers be pointed. I don't care. The world is a crossroads ... let all the secrets of my life come out in the open ...

My life will be destroyed ...

Let it be destroyed ... Give back my own flesh ... Don't take away part of my soul ... You don't know how very precious it is ... It's a pearl granted to me by those moments, moments which collected bits of my being to complete someone else, and which thought he had left me incomplete ... I have been consummated today.

I agree with it, I agree with it ... Ask the void in my womb ... Ask my milk-filled breasts ... Ask those lullabies which are waking up after calming down the sobs in every part and every pore of my body ... Ask those cradles that are being put up in my arms ... Ask the pallor of my face that has let this lump of flesh suck all its ruddiness ... Ask those breaths that have furtively delivered it its share.

Fingers ... let fingers be raised ... I'll cut them off ... If there is an uproar, I will pick up these fingers and stuff them in my ears ... I'll become dumb, deaf and blind ... My flesh will understand my signs ... I'll recognize its touch.

Don't take it away ... Don't take it away ... It's the sindoor of my womb ... It's the bindiya on the forehead of my love ... It's the bitter fruit of my sin ...

People will spit at her?

I'll lick it up, let them spit.

Look, I plead with folded hands, I lie at your feet ... Don't turn over the pots filled with my milk ... Don't set fire to the soft and tender swaddling made out of the carded blood of my heart ... Don't break the ropes of the cradles in my arms ... Don't deprive my ears of the songs that I hear in its cries.

Don't take it away ... Don't take it away ... Don't separate it from me. For god's sake, don't separate me from it.


Lahore: January 21. The police discovered a shivering, newly born baby girl in Dhobi Mandi and have taken her under their protection. Some merciless person had tied a cloth tightly round her neck and a wet cloth around her naked body to kill her from cold. But she is alive ... The girl is very beautiful. Her eyes are blue ... the girl has been admitted into a hospital.

"By The Roadside" has been translated from "Sarak ke Kinaré," in *Sau Kendil Power ka Bulb: Sa'adat Hasan Manto ke Ikkis Muntakhab Afsane*, Modern Publishing House, New Delhi, 1980.

# Sonorol

When Bushra attempted to commit suicide for the third time by swallowing thirty two Sonorol sleeping pills, I began to wonder. If she must die, there's arsenic and opium. There are other kinds of poisons readily available too. Why take Sonorol every time? An overdose of sleeping pills leads to death, no doubt about that. However, I thought there must have been a deeper reason behind Bushra's tenacious recourse to it for the third time. My thought ran like this – since she didn't die after swallowing it on the first two occasions, she must have taken it the third time around without any real sense of danger, and thus derived the pleasure of an attempted suicide without actually committing it. But it could be dangerous. The game was not one hundred percent safe.

Her third attempt took place in the house of her third husband, an overseer with the Public Works Department. At six thirty in the morning, he discovered her lying immobile on the bed like a paralyzed buffalo. She had probably taken the pills three or four hours earlier.

The overseer came to me, nervous and trembling. It was a surprise because after marrying Bushra he had forgotten about me altogether. He used to come every day before and we use to have beer or whisky together. He was not well-off and used to go to office on a bicycle. But when he began to court Bushra and eventually brought her home as his wife, a great transformation could be seen in him and his house.

Now he sported a fine suit and went about in a car. The house got the choicest furniture. He started gambling at the racecourse. Scotch whisky replaced his country rum. Bushra also drank heavily, so they both lived happily.

Qamar Sahab, the overseer, was about fifty. Bushra was probably five years older. She might have been pretty once, but now she looked horrid. She wore heavy make-up over her wrinkled complexion and dyed her hair. Every part of her body had come loose like a soaked kite. With her distended belly, her breasts pulled up by the crane of brassieres, and her thickly kohled eyes – she always looked like a caricature of femininity to me.

I wondered what Qamar Sahab saw in her, except that she was rich. She had inherited a lot of land from her wealthy zamindar father in Punjab. She had a monthly income of six or seven hundred rupees from it. On top of that she had a bank balance of ten or fifteen thousand. And Qamar Sahab? He was an indigent overseer. He had a wife and six children. His two sons were studying in college. His house presented a picture of abject poverty. He loved luxury and was a poet to boot. His evening liquor was essential for him. It was apparent, given his weakness for the better things in life, very little money was left for the upkeep of his family.

Qamar Sahab gave the impression that he had lawfully wedded Bushra but I suspected otherwise. He was a clever and farsighted fellow. In the fifty five or so years of his life he had experienced many vicissitudes. He was unlikely to entangle himself in a marriage with Bushra with its attendant responsibilities.

The union with Bushra improved the condition of his family immensely. His three daughters, who had loitered around in the lanes before, were now admitted to a missionary school. His first wife got better clothes to wear. The quality of Qamar Sahab's drinks also showed a marked improvement.

I was happy. It was his second marriage, but so what? Bushra had got a husband who was competent and worldly-wise. Qamar Sahab had got a wife who, though ugly, was fairly rich.

However, this conjugal bliss was short lived. One day, word got around about a violent fight between them. It came to such a pass that both of them took a good number of Sonorol pills. Qamar Sahab was lying on the floor unconscious, and his respectable wife lay like a corpse on the bed.

The two were rushed to the hospital immediately. The following day they were all right and returned home. But hardly a fortnight had passed when both of them again took recourse to Sonorol. I have no idea whether they were taken to the hospital or treated at home, but both survived. After that nothing was heard on that front for about a year. Then one day, at the crack of dawn, I was informed that Bushra had swallowed as many as thirty two Sonorol tablets.

Qamar Sahab was badly shaken and looked woebegone. I rang up the hospital for an ambulance and Bushra was rushed there. The house surgeon was at his home. I called there, briefed him on the case and urged him to rush to the hospital. My impassioned plea had no effect on him. He said nonchalantly, "Manto Sahab, let her die. Why do you worry?"

He knew that Bushra had already been to the hospital twice

because of her suicide attempts. I didn't ask him anything about Bushra and after a little while returned home.

I cannot say that I was not aware of Bushra's circle of friends or her earlier life. We had met quite a few times. She addressed me as Bhai Sa'adat. We had also shared drinks on several occasions.

She had a daughter, Parvez. I first saw her photograph on the day she entered Qamar Sahab's house as his wife. The two rooms on the ground floor were being renovated. I saw a charming young woman's photograph mounted in an ordinary frame, on the mantelpiece. While we were enjoying beer, Bushra told me that this was her daughter Parvez, who had committed suicide. When I delved deeper, both Bushra and Qamar Sahab shared their memories with me. I wanted to know the reason behind her suicide. What Bushra and Qamar Sahab told me may be given the semblance of a narrative.

Parvez was Bushra's daughter from her now dead first husband. He too, had been well-off. I came to know from another source that Bushra's first husband, Allah Bakhsh, did not trust her. This was a few years after their marriage when she had begun to fool around with some other man. The upshot was that Bushra's husband had begun to ignore and hate her. To escape his wrath, Bushra had to live separately. On his death, Allah Bakhsh did not leave a penny to her, though he did set aside some property for their daughter, Parvez.

Bushra remarried. As she was an enlightened lady, a successful barrister from Peshawar fell for her. They had two sons. But she was not happy with her second husband either and thus divorced him. She wanted to live freely.

The barrister is still alive. The two sons have grown up and live with him. They do not visit their mother as they do not approve of her conduct.

This is a short sketch of Bushra's life. The story of her daughter Parvez, however, is a long one. Her childhood was spent largely in the countryside. She was a delicate child and used to play in the lush green fields all day long. She had no friends. Her parents did not approve of her mixing with the children of the neighbourhood. When she got older, she was sent to a school meant for the children of affluent families in Lahore.

She was both intelligent and graceful. By the time she left school and entered college she had grown into a very beautiful woman with her restless mind and heart in quest of an ideal. She had a rich, melodious voice – it was a treat to listen to her. She had learnt dancing too. When she performed, spectators would stand transfixed. Her limbs were very supple. People say, when she danced even the faintest movement of her body established an immediate rapport with her audience.

Like most villagers, she was simple and naive. She studied in an English college, where she had several mischievous, snooty girls among her friends. But she was different from them. It was as though she lived beyond the world of clouds, where everything was pure and refined. She never cared for money or wealth. She dreamt of meeting a youth who would become her god and she would spend her life worshipping him. She was a totally dedicated soul at the altar of love.

Her mother had taken her to Abbotabad, to give a dance performance before an assembly of men and women. She looked out at the spectators and saw a handsome Pathan youth in a far corner. His face had a special glow and his eyes sparkled. Parvez could not take her eyes off him for some time. The young man seemed to communicate something to her through his eyes. She forgot her reluctance and began to dance bewitchingly. Through the tiniest gestures of her attractive, limber body and her delicate complexion she began to unravel, as it were, the hidden yearnings of her soul, layer by layer, and lay them before the fascinated eyes of the young Pathan.

The Pathan youth was called Yusuf Gulzai. He was a worthy member of a well-to-do tribe. After finishing school he had begun to take an active interest in politics. He was not a stranger to women, but Parvez had him totally under her spell. Eventually they were married with great pomp and show, and began to live at Abbotabad. Parvez was deliriously happy – she felt like dancing all the time. Melodious songs flowed from her lips like cool springs of water.

He was Yusuf, and Parvez was no less than his Zuleikha. All day long she looked after his comfort. She laid all her feminine assets at his feet. What more can a woman do?

In the beginning she was ecstatic, so ecstatic that she didn't realize how three years of married life slipped by. Though she had a daughter, she would very often become oblivious of her, drowned as she was in Yusuf's love. One could only guess the extent of her love. It was hardly surprising that when her daughter was born, she felt it was not the baby but Yusuf who was born out of her love and had emerged from her womb.

But then her god fell from his pedestal. He was by nature a philanderer. He was not like a fly that prefers to suck only candy. He was more like a honeybee that wants to suck nectar from every bud in the garden. As time went by, he broke the bond of love with Parvez and went back to his previous life of indulgence.

He had wealth and youth in abundance. He also had a pleasant personality. All this contributed in making him a rising star in the political firmament of the country. He began to regard Parvez's all-embracing love for him absurd. He got tired of her kissing and cuddling all the time. He didn't want to remain trapped like a fly caught in a web ... to turn into powder and used as snuff.

Parvez got a rude shock when she discovered that Yusuf was not hers alone anymore. She remained dazed for several days, feeling as though someone had shattered her idol.

She didn't say anything to Yusuf, nor did she complain about his infidelity and indifference. She just wanted to take a decision. She reflected on it for a long time by herself. It was not difficult to get a divorce, but she could not bear being separated from Yusuf. It was she who had elevated him to the status of a god. How could the devotee destroy the god? Once she had sincerely accepted his godhood, she was ever ready to surrender herself to him.

She decided to stay with him forever – not for him, but because of the way she had once felt towards him, making him her god. She was ready to make even greater sacrifices for this.

People say that she made it easy for any woman who wanted to warm herself in Yusuf's embrace for a while. It was certainly a shameless act on her part, but she resorted to this kind of escapism and bore the shame because she wanted to save her shattered ideal from total destruction.

She treated his numerous fancy women with affection and looked after their comforts. She put up with their tantrums, willingly provided them and her husband suitable opportunities, and did not intrude in their lovemaking. She smothered her innermost feelings and prepared sumptuous dishes for them. When her husband ordered her to dance and sing to entertain those loose women, she controlled herself with great effort. She dried her tears, consoled her wounded heart, forced a smile on her lips and, shaking with anger and pain, would sing powerfully of joy and happiness, dancing gracefully. Then, in the seclusion of her room she would cry her heart out and have such bouts of melancholy that she felt she could not hold on to life anymore. But after such tempests she would find a new power of endurance and would begin to humiliate herself once again to please Yusuf. She pretended that it was not her shame but her triumph.

During this period her mother came to visit her on several occasions. Parvez never complained to her about her husband. She didn't want to share her private sorrow or discuss her husband with anyone else. She would tell herself – he's my husband and this sorrow is also my own. If he inflicted the same sorrow on others that he inflicts on me, I would have a reason to feel jealous. As he is not doing that, I should be happy.

During those days, Bushra was not attached to anyone. That is to say, she hadn't yet acquired a new husband for herself. She was roaming around enjoying herself as a free woman. She would come to stay with Parvez in Abbotabad for ten or fifteen days at a stretch and would go running around with Yusuf. They liked each other. When she was there, Yusuf didn't bring any other women into the house. For hours they played cards together in a separate room while Parvez looked after their comforts. She wanted her mother to stay on so that those loose women, worse than brothel whores, stayed away from her home. But her mother could not stay in the same place for very long. With her departure, Yusuf would go back to his old ways. Parvez too, would resume her self-imposed role of footstool for his new found girlfriends.

Slowly she got used to her new life and stopped feeling as miserable as she had initially. The great pain caused by her initial disappointment gradually dissipated. She began to pay more attention to her child and felt happy.

One day she had gone to Lahore on some urgent business and returned after two days. It was evening. Yusuf's door was closed but she could hear his drunken peals of laughter coming from inside the room. Parvez peeped in through the door and stood transfixed. Her pink complexion turned white as a sheet of paper.

I came to know about this through very reliable sources. But Bushra's account was different. She said that her husband's neglect silently ate into Parvez's heart and she lost all zest for life. Parvez had resolved to put up with all sorts of humiliation for Yusuf, but there was a limit. One night when he was with one of his women, dead drunk, he asked Parvez to dance nude. She never disobeyed him, he was her god. So she danced. Tears flowed from her eyes continuously while her naked body moved to the rhythm. When the dance ended, she put on her clothes without speaking, went out of the room and swallowed poison.

I don't know the exact truth. But this is what could be gathered from reliable sources – Parvez had peeked into Yusuf's room and resolved right at that moment that she could not live anymore. She took the car, went straight to a chemist's shop and asked for a full packet of Sonorol. As she was going to pay she realized that in her agitation she had left her purse home. She said to the chemist, "I am Mrs Yusuf Gulzai. I forgot to bring my purse. Please send the bill. Yusuf Sahab will pay it."

When she got home, she asked the maid to grind the tablets. She mixed the powder with warm milk and swallowed it.

In a little while a servant came and told her, "Your mother has come. Yusuf Sahab is calling you."

Parvez's eyes were dry. But she felt dizzy as the poison had begun to work. She washed her face and tucking her hair into a bun, joined them. She hugged her mother and sat down on the carpet with Yusuf. As she was talking to her mother, her head spun and she fell unconscious on her side. Her mother got worried as Parvez's complexion was turning blue. But Yusuf, dead drunk, showed no concern and said to Bushra, "Nothing has happened to her ... she's just faking." Then he caught Parvez by her shoulder, shook her violently and said authoritatively, "Get up. I don't like these histrionics." Bushra also tried to revive her, shaking her vigorously. Eventually the doctor was called in, but by then Parvez had departed for her heavenly abode.

Several stories circulated regarding her suicide. The version I came to know from my reliable sources seemed credible to me so I kept quiet and waited for it to be confirmed.

I met Qamar Sahab when he brought Bushra back from the hospital. Their car was not there. When I asked him about it, he said with his poet-like indifference, "The owner has taken it away."

"What do you mean?"

"I mean, it didn't belong to me. It was hers. I stopped using it some time ago. I've been going to the office on my bicycle. Of course, whenever she needed a driver I offered my services."

I tried to comprehend the situation. "So there's been a tiff?"

"Well, more or less. I've divorced her."

Later, when he elaborated on this I learned that they had indeed never married. He wrote the talaaqnama simply because he did not want people to know that he had been living in sin with her for almost two years.

I did not want to delve deeper. The real cause of their violent fight was that his so-called wife had established a physical relationship with an aristocratic Mohajir of declining years from Hyderabad. Once Qamar Sahab had dazzled her eyes, but now he did not have the same attraction for her anymore.

I felt sorry when I later learnt that Qamar Sahab withdrew all three of his promising daughters from school. His Gold Flake cigarettes gave way to the cheap Bagla. For a while he had lived in the lap of luxury, but now he roamed about like a camel without a leash.

He told me a lot more about Bushra. But I couldn't understand why Bushra had to swallow thirty two Sonorol pills when her separation from Qamar Sahab had already been decided upon, and she had already begun sleeping with the aristocratic Mohajir. Ostensibly it was a reaction against Qamar Sahab's objection to her ways. But honestly, I could not convince myself that this was reason enough to drive her to suicide. Qamar Sahab could not shed any more light on it either.

One day, as we were talking, I ventured to ask, "This tradition of swallowing Sonorol pills established by Parvez, Bushra's daughter, and then continued by you and Bushra ... But please tell me, what was the real reason behind Parvez's taking such a drastic step? You've told me several times that Parvez had grown accustomed to Yusuf's illicit liaisons, even helped him in this. When a woman reaches the limit of such humiliation, the thought of suicide does not occur to her. I think, actually I'm convinced, that Bushra and Yusuf had established an illicit relationship."

Qamar Sahab's confirmation came in these words, "You're right. One day drunk, she confessed and wept bitterly."

That evening I found out that the aristocratic Mohajir from Hyderabad had taken twenty four Sonorol pills. Bushra, as usual, took thirty two. Both of them were lying unconscious in the hospital. On the second day, the aristocrat died. He could not endure twenty four pills. Bushra survived.

These days she is mourning her dead husband. The fellow who bought her car, stays with her day and night to cheer her up.

---

"Sonorol" has been translated from "Sonorol," in *Manto ke Gumshuda aur Ghairmatbu'a Afsane,* Modern Publishing House, New Delhi, 1992.

**Asha Puri** taught French at Jawaharlal Nehru University and Jamia Millia Islamia, Delhi, and is the translator of many French and Spanish literary works.

**M Asaduddin** writes on aspects of Indian Literature(s) and culture, and translates from Asomiya, Bangla, Hindi and Urdu into English. His recently published (translated and edited) books include, *Short Stories from Pakistan; Lifting the Veil: Selected Writings of Ismat Chughtai; For Freedom's Sake: Stories and Sketches of Sa'adat Hasan Manto*; and (with Mushirul Hasan) *Image and Representation: Stories of Muslim Lives in India*. A recipient of the Katha Award and Dr A K Ramanujan Award for translation, M Asaduddin has been a fellow at the British Centre for Literary Translation, University of East Anglia, UK. He currently teaches English literature and Translation Studies at Jamia Millia Islamia, New Delhi.

**Moazzam Sheikh** is a creative writer, born in Lahore and now settled in San Francisco. His stories have appeared in the US and Canada. *A Dragonfly in the Sun: Fifty Years of Pakistani Writing in English* (Oxford) and *Katha: An Anthology of South Asian Writers in the US* feature his work. He has recently finished his first novel, *Sahab*.

**Muhammad Umar Memon**, Professor of Islamic Studies, Urdu and Persian, at the University of Wisconsin, Madison has done his Masters in Near Eastern Languages and Literatures from Harvard University and a PhD in Islamic Studies from the University of California at Los Angeles. His writings include fiction and criticism in Urdu and English. His book on religious polemics, *Ibn Taimiyya's Struggle Against Popular Religion*, was published by Mouton (The Hague and Paris) in 1976, and a collection of his Urdu short stories, *Tareek Gali*, was published by Sang-e-Meel, Lahore, in 1989. An avid translator, he has translated extensively from modern Urdu fiction, including *Intizar Hussain: The Seventh Door and Other Stories; An Epic Unwritten: The Penguin Book* *of Partition Stories; Abdullah Hussein: Downfall by Degrees; Domains of Fear and Desire: Urdu Stories; The Colour of Nothingness, Contemporary Urdu Short Stories;* and *Abdullah Hussein: Night and Other Stories.* He has also edited Studies in the *Urdu Ghazal* and Prose Fiction and is the General Editor of the Pakistan Writers' Series, Oxford University Press; Editor, *The Annual of Urdu Studies;* Associate Editor, *The Journal of South Asian Literature.* He serves on the Editorial Board of several professional journals, including the *Edebiyat, Journal of Middle Eastern Literature, Bridges* and *Toronto Review of Contemporary Writing Abroad.*

**Ralph Russell**, among the most prominent scholars of Urdu in the West, is currently Reader Emeritus at the School of Oriental and African Studies, University of London. His publications include *The Pursuit of Urdu Literature: A Select History* and, with Khurshidul Islam, *Three Mughal Poets* and *Ghalib – Life and Letters.*

**Ravikant** works with Sarai, at the Centre for Studies in Developing Societies, Delhi. "Remembering the Past," his translation of "Ateet ki Smriti," an essay by Ramchandra Shukla, appeared in *Hindi: Literature, Discourse, Language,* vol. 1.1 (2000). He has co-edited *Translating Partition: Stories, Essays, Criticism* which was published by Katha in 2001.

**Shikoh Mohsin Mirza** was born in Lucknow. He teaches English literature at Jamia Millia Islamia, Delhi. He specializes in Narratology.

**Tarun K Saint** teaches English Literature at Hindu College, University of Delhi. His poetry has been published by *Wasafiri* (University of London). He has co-edited *Translating Partition: Stories, Essays, Criticism* which was published by Katha in 2001, and has edited *Bruised Memories: Communal Violence and the Writer,* an anthology of writing which was been published by Seagull Books in 2002.

# ABOUT KATHA

India has always been a land of storytellers. Over the centuries, we have honed the fine art of telling the short story – be it in our epics, our mythologies, our folktales or in our more recent writings. Told by traditional Katha vachaks, village storytellers and one's favourite grandmother, we have all heard stories that have taught us our values, our morals, our culture. "Katha" or the narrative is a special legacy that continues to exist in our country as a rich and fascinating tradition, moving with grace and felicity from the oral traditions to the written texts, from the heard word to the read.

We at Katha endeavour to spread the joy of reading, knowing, and living amongst adults and children, the common reader and the neo-literate. Katha has striven to establish a code of excellence in all that it does, to enhance the quality of life in every project it has attempted.

Katha's main objective is **to enhance the pleasures of reading for children and adults,** for experienced readers as well as for those who are just beginning to read. And, inter alia, to –

- Stimulate an interest in lifelong learning that will help the child grow into a confident, self-reliant, responsible and responsive adult.
- Help break down gender, cultural and social stereotypes.
- Encourage, foster excellence, and applaud quality literature and translations in and between the various Indian languages.

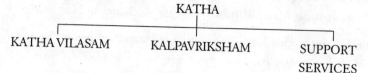

KATHA

KATHA VILASAM     KALPAVRIKSHAM     SUPPORT SERVICES

**KATHA VILASAM**: The Story Research and Resource Centre was created in September 1989 with the following main purposes:
- To help capacity build in writers, translators and editors. To organize and promote, wherever required, the study of those subjects through lectures, demonstrations/workshops etc.

- To offer a decentralized research and a centralized documentation service on Indian literature, focusing on short fiction. The idea is to collect and have for larger use research papers, writings and other forms of scholarship on writers and writings.
- To publish quality translations of good writings from the various Indian languages, in English.

These goals have crystallized in the development of the following areas of activities:

- **Katha Books**: Publishing of Quality Translations
- **Academic Publishing Programme**: Books for teaching of translation and Indian fiction
- **Applauding Excellence**: The Katha Awards for fiction, translation, editing
- **Kathakaar**: The Centre for Children's Literature
- **Katha Barani**: The Translation Resource Centre
- **Katha Sethu**: Building bridges between India and the outside world
  - **The Katha Translation Exchange Programme**
  - **Translation Contests**
- **Kanchi**: Katha National Institute of Translation was started in 1994 with the Vak Initiative for enhancing the pool of translators between the various bhashas.
  - **Katha Academic Centres.** In various universities across the country
  - **The Faculty Enhancement programme.** Workshops, seminars, discussions
  - **Sishya:** Katha Clubs in colleges; workshops, certificate courses, events and contests
  - **The Katha Internship programme** for students from outside India
  - **Storytellers Unlimited:** Stotytelling – the Art and Craft
  - **KathaRasa:** Performances, Art Fusion, events. Katha Centre Activities

**KALPAVRIKSHAM**: The Centre for Sustainable Learning was created in September 1989 with the following main purposes:

- To foster quality education for children from nonliterate families that is relevant and fun
- To develop teaching/learning materials that see the story as the basis, for fostering lifelong learning skills and knowledge in our children that will make classroom teaching rememberable and understandable.
- To find, foster, and applaud good teaching of our children, through inservice and preservice training.

These goals crystallized in the development of the following areas of activities:
- **Katha Khazana**
  - **Katha Student Support Centre.**
  - **Katha Public School**
  - **Katha School of Entrepreneurship**
  - **KITES**. Katha Information Technology and eCommerce School
  - **Iccha Ghar. The Intel Computer Clubhouse @ Katha**
  - **Hamara Gaon**. Community revitalization and economic resurgence.
  - **The Mandals**: Maa, Bapu, Balika, Balak, Danadini
  - **The Clubs**: Inducement to activity clubs like Gender Club, Mensa Club etc.
  - **KathaRasa,** Artistic education, performances, events.
- **Shakti Khazana**: Skills upgradation. Income generation activities. The Khazana Coop.
- **Kalpana Vilasam:** Regular research and development of teaching/learning materials, curricula, syllabi, content
  - **Teacher training.**
  - **TaQeEd — The Teachers Alliance for Quality eEducation.**
- **Tamasha'S World!**
  - **Tamasha! the Children's magazine**
  - **Dhammakdhum!**
  - **www.tamasha.org**
  - **ANU — Animals, Nature and YOU!**

# BE A FRIEND OF KATHA!

If you feel strongly about Indian literature, you belong with us! KathaNet, an invaluable network of our friends, is the mainstay of all our translation related activities. We are happy to invite you to join this ever widening circle of translation activists. Katha, with limited financial resources, is propped up by the unqualified enthusiasm and the indispensable support of nearly 5000 dedicated women and men.

We are constantly on the lookout for people who can spare the time to find stories for us, and to translate them. Katha has been able to access mainly the literature of the major Indian languages. Our efforts to locate resource people who could make the lesser known literatures available to us have not yielded satisfactory results. We are specially eager to find Friends who could introduce us to Bhojpuri, Dogri, Kashmiri, Maithili, Manipuri, Nepali, Rajasthani and Sindhi fiction.

Do write to us with details about yourself, your language skills, the ways in which you can help us, and any material that you already have and feel might be publishable under a Katha programme. All this would be a labour of love, of course! But we do offer a discount of 20% on all our publications to Friends of Katha.

Write to us at –
Katha
A-3 Sarvodaya Enclave
Sri Aurobindo Marg
New Delhi   110 017

Call us at: 2652 4350, 2652 4511
or E-mail us at: info@katha.org